# BLOOD JUSTICE

ALSO BY TERRY J. BENTON-WALKER

*Blood Debts*

# BLOOD JUSTICE

TERRY J. BENTON-WALKER

TOR PUBLISHING GROUP
NEW YORK

This is a work of fiction. All of the characters, organizations, and events portrayed in this novel are either products of the author's imagination or are used fictitiously.

BLOOD JUSTICE



A Tor Teen Book
Published by Tom Doherty Associates / Tor Publishing Group
120 Broadway
New York, NY 10271

www.tor-forge.com



The Library of Congress Cataloging-in-Publication Data is available upon request.

ISBN 978-1-250-82595-7 (hardcover)
ISBN 978-1-250-82596-4 (ebook)



First Edition: 2024

Printed in the United States of America

0 9 8 7 6 5 4 3 2 1

*For the Black Queer community.*

*When existing at the intersection of Blackness and Queerness becomes too difficult, remember that gods are often found at crossroads.*

# AUTHOR'S NOTE

As I pen this letter, some of the most vulnerable people in our nation, the LGBT+ community, and especially the trans community, are under attack by the very systems we're told are meant to "protect" us. This is one of the many reasons why I *never* want my art to be separated from me or my identity. Every day, I choose to fight with my pen and my platform by telling stories that I hope, more than anything, encourage Black Queer people and Black young adults to stand up for themselves and their communities—even in the face of insurmountable odds.

*Blood Justice* continues exploring the pursuit of justice that began in *Blood Debts*, but this time, we see what happens when those seeking justice become frustrated—to the point of desperation—not only with the systems of oppression but with the people who prop them up to benefit from the suffering of others.

Once more, I ask: How far you are willing to go for justice—and is there such a thing as too far?

Welcome back to New Orleans.

Royal regards,
Terry J. Benton-Walker

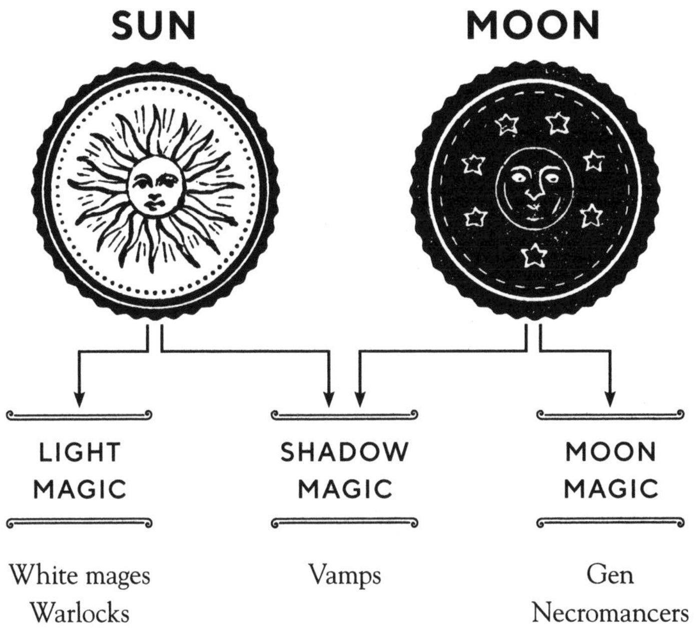
SUN
MOON
LIGHT MAGIC
SHADOW MAGIC
MOON MAGIC
White mages
Warlocks
Vamps
Gen
Necromancers

# DUPART–TRUDEAU FAMILY

Rinalt Montaigne
1960–

m

Vanessa (Glapion) Montaigne
1958–2010

Justin Montaigne
Gen Council Root Doctor
1990–

Cristine (Glapion) Dupart
1960–1989

m

Baptiste Dupart
1960–1989

David Trudeau
1982–2018

m

Marie (Dupart) Trudeau
1983–

Ursula Dupart
1984–

Desiree Dupart
1985–

Jacquelyn Dupart
1987–

u

Arturo Savant
1980–

Rosalie Dupart
1988–

Cristina "Cris" Trudeau
2003–

Clement "Clem" Trudeau
2003–

Baptiste Dupart
2018–

## SAVANT FAMILY

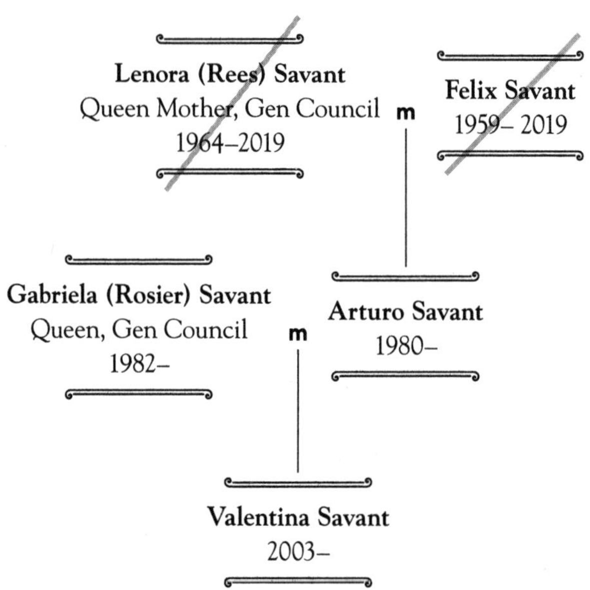
Lenora (Rees) Savant
Queen Mother, Gen Council
1964–2019
m
Felix Savant
1959– 2019
Gabriela (Rosier) Savant
Queen, Gen Council
1982–
m
Arturo Savant
1980–
Valentina Savant
2003–

## DELACORTE-STRAYER FAMILY

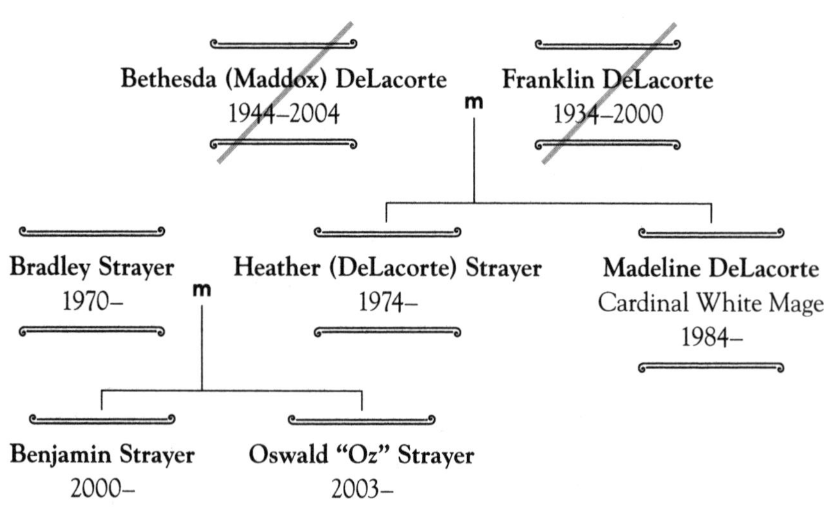
Bethesda (Maddox) DeLacorte
1944–2004
m
Franklin DeLacorte
1934–2000
Bradley Strayer
1970–
m
Heather (DeLacorte) Strayer
1974–
Madeline DeLacorte
Cardinal White Mage
1984–
Benjamin Strayer
2000–
Oswald "Oz" Strayer
2003–

## BEAUMONT FAMILY

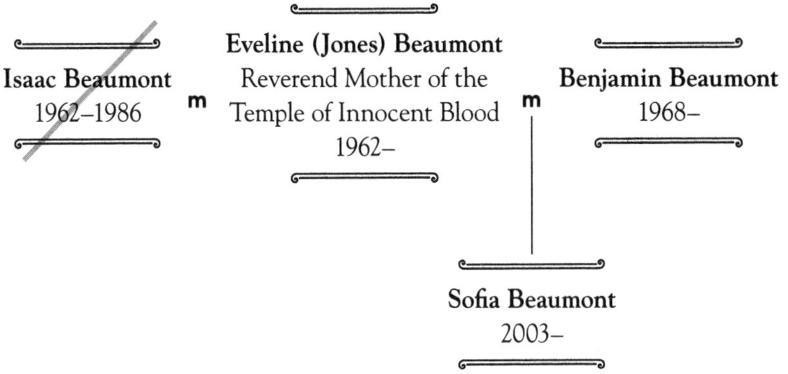


## VINCENT FAMILY

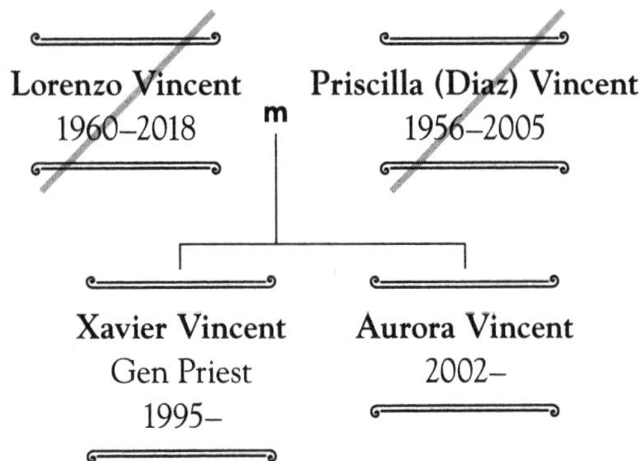

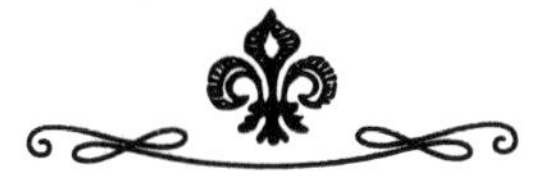

# PART I

I'm no longer accepting the things I cannot change . . .
I'm changing the things I cannot accept.

—ANGELA DAVIS

# MAYOR OF NEW ORLEANS CALLS IN REINFORCEMENTS TO CRACK DOWN ON MAGICAL CRIME

**By Sharita L. Green, academic fellow**

Today marks one week since a fire aboard the *Montaigne Majestic* tragically ended the lives of fifty-one people, including Lenora Savant, [former] Queen Mother of the Generational Magic Council of New Orleans, and her husband, Felix Savant, owner of several local capital investment and real estate firms. The New Orleans Police Department has concluded their investigation and ruled the incident "an unfortunate accident." However, members of the community are not pleased with the police response.

"Magic is a deadly weapon," says Tabitha Edgewater, leader of the Redeemers, an activist group lobbying local elected officials to implement magical regulation. "In light of recent events that were clearly the result of magical hijinks, I see a need now more than ever for strict magical law enforcement, which should begin with the registration of *every* magic user." Edgewater also stated she hopes to join forces with Eveline Beaumont's newly established Magical Regulation Bureau; however, Edgewater claims to have not been able to secure a meeting with Beaumont, who has also not responded to our invitation to comment on the matter.

In a statement to the *Herald* from the mayor's office, we've learned that Mayor Beaumont has been granted a high-priority request for the transfer of Detective Jeida Sommers to New Orleans from her current position in the Miami Police Department. Under Sommers's leadership, her team took down the South Florida arm of the Divine Knights, a shadow magic cartel who'd used their power and influence to control the drug and party scene in the city for the past three decades. Prior to Sommers's work in Miami, the Center for Magical Data Analysis and Reporting *from p.1*

(CMDAR) released an essay in 2018, in which researchers claimed "it is estimated that anywhere from 75–85 percent of the unsolved murders in Miami-Dade County and surrounding areas could be linked to the Divine Knights' operation." Sommers will leave behind an impressive legacy, where she and her team reduced the number of unsolved homicides by more than *half* through their work crushing magical gang activity in Miami [Source: CMDAR data].

Mayor Beaumont gave the following official announcement: "[The mayor's] office and the Magical Regulation Bureau are pleased to partner with Detective Sommers and the New Orleans Police Department to crack down on magical foul play in New Orleans. Let's make our city safe again."

# PROLOGUE

## VALENTINA SAVANT

### ONE MONTH AFTER THE INCIDENT ABOARD THE *MONTAIGNE MAJESTIC*

Granny was dead, and no one gave a damn—a truth that Valentina Savant choked on for the entirety of her grandparents' poorly attended joint funeral service.

Lenora Savant, Queen Mother of the Generational Magic Council of New Orleans, had single-handedly pulled their community out of the muck of scandal the previous Queen, Cristine Dupart, had rolled around in like a sloppy pig—until Granny sent her to the slaughterhouse. Since Granny's death, grief had swollen inside Valentina, taking up nearly all the space in her chest, and now she had to somehow make room for the unwelcome fact that Granny had already been forgotten.

The church where the droopy-faced bishop gave her grandparents' eulogy was so empty that the man's sleepy voice echoed in the cavernous sanctuary—and Valentina's hollowed heart. It was hard for her to sit still while trying to wrangle all the emotions fighting for her attention. She hardly got much use out of the black kerchief she'd brought, which she'd taken from her mom's closet. Valentina had already cried enough.

The closed casket helped too.

If Valentina had had to sit and stare at her grandparents' corpses for the entirety of the service, she would've broken down and crumbled into ashes on the spot. But she managed to hold it together because she'd developed a sturdy callus to the pain of absence; so, instead of acting out like her dad, who wailed until Eveline Beaumont sat beside him and rubbed his back, Valentina sat still, with quiet rage stewing inside her.

What happened on the *Montaigne Majestic* that night had not been an "unfortunate accident." And Valentina had a pretty good idea who was responsible for the deaths of her grandparents. It made sense after everything that'd happened last month, which began with the confrontation between Granny and Cris's ratchet-ass aunt Ursula at the pier. Valentina should have known Cris and her family would be out for blood once they learned the truth about the hex doll that almost killed their mother. Thanks, Oz.

But then Granny had gotten sloppy, and of course, Cris and her family had taken advantage of that misstep.

There was no way in the infinite realms of the universe Valentina would let those bitches get away with what they'd done. She didn't know how yet, but one day, she would make Cris and her family repay the blood debt they owed her.

But first, she'd have to survive the rest of the funeral. She would have plenty of time to sort out her enemies once she was Queen.

After the church service, there was no elaborate jazz funeral march with blaring brass instruments swinging back and forth, glinting in the sunlight, followed by a winding, blocks-long second line of folks dancing and grinning in celebration of Granny's life and legacy. Instead, Valentina and her father ducked into the black car provided by the funeral home and rode to the cemetery together.

Several quiet moments into the ride, Dad let out a choked sob and proclaimed, "I don't know if I can do this."

Valentina felt her face twist, wrinkling her nose, and she clenched her teeth to keep from saying what was on her mind.

Dad sucked in a shaky breath and turned to the window.

*Such a fucking child.*

They rode in throttling silence the rest of the way.

Dad had already been a pitiful mess after learning of Granny's and Grandpa Felix's deaths, but when the police told Dad they couldn't locate Granny's head and she'd have to be entombed without it, he went flailing over the edge. Afterward, he drank himself into an emotional hurricane, ripped down all of Mom's clothes and shoes from the closet, and disappeared for three days—most likely holding down a grand suite at the House of Vans, complete with bottle and body service. Valentina wondered if he'd deteriorated so fast because Mom was still missing.

Neither of them had heard a word from Gabriela Savant since the morning she'd packed an overnight bag and stormed out of the house. At times, Valentina wondered if Cris's family had taken her mother too. Or maybe Mom had finally realized Dad would never love her the way she wanted, so she'd gotten the hell out before she couldn't save herself anymore.

*But why leave me behind?*

The question plagued Valentina more than she cared to admit. She wondered if Mom had gone back to California, where she grew up, where Valentina's maternal family still lived—the family she'd never been able to form a connection with because Mom had iced them out before Valentina was born for some reason she never wanted to talk about.

After Mom had left, Valentina learned what true loneliness felt like. And in that lonely state, her hatred for her dad festered and spread, because she didn't understand how he wouldn't do more to find Mom or at least find out what happened to her.

It wasn't until Mom's absence that Valentina realized that although she loathed her mother most times, she'd grown accustomed to her presence. Gabriela was very far from a perfect mother, but, unlike Dad, she'd been present—in body, at least, if not always in mind. Valentina often wondered what kind of mother Mom could've been without shouldering the trauma of Dad's bullshit. However, in the quiet weeks following her grandparents' passing, Valentina grew to hate her mom almost as much as her dad for abandoning her. And the hate continued to burgeon until Valentina began hating herself for missing her mom. And so, she often sat for hours on end, blasting through leaderboards on Xbox, mentally and emotionally spiraling in an endless cycle of anger and sadness.

However, the entire morning of her grandparents' funeral, Valentina had felt something new. It floated on top of her grief and depression, a glistening oil sheen on water.

Anxiety.

When they arrived at the cemetery, Dad stepped aside to speak with the funeral director, and Valentina made the short walk to her grandparents' final resting place. She was grateful Granny had had the forethought to have a grand mausoleum erected for her and Grandpa Felix, though she'd bet Granny hadn't considered she'd recoup her investment so soon.

Valentina stopped in front of the massive stone crypt with its double oak-and-brass doors propped open. A cold chill wafted from within, stopping her on the threshold. Sadness had lived inside that place from the moment it was constructed, long before her grandparents' bodies moved in. And, like the master of a home, Valentina would never be able to visit without acknowledging the grief that not only owned that place but would remain there until no one left alive remembered the dead inside.

She took a deep shuddering breath and stepped through the doors.

The black Louboutin heels Granny had bought Valentina for her birthday last year clicked against the mausoleum's polished stone, and the sound echoed off the walls. Candles burned along the floor and on pedestals toward the back of the space, which was about a quarter the size of Valentina's bedroom at home. Eerie orange light danced inside the crypt, tossing shadows across the sealed tombs where her grandpa's and her headless grandmother's bodies had been laid to rest.

Tears pricked her eyes, and she gripped both bouquets of black roses she'd brought along with her before setting one atop each tomb, rectangular stone caskets set beside each other on a raised dais in the center of the room.

Valentina ran her satin-gloved fingers across the engraving on each.

LENORA SAVANT

1964–2019

A FORCE. FOREVER QUEEN. BELOVED MOTHER AND GRANDMOTHER.

MAY HER LEGACY BE UNDYING.

MAY HER SPIRIT BE ENDURING AND MERCIFUL.

FELIX SAVANT
1959–2019
HERE LIES A GOOD MAN.

Valentina bit her lip and tasted the bitter coating of lipstick, then sucked in a shaky, anxious breath. *Be better*—the promise she'd made to Granny. She intended to keep it. She *needed* to keep it. But how could she? Cris's family had not only snatched both Valentina's grandparents but also her granny's legacy.

She would *never* forgive Cris for that. Not even (finally) sitting on the throne of the Gen Council would soften Valentina's contempt for her ex-bestie.

But maybe she could focus on building her own legacy and being better, and with time, those raw feelings would fade. Or perhaps she'd bury Cris alive beneath the dais in the throne room.

The shuffle of footsteps accompanied by a dramatic sob set Valentina's skin crawling. Her father shambled into the mausoleum, reeking of tequila. His light-brown cheeks were wet with the tears that still free-fell from his swollen red eyes. He reached out for her, but she ducked under his arm and headed for the door.

"Valentina, *please*," Dad whimpered. "Can you just stand here with me, at least?"

She frowned over her shoulder at him and shook her head before stepping back into the sunlight.

"You okay, Val?"

Sofia Beaumont's voice had always been gentle while still maintaining a sturdiness that was so solid at times, it'd felt like Valentina could physically cling to it. Sofia loved to remind her it was because she was a triple water sign—whatever the hell that meant. Regardless, Sofia's presence was comforting, which Valentina gladly folded into as she leaned against the stone façade of the mausoleum beside her one remaining friend.

"That's a loaded question right now," Valentina answered.

"I get it." Sofia took a long pull on a weed vape she produced from nowhere like a street magician.

"You know that vaping shit's bad for you."

Sofia scoffed. "I'll *know* when to quit."

Valentina turned to side-eye her friend properly but had to stop and blink several times to make sure she *actually* saw what she thought she was seeing. "Sofia . . ." she said. "Why the *fuck* are you wearing *yellow* to my grandparents' funeral?"

Albeit disrespectful, the yellow linen pantsuit and skinny black tie Sofia had put together were striking. Valentina didn't care for the yellow Chucks, but she'd never waste her energy sharing that critique with Sofia because Sofia generally didn't care what people thought about her. Never had. Well, unless that person was her mother—Eveline Beaumont.

"This morning, my cards predicted you'd need some warmth, so I decided to look the part," Sofia said, sucking smoke in a river from her parted lips into her nose and out again. "And I was right, which I typically am, long as I have these." She coughed and tapped two fingers on the small golden-brown satchel draped over one shoulder, which concealed her handy-dandy tarot deck. Sofia often forgot her phone or keys or literally anything else, but she never, *ever* left her cards behind. Not even once.

Valentina rolled her eyes and leaned back against the mausoleum's outer wall.

Beside her, Sofia lowered her gaze. "You have magic, and I have my cards."

And there it was. Sofia was an emotional creature, another trait she attributed to being a triple water sign—Valentina made a mental note to google that later—but what that really meant was that whenever they got together, it was always only a matter of time before Sofia would lay her emotional wound bare to Valentina, the only person Sofia had left in the world to confide in about her biggest shame.

Sofia Beaumont, daughter of the Reverend Mother of the Temple of Innocent Blood, was shunned from generational magic, which meant she was unable to wield the power of her ancestors like Valentina or Cris.

Besides Valentina, the only other people who knew were Sofia's mother and Cris. But Sofia had nothing to worry about, as Valentina imagined Eveline wouldn't want to go around town blabbing about her daughter's ineptitude in magic, and Valentina and Cris had both vowed to keep Sofia's secret. As much as Valentina hated Cris, she couldn't deny Cris was a girl of her word.

And so was Valentina.

Sofia always had Valentina's back; she even stuck around after the fallout with Cris. Sofia also had her eccentricities—of which there were more than a few—but, most importantly, she was trustworthy and loyal. And that mattered to Valentina. Now more than ever.

Sofia looked up at Valentina with light-brown eyes that complemented her gentle voice like honey on warm biscuits. "Would you like me to do a pull for you? It might help you feel better."

*Not really*. "Sure," Val said unenthusiastically, although Sofia either didn't notice or didn't care.

Grinning, she opened her purse and carefully retrieved her tarot deck with the same care as if she were handling a precious gemstone. She removed the cards from their case, which was made from wood and bone. Her mom had gotten it hand carved by a local artisan for her this past Christmas.

Sofia gave the cards a hearty shuffle. The flapping of their plastic edges rooted Valentina to the present, even though her mind yearned to swim off to anywhere other than here in the thick humidity of the summer Louisiana air. And with as much as Valentina was sweating, she felt like she'd already been swimming. The afternoon Sun was relentless, and she was grateful she'd chosen to wear the wide-brimmed black hat she'd borrowed from her granny's closet. She hoped Granny was watching from the spiritual realm—and was proud of her.

There weren't many funeral attendees who stuck around for the final goodbyes to Granny and Grandpa Felix at the cemetery. Benjamin Beaumont was at the church service earlier but jetted before the bishop hit the second syllable of "amen" during the final prayer, leaving his wife and daughter behind. Valentina had wondered how Eveline felt about that, but since Eveline always looked annoyed, it had been truly hard to tell.

In the shade of a lofty tree not far from where Valentina stood, she noticed Eveline and Jack Kingston speaking in hushed voices despite what appeared to be a tense conversation, judging by how Eveline jabbed her finger in Jack's chest. He threw his arms up, and the red flush of his face deepened.

Eveline wore her hair pinned underneath a black hat and half veil with a simple yet elegant black skirt and blazer. Jack's dark gray suit was wrinkled and distressed, and his well-worn casual black shoes curled upward at the toes. His dirty-blond hair was also messy, likely owing to how he wouldn't quit raking his hands through it in frustration.

Valentina was keenly interested in what those two were chatting about. Granny sometimes hired Jack to consult for her privately. She'd called it "mud work," but Valentina had watched enough television and played enough video games that she knew damn well what that meant.

"All right," Sofia said, fanning the deck out in front of her. "Pull one card and show it to me."

Valentina slid her finger along the slick surfaces of the overturned cards, stopped on a random one, and pulled it out. Sofia had done this for her a hundred times over, and Valentina had never felt anything before, during, or after picking a card. Sofia's readings were always general enough that everything mostly came true, but to Valentina that was as useful as predicting they'd have homework on any given school day. But she placated her friend because tarot occupied the space in Sofia's life that real magic had left vacant.

Valentina turned the card over and rolled her eyes.

"What is it?" Sofia asked.

Death. Valentina gave the card to her friend, who immediately launched into an excited explanation.

"It's not literal—"

Valentina waved a hand. "I know, I *know*. Not a physical death, but it means the end of something else, yada, yada, yada. You told me already, Sof."

"I was just trying to help," Sofia muttered under her breath as she carefully returned her cards to their carrying case.

Someone standing at the crossroads of the path leading to Granny and Grandpa's mausoleum drew Valentina's eye. A Black woman with medium-brown skin and a shoulder-length bone-straight silk press that was all business. The black suit and modest-heeled shoe she wore drew a skeptic look from Valentina. The woman was too far away for Valentina to be sure, but she could've sworn they locked eyes for a moment.

"How long has that lady been standing over there?" Valentina asked Sofia.

"Since before we got here," Sofia replied. "She's just been lurking."

"Do you know who she is?"

"Some detective. She's working with my daddy on something. She stopped by our house the other day, and I overheard her talking with my parents."

A spark of intrigue zipped up Valentina's spine. "About what?"

Sofia shrugged, and Valentina wanted to strangle her. "Boring politics. I wasn't interested."

Valentina sighed. She genuinely loved Sofia, but it would always annoy the shit out of Valentina that Sofia *never* knew when to pay attention.

"Why do you care?" Sofia asked.

"*Fuck!*" Jack shouted, drawing Valentina's and Sofia's attention. He stormed off, leaving Eveline standing alone underneath the tree.

"I don't," Valentina said, and started toward Eveline.

"Hey!" Sofia called after her. "Where you going?"

Valentina waved a hand over her shoulder without turning back.

"Hey, Mrs. Beaumont," she said as she stepped into the marginal coolness of the aged tree's shade.

"Valentina," cooed Eveline. Even when trying to be comforting, Eveline's voice still bore an unavoidable sharpness around the edges. No wonder Sofia's relationship with her mother was so messed up. Relatable. "How you holdin' up, hon?"

"I'm here," Valentina said, then pointed at Jack, who'd just gotten into his SUV and slammed the door. "Is everything okay?"

Eveline tilted her head slightly and narrowed her eyes at Valentina, as if measuring the audacity of the girl who dared dip a toe into adult business. But Eveline was going to have to get used to that because Valentina wasn't going anywhere.

"Yes, yes, never mind him." Eveline waved him off.

"I wanted to talk to you about the Gen Council," Valentina said. "I assume with my granny's passing and my mom's disappearance that I—"

"Oh, Valentina, dear," Eveline interrupted, pity dripping from the razor's edge of her voice. "I wanted to wait until after the burial when everything was settled before I told you this, but your family's sovereignty has officially been revoked. Marie Dupart is Queen now." She tucked her black handbag into her armpit, then held both Valentina's shoulders in such a condescending gesture that Valentina had to bite down hard on her lips to keep from twisting out of her grasp. "It's just as well too, Valentina. You're only sixteen and don't need the responsibility of ruling weighing on you right now, not with all you're going through. Take my advice: Use this time to grieve, heal, and focus on yourself and your future." She rubbed Valentina's shoulders before cupping her hands around her mouth and calling to Sofia, who'd maintained her post beside the mausoleum.

Valentina stumbled backward until her back found the trunk of the old tree. She reached behind her and placed her hands against the rough bark, gripping it until the pads of her fingers burned. She shut her eyes and swallowed the mighty shriek she wanted to let rip from her core. This had officially become the *worst* day of her life.

As if losing both her grandparents *and* her mother in the same weekend wasn't horrible enough—

Valentina Savant would never be Queen.

# ONE
# CRISTINA

### PRESENT DAY

It's been nearly nine months since the people who thought they could play chess with my family's lives fucked around and found out, and I'm *still* angry about it.

I was in a completely different place at the start of last summer than I am now. I'd broken things off with magic because I thought the Scales of Justice, a spell I conjured from my great-grandmother's old spell book, killed my dad. Not only that, but over the years, I'd begun to believe the rumors about my grandmother, Cristine Dupart, former Queen of the Generational Magic Council of New Orleans, that she'd murdered the mayor's daughter in a magic ritual in the Council Chamber hidden in the basement of St. John's Cathedral—where the police had found the woman's body the next day.

However, by the end of last summer, I found out my grandmother had been falsely accused of the crime that conjured the mob that lynched her and my grandfather on their own front lawn, in sight of their five young children—my mother and her sisters. Through some clever sleuthing and with help from my twin brother, Clem, and a new friend, Aurora Vincent, I uncovered proof that my grandmother's best friend had orchestrated the whole ordeal.

Thirty years ago, Lenora Savant wove a blanket of lies she then used to smother my grandmother's legacy and ascend *her* throne. And when my dad got too close to the truth, Lenora had her goons murder him. That old crone took our dad from us, and because of her, I carried that guilt, thinking it was my fault for over a year.

So, on the thirtieth anniversary of her grand deception, I, along with my family and with the blessing of Papa Eshu, called in the egregious blood debt Lenora Savant owed us.

We took her life. And her head.

Her husband, Felix, is dead too. We let him keep his head though.

And we snatched back our throne, which should've never left our family in the first place. An unexpected gift of that whole hellacious journey is that I reconnected with magic, an old friend I incorrectly thought had turned on me.

Now Mama's Queen of the Gen Council, and I'm next in line.

I should be happy and at peace, but I haven't been for months. Instead, I'm still angry and . . . unsatisfied. No matter what attempt I make at pushing forward, unresolved anger's always buzzing around my thoughts like an annoying housefly that suddenly resurrects every time I think it's finally died. I've wondered if I should ask Mama about restarting therapy sessions with Dr. Omar, but I'm still not ready to swallow the concept of accepting things I "can't" change. Maybe because that's not completely true; there are some things I have the power to change, if I'm willing to use it—my power, that is.

Since the night on the *Montaigne Majestic* when we ended Lenora Savant's reign of terror, I've run my fingers along her web of deceit many times, lingering on the names attached to each thread and tracing them back to the rage chained up inside me, bucking to break free. So many people had their hands in betraying my family—betraying *me*.

And they *all* got away with everything.

That will never sit right with me.

*Dr. Gregory Thomas*. The quack physician who upheld the farce that Mama was deathly ill, while Lenora magically poisoned her with a hex doll that'd been planted by my snake of an ex.

*Eveline Beaumont*. A silent partner in Lenora's treachery. I don't have solid proof of her part in what went down three decades ago, but I've learned that where one rat can be found, there are typically more. And besides, if God themself descended from the spiritual realm and tapped that woman on the shoulder, I still would not trust her.

*Xavier Vincent*. Another of Lenora's tools—and an actual tool—who magically incapacitated his younger sister and stuck her in an asylum, which I freed her from.

*Oswald "Oz" Strayer.* The aforementioned snake of an ex, who'd been conjuring love spells on me until I exposed him last summer.

I've thought long and hard about adding two more names to that list. Starting with Lenora Savant's daughter-in-law, Gabriela Savant. But when I really thought about it, I realized her only crime was allowing herself to be a royal pawn. As far as I know, she's still missing, which is fine by me. Her weakness is her penance.

And then there's Lenora's granddaughter, Valentina Savant (*ex-heiress* of the Gen Council), who also happens to be my ex-bestie. Yeah, fate has a real jacked-up sense of humor. Valentina and I will never be friends again, but I'd be a monster to not acknowledge the grief she must be feeling after what we did to her grandparents. It's probably similar to how I felt when her granny murdered my dad. Valentina's navigating her own personal hell right now, and I'm good with leaving her to it.

She's not the one I'm angriest with right now.

Nor is she the one whose house I'm sitting outside, attempting to talk myself out of doing what I know damn well should've been done a long time ago.

Oz Strayer needs to be put down.

Oz's mom has been posting pictures to her Instagram since she and her husband took off for Vegas early this morning. Every year, Oz's parents spend their anniversary there, where they eloped many years ago, which, mind you, enraged his grandmother, who was the Cardinal of the white mages at the time. She preferred her daughter be with a warlock. After his grandmother passed, his mom's older sister, Madeline DeLacorte, became Cardinal but never married or had kids of her own, which means she has no one to name as her successor. But I'm not concerned with white people's problems today.

Oz's older brother, Benji, never wastes an opportunity to frolic during this guaranteed free weekend every year, so he hit the streets hours ago, while the Sun was still out.

A past version of me would've cherished an entire weekend of private time with Oz. But that girl was under a spell. And she's gone now because all the jerks who took advantage of and abused her eventually burned her at the stake like a white mage. Unfortunately, for them, *I* rose from those ashes, a gen queen who stands proud atop a legacy built by a long line of extraordinary Black people, especially Black women.

However, present me is still happy to find Oz home alone tonight, confirmed by his car out front. I grab my bag of conjuring supplies and get out of my car, which I parked on the street at the edge of the driveway. The chill in the nighttime air nips at the exposed skin of my neck, so I throw up the hood of my hoodie. I take a step and stop, narrowing my eyes at the old beat-up white pickup parked farther down the street on the opposite side. Something about it feels out of place, but maybe I'm just being paranoid.

The spare house key is in the same spot: inside the outlet cover by the front door. Oz's parents had to start leaving an extra outside because he couldn't quit losing his. There are probably a dozen keys to his family's home scattered throughout New Orleans like Dragon Balls. Also, last winter, Oz's dad removed the doorbell camera because Oz's mom wouldn't stop spying on her family's comings and goings with it like the NSA.

I grin with gratitude for this family's dysfunction, which makes it so freaking easy to do what I came here to do tonight. I unlock the door and step into the dark foyer.

The bottom floor is dark and quiet. I stop at the bottom of the staircase and listen for several moments. Nothing. Oz must be upstairs in his room. I check the time. Only a little after midnight. He adores being up at this hour because then he can be a creep without worrying about judgment from woke people.

I sneak up the stairs, sticking to the far sides to prevent them from creaking. At the top, I release the breath I held the whole climb and inch toward the dim light glowing from underneath Oz's bedroom door midway down the hall.

I swallow the paranoid lump in my throat that's telling me this is a mistake and to turn around and go back home. But that's just propaganda pushed by the spirit of the old me, who thought it was wrong to stand up for herself like this, to swing back at the people who swung at her first.

So . . . I step back, take a deep breath, and kick the door open.

Oz, sitting in bed, yelps and yanks the blanket up to his waist, leaving his familiar naked torso exposed and as blanched with surprise as his face. He stares at me through terrified wide eyes.

"Cris?" He blinks and shakes his head. "What are you doing here? How'd you get in my house?"

I step inside his room, ignoring his questions, and push the door closed behind me.

His phone is in his hand, the screen dark, locked. His other hand's hidden beneath the blanket. I approach his bedside, close enough to notice his slight tremble. I can almost smell the tangy, acidic scent of fear on him. *Mmm.* Nature's cologne. It's like a pheromone.

I rip the blanket away, and his face burns bright red as we both stare down at his shame. At least he's wearing shorts.

Between his legs lies a group of hex dolls he must've been fastidiously sewing shut. I tilt my head and flick my eyes to his.

"I-It's not what you think," he stammers.

I scoff under my breath and double back to his desk across the room, near the door. He doesn't move an inch.

"Cris, please say something," he begs. "You're really weirding me out."

I sweep one arm across his desk to clear the surface for my work, sending all his belongings crashing to the floor. He jumps with a start and swings his legs over the edge of the bed, but I turn and hold up two fingers at him. He stops at once.

"Sit your ass back down." When he doesn't move, I raise my voice. "*Now!*"

He scrambles back onto the bed and hugs his knees to his chest, his long legs bent double. "What are you doing?" he asks. "Can we just talk? Please?"

"Sure," I say.

He relaxes and releases a shuddering breath. But he tenses again once I set my bag on the desk and begin unpacking the conjuring items I brought with me.

A mirror chamber, made from a thrifted old wooden jewelry box, inside of which I glued mirrors to each wall.

A plain hex doll.

A large sewing needle.

A string of hemp dyed purple.

A bit of snakeskin.

A small container of liquid fire, a concoction of various oils, peppers, and spices that probably tastes like molten lava. One sniff of this stuff could clear someone's sinuses for a week.

And, last, a lavender-colored candle.

I set the candle on the desk and light it with the matches I also brought.

"I need this to burn a bit for the wax," I explain. "In the meantime, I'm going to talk, and you're going to shut the fuck up and listen. Do you understand?"

"Cris. What *is* this?"

"So, you *don't* understand?"

His Adam's apple dips as he swallows hard. "Are you going to kill me?"

I stalk over and grab him by his skinny throat. He's stronger than me, so he easily yanks my hand away, but not before I snatch a few strands of his ginger hair.

He curses and holds his head, scuttling out of my reach.

"You have no shortage of faults, Oz," I tell him, "but you were right about one thing. I shouldn't have ever turned my back on magic. When my mama became Queen, I gained access to a part of my world I never imagined I'd get to see. And over the past nine months, I've finally come to understand how fortunate I am to be gen."

Oz's face twists into an ugly grimace.

"And one of the benefits of being heiress to the Gen Council is that I get access to the extensive Council Library." I raise an eyebrow at him. "I've learned a lot of really cool shit in just that short amount of time."

His muscles tense, and his eyes flit to the door and back to me.

I shake my head at him. "That would be a waste of time."

I don't really know what I'll do if he does try to flee. He only needs to believe I do.

"I won't bore you with the details of everything I've learned, but there is something very intriguing I discovered and want to share—because it pertains to our situation." I stuff Oz's hair into the hex doll via an opening in its side, thread the needle with the purple hemp string, and stitch the doll closed while I talk.

"Way, *waaay* back in the day, there used to be a full-on god of justice. He was around even before Papa Eshu. His name was Oberun, and there's not a lot on record about him, but what little I found was clear about one thing: He never agreed with turning the other cheek. In fact, he believed that when someone fucked with you, you fucked with them *harder*. And when they messed with your family . . . well . . . you see where this is headed. He was also first to coin the term 'blood justice.'

"But Oberun was misunderstood by mostly everyone. People thought he was too aggressive, too destructive, too radical, too *angry*. So it's no surprise they faded him out of mainstream Moon-magic lore over the past century. Respectability politics have a way of erasing Black people's history like that." Oz's brows pinch, and I add, "Don't strain. I expected you might not get it straightaway."

He digs his nails into his legs and presses his lips into a thin line but remains quiet, though I see in his sharp stare that he wants to fire back at me.

I finish my needlework and hold the doll up to the candlelight to examine it. Not perfect but good enough. It's hard to sew while having to keep one eye on Oz and trying not to skewer my fingers with this big-ass needle. And it also doesn't help that my fingers are shaking from nerves.

"There's no record of what happened to Oberun or where he's gone, and no traditional magic users call on him today," I continue. "But I was curious, so I gave it a try. And this is where *you* come in." I point the needle at Oz, and he flinches.

"I prayed to Oberun a *lot*," I say. "I craved guidance from someone who might understand me better. I had so much anger inside me because of what you and all the other people you conspired with did to me and my family. Y'all stole the most valuable things I had: Time. Memories. Grief. Things I'll never get back, not even with magic. I just *knew* Oberun would understand that.

"I wanted him to give me permission to unchain my rage. To feel it. To let others taste it, the ones who think my life is a token for them to play with—people like you. I wanted you all to glimpse the monster I can be when I stop being nice."

"This isn't you," Oz says. "You *are* nice."

"*Was*," I correct him. "Abusers like you require niceness from their victims, a never-ending turning of cheeks, because that makes it easier for y'all to keep doing what y'all do best—exploiting and destroying. But *you* don't get to do that anymore, Oz. A nice person was never going to stop you, but I am now." I grimace at the pathetic hunched sight of him. "Did you really think I was going to let you get away with conjuring love spells on me and almost killing my mama?"

I wait for him to say something, but he's silent. And then the sharp smell of urine stings my nose. His jaws clamp tight, his face ashen, highlighting the ginger freckles across his nose and the tops of his cheeks.

"P-please don't kill me." He sniffs and wipes the single tear that rolls down his cheek. "I'm so sorry, Cris. Please b-believe me. I won't bother you or your family again, I swear."

"Oh, it's much too late for that," I reply, deadpan.

I open the vial of liquid fire and dip the hex doll's tiny round hands and feet inside, coating them with oil, careful not to let a single drop of the stuff touch my bare skin. The last time it got underneath my nails, my nail beds felt like they were on fire for three days.

"You almost did get away with it, y'know," I tell him. "I came *real* close to buying into that whole concept of 'radical acceptance and moving on.' And I felt bad about going back on my promise to 'let go' at first, until I realized I'm allowed to change my mind. I don't want to just be okay with scum like you getting to hurt people—especially Black girls like me and Valentina—as you please and without consequence. That's not justice." I shake my head. "So you don't get to do that anymore. And if I have to be the gotdamned reaper to make sure that happens, then so be it."

"But you don't even *like* Valentina!" he cries. "I did that for *you*!"

"Oz, I can't stand your mama either, but that doesn't mean I want her run down by a car."

"I don't understand why you're still coming after me though. I *said* I was sorry, and I *am*! I'm really, *really* sorry, Cris! You're better than this!"

"You see, that's *exactly* why I'm here tonight. If not for me, you'd never take accountability for your shit. You, and white people like you all over the world, act the same. When y'all do awful things to people of color, y'all *always* expect us to take the high road, forgive and forget, except that's the only time y'all ever afford us a sliver of humanity—any other time we're 'savages' and 'thugs.'

"But what happens when the oppressed stop being nice? What will y'all do when Black women collectively, across the world, all wake up and decide we're no longer taking y'all's bullshit? What if we choose violence instead of forgiveness? *Then* what?"

Oz hugs himself. "Sooo . . . you're just going to murder me in cold blood? Cris, please be serious. You're not trying to go to prison for real."

I chuckle softly. "That would require me to get caught."

The faint, strangled whimper that comes from him is euphoric to me.

"Anyways," I say, "we've gotten off track. So, I prayed and prayed to Oberun, but he never answered, not even with a single sign. I started to doubt why I ever thought he would. I mean, he's been MIA for centuries, and who am I?

"But I started looking for the perfect spell for you on my own, something fitting for your crimes. I searched the Council's library for *months*, digging through dusty old books for hours at a time, raw anger keeping me motivated. And then I finally found the right one, but it called for a rare ingredient that I, unfortunately, could not get my hands on and could not substitute. The shed snakeskin of a black mamba. What were the chances? I took that as a sign to give up and finally let it go—let *you* go.

"But then, a few weeks ago, on the first warm day we had since October, I had my bedroom's balcony doors open, and a raven swooped into the room and dropped the snakeskin on my bed, then turned and flew back outside. It scared the shit out of me until I realized the gift it'd left. It was the black mamba snakeskin. He actually answered my prayers, Oz. Tonight's ritual has been blessed by Oberun himself."

I wrap the hex doll from head to foot in the grayish-black snakeskin, which crackles and flakes as I twist it around and around until the doll looks like a miniature mummy. I open the mirror chamber and pour a bit of the wax from the candle inside, then place the doll in the center of the small glob and press it there until the wax hardens.

"I bind you, Oswald Strayer, from doing magical harm to others. And, with the blessing of my ancestors and Oberun, god of justice, I sever your connection to the spiritual realm—thus draining your flow of Moon magic—*forever.*"

"Cris! No! *What the fuck?*" Oz cries, holding his hands in front of his face as his fingertips glow with soft blue light; it trickles up from them like inverted rain and floats across the room toward the mirror chamber. The magical light deposits around the rim of the open box like drops of morning dew, and when the last one lands, the lid snaps shut with a *click.* The seams glow bright, sealing the mirror chamber shut and transforming it into an impenetrable block of wood with Oz's hex doll forever trapped inside.

"It's not exactly blood justice, but it'll do for now," I tell him, as I place the box and the rest of my belongings inside my bag. "However, if you fuck with me or my family again, Oz, I *will* kill you."

He frowns, wrinkling his nose at me. "I hate you."

I shrug. "Well, now you'll have to do it without my ancestors' magic."

He glowers at me as I leave his bedroom.

I hurry down the stairs into the dark lower level of Oz's home. My heart races, but he doesn't follow me. Once I'm out the front door, I breathe a relieved sigh, return the key to its hiding place, and head to my car.

I take a detour across the Huey P. Long Bridge—which is relatively deserted this time of night—turn on my hazards, and pull over. I grab the sealed mirror chamber from my bag and get out of the car.

I step up to the side of the bridge, and a shock of frigid air, chilled by the Mississippi River below, whips across me. I stare down into the murky water for a second, then chuck the mirror chamber in. It hits with a pitiful splash and sinks into the depths.

I make a fist, kiss the side of my knuckle, and lift it to the sky. "Thank you, Oberun."

When I pull onto the road again, I let out a scream of pure joy and satisfaction. I bang on the steering wheel and release another cry of triumph. Tears well in my eyes, and I wipe them on the back of my hand and smile until my cheeks ache. I blast Megan Thee Stallion and cruise the nighttime streets of my city, too hopped up on adrenaline to rush back home. I'm filled with a tingling brightness that courses through me; it's energizing, like my heart's become a miniature sun, pumping rays of sunshine through my veins—and I wonder—

Is this what power feels like?

Is this what it's like to take justice into my own hands?

If so . . . it feels fucking amazing. So . . . why should I stop here?

*Dr. Gregory Thomas.*

*Eveline Beaumont.*

*Xavier Vincent.*

*Blood justice will soon come for each and every one of you.*

# TWO
## CLEMENT

Nine months ago, I found real love with a boy who shone more brilliantly than raw moonlight, a boy I would've lost forever were it not for the remarkable gift of dark Moon magic.

And . . . I think I fucked up.

Because now it's hard to look at Yves Bordeaux for fear of invoking the sensation of frigid fingers grazing my skin before abject terror grabs hold of me. The fear grew from my conflicting thoughts the day I realized that when it comes to the matter of restoring Yves's severed soul, the odds are definitively *not* in my favor.

And I'd rather have my heart gouged from my chest with a rusty ice-cream scoop than default on my promise to Yves. I'd give anything to save him.

If only I knew how.

The riddle's swallowed me whole, and now escaping this tortuous captivity has monopolized my every waking thought and dream not pertaining to school. Even when I try to push the topic of Yves's fate to the bottom of my mind, it buoys right back to the surface. The only way to keep myself from obsessing over the one problem I have no idea how to fix is to hyperfocus on the one I can—schoolwork.

Mine *and* Yves's. I release a heavy sigh.

We're supposed to be studying right now, actually. But, instead, I'm downstairs pulling out the cushions of Jean-Louise's leather couch, searching for Dad's knife. I can't believe I lost it again. I know, I *know*. But I don't need to browbeat myself over this shit too on top of everything else going on.

As I reassemble the couch cushions, I try to think back to the last time I remember seeing my "blessed blade." I haven't laid eyes on it in a few weeks now, a problem I've ignored until this morning. However, today's steadfast search is merely a subterfuge. I really just needed to escape that stuffy room. The air inside was stifling with obligation, and my anxious brain was gasping for breath.

I slam the last cushion back into place with a huff.

*Where the hell is my knife?* I swear to the gods, I'm going to put a GPS tag on that thing when I find it again.

I try the kitchen next. Jean-Louise might've mistaken my knife for one of his and stuck it in one of his several junk drawers. It must be around this house somewhere. Maybe it'll turn up when it's good and ready like usual.

I left Yves upstairs reading his world history textbook. ~~He has~~ ~~We have~~ I have a test on Monday, and I also have calculus and English homework due too.

There's no way Yves can attend school in his condition, so I had to find a workaround. At the end of last summer, I signed him up for New Orleans International Magnet High School's HI program—and that's "HI" as in "homeschool integration," not drugs. I don't know why the administration never asks our opinions about these things before they roll them out, but that's neither here nor anywhere as far as I'm concerned.

Once I took care of school for him, I had to tackle the much bigger issue of Yves's older sister. I was able to convince Fabiana Bordeaux that Yves had been awarded a coveted spot in an international bridge program where he'll get all his high school credits for junior year *and* earn some early college credit too while studying abroad in Paris through June. I was proud of my well-crafted lie for all of five seconds before guilt started nibbling on my decomposing conscience. But this deception was necessary because it at least bought me a few more months to figure out how to save Yves.

Despite his being technically only *partially* alive, Yves's biometrics still work to unlock his phone, which became an important asset to my scheme. However, Yves has developed a strange aversion to his phone since we brought him back. I wish he could tell me what's going on inside his head, but communication has been practically impossible between us in his fractured state.

But it's fine. I'll deal.

Alternatively, my interactions with Fabiana were (surprisingly) much easier; however, I still crafted every exchange with the delicate precision of an artisan. Every word I typed was strategic and deliberate, and conversations were carried out sparingly and deftly, as if I were defusing a bomb. I mean, technically, I was. After what I learned about Fabiana last year, I have zero desire to be on her bad side. She scares me almost as much as the Moon King.

*Almost.*

I slam the first junk drawer shut and move on to the next. The ruckus I'm making in my search is immaterial to anyone else in this house. Lately, I've started to feel like the only living person in this bitch, and it's getting annoying. The world is cracked and crumbling all around us, yet I seem to be the only person who can be bothered.

My knife's not in the second drawer. I move on to the last one, sifting through screwdrivers, restaurant condiments, random bits and bobs from who knows what, and—

I breathe hard and slap the drawer shut with a loud bang that echoes in the kitchen. I'm frustrated because I can't shake the encroaching feeling that this tremulous house of cards I've built is about to come crashing down in an epic way. And that makes me anxious as hell because I don't know how to stop it. Or if I can.

Unbeknownst to me at the time, my doomsday clock started ticking right before Thanksgiving, when Fabiana mysteriously stopped responding to ~~Yves's~~ my messages after sending a strange text about going out of the country on a business trip. I didn't think much of it at the time because I was relieved that she'd be too busy to press for video chats with her brother during the holidays, a time when I was busy struggling to use what little emotional gas I had to power me through forced appearances with my family while concealing this bulging secret beneath my cloak the whole time.

But Fabiana's silence has lingered long enough since that I've started to wonder if something more serious might be going on.

I haven't mentioned his sister's "absence" to Yves because I don't want to worry him. And the deeper I burrow myself into the charge of making sure he doesn't fall behind in school (so I don't *completely* ruin his life), the easier it becomes to sideline the issue of Fabiana's uncharacteristic disappearance. Staying on top of my own classwork while teaching myself Yves's coursework so I can then teach *him* has been brutal as fuck; but meeting that challenge has also been exhilarating and, most importantly, distracting from the anxiety-inducing tick of the doomsday clock in the background of my mind.

I take the search for my knife outside next, through a back door in the laundry room/mudroom that leads to Jean-Louise's small, unkempt backyard. The grass is overgrown, and a small metal shed at the far end of the space looks like where a serial killer might hide their victims until they are ready to murder them. Except there are just a bunch of old boxes and other junk stashed in there. My imagination's apparently found other ways to keep busy since I haven't had time to read for pleasure lately.

I've been practically living part-time at Jean-Louise's ever since Yves's resurrection, which makes it easier to tutor him—and forces me to face my guilt. Yves was once the most gorgeous representation of a human I'd ever laid eyes on, from his mischievous good looks to his pure-gold core; but now my punishment resides in the perpetual agony of looking at the shell of who Yves Bordeaux once was and knowing I might've irrevocably broken him. And what's worst is that I don't know how to fix him again—or if I even can.

And that *torments* me.

My only hope for relief lies with Jean-Louise Petit, the grumpy sleepy-eyed necromancer whose life I barged into last summer and refused to leave. He's vowed to help me find a way to restore Yves's soul, probably because he's also living with his own semi-resurrected lover by the name of Auguste Dupre, who died several years ago in an experimental necromancy ritual that went terribly wrong. Jean-Louise's support has been the only thing propping me up all these months.

The sky's been dreary and cloudy all morning (twinsies!), but it seems the Sun's finally peeking through some of the thick cloud cover. I glance up at the window of Jean-Louise's bedroom. A door beside it opens to a sliver of balcony only large enough for maybe a small stool and table to enjoy a coffee and smoke at sunset, though Jean-Louise has left it bare. I squint at the door's frame, which looks to have been broken and shoddily repaired at some point. *Was it always like that?*

I can't remember. Don't really care, honestly.

Yves and I come out here from time to time to get fresh air. The backyard isn't very inviting, but it's private and gets good moonlight and sunlight—which reminds me! I grin and snap my fingers, remembering I left Dad's knife out here a few weeks ago so it could recharge in the light of the full Moon.

I scan the area around the door and the two rickety patio chairs where Yves and I often sit and stare up at the nighttime sky in silent reverie together.

It's not here.

I stare down the yard at the metal shed and realize the door's unlocked. That's strange. Jean-Louise never leaves it open.

As I approach the shed, I glance back at the window of Jean-Louise's bedroom. It's early afternoon, and his blackout curtains are still closed, which is unlike him. He's not a morning person (or an afternoon or an evening or a night person—yeah, he's pretty much grouchy twenty-four seven), but most days, he's usually up and moving around by nine—at the latest. Yet, for the past month, it seems Jean-Louise hasn't been engaged in much of anything, especially our joint quest. In fact, he's been downright aloof and avoidant (more than usual).

He hasn't attempted to find the Kahlungha in *months*—at least not to my knowledge. Right before Christmas, he created the experimental elixirs, using up all the narcotics I'd gotten from the ER last year after the car accident—and he'd refused to let me try them. He claimed he would hit up that same sketchy Russian guy who'd gotten us the fifty cadavers to restock so we could keep trying. But then one day, out of nowhere, he just . . . changed.

It was early January, and I came home from school and found him in bed with the door shut. It was a bit weird, but I assumed he was just taking a nap. It kept happening, and I kept overlooking it because I already had too much to deal with to babysit him, so I let him be. But it's been weeks now.

Something's wrong with Jean-Louise.

I feel on the verge of panic because my lifeline is in danger of snapping. I cannot free-fall again. I barely survived after Dad. I'm not sure I can this time.

Not with this.

My phone vibrates in my pocket with a new text. I pull it out to see who it is, preemptively annoyed.

It's Cris. Some of my sourness wanes.

You still coming to Rosalie's party at Vice Hall tonight?

Irritation reinstated. I respond immediately.

Sorry. Not in a party mood. Talk later. Have fun!!

K

I put my phone away and open the creaky door of the rusted metal shed. Muted sunlight floods the space that's packed to capacity with wilted cardboard boxes teeming with various odds and ends from Jean-Louise's life.

I sneeze from the dust and then groan loud enough to startle some of the spiders nesting at the back unit into skittering deeper into the shadows.

*What am I thinking?* My knife clearly isn't in this mess.

I'm backing out of the shed and reaching for the door when a small box beside my foot catches my attention. I kneel to check it out, and my breath catches.

I pull items out of the box one by one, growing more unwound and angrier with each. I distinctly remember all this stuff from when Yves and I first discovered Jean-Louise's "necromancy office" last summer. All the books on dark Moon magic, vials and jars filled with colored liquids and herbs—and the notebook with the broken spine in which Jean-Louise recorded notes regarding our effort to restore Yves's and Auguste's souls. I pick it up and flip through the pages. The last documented attempt was on December 13, which I remember as being right when we ran out of opiates. The pages beyond are blank.

Why would he throw this stuff out?

My chest constricts, and my breaths shorten as the air thins around me. The skin of my forehead tingles as cool beads of sweat push through my pores.

*That* fucking *liar. I can't believe he'd do this to me. I* trusted *him.*

He knows how much of a strain it's been on me to hide Yves's condition, aside from the emotional turmoil of seeing Yves like that. Was Jean-Louise just going to let me go on suffering and thinking he was actually helping when he'd already abandoned us?

Of all people . . . how could *Jean-Louise* do this to me?

I snap the notebook shut and storm back inside the house. I take the stairs up, two at a time, which leaves me winded by the time I reach the top but still too mad to slow down. I throw open Jean-Louise's bedroom door, and he sits bolt upright in bed.

His heavy-lidded eyes look extra intense, wide with the sudden shock of my intrusion. His hair's grown out and knotted. He looks like a ghost, sitting with the blankets pulled up to his waist and the ratty tee he's wearing bunched and wrinkled around his hulking frame.

His bedroom is dim, hardly lit by the pale light spilling around me through the open door. And it smells like musty armpits and salted balls in here. *When's the last time he showered?*

I fling the book at him, and I'm extra annoyed when he catches it with one hand.

He frowns down at it and then at me. His mouth prunes, but he doesn't speak. He knows he's in deep shit.

"Why the hell did you throw out our work?" I ask, poised in the doorway like a furious parent. When he doesn't answer, I add, "What happened to you?"

"Nothing, Clem," he says, his tone clipped, which only pricks me more.

"You're lying," I say.

"I'm just taking a break."

"Another lie."

"It's not!"

"What's going on with you, Jean-Louise?" I ask, afraid of the answer given the fight he's putting up. "You've been acting strange for *weeks* now. Are you depressed? Because join the crowd—"

"No," he says. "I mean, maybe, uh, I don't fucking know, Clem! It's way more complicated than that."

"Okay, whatever." I roll my eyes. "I thought you were different, but turns out you're just as selfish as everyone else." His face falls, and I hate that I find pleasure and satisfaction in hurting him back. "If you won't help with Yves's and Auguste's souls anymore, I'll just do it myself. I don't need you anyway."

"*No!*" Jean-Louise flings the cover off him, swings his big, trunk-like legs over the bed, and thunders up to me. I flinch when he grabs my shoulders in both his meaty hands. "You *cannot* do that," he says, gripping me tighter and giving me a little shake that rattles my brain in my skull. "It's too dangerous now."

"Thanks, but that warning's just vague enough to be meaningless—"

He shakes me again. "Stop being a smartass and *listen* to me for a minute, boy!"

I twist out of his grasp. "I *am*, but you're not saying anything worth hearing, *Jean-Louise*!"

I resent being called "boy," but I don't need to steer off topic.

"I did it," he proclaims only a splinter above a whisper, but the words still knock me back a step.

"Huh?"

"You heard me. I've been to the Kahlungha."

"What? *When?* And why didn't you tell me?"

He casts his eyes down at his ashy feet and his toenails, which are overgrown like his lawn. "Because I found something evil there."

I frown up at him. "What do you mean?"

"A few weeks ago, I astral projected to the Kahlungha. It was a strange place. There was a black-sand beach that went on forever in one direction, water in the other. It was a realm trapped in perpetual night with a starless sky, and this glowing orb that looked like the Moon—but definitely was not."

*Oh, God.*

Goose pimples rise on my arms and prickle along the back of my neck.

I've already been to the Kahlungha.

I reach an unsteady hand to my shoulder, the same one the Moon King grabbed in what I thought at the time was a dream or vision. The phantom chill of his grip makes me shudder.

"I met a dark presence there," Jean-Louise says, "a god who latched on to my soul and hitched a ride back to this realm." He shakes his head. "Going there was a mistake. I brought something evil back to this world, and I'll never forgive myself for it."

"But why not tell me?" I ask. "Why keep it a secret?"

He hangs his head. "A lot of reasons, none I can give a proper name to right now, but I was . . . terrified. Especially because I think he's after Yves. I never wanted to do anything to put you boys in harm's way."

I'm genuinely shocked despite my frustration at Jean-Louise for keeping such an epic secret from me for so long. "Huh? Why do you think the Moo—I mean, why's he after Yves?"

"I think he can sense powerful dark Moon magic, and our resurrection ritual that night must've called to him somehow. He kept saying he wanted 'the boy' but never said a name. Maybe he tasted the part of Yves's soul that we severed, and now he wants the rest—hell, I dunno."

My heart plunges at the thought of the Moon King snacking on Yves's soul. Dear gods, I hope that's not what happened. That can't be true. Jean-Louise is just spitballing wild theories now.

"But what I *do* know," he continues, "is he scared the shit out of me, and now he's loose in the natural realm—and it's all my fault."

"Loose?" I ask. "What do you mean, '*loose*'?"

"He seemed more monster than god. When he tethered himself to me, I felt so much fury and pain and sadness all at once." Jean-Louise shivers despite the stifling warmth of his bedroom. "When I came to, I was back in this realm, in my bedroom—and so was he.

"He stood over me—he had to stoop because he was taller than the ceiling—and grabbed my face in one hand." Jean-Louise mimics the motion of clutching his face like LeBron palming a basketball.

My soul would've left my body if that'd been me.

"He lifted me off the floor," Jean-Louise says, "but luckily, my magical wards kicked in and flung him straight through the patio door." He folds his arms over his broad chest and nods at the mended door.

So *that's* what happened to it.

"When I looked outside, he was just standing on the ground below, on the patio where you and Yves hang out sometimes, grinning up at me with those freaky glittering teeth. Then he vanished on the spot, literally melted into a puddle and evaporated into nothing.

"Thanks to my wards, this house is the only place we know that's safe from him—for now. We can't risk drawing his attention again. I won't let him have what's left of that kid."

I want to sink into the floor and disappear. Jean-Louise is sadly misinformed. The god he met in the Kahlungha is none other than the Moon King—and he's after me, not Yves. My mind harkens back to the ominous forewarning Grandma Cristine gave me last summer before Papa Eshu disappeared her back to the spiritual realm.

*Clem, the Moon King is coming for this realm.* Her words still haunt my memory banks.

I don't know what the Moon King could possibly want with me, which is no less terrifying, but I'm not going to let that stop me from saving Yves. I *promised* him.

Jean-Louise turns a stern stare onto me. "No more magic of *any* kind is allowed in this house lest we draw the Moon King back here. I need you to sit tight until I can come up with a plan."

"And how long is that gonna take?" I ask.

"I dunno." He sighs.

"A week?"

He shakes his head.

"A month?"

He shrugs.

"A *year*?"

*"I don't know, Clem!"* he shouts.

"You swore you'd help," I say. "And here you are, throwing me away too."

"That's not fair—"

"Life isn't fair, Jean-Louise!" It's my turn to yell.

He holds up his hands in front of him. "This is serious. I won't let you boys get hurt on my watch. And if you can't chill out, I'm going to have to rethink you hanging out here so much. It'd only take one call to Marie. Please don't make me do that."

I cross my arms. "And I'll tell her the real reason I'm over here all the time, and then she'll be pissed at you too."

"I don't give a shit, Clem." Jean-Louise tosses his hands up and slaps them onto his hips. "Not sure if you can tell, but mutually assured destruction doesn't work on people who ain't got shit left to destroy. I meant what I said. No more Kahlungha talk. And no magic in my house until further notice. Now leave me alone. I need to think."

*He's. Still. Fucking. Lying.* He's already had *weeks* to think.

I glower at him one last time before leaving and slamming the door behind me.

Hopelessness bears heavy on my back and shoulders as I trudge across the hall to Yves's room. I find him sitting on the floor criss-cross applesauce, bathing in the feeble light coming in between the curtains. His textbook sits open on his lap to a page on the French Revolution. His brown skin no longer gleams but pales even in natural light, and the gateways to other worlds that once existed in his dark eyes are now sealed shut.

The moment he sees me, he sets his book aside and stands, his own face twisting when he sees the dejection in mine. Yet another thing I hate about this predicament. Even though Yves is not wholly himself and has every right to hate me for it, he still bothers to suss out my every emotion so he can attend to them even when I'm trying my damnedest to hide them from him.

He grabs a throw blanket and points at the recliner. He wants me to sit.

I shake my head at him. He does this a lot, urging me to nap or rest in that little raggedy chair Jean-Louise found at Goodwill and dragged up here for Yves. Neither he nor Auguste sleeps anymore, so they have no need for a bed, but the reclining chair at least ensures he can be somewhat comfortable in his misery while he spends his days and nights cooped up, reading and lamenting the life he's lost.

I start unloading my own books from my bag and organizing them so I can study too—even though I know good and damn well I'll never be able to settle my mind enough to comprehend a single sentence after the fight Jean-Louise and I just had.

I'm so damn tired.

When I open my eyes every morning, I wonder if this will be the day I finally fizzle out like a star that's burned too intensely for too long. The thrill of accomplishing the impossible, resurrecting Yves, has dwindled significantly over the past couple weeks, leaving me less motivated, more exhausted, and even grumpier.

Yves puts a tepid hand on my arm. The coolness of his touch startles me out of my reverie, and I jerk away from him without thinking. His desolate face darkens even more. Despite looking wounded, he still shoves the blanket toward me, silently pleading with me to take a break.

But he doesn't understand that I can't relax yet. My back is against the last section of crumbling wall that's gonna crush us both unless I keep holding it up. Naps and daydreams are a luxury I just cannot afford right now.

I shake my head again, but Yves insists, pushing the throw into my arms.

I snatch it and toss it across the room. "I said *no*!" I shout, then clamp my mouth shut, instantaneously ashamed.

Yves recoils. His eyes waver but don't well because he doesn't cry anymore. I don't think he can.

Gingerly, he stoops to pick up his textbook, then straightens, clutching it to his chest, and heads for the door.

"Yves, wait," I call after him. "I'm sorry."

He glances back at me and half nods before disappearing into the hallway. A moment later the door of Auguste's room creaks open and then softly clicks shut.

I crumple to the floor in a heap, a wind of emotion kicking up inside the empty cavern of my chest. I hate that I've become so mean and impatient. Sometimes it feels like I don't know myself anymore.

At least Yves has Auguste. They hang out and bond over their trauma sometimes, mostly reading books—their own selections or sometimes they'll trade with each other, like how Mama and I used to do before my life got significantly more complex.

I need help. And Jean-Louise has effectively deserted me. Looks like I'm going to have to call in reinforcements.

Not Fabiana though. I'm terrified she'd skewer me on the spot.

Aunt Ursula is likewise out of the question. She's already made her stance on necromancy perfectly clear, and I'm willing to bet she'd only make this situation worse.

I'm not close enough with any of my other aunts to ask one of them—not that they'd be helpful anyway.

And despite what I said to Jean-Louise earlier, I can't be honest with Mama for many reasons, the most threatening being my fear of what she'll think of me. I don't want to disappoint her, not that she's ever made me feel like I have. But when you're so used to being thrown away by people you love, hiding any reason for them to discard you becomes a second-nature survival tactic.

I take a deep breath in through my nose and blow it out my mouth. There's only one person I can rely on. But asking my twin sister for help means I'll have to divulge that I've been keeping secrets from her despite vowing to be truthful, a crime which I've sufficiently reproved her for when she hid that whole Scales of Justice fiasco from me for so long.

But one thing's certain: I cannot tell Cris about the Moon King.

My sister would never agree to help me restore Yves's soul if she knew it might put me in danger. I suppose it's going to be utterly impossible to stop keeping secrets. But I can only pray at this point that the outcome of all this will vindicate my sometimes-sketchy means.

Welp, guess I'm going to a party tonight after all.

# THREE
## CRISTINA

The magical community of New Orleans has been somewhat peaceful under Mama's rule, the legitimacy of which was never questioned, outside the occasional antics by Redeemers. I may be biased, but I've felt our community take back some of its strength in the months since Mama ascended the throne.

Maybe it had something to do with her and I hand making and distributing protection gris for small-business owners who'd been past targets of Redeemer assholes. We even spent an entire weekend mixing a ten-gallon bucket of protective brick dust to line the thresholds of their buildings (and we gave them a little extra for home too).

It's not until late on Saturday morning that the clouds vanish, leaving the Sun uninhibited to warm all the smiling faces in the crowd of people attending the local magic festival that Mama and I spent weeks planning and all morning setting up.

The whole thing was Mama's idea, and I helped her bring it to life. She wanted to do something to celebrate and uplift the Black magical community, to give a sign that the Gen Council had returned to what it once stood for when my grandmother, Cristine Dupart, ruled as Queen: an organization that promotes peace, prosperity, and justice within our communities.

I feel a powerful sense of pride getting to impact meaningful change in my neighborhood, which has kept me energized all morning as I've been zipping back and forth helping Mama knock out the million tiny tasks that neither of us realized come along with hosting an event of this magnitude. But the hustle is worth it.

This is Mama's legacy—and I'll have my own someday. In the short span of her rule, Mama's already recruited magical volunteers to support local gen and their businesses who've faced external hardship and created counseling and support groups for victims of magical abuse (that one was my idea).

And we're just getting started.

Mama's worked really hard to paint generational magic and gen in a positive light to detract attention from the negativity spewed by the Redeemers and their supporters, especially after the *Montaigne Majestic* incident, which led to the appointment of that new detective who's allegedly taken a personal vow to "end magical crime."

*Tuh. If only she knew.*

But I'm not focusing on drama today. The purpose of this event is for all official branches of magic to come together to celebrate one another and exist in *harmony*. From inception, all were welcome, though there are only a couple of vamp- and white-mage-owned booths here. I guess Mama's vision of a euphonious existence among *all* magic practitioners is gonna take some time.

The festival is at the southern end of City Park, where dozens of vendors have erected tented booths along the perimeter of a sectioned-off area with larger tents and activity spaces in the center. There's a little something for everyone: Diviners are doing palm readings, tarot, charting, and more. Firefly Supplies arranged a massive minimarket and is offering free samples of herbs, potions, and healing tonics. Magic bookstores have brought out several authors of magical fiction and nonfiction books for signings. A couple of young white mages even showed up with several display cases filled with breathtakingly stunning crystals for charging.

I'm about to step up to their table and look around when someone across the aisle snags my attention. He's waiting in front of a booth for Oscar's Oddities and Rare Magical Effects, a vamp-owned antiquity shop that's showcasing a collection of old spell books and other relics encased in glass. He's overdressed for an outdoor market in his slim-fit cream suit and chestnut Chelsea boots. Before, when someone described a man as "tall, dark, and handsome," I would always imagine someone like Winston Duke or John Boyega; but it was only recently that I learned they really meant *white* men with dark hair, a five-o'clock shadow, and a face that's as enthralling as it is untrustworthy—or in other words, this guy.

Mr. Tall and "Dark" *is* handsome, though he looks to be in his late twenties, which is a bit *old* for my tastes. He catches me observing him, and his brow tenses, but then his eyes wander up to my satin tignon tied into a seven-knotted crown resembling Mama's.

His face lights up with sudden realization. "Cristina Trudeau, is it?"

I narrow my eyes at him suspiciously. *How does this random-ass white man know my name?*

He walks over and extends his hand for me to shake, which I do, albeit with caution. "Karmine Delaney," he says. "U.S. Vamp Dejoir. I serve on the board of MASC with your mother. I'm based out in L.A., but I'm in town on business for a while." He spreads his hands and gestures toward the market teeming with people. "Your mother has fashioned quite the event. Very impressive."

"Thanks," I say, immediately hating myself for the pride the Vamp Dejoir's validation evokes in me. Aunt Ursula's voice echoes in my head: *Pining for powerful white men to cosign your existence is a slippery slope, beloved.*

"Maybe we can work together in the future to get more vamps to participate as vendors," I tell him.

"I'd be delighted," he says, without hesitation.

"Mr. Delaney, I got you all set," announces a squat, balding white Cuban guy, gesturing for Karmine to return to his counter. Curious, I approach too.

I remember Oscar from registration because he was one of only two shadow-magic practitioners who showed interest in the festival. The other stood us up.

Oscar hands Karmine two large thin packages wrapped neatly in brown paper and tied with twine.

"Thank you, sir," Karmine says, and takes his purchase.

Oscar leans closer and lowers his voice. "And if I get wind of what we, uh"—his eyes scour me for a split second—"discussed, I'll give you a call straightaway."

"Please do," coos Karmine, before turning back to me.

I point to the packages in his hand. "What'd you get?"

He tucks them both under one arm and grins. "I'm a connoisseur of rare magical artifacts. These are twin paintings, a one-of-a-kind set, by Bellamy Corbin Moreau, a vamp who lived in the early 1800s and developed a technique to imbue his paintings with shadow magic."

"And what will you do with those?" I ask.

Karmine studies my face, but his eyes shift past me and narrow. I turn to see who he's glowering at and immediately notice the Black woman standing a few dozen feet away, not bothering to hide that she's staring at Karmine.

I recognize Detective Jeida Sommers from her headshot in that *Herald* article from a few months ago. I remember that picture because it turned my stomach, seeing her hugged up and grinning wide alongside Ben Beaumont. Today she's dressed in a black suit with a plain white button-up, and her jet-black hair hangs straight and compliant. She watches now with similar intense focus, which sets off a subtle unease within me. Something tells me I should keep my distance from this woman, but something else warns me that perhaps I should also keep an eye on her.

Still glowering at the detective, Karmine mutters, "Enjoy the rest of your day, heiress." Then he dips between two stalls and disappears.

I glance back to where Detective Sommers was standing and realize she's gone too. *What's up with those two?* I wonder if it has anything to do with the "business" that brought Karmine to New Orleans.

I did a little research on Detective Sommers and her beef with the Divine Knights, an elite shadow magic cartel with bases of operation in Los Angeles and Miami—or rather, just L.A. now, thanks to Sommers. Over the years, there were all sorts of rumors about Karmine and his family's involvement in the cartel, but no one could ever prove it. After a while, it publicly became as ridiculous an insinuation as Beyoncé being part of the Illuminati—although I never believed that one. Can't say the same for the allegations against Mr. Tall and Dark.

Karmine Delaney is absolutely suspect. *So what is he* really *doing here?*

"Cris!" Aurora Vincent walks up from the opposite direction with her best friend, Remi Prince. "Hold it right there, miss mamas!"

Last summer, I found Aurora gaunt and abandoned in Chateau des Saints, and I freed her from the spell that was literally sucking the life out of her. Then we became friends. For a very short time after, I got to witness the light rekindle in her eyes and the color return to her cheeks, which also plumped thanks to Odessa's and Mama's cooking. But now something else is draining her. Dark circles color the puffy skin beneath her eyes, and the rest of her face is pale and ghostlike.

I greet my friend and wave at the boy standing beside her. "Hi, Remi! I'm glad you came!"

Remi's a couple of inches taller than me and has acne-prone fluorescent-beige skin, thick black curls that look auburn in the sunlight, and full pink lips that are irresistible when he makes this adorable pouty face that typically works in breaking down Aurora's defenses. Thankfully, I'm immune to such charms.

I've gotten to know him a bit better by way of Aurora over the past few months, and I've mostly found Remi to be kind and quiet—not shy but also not the type of person who needs to yell or take himself too seriously. His mom's Black, but she's not in his life anymore, by her choice, the details of which he's never shared, understandably so. Remi's dad is Michael Prince, the Chinese American Democratic candidate for mayor who lost to Ben Beaumont last fall.

"Hey, Cris," Remi says, grinning and exposing his braces.

It's impossible not to smile back. I've also come to understand why he's Aurora's best friend. Remi effuses a natural positive energy whenever he's around. Only problem is, I struggle to trust my judgment in that area after Oz.

"I've been trying to catch up with you," Aurora says.

"Sorry," I say. "I've been running around since seven this morning, helping everyone get set up."

She winces. "I feel bad—"

"No, it's okay!" I tell her even though I'm not sure if it is, indeed, *okay*.

I'm frustrated with Aurora, which makes me feel like an ass because she's already explained how overwhelmed she's been. I've tried to be there for her, but she keeps shutting me out. I thought the holidays would've been tough for her, with her mother and father both being gone and her being at odds with her only brother, but she still declined my invitation to celebrate with my family at the main house. Each time, I took loads of food to her and stayed a while to keep her company, only to end up leaving after about an hour when she folded into herself and faded into the background of the room.

Aurora and I started writing our own book of original spells we created together, much like my great-grandma Angeline's—the one where I found the Scales of Justice and the spell that uncrossed Aurora. My very first contribution was a re-creation of the famous conjuring that saved Henri Eshu's life back when he was human, before he became Papa Eshu, Guardian of the Crossroads: a magical dust that could render someone coated with it invulnerable to physical attack. I made my own batch and soaked the oversize black cable-knit sweater I'm wearing in it for a whole day and let it dry for another. I'm planning to test the limits of it later this afternoon after the festival wraps, though I don't mention that milestone to Aurora.

We haven't talked about our spell book in a few months. She feels bad about abandoning me—she's told me as much—but that doesn't make it hurt less. We promised we'd name our book together once we finished, but then Aurora became so distracted and withdrawn that I'm not sure we're ever going to complete it.

My phone vibrates with a text notification from Clem. I check it and groan under my breath. He's bailing on me for Rosalie's thing tonight. *Great.* I roll my eyes and shove my phone back into the pocket of my jeans.

"Everything okay?" Aurora asks.

"Yeah," I say. "Do you wanna come to a party at Vice Hall with me tonight?"

"Don't you have to be twenty-one to get in there?" asks Remi.

"In general, yes," I explain, "but since it's a soft launch, my aunt Rosalie says we're good."

"Ah, gotcha," he says.

"I wish I could come." Aurora sighs and glances at her feet. "But I need to try and catch up on all the schoolwork I missed while at

Chateau des Saints, otherwise I won't be able to graduate with your class next year—a whole year later than I was supposed to." She cuts her eyes to the sky. "Gee, thanks, Xavier."

The worst thing about all this is none of it is Aurora's fault. Her brother, Xavier Vincent, set her entire world ablaze, and now she's trying her best to see what she can salvage from the ashes. Meanwhile, she's caught up in a nasty legal battle with him over her father's estate, which Lorenzo bequeathed solely to her, shutting Xavier out of everything. And that's why I feel so awful for being exasperated with my friend, but I don't know what else to do when she won't let me be there for her.

"I'm so sick of all the fighting and scheming and politics in this damned city," Aurora grumbles. "I'm beginning to think there's no such thing as justice for real."

"Huh?" I raise an eyebrow at her. "What do you mean?"

"The people in charge of administering justice are the most corrupt," Aurora says. "True justice can't exist in a system like this."

Remi shrugs and bites his lip nervously when he catches me frowning at him. "She kinda has a point."

"That feels like a weak perspective to have considering the position you hold in your community," I say. "Maybe we should be getting justice ourselves instead of relying on the powers that be to spoon-feed us."

Aurora chuckles softly. "So, what, you're a vigilante now? Should we all just go around executing anyone who crosses us?"

I fold my arms, my gaze locked on hers. "Striking back isn't always bad, especially after someone does something like what Xavier did to you."

"Yeah, well he's my *brother*, Cris," she says. "I hate him enough for the both of us, but I don't want him dead." She sighs deeply, her shoulders sagging. "Is there coffee anywhere around here?"

"The Bean has a mobile café over by the registration table," I say, and point her in the direction.

"Thanks," she says, and whisks away, leaving me alone with Remi.

I take a deep breath and grind the toe of my boot into the grass.

I despise moments like this, when I'm made to feel bad about how angry I am. I can't let it go. How can I, when it's constantly thrown back in my face? How can I not want to murder Xavier as I watch him whittle my friend down to nothing after what he *already* did to her?

Where's the fucking justice in *that*?

"Don't read too much into that," Remi says, in a quiet, conspiratorial voice. "I, too, have to remind myself to cut her a break at times because of everything she's going through with her jackass brother. Annnd, if we're being totally truthful here, I might be just a tinch"—he pinches his thumb and forefinger in front of his face—"responsible for her mood this morning." He winces then, arching one of his bushy, overgrown eyebrows, those delightfully unkempt beasts that've somehow grown on me while I wasn't paying attention.

"And how is it *your* fault?" I ask.

"Well, we planned to swing by the Bean on the way in, but I was running late picking her up, and she was antsy about getting here to help and didn't want to stop anymore, so, uh—"

"Then it sounds like you owe us *both* a coffee," I say.

"I can offer something even better." Remi grins, and I catch myself wondering how his smile could possibly get any better than what's in front of me right now, even though he's supposed to get his braces taken off just in time for graduation in a few months. "Aurora also turned down my offer to hang out tonight, and since it seems we're both suffering through Aurora absentia, I was wondering if maybe I could be your date to the party at Vice Hall?"

I look away from his beguiling stare and steel the emotions already riling inside me. Remi is cute and kind and so much more, but I'm just not ready to trust someone on that level again. Besides, he's a senior. Before the end of the year, he'll be setting out into the world and gradually severing the ties connecting him to the life he's leaving behind in New Orleans. It seems illogical to even entertain the thought of crushing on Remi—

*What the hell am I doing?*

"I'll pass on the party," I tell him, "but I was serious about that coffee."

His smile widens, and he stumbles backward, clutching his hands to his chest dramatically. "Cold-blooded," he says.

"Bye, Remi!" I wave him away and head off, still chuckling.

I head back to the mini command center Mama set up next to the registration table to check in. Last I saw her, she was arguing with the fire marshal about someone's tent placement, so I did a quick walk around and made sure everyone else was compliant so we wouldn't have any more problems.

The fire marshal's gone, and now Mama's hovering over a clipboard with one of the volunteers when I approach. She's wearing the casual teal dress I set out for her, along with her bright gold royal tignon that makes it seem as if the Sun is rising from the crown of her head.

But I don't make it to her before an amplified voice echoes from the opposite end of the park, stopping me and simultaneously snatching the attention of everyone in the vicinity. Suffocating heat pumps through my chest when I realize what's going on.

Fucking Redeemers.

I take a deep breath and pinch the bridge of my nose. It's not just them.

They brought the Mega Bitch™, none other than Ms. Tabitha Edgewater herself. Back in the day, she was married to a local pastor of a church that was infamous for being racist, but he divorced her because even he got sick of her radical pursuit of magical oppression.

"Witches are domestic terrorists, and magic is a weapon of mass destruction!" Tabitha shouts into the megaphone pressed against her razor-thin lips.

She's dressed in a hooded gray sweatsuit with REDEEM NOLA. REGULATE MAGIC. NOW. on the front. Her stringy gray hair is pulled back into a ponytail, and the wrinkled pale skin of her face has gone red from all her yelling.

A large gang of her supporters, a collection of mostly white faces with a sprinkling of others here and there, wears various Redeemer paraphernalia and pumps hand-painted signs in the air, cheering on Tabitha's foolishness.

MY TAX $$$ SHOULDN'T FUND MURDER

WITCHES ARE TERRORISTS.
AND WHAT DO WE DO WITH TERRORISTS???

BACK IN THE GOOD OLE DAYS,
WE BURNED OUR WITCHES!

This feels different from the protests last summer. They've escalated. I scan the angry, screaming faces in the crowd of protestors, and I'm so confused, it's almost making me dizzy.

This was a peaceful magic festival. Why are the Redeemers so pressed about what we're doing when we're not bothering anyone?

A group of people, vendors, patrons, and volunteers alike, bunch together in front of the registration table, creating a human barrier between Mama and the Redeemers. But Mama pushes her way to the front and stands rigid with her hands on her hips, her face defiant and unyielding.

I clench my fists at my side, and the whistling rage boiling inside me drowns out the surrounding ruckus. I'm so sick of this bullshit. We were just trying to do something positive for our community, but these Redeemer jerks won't even let us have this small speck of happiness. And after wrecking our event, they get to go back to their peaceful neighborhoods and rest their bigoted heads soundly in their beds.

Where's the justice in *that*?

I storm to the front of the group and stand next to Mama. I turn an iron-hot glare toward Tabitha—who smirks back at me.

All this is amusement to her. Our trauma is her entertainment.

I step forward to light into her, but Mama swings an arm out, stopping me. I glance up at her, and she looks back at me with an annoying calmness and shakes her head.

The megaphone squawks as Tabitha presses it to her mouth. "The good people of this city won't sit idly by while you start a violent cartel in our backyard!"

I look around, searching for Detective Sommers. She was prowling only a few minutes ago. How convenient she's nowhere to be found now. Typical.

A protestor shouts, "Magic regulation now, or we'll burn the witches to the ground!" and others repeat after him until the entire mob at Tabitha's back chants the threat over and over.

"Marie Trudeau," Tabitha says into her megaphone. The way my mama's name sounds coming out of her mouth, with such disrespect, as if it's something nasty, makes my fingers itch to wrap around her throat and make her choke on it. "You may fancy yourself a queen among those people, but the Redeemers see you for who you *truly* are. Your mother was nothing more than a corrupt gang leader and a thug too, and she—"

The megaphone scuffs loudly and squawks again when a shoe zips through the air and hits the side of Tabitha's head.

A single quiet moment follows where I'm unsure exactly what's going to happen next, and several potential scenarios shoot through my mind in that moment, but none of them involve a *second* shoe.

But Tabitha blocks that one.

I pray the universe protects the barefoot queen standing somewhere on our side, whoever they may be.

Protestors jostle one another behind Tabitha, who quickly recovers from the assault and holds up a hand. But she doesn't get a chance to speak because a group of police officers in full riot gear jog onto the scene, yelling into their own megaphones for everyone to disperse from City Park before they gas us all.

No one moves for a tense moment. Two dozen or more police officers, resembling a troop of mercenaries from a video game, stand between the innocent people who were just trying to have a civilized Saturday morning and this Redeemer gang, who seemed dead set on disruption and chaos since they showed up.

Mama turns to our group and lifts her hands. "For the safety of everyone, I'm canceling this event." My heart drops to my toes. People from our side cry out and jeer with disappointment, but a single wave of Mama's hand quiets them. "I'm sorry, but your well-being is my primary concern. This is not the end, nor was it a total loss! For centuries, we have been holding on to our joy despite the best efforts of our enemies—and today is no different. Today we've shown ourselves what we can accomplish as a community. *They* will not intimidate or weaken us; instead, we grow stronger *in spite of* them."

Our side explodes in a raucous thunder of cheers and whoops, but I can't help frowning. I love and respect my mama so much, but at times, I hate how accommodating she can be to our oppressors. Why do we always have to be compliant and forgiving and kind and magnanimous and all that other *bull*shit?

The lead officer stomps up to Mama and hollers into his megaphone, "DISPERSE! NOW!"

Mama collects herself and turns to the officer, the muscles in her jaw tight and her eyes narrowed and intense. The sight of her steals my breath, and fear paralyzes me.

"Officer," Mama says in a voice as bold as it is calm. My eyes jump between her and the blue-eyed cop who stares her down from behind his face shield. "Even though we have the necessary permits to be here, we are going to leave. I just ask that you give these folks time to secure their belongings—safely." She nods at the pulsing mob of protestors that hasn't given up an inch of ground since the police showed up.

"Make it quick," the cop growls. "I want this park cleared out in fifteen minutes."

He walks over to Tabitha, but they smile and greet each other as if they're family friends. She pats him on the shoulder as he leans in and whispers something in her ear. She nods and whispers something back, and they both laugh.

Tabitha turns and lifts her megaphone. "All righty, Redeemers! Time to move out! Today's mission was a success! Excellent work. Expect an email from me tonight."

Mama glances over her shoulder at Tabitha and pauses a moment as if debating whether to respond. But, after a second, she only shakes her head and goes back to helping the volunteers break down the registration and command-center tables.

I don't know how long I stand there, my fists balled at my sides, my heart pounding wildly, watching Tabitha and her troop of racist bullies trickle off back to their miserable lives as if they're leaving a Saints game. This is so fucking unfair.

The lead cop notices me watching and glowers before shooing me with one hand.

"You bet," I mutter, and hurry to help Mama and the other vendors tear down months of hard work.

Mama's choosing to pave her legacy of tolerance along the high road, which is totally awesome for her—but we'll never see justice in our lifetime this way.

Fuck tolerance.

Because what if sometimes violence *is* the answer?

I consider the possibilities as I work diligently alongside the heartsick and frustrated gen who pack up their belongings and their trauma and return to their homes to salvage what remains of their weekend and their humanity.

# FOUR
## CRISTINA

Despite the officer's ridiculous warning, it takes an hour for everyone to vacate City Park, and Mama and I are the last two remaining, hanging back to make sure everyone was able to leave safely. Aurora and Remi offered to stick around and help, but I convinced them not to let the Redeemers steal any more of their Saturday.

All that's left of our festival are four tote bags of random supplies Mama brought from home this morning. She stands to one side, frowning down at them.

"We have to do something about the Redeemers, Mama," I tell her. "We can't let them keep terrorizing us like this."

She shuts her eyes. "Unfortunately, that's not an easy task, baby."

"Then what's the point in being Queen?"

Mama's eyes shoot open and narrow at me. The force of her gaze hits me like a shock wave, but I stand firm. "What would you have me do, Cristina? Start a war with those people? I do not want to be the Queen of Violence and Death. I'm trying to *heal* our community, not bloody it even more than *they* already have"—she lowers her voice and leans closer to me—"than *we* already have."

"Lenora Savant got exactly what she deserved," I retort. "And that has nothing to do with this."

"Oh, yes, it does," Mama says, her voice even and emboldened by conviction. "When you spill blood in your community, it impacts that community, whether you feel it directly, indirectly, or seemingly not at all. Deserved or not, we took two people's lives, Cristina. You had better start being mindful of the consequences of your actions, *especially* if you think you're going to sit on the throne one day. Tearing down oppressive systems takes time most of all, and I've been Queen for barely nine months. We will not be the villains they want us to be, no matter how hard they push us toward it."

It terrifies me to admit how wrong she is. Pleasantry is far too gentle to break chains—and that's by design. It gives us an excuse to overlook people playing in our Black and brown faces on the daily. Like the police, who yelled in Mama's face today, but showed up on a Sunday afternoon weeks ago to protect a "Big Hat Brunch" for the white mages hosted by the Cardinal Mage, Madeline DeLacorte. It's not worth pointing out the hypocrisy to Mama. I've already tried more than once.

She's chosen her path. And I'm choosing mine.

I lift my hands on either side of me, slack with frustration. "After today, I'm not sure we'll get so many people to participate in an event like this again."

People were already skeptical of participating in the festival when we first announced the idea. Mama and I had to put in *work* to earn the community's trust—which the Redeemers just shit on. We can't continue living like this.

I *won't* live like this.

Mama startles me out of my angry musing by pulling me into a hug. I wrap my arms around her when she squeezes me.

"Everything's gonna be okay, baby," she says when we part.

I nod. "I know."

She forces a smile, but I don't bother.

Mama and I collect the rest of the bags and head to the parking lot. As we're loading the trunk of Mama's car, I catch sight of Tabitha Edgewater, a block away, chatting casually with the cop she was all buddy-buddy with earlier. There's a certain narcissistic arrogance in her lingering to make sure her destruction was absolute.

Mama slams the trunk shut. "See you at home?"

"I'll be there later to get ready for Rosalie's party, but I need to run an errand first."

"Okay," she says, opening her car door. "Be careful, baby."

I nod. "Yes, ma'am."

After Mama pulls away, I hurry to my car. Once inside, I pull off my tignon and fix my hair, then drive out to the main road and pull to one side—not far from where Tabitha walks alone—and wait.

* * *

My patience wanes after the fourth hour of stalking Tabitha while she meanders around town, from light shopping at Walmart to a post office run and a quick stop by the Popeyes drive-through before finally steering her Ford Escape into the garage at the back of her two-story white brick home in a southwestern suburb of New Orleans. It seems she makes quite the daily commute to the city to cause trouble for people of color.

I park my car a couple of houses down and get out before closing my door softly. An eerie gust of warm air blasts past me, making the back of my neck prickle. I whirl around, scanning the area still lit by the golden glow of late evening. I'm alone on the street, and the curtains of the nearby homes are all drawn. I run my hand across the gooseflesh on my neck while I hurry to Tabitha's house.

As I make my way down her badly cracked driveway, I take in the weed-infested, malnourished front lawn. Up close, the white façade of the house appears eggshell colored and in similar disrepair as the drive. I wonder what other parts of this woman's life she's neglected in her daily pursuit of harassing gen.

A thick shadow cuts across the edge of my vision and disappears around the corner of the house. I stop and listen while giving the area a quick once-over, but no one's out here. I hope my paranoid mind's not making me see things. Now's not the time.

I sneak into Tabitha's expansive backyard that's protected from the surveilling eyes of her neighbors by a privacy fence and high shrubbery. I climb the short stairs of a raised wooden deck and find the glass sliding doors leading inside the house open, the curtains on either side parted a hand's width to allow the evening breeze—and me—access to her home. I peer through into the dimly lit dining area and kitchen, which appear to be deserted. I sweep the curtain aside, but before I can step through, that familiar warm air whips by, brushing against my knuckles and swaying the curtains.

I leap back, my heart pounding.

*Am I making a mistake coming here tonight?* I glance back down the deck stairs and consider turning back.

But then I remember the smug look on Tabitha's face after she destroyed our magic festival, and I ball my fists, take a deep breath, and peer back inside the house.

Directly in front of me is a six-seat dining table, atop which are stacks of various mail and other loose papers that spread across the surface like a miniature mountain range of chaos. Just looking at it makes me anxious.

Footsteps thump upstairs, and my eyes dart to the ceiling. Tabitha lives alone. Her husband and three kids left her a couple of years before she restarted the Redeemer movement, and she never remarried. *I can't imagine why.*

I turn to the pale Moon in the sky and lift my hand toward it. When I rotate my wrist as if unscrewing a light bulb, faint strands of azure moonlight spiral down to our world like shooting stars. They land and pool at the bottom of the deck's staircase, and then, in a glimmering rivulet, they flow up the stairs toward me, hovering an inch above the floor in the image of a magical serpent.

I push the curtains aside and step through into Tabitha Edgewater's home, the moonbeams trailing me. Immediately, the small hairs on the back of my neck rise as if sensing someone else's presence in the room with me—but there's no one here. Somewhere upstairs, a toilet flushes, and water rushes in the pipes behind the walls.

The interior of Tabitha's home is no more comforting than the outside. Notwithstanding the very small collection of photos pinned to a single corkboard hanging on a kitchen wall, there are no other pictures of her or her family. I step over to the board and examine the ones there, all of which seem to be at least two decades old, judging by the dated hairstyles and clothes. Tabitha most definitely looks younger in these pictures. In one, she and her husband, a stout white man with cartoonishly small facial features and thick chocolate-brown facial hair, stand in front of two boys I assume to be their sons, the oldest of whom looks to be a preteen. If they're still alive, they'll be adults now.

Yet she doesn't have any recent pictures of them, which makes me wonder if her family completely cut her off.

I'm contemplating what she could've done to them and if their abandonment might be why she's so nasty to everyone now when she whisks into the room, not noticing me at first, though quickly sensing my presence. She jumps back with a start.

"Who are you?" she demands, the pale white skin of her face flushed bright red. "And what the *hell* are you doing in my house?" She looks down at the bit of moonbeams at my feet and dashes for the knife block on the nearby counter. She yanks out a butcher's knife and brandishes it in front of her with trembling hands, the silver blade glinting whenever it catches the sparse light.

"I'm here to talk to you about the Redeemers," I announce, keeping my voice calm and even amid the fear and anger battling to unseat my resolve. "What happened at City Park today *cannot* continue."

Tabitha blinks several times and frowns. "Excuse me, little girl, but who exactly do you think you are, breaking into *my* home and threatening *me*?"

I lift my hand to waist level, my palm facing the floor, and the serpentine beam of moonlight twists through the air and orbits my hand. "I haven't threatened you"—the gentle blue light spins slowly at first, then gradually increases speed at my unspoken command—"*yet*."

I watch the raw moonlight reflect in Tabitha's greedy eyes and don't miss the way her lips prune, accentuating the deep craters branching out from her mouth. She's damn near salivating. *That's* interesting.

"I know who you are now," Tabitha says, jabbing the point of the knife toward me. "You're *her* daughter. Does she know you're here?" She steals a quick glance over her shoulder and around the room, worry on her face.

"This business is between you and me," I tell her.

I glance at the moonlight encircling my hand and will it to spin faster, feeling every particle as if it were a tiny crumb of me as the increased velocity heats them to a dangerous temperature. Each one vibrates and hums with hot excitement, turning from a gentle blue to a dull white and emitting subtle heat that warms my skin as I remove my hand from the spinning ring between us. A trick I picked up from Aurora: how to tap into generational magic on a micro-level, which we're able to do because it lives inside us and flows strongest in those it's been passed down to through generations.

Tabitha's focus drifts back and forth between my magic and me. "What do you want?"

"End it," I say. "All your Redeemer bullshit. The protests. The harassment. All of it. Please, leave us alone."

She scoffs, then laughs in my face. "You're trespassing, you know. I could kill you right here, right now. Imagine the story the *Herald* would spin for me about how the Queen's daughter attacked me in my home for exercising my legal right to free speech."

"I didn't come here for violence," I say. "I thought we could have a civil conversation, one that ends with you leaving my community the fuck alone."

Tabitha studies my face a moment before lowering her knife. "I might consider that if you were to do something for me."

"What is it?" I ask.

She nods at the moonbeams swirling around my hand. "It used to work for me. When I was a little girl." The haunting reverie drags her voice lower. "And after that night thirty years ago—*poof*—it was gone. Stolen. And I didn't deserve that."

I knit my eyebrows, curious. "What did you do?"

"I was there—that night," she says. "I was part of the group of folks who marched to your grandparents' estate with Gerald Lancaster. You see, my and Gerald's families were acquainted through church, so my parents got the call to arms after the news broke about the murder of Gerald's daughter. By that point, the feud between your grandmother and the Lancasters was well-known, and I couldn't contain my curiosity. My parents declined to participate, but I snuck out." She shrugs, and I frown, wanting badly to heat this moonlight to boiling and baptize her in it.

"But after we got to the house, the situation escalated out of control, and then the earthquake happened. Out of nowhere, the ground split, and all kinds of snakes, the width of some larger than one of my calves, slithered up from what must've been hell, the way steam rolled up along with them and blanketed the area in a thick hot fog. Hearing grown people scream like that . . . Sometimes, if it gets too quiet, I can still hear them. TV will never be able to accurately emulate the sound of real-life terror."

She lets out a shaky breath and adds, "I knew magic when I saw it. It was the Queen's revenge. So I ran. I was the only one to escape that night, and I was too afraid to let anyone else know I was there. The next evening, we had a candlelight vigil at the church for Gerald and his wife, Deborah, and the others who died. At the service, Gerald's mother gave a speech that introduced me to a new kind of fear.

"That woman stood below the pulpit in front of a gigantic statue of Jesus on the cross and vowed to do everything in her power to protect her community from people like Cristine Dupart. She preached that we couldn't allow you people to control something that would give y'all supremacy over us—it went against the natural order of things. And after what I'd seen with my own eyes, I couldn't have agreed more."

It's my turn to scoff in disbelief. "Even if I could share the gift of generational magic with you, I would *never* let you have it because you don't deserve it."

This pitiful excuse for a human is no different from Alexis Lancaster or Oz. They're all the same. History just keeps repeating itself over and over. The same murderous cycles again and again ad nauseam. When will it end?

"Have you considered that maybe the gods took your magic because you betrayed your Black and brown sisters?" I cock my head at her, studying the way her chest heaves and her face burns an even brighter shade of red. I spin the moonbeams faster, until they glow bright orange with molten heat and cast an uncanny light across Tabitha's face.

She lifts the knife again and steps around the counter, approaching me slowly. I launch the now-molten moonbeams above my head, where they reform into the shape of a red-hot spear, rolling in place where it hovers, aimed at Tabitha's left eye. She stops close enough for me to get a good look at them both, silvery blue green and evil.

She holds the butcher's knife out between us, the blade trembling in her white-knuckle grip, and stares at me with an expression of revulsion. "My mama and daddy always told me I was lucky to be born white," she muses aloud, almost fondly, which turns my stomach. "They said every little white girl was born a princess, and the world was created for people like us—like me. And all I needed to do to inherit my kingdom—and all the opportunities and privileges and riches that came along with my place in the upper echelon—was to remain quiet and meek and pliant and proper. A good girl, who would become an even better wife and mother. I waited patiently for decades for what was promised to me." She waves the knife, gesturing around her. "And, as you can see, this ain't it. My magic *and* my dreams were *stolen* from me.

"So imagine my surprise all those years ago, when little teenage princess me saw your grandmother, proud, bold, ungovernable . . . *Black*"—the way she says the word with a pronounced sneer makes me bristle—"with unfathomable power at her fingertips."

"But didn't you have magic then?" I ask.

She sucks her teeth. "My conjurings were petty parlor tricks compared to what that woman could do. And that's when I first started to wonder if I'd been cheated. I never blamed Alexis for hating Cristine Dupart. Who was that woman to decide who got access to magic? Who the hell was she to tell women like me and Alexis that we couldn't have what we wanted?"

The mention of my grandmother's name draws my back straighter and pushes my shoulders back. Grandma Cristine couldn't give people magic, but she damn sure could take it away. I wonder if she'd be on my side about how I dealt with Oz and how Mama *should be* handling the Redeemers. And I wonder what would she think about what I'm doing tonight.

"And if y'all can't have the power of gen magic, then no one should?" I ask.

Tabitha slams the butt of the knife down hard on the counter and lets out a frustrated breath. "WHY CAN'T YOU SELFISH BLACK BITCHES JUST SHARE?"

I laugh in her face. "You have *some* nerve—"

"Fine!" she screams. "Then I'll carve the goddamned magic out of you myself!"

Tabitha roars and leaps for me, catching me off guard. I stumble backward, and my feet and my concentration both slip—and so does my spear of molten moonbeams.

The woman jabs the knife into my stomach with the full force of her body weight, which slams me against the wall. The laser-hot moonlight spears her left eye and exits the back of her skull before it evaporates. Her eyeball sizzles and melts, and her charred flesh crackles.

I gasp, and the scream I want to release curdles in my throat as I shove Tabitha back. The knife slips from between us and clatters at my feet. Her body flops backward onto the kitchen floor. I grimace at the gaping hole in the woman's head and the blood spreading around her, adding notes of copper to the pungent smell in the room.

Remembering her attack, I lift my sweater and check for a stab wound—but find nothing. I look down at the knife on the floor and raise my eyebrows in surprise. The blade of the butcher's knife is bent into a U shape. My spell worked.

I let out a shuddering sigh, make a fist, press the edge of it to my lips, then hold it up. "Thank you," I tell my ancestors. "And thank *you*, especially, Oberun, god of justice."

But then it hits me. *Oh, gods.* I just killed someone.

Not just anyone—the head of the Redeemers.

My stomach lurches, but I press my arm against my mouth and bite down on the heavy knitted sleeve of my sweater, swallowing the rising bile. I can't vomit. Not here.

This is a crime scene now.

*Oh, fuck. What have I done?*

My head swims. I stagger back and reach for the wall to steady myself but yank my hand back just before my fingertips brush the surface. I clutch both my hands against my rapidly beating heart. I need to get my shit together. I can't leave any evidence I was ever here—especially not with Detective Sommers prowling for magical criminals.

A chill wind blows through the open patio door, bustling the curtains. The strip of sky visible beyond has darkened already. The Sun must've set around the same time Tabitha took her final breath. The room is dark now, making it harder to see the details of the dead woman's face and the growing puddle of blood beneath her head.

I take a moment to gather my wits. Now's not the time to freak out and fuck up even more than I already have. What's done is done.

Tabitha Edgewater is dead.

But . . . why don't I feel worse about it?

*"It's what she deserved."*

The deep rasping whisper makes me jump and spin around. I peer in the direction the voice came from but find no one. Only darkness.

I turn on my phone's flashlight and aim it across the room. The shaky beam dispels the thick shadows on either side of an old china cabinet. Could I have imagined that voice?

*"She deserved it."*

This time, it's right beside me—so close that I feel a familiar rush of warm air against the nape of my neck.

I yelp and turn around. Nothing.

I need to leave.

I slip into the night through the patio door and hold my breath on the short jog down Tabitha's driveway to my car.

I can't get out of her neighborhood fast enough. Driving on the highway feels like a dream.

*I murdered someone*, I repeat over and over in my head. There's no going back now.

But where do I go from here?

I need to get my head *and* my story together.

And then I have a party to get to.

# FIVE
## VALENTINA SAVANT

The Sun sank in the sky, painting the horizon a steampunk array of pinks, oranges, and purples as Valentina Savant sat on the front steps of her recently inherited McMansion, grieving the death of her granny's legacy—and her own future. Meanwhile, she imagined her rage boiling inside an iron cauldron, into which she dunked Cris and her entire family, one by fucking one.

It had been on that same step, about eight months ago, that she fell asleep waiting for her grandparents, who never came home again. The growl of her dad's Maserati startled her awake. Her phone had died sometime after she'd drifted off, so she had no choice but to get in the car with him and return to the shithole she'd thought she'd escaped.

On the way back home, she confessed she suspected something bad had happened to her grandparents. But she hadn't told Dad about the fathomless sinking feeling in her stomach. That secret was hers alone. And later that same night, when Dad had called around and discovered that Granny and Grandpa Felix had been onboard the *Montaigne Majestic* when it sank, Valentina had plummeted into an endless pit of darkness herself.

She took up the saucer and cup with the lavender, orange, and chamomile tea she'd made for herself—just like Granny used to. In fact, the teacup she drank from was Granny's favorite. *Used to be* her favorite. None of this was Granny's anymore. It all belonged to Valentina now.

The bright white lights of a mint-green Prius swung into the driveway as the car quietly glided up to the house and parked. Sofia got out, the tight curls of her long hair back in a ponytail and an old leather knapsack with her tarot cards inside strapped around her waist.

"Hey." Sofia's keys jingled in her hand as she locked the car with a muted chirp. "Why are you sitting outside?"

"Needed some fresh air," Valentina said, gathering her things.

"Thanks for inviting me over," Sofia said. "Mom and Dad are at some swanky party at Vice Hall all night, so I was home by myself."

Valentina ushered Sofia inside the gargantuan home that belonged to her now, and Sofia's eyes widened as they wandered over the lavish interior decorated with all the oversize furniture that made it look as if Granny had a giant for an interior designer.

"I still can't believe this is all *yours*," Sofia exclaimed quietly.

"Me neither," Valentina replied, and dipped off to the kitchen to deposit her dirty dishes. "Dad's still pissed, but his attorney agrees with Granny's that there's nothing he can do about it."

After Dad had rejected Granny's offer of succession to the Gen Council throne, she'd changed her will so that her and Grandpa Felix's entire estate went to Valentina, except Grandpa's realty business, which Dad now owned 80 percent of—the remaining 20 percent belonging to Benjamin Beaumont, *alleged* silent investor. Valentina had chuckled to herself when the estate attorney revealed that juicy tidbit at the will reading. Powerful white men like Ben Beaumont had a hard time being "silent," and Arturo Savant hated nothing more than being told what to do. But that was his problem now because Granny had curved him in death the same as he'd done her in life.

Granny didn't believe in turning the other cheek.

And neither did Valentina.

"So you moved in here to twist the knife," Sofia suggested, with a naughty, childish glint in her eye that made Valentina's skin prickle. "Brutal."

"It's more complicated than that, Sof."

Valentina gave her friend a disarming glare she had to keep in her base load out whenever Sofia came around lately because for whatever reason, as brilliant as Sofia was, boundaries still fucked her up from time to time. But Valentina exercised patience because she couldn't obliterate Sofia where she stood. Not today.

She needed her bestie a little longer.

"Actually, my daily reading this morning foretold I'd have a tense day with a close friend over complex issues," Sofia said, with a gentle confidence that needled Valentina even more than if she'd outright insulted her.

"Well, let's thank the gods for that divine insight," Valentina said, which drew a grin from Sofia that quickly wilted once she realized it wasn't meant as a compliment. "You want something to drink or anything else before we go upstairs?"

Sofia shook her head, and Valentina led her up the grand curved marble staircase to the second floor. "Are you not scared to be in this big-ass house all by yourself?" Sofia asked along the way.

Valentina shrugged one shoulder. "Being alone is about the *least* scary thing I've had to deal with so far in life."

"I can sleep over sometimes," Sofia offered, "you know, if you want. Just lemme know."

"That would be cool," Valentina said, thinking that it truly would be nice to have some company to distract her from missing her granny, especially seeing as how *everything* in that house reminded Valentina of Granny.

They passed through the double doors into the owner's suite, and Sofia *ooo*-ed under her breath at the stately bedroom that was easily five times the size of Valentina's at her last home—the one that reminded her of a prison cell.

The bulky furniture all looked like it weighed a ton, particularly the four-poster bed with the great oak columns wider than Valentina's head. The only dainty piece in the room was an opulent wooden footstool on Granny's side of the bed. It was a one-of-a-kind piece she'd had handcrafted as a gift to herself. Every time Valentina had watched Granny step onto the face of the stool and press her stubby toes onto the elaborate carvings of a celestial landscape filled with moons and stars and miniature suns, then listened to the tiny bones in Granny's delicate feet popping as she climbed onto her bed, Valentina wondered how Granny could tread on something so beautiful. Granny's house was full of little treasures like that, things she treated like mere trinkets; and now that they belonged to Valentina, she felt silly for cherishing them.

"Do you sleep in here?" Sofia asked.

Valentina shook her head. "I'm staying in the room they kept for me whenever I visited. Moving into this one would make it feel a bit too real, and I'm not sure if I'm ready for that yet."

Sofia squeezed Valentina's hand, and Valentina squeezed back. As annoying as she could be at times, Sofia was a good friend.

Valentina hated being in such a mixed-up mental space. Since Granny and Grandpa Felix died, she'd felt like someone spun her around and threw her into a mirror dimension. And it fucking sucked there.

That's partly why she'd called Sofia over tonight—not for comfort though. Valentina needed another soul present to strengthen her connection to the spiritual realm.

Valentina led Sofia through the bedroom and into the owner's closet, a space large enough to host a very small gathering of friends, complete with glass-paneled wardrobe cabinets, golden-handled drawers, and tilted shoe displays. There were even two really cute plush chaises poised beneath a glittering crystal chandelier, a twin to the one above the stone-capped closet island on the opposite end of the rectangular space. "We'll do the conjuring in here."

She'd already set up the room. The first thing she'd done was remove the empty vase from atop the closet island. She'd already thrown out all the wilted flowers throughout the house that'd filled the rooms with the stench of decay. Valentina had organized a small collection of thick black and white candles into a crescent shape on one end of the closet island. In front of the candles was a crystal bowl she'd filled with spirit water, which Granny had taught her to make when Valentina was ten. In the bottom of the bowl, she'd muddled anise herb, several pinches to personal taste, and angel root, one dash usually, two if summoning a femme spirit. Valentina had opted for two and an extra dusting for good measure because that's what Granny would've wanted. And for the final ingredient, she was unable to conjure raw moonlight from the Moon like Granny or Cris—no matter how hard she tried—so she used moonglo.

Valentina had invented moonglo via trapping reflected moonlight on the surface of water by sprinkling it with powdered blessing salts and harvesting it from there. It worked nearly as well as the raw stuff.

Lying on a velvet cloth in front of the crystal bowl were the offerings Valentina had personally and thoughtfully curated.

One teabag of the same lavender, chamomile, and orange tea she'd had earlier on the porch.

A single white-and-pink flower that always reminded Valentina of the tip of a pink dragon's tail. Snapdragon. Granny's favorite.

A pair of sapphire earrings. A birthday present from Granny. The same ones Valentina had worn to her first visit to a Council meeting last summer.

Sofia gave the countertop a once-over and pointed at a small woven bag about the size of a golf ball lying in the corner. "What's that?"

"You can touch it." Valentina nodded at her. "I call it Protection Potpourri."

Sofia held it to her nose and inhaled, closing her eyes. "Mmm . . . Smells like cinnamon and . . . something more . . ."

"It's a dehydrated mix of garlic cloves, aloe, mint, and one bay leaf, all of which I tossed in a generous dusting of cinnamon powder," Valentina explained. "Strongest when blessed under a full Moon."

"Did your granny teach you that?"

Valentina shook her head. "I invented it."

"Badass," whispered Sofia.

"That one's yours. I already have mine." Valentina patted the slightly bulging pocket of her sweats, and Sofia pocketed hers too. "I stashed a few more around the room for extra protection."

Sofia spun in place, taking in the few dozen black and white candles and frankincense sticks Valentina had set up along the base of all four walls. "Val," she said, "why do we need so much protection? What exactly are you conjuring tonight?"

"We're going to summon my granny from the spiritual realm," Valentina said.

Sofia's brows shot up, and Valentina braced herself for the sting of judgment and rejection. She'd considered this might happen. She'd even prepared for it.

But . . . Sofia didn't recoil. Instead, she asked, with an innocent curiosity and a dash of delight, "Is this . . . necromancy?"

"Would you be cool if it were?" asked Valentina.

Sofia frowned, concentrating so hard, Valentina could almost hear her thoughts. "I've always wondered why it was shunned. I never believed it was bad."

"Exactly," Valentina said. Her spirits lifted, which made her feel weightless and light-headed for a split second. "Necromancy and gen magic are siblings, cut from the same cloth of Moon magic. The War of the Moons began in part because of necromancy. Feebleminded light magic practitioners didn't like that Black and brown folks had so much power at our fingertips, especially at that particular time in history, seeing as how we were wanting our freedom and shit. So they tried to take that power from us."

"Whoa," Sofia said. "I didn't know all that. If generational magic and necromancy are so closely related, how'd necromancy get such a bad rap?"

"The war ended in a stalemate, and both sides had to give up something in the end. Moon magic split off into gen and necromancy, and gen had to disavow necromancy forever in exchange for control of the Magical and Spiritual Coalition—or MASC—that was created by the Treaty of Moons. The shitty thing about the way things turned out is that no branch of magic is inherently evil or bad—especially not ours. *People* are evil, and they use magic as a tool to do foul shit—just like white mages do with light magic and vamps do with shadow magic every day, except *our communities* are the only ones ever formally penalized for it."

"Let's do this shit then," Sofia said. "Fuck the system."

Valentina smiled at her best friend. She appreciated being validated, especially considering how she'd had to bust ass to come up with this spell. Being cut off from the extensive (and exclusive) magical library in the basement of St. John's Cathedral really sucked. And now the library was overseen by Aurora Vincent, new Gen Priestess and new bestie to Cris, which meant Aurora damn sure wasn't letting Valentina renew her library card anytime soon. Convincing Aurora to change her mind was not in the cards either (pun definitely *not* intended, Sofia) as neither of them had been in each other's orbits much at all at school or otherwise.

Instead, Valentina had had to excavate information from the darkest corners of the internet and the dustiest basements of magic bookstores throughout New Orleans *and* Baton Rouge.

But she'd done it.

She picked up one of the wand lighters she'd laid out earlier and tossed it to Sofia. "Help me light the candles and incense, and then we'll get started."

Once they were done, Valentina turned off the lights, plunging them into an otherworldly ambiance that hung thick in the space despite them not having even started the spell yet. Candlelight flickered against the walls, throwing long shadows that made Valentina flinch. She caught Sofia staring at the goose bumps on her bare arms, and Valentina looked at her own and realized she'd had the same reaction.

Necromancy might not have been evil, but the creep factor was undeniably off the charts.

Valentina took up a spray bottle she'd filled with moonglo earlier and misted the room.

"What's that for?" asked Sofia.

"Charges the air," Valentina replied. "Makes the space more welcoming to a soul summoned from the spiritual realm."

"But what if you contact the wrong soul . . . or the wrong *realm*?"

Valentina gestured at the offering items displayed on the small velvet drape. "These items together are like dialing the number to Granny's phone in the spiritual realm. I curated this conjuring specifically for her palette. She'll come."

"But what if she doesn't?"

"Well, I guess we'll find out then, won't we?" Valentina cocked her head, trying desperately to hide her encroaching annoyance. "Last chance to bail, Sof. You in or out?"

Sofia swallowed hard in the staunch quiet, then nodded.

Valentina turned to a nearby wardrobe and swung the doors wide, revealing a treasure trove of satin scarves hanging from the many display hooks arranged inside. She selected a simple black sateen one that shimmered in the candlelight as she swept her hair into a high bun and tied the tignon atop her head. She wore the crown with the knots sticking up, the same way Granny had. Valentina had done it so much over the years that she could tie it with one hand behind her back *and* her eyes closed.

On her phone, she started a heavy jazz song with sad bleating brass tones that Granny often played on Sunday evenings after dinner.

"I didn't know spells used music," Sofia said.

"Incantations alone aren't always enough." Valentina misted the air with moonglo once more, which made the fires atop the candlewicks stand a little taller. "Sometimes you have to create an *experience*. The offering. The spirit water. Granny's favorite song. She won't be able to resist."

Valentina took Sofia's hand and led her to the back side of the closet island, where they had a clear view of the rest of the room. "It's time," she told Sofia, who gave a blunt, anxious nod.

Valentina cleared her throat and lifted her chin before speaking. "GODS! ANCESTORS!" she bellowed. Sofia startled, but Valentina clung tighter to her hand. "Heed my plea across realms. Part the spiritual sea of souls and call forth my blood, my ancestor. The living gathered here tonight seek to summon Lenora Savant, once Queen of the Generational Magic Council of New Orleans. I beseech you, light the beacon beyond worlds so that we may speak with her once more."

Wind whipped through the windowless space, fluttering the fires atop the candles throughout.

"LENORA SAVANT!" Valentina intoned and waited.

But nothing else happened. The wind dissipated as quickly as it'd come, and they were still alone. Valentina's stomach bubbled with embarrassment. She'd worked *so* fucking hard on making sure every detail of the spell was perfect. Why wasn't it working?

Sofia clung to Valentina's arm. "Val . . . I have a bad feeling . . . You've never done dark Moon magic before, right? Are you *sure* about this?"

Valentina snatched her arm away from Sofia, picked up the moonglo, and spritzed the room until the spray bottle was empty; then she tossed it aside. She clasped her hands in front of her, dropped to her knees, and shut her eyes again. She felt Sofia's presence beside her, but she didn't falter.

"Please," Valentina whispered. "Granny . . . I *need* you."

Valentina opened her eyes just as the light of every candle was snuffed out and darkness devoured them. She leapt to her feet, and she and Sofia held on to each other, both trembling and unsure what to do, their breaths shaky and shallow in the dark quiet.

Then Valentina heard something else. It wasn't Sofia's soft whimpering from beside her, but something . . . peculiar.

Valentina clamped a hand over Sofia's mouth and whispered for her to shush, which Sofia did; and once she quieted, Sofia dug her nails into Valentina's arm.

Sofia heard it too.

A faint phlegmy crackle echoed from the shadows on the opposite end of the room near the twin chaise loungers. The breaths were measured, shallow, and labored . . . as if . . . they hurt.

"Hello?" Valentina called out softly. "Granny?"

Sofia elbowed her in the ribs. "How do you know that's your granny, Val? I'm not trying to get murdered by an evil spirit tonight!"

Valentina didn't immediately tell Sofia to shut the hell up because she was scared too. But fear loses much of its bite after a person's been stuck in survival mode for too long.

Valentina thought to turn on the lights, but before she could move, tiny pearls of flame blinked into existence, perched on the tips of every candlewick in the room. Valentina's heart sprinted, and Sofia gasped as the flames grew, not to full size, but just large enough to cast a creepy, dim orange glow in the room—illuminating the hunched figure standing to the other side, facing the wall with their back to them.

Sofia gasped and scrambled a few paces back, her hands clasped over her mouth.

A stooped woman stood behind one of the chaises, the top of her head pressed into the corner. Her back rose and fell with deep breaths that crackled in her throat like static. She wore a white embroidered floral dress with flowing arms lined in delicate lace and a string of the finest pearls around her neck—the outfit Granny had been entombed in.

But something was off.

The dress bulged in some places, like across her humped back, where the stitching down the spine had stretched so taut that the fabric had already begun to tear. Or in the rear of the dress that fell flatly and bunched on the ground.

Sofia shook Valentina's arm gently. "Val—"

Valentina put up two fingers. "Chill. I got this."

Gingerly, so as not to startle their visitor, Valentina pulled out the single drawer in the closet island that Granny had failed to fill to the brim with jewelry. Having thought ahead, Valentina had hidden a jar of brick dust there earlier, which she'd enhanced with additional conjuring herbs for extra strength—and had hoped not to have to use. The shitty part about always being prepared was that she had to constantly face her failures, even if only theoretically. And Valentina hated losing.

She removed the lid, plunged her hand inside, and grabbed a fistful of the rough, grainy dust the color of a blood-orange sunset.

The woman's loud breathing halted. The bones of her back cracked as she unfolded from the corner and began a slow turn toward them.

Sofia shrieked and leapt backward, her back thumping into the closet door.

Sounds of fabric ripping and the throaty, gravelly breathing of the spirit filled the room. The beautiful white burial dress fell in tattered pieces to the floor and caught fire. The flames glowed bright for a moment, burning nothing but the ruined dress until it was gone, which took just long enough for Valentina to get a good look at the raggedy motherfucker who'd somehow slipped from the never-realm into this one—and was definitely *not* Granny. Valentina took a step toward her, sneering, while Sofia's trembling limbs clattered a drumbeat against the cabinet doors at her back.

What stood before them might've been a woman once, but Valentina wasn't so sure if she'd summoned a spirit or a demon. The woman's skin was pallid and gray, and her teeth that remained were broken and diseased; her eyes were but silver orbs shifting uselessly in their sockets. Measly strings of gray hair clung to her misshapen skull and hung long and limp over both shoulders.

In all of Valentina's research, she'd learned a lot about the spiritual realm and the never-realm, particularly that when a soul left the natural realm (the one she and everyone else lived in), no matter where it went, it would *never* be the same. And the longer the soul remained in either place, the more drastic the transformation. She wondered how long this person had suffered in the never-realm. They looked nothing like Granny. Even *if* her spirit had gone to the never-realm, she wouldn't have been there long enough to have made such a grotesque transformation.

Valentina and the crone moved at the same time.

Valentina slung a solid line of brick dust across the width of the room, splitting the space in half. The crone launched for her like a lioness leaping to tackle a gazelle, then slammed into an invisible wall at the protective line and fell backward, snarling and spitting at Valentina.

She took a step closer, glowering at the pitiful spirit in front of her. "I didn't call you."

The crone stopped growling and pushed up to its knobby knees. It turned a rotted grin up at Valentina and hissed with phlegmy laughter.

Valentina's frown deepened. *The fuck is so funny?*

"Ohh, ho, *hooo*"—the crone spoke in a low, rasping voice—"you most definitely her granddaughter."

"Do you know my granny? Lenora Savant?" When the crone didn't respond, Valentina clenched her fist in front of her. "Tell me. *Now.*"

"Or what?" The crone spat maggots on Valentina's protection line, but they could not cross either. "You *just* like her. And you gon' end up like her too."

"What are you talking about?" Valentina asked. "Where's my granny's spirit?"

The crone laughed again. "She nowhere. Trying to call her a

waste of time. Now . . . don't let those nice offerings over yonder go to waste. Let me have them."

Valentina narrowed her eyes. "You can choke."

"Much too late for that."

Valentina turned back to the counter and grabbed the bowl of spirit water, briefly catching Sofia's terrified wide eyes from where she huddled in the corner, her knees tucked up to her chest. Valentina couldn't be mad at her friend for being afraid. When you've been pampered and protected your entire life, fear can become as close as a sibling. But for Valentina, fear was one of the first minibosses she'd had to defeat early on.

"Don't you *dare*, you little bitch!" the crone screamed when Valentina crossed the protection line. Glaring at the bowl in Valentina's hands, the crone blurted, "You a fool, chasing death—both of you." She pointed a knobby gray finger at Sofia, then turned her milky-eyed gaze onto Valentina. "You *never* getting what you want. *Never!* You think you got power over me when you don't even got power over your*self*!" Valentina hesitated, and the crone flashed her repulsive smile again and looked straight through Valentina's eyes into the core of her soul. "You can't see the strings on you, gal, and you can't cut them neither, 'cause they strummed by the gods." The crone broke into manic laughter that rang in Valentina's ears. "You foolish girl!"

She splashed the spirit water in the crone's face, and the unwelcome spirit went from guffawing to howling. Valentina grabbed a black candle and a white candle, hot wax spilling over the sides and burning the thin flesh of her knuckles, but she was too enraged to even flinch.

She stood over the crone, who'd gone to writhing and screaming on the floor like a water bug doused in pesticide. She knelt and looked into the spirit's grotesque eyes.

"Get the fuck out of my house," Valentina said, then touched the flames of both candles to either side of the crone's still-wet face. It caught fire, the spirit water acting as an accelerant.

Violent flames whooshed and engulfed the crone, startling Valentina and knocking her back. The crone's body ruptured down the center and burst open, spilling more maggots and other fat grubs onto the carpet, only for them to wriggle with minute screams as they sizzled and crackled in the flames. And in a matter of moments, the crone was reduced to ashes and then nothing, all traces of her visit to this realm completely gone.

The candles all winked out, enveloping the room in stomach-wrenching darkness. Several nervous seconds passed before the lights flashed on, temporarily blinding Valentina. She threw one arm across her eyes until they focused, then got to her feet.

Sofia stood next to the light switch, scowling. "I *told* you," she said smugly.

"No," Valentina said, "you don't understand. I didn't do anything wrong. Something's going on with my granny's spirit."

Granny's soul wasn't at peace. Then where was she?

Valentina hadn't thought it possible she could feel even more hollowed out than she already had, but maybe the limit on her pain didn't exist.

"Now you're talking in riddles exactly like whoever's fucked-up nana that was you just summoned," Sofia said.

Valentina stood and dusted off her hands. "I don't think my granny can find peace because she's missing her head."

The tightness in Sofia's face and shoulders slackened, but she didn't say anything.

Valentina started clearing the offerings from the velvet drape. "We have to do it again. But we need to call Grandpa Felix this time—"

"Hell no," Sofia snapped. "I'm not doing that shit again! Maybe in some weird, twisted way, the Treaty of the Moons was right. I don't think we should be fooling with necromancy."

"So, you're abandoning me?"

"Val, really? Don't do that. That's not fair."

"Fair?" Valentina scoffed. "Trust me, *you,* of all fucking people, don't wanna have a conversation with *me* about what's fair, Sofia Beaumont."

Sofia took a deep breath and clasped her hands in front of her. "Look, babes, if you wanna conjure homicidal spirits from the never-realm for tea and a ki, I won't judge you, but please leave me out of it."

Valentina stepped up to Sofia and took her hand. "Please, Sof. I don't have anyone else." Her voice wavered, and she bit back the tears she hated for telegraphing how *not okay* she really was. "If something's wrong, I might be the only person who can give her peace."

Sofia stared at the floor, chewing her bottom lip as her grip on Valentina's hand slackened gradually until she pulled away.

"What is it?" Valentina asked, afraid of the answer.

"Nothing," Sofia said, smiling weakly and obviously lying. "I have an idea!" She unzipped her bag and pulled out her tarot deck in the fancy case. "Let me do a reading for you. That might give you some insight—"

Valentina slapped the box out of Sofia's hand. It thumped against the wall and fell to the floor, opening and spilling Sofia's precious gold-foiled cards.

"That fake shit doesn't matter to me, Sofia!" Valentina shouted while clapping her hands in front of her for added emphasis since it seemed Sofia couldn't get it. "*God!*"

Sofia pursed her lips, and her eyes brimmed with tears, but none fell. She collected her cards, returned them to their box, and placed it back inside her bag.

"You know," Sofia said calmly, "you *and* your granny did a lot of fucked-up stuff to Cris and her family. Maybe your granny doesn't deserve peace. But it's not too late for you to find some for yourself."

Valentina scowled, stabbed straight through the heart by Sofia's words, the last her friend spoke before showing herself out and leaving Valentina alone.

# SIX
## CLEMENT

Odessa meets me at the door when I make it home to get dressed for the party. She lets me know that Mama left early to help Rosalie set up. She also drops tea that neither Ursula nor Jacquelyn have been back home in a few days, which I find interesting, but I don't have time to dig into it.

Much to my dismay, Odessa forces me to shower and steams my outfit for tonight while I'm getting clean. I already feel guilty that, for some odd reason, Cris has taken a keen interest in doing my laundry, which I don't mind because I appreciate the help—I just don't want to be any more of a burden to the people in my life than I already am.

The only outfit that I have the mental capacity to throw together is a collared shirt, some dark jeans, and black leather sneakers, which is hopefully snazzy enough that I won't look too out of place at the event.

I arrive at the soft opening of Aunt Rosalie's new business, Vice Hall, not long after the festivities begin. It feels strange being at a celebration while Yves is shut away at Jean-Louise's.

I'm happy for Aunt Rosalie though. She fought really hard for a long time to carve out her spot in the world, and I think she might've finally done it. I just wish I were in a space to be joyful with her instead of feeling guilty for being so sad all the time.

Vice Hall is in an old converted warehouse in the business district of the city. It has its own parking, but the lot is full, so I stash my car in a nearby surface lot behind some local shops. There are more than a few Black-owned businesses in the area, like a bakery, barbershop, café, and dry cleaners, though none of them cater to the nightlife like Rosalie.

It's a short walk to my destination, where I'm met by a grand stone staircase that climbs to the main entrance, over which a large neon sign hangs that reads VICE HALL. There are no other signs advertising tonight's event because it's closed to the general public—invite only (unless you're an *extra* special VIP like me).

Beyond the first set of doors is a sizable vestibule and two sets of large oak double doors. Branded into the face of each is a four-paneled mural of various people. Upon closer inspection, I recognize these aren't just regular folks but gods. I spot Black Wolf first. The only color in the mural is from the haunting highlights of bright blue in the Marks of the Gods on certain gods' wrists or the blue-ringed irises of others, like Black Wolf, whom I then realize I've never seen in real life without his sunglasses. At the bottom of each panel is a brand with a familiar signature. Ayden Holloway. He's the artist who did the magical-history art exhibit Yves took me to last summer. Rosalie must've commissioned him for this mural, which slaps.

I could stand in the stuffy vestibule and lose myself in Ayden's artwork all night, but I peel myself away, tug open one of the great doors, and head inside.

Vice Hall is a wonder to behold.

In front of me is a towering cylindrical bar that's so bright with colored lighting that the other glittering modern fixtures hanging throughout the main room seem pointless. The bar is two levels, stretching upward to the open-air second floor. There's a DJ booth perched at the back of that level. There must be a dance floor up there somewhere too.

On the ground level to my right, an arched alcove leads to a revolving door. The space beyond is dark and looks unfinished from what little I can see. A sign sits out front that reads: RESTAURANT COMING SOON! Next to the future restaurant is a set of double doors labeled the HIGH ROLLERS ROOM. To my left, another gambling room takes up the entire western wall, accessible through intermittent archways, each roped off for tonight's event. The various slot machines and gambling tables are arranged and ready for Rosalie's grand opening.

This place is pretty packed for a soft opening. There must be at least a hundred people here, easy. New age jazz blasts from overhead speakers, giving the space a classy lounge vibe that's infectious. I feel a bit lighter already. And then I realize where that sensation might be coming from.

Girthy industrial piping snakes throughout the rafters beneath the ceiling, and its air ducts emit puffs of pale blue smoke. I notice it at first because it reminds me of raw moonlight—if moonlight were a semi-intoxicating gas. But then I remember something else: the bewitching scent of Fabiana Bordeaux's Ho-Van Oil, which I'd smelled on her when we first met last summer. Rosalie must have something similar pumping into the air in Vice Hall. It makes me feel a bit floaty and giggly.

Servers carry trays of drinks around the room, which I recognize as the signature cocktails on the humongous posters hanging from the balconies of the second level and surrounding the bar. They're named after three major vices.

Vanity. A pink-tinted drink in a tall skinny glass garnished with a nest of mint leaves and pink and white flower petals.

Pleasure. A squat glass half filled with an amber liquid and one tennis ball–sized sphere of ice and a twisty orange peel. The rim of the glass is alight with blue-green flames.

Ambition. A champagne flute filled with a lavender-colored sparkling drink, a thin wedge of dragon fruit floating sideways in it.

Heavily made-up, costumed servers hand out cocktails to the adult guests, which, now that I look around, is everyone *but* me—unless Cris beat me here. It feels a bit strange being the only underage person here, but Aunt Rosalie wouldn't have invited me and Cris if it weren't cool for us to be here. Besides, as far as drinking's concerned, this event is quite tame compared to a high school party.

I'm looking around for Cris when I see Aunt Desiree standing several feet away. She doesn't notice me because she's too busy schmoozing with the group of people she's entertaining. A diamond engagement ring glitters on her ring finger as she talks passionately with her hands. We make eye contact briefly, but she doesn't bother breaking character to acknowledge me.

*Whatever.*

I start making my way through the crowd and catch sight of Mama and Rosalie talking toward the back of the main room, in front of the stately entrance to the theater, which has also been cordoned off. I should go over and say hi.

Along the way, I spot Eveline Beaumont and her husband, Ben, current mayor, who've also retreated to an out-of-the-way spot in the room. Eveline's pulled one of the waitresses aside for a semiprivate chat as if they know each other. Ben stands beside his wife, disengaged from the conversation—and seemingly, the event as a whole—preoccupied with glaring into the watered-down Pleasure cocktail he's nursing. Every so often, he'll glance around the room, frown harder, and take an angry sip of his drink. He clearly doesn't want to be here.

The waitress breaks away from Eveline and returns to the bar to drop off her empty tray. My cousin Justin Montaigne works behind the bar tonight, helping the other two bartenders make cocktails and load them onto the trays the servers exchange for their empties. The sleeves of his plain white button-up are rolled up and the top buttons are undone, his signature look revealing the patch of curly chest hair over his brown skin. He looks up, and our eyes meet. For a moment, he resembles a squirrel, halting in the middle of gathering acorns to stare at something he finds intriguing across the way. He waves at me, and I dip my head in greeting. His face falls, and he returns to mixing drinks.

We're not friends. And I'll never give him the chance to hurt me again after I came out to him all those years ago, and then he selfishly abandoned me. He's also gay, just too self-absorbed to give a damn about anyone else. But I'm at least cordial, and if that's not enough for Justin, I don't know what else to tell him.

I'm walking, minding my own Black gay business, when a sharp tug on my arm almost pulls me off my feet. I whirl around and almost curse out loud before I realize who has hold of me.

"Now I *know* you not gonna pass by your favorite auntie without saying hello," chides Aunt Ursula.

"Oh, I'm sorry," I tell her. "I didn't see you. I swear."

She pulls me into a hug. I have to turn my head to keep from suffocating in her bust, which is more voluptuous than usual tonight and front and center in the low-cut fitted black dress she's wearing that hugs and flares in all the right places as if made specifically for the unique contours of her body.

"I want to introduce you to LaShawn Daniels," Ursula says, grinning as she places a friendly hand on the lower back of the tall, richly brown-skinned man standing beside her.

LaShawn's smiling too, which I can tell he does a lot, judging by the well-worn lines on either side of his mouth. Jean-Louise has those too, but his are from frowning too damn much.

LaShawn reaches out to shake my hand, and when I put mine in his, I'm taken aback by how soft they are despite the crushing handshake he gives me.

"This is my nephew, Clem," Ursula announces with a loving rub on my shoulder.

"Nice to finally meet you, Clem," says LaShawn. "Your aunt talks about you all the time."

I smile and raise my brows with feigned intrigue.

My aunt and her date remain in each other's personal space and don't stray more than a shoulder's breadth apart. It's sorta cute in a sickening way. Or maybe I'm just jealous because I miss having a normal relationship with Yves.

"How'd you two meet?" I ask.

"We've been friends since high school," LaShawn replies, turning his ever-present smirk to Ursula.

She nods. "And now LaShawn is commissioner of the Office of Tobacco and Alcohol Regulation for New Orleans. We reconnected when I went to him for help last June after that moron, Jack Kingston, had my bar temporarily shut down."

"Oh, yeah," I mumble.

I remember that day: my aunt and I toasting the destruction of Jack's bar—Spirits of NOLA, where my dad had died—thanks to some godly assistance from Black Wolf.

Won't ever forget it.

I watch Aunt Ursula and LaShawn flirt with each other and wonder if it's a relationship of convenience for my aunt. I didn't think she played those sorts of games, but then again, I'm not as good at figuring people out. Not like Cris.

But it seems Aunt Ursula and LaShawn are both genuinely into each other. I can tell by the way they can't stop making eye contact and touching each other and giggling at jokes only they seem to hear and get. If nothing else, the way LaShawn can't stop biting and licking his lips whenever he catches fleeting glimpses of Ursula's figure—though I have to admit, her body goes *off* in that dress—suggests they're at *least* fucking, and if not, they will be soon.

"I'm gonna go say hey to Mama," I tell them.

"Okay, baby," Ursula replies. "We might be getting out of here in a few minutes anyway. We just wanted to stop by and congratulate Rosalie."

"'Kay," I say.

"See you around, Clem," LaShawn tells me.

"Nice meeting you," I say, and leave before they spark up another conversation.

I finally make it to Mama and Rosalie, who're thankfully still where I first saw them next to the theater entrance and a short darkened hallway that I'm guessing leads to the back office.

Mama's not wearing her tignon tonight, so her hair's down in loose curls, and she's wearing a black evening gown and some strappy pumps. Rosalie's hair is pulled back in a lengthy ponytail that would seem simple were it not for the gemstones of different sizes placed throughout her head that make it look as if she's wearing the nighttime sky as a headpiece. It's gorgeous. She's dressed in a gold-and-cream pantsuit with a cream blazer and gold platform heels, and her makeup is flawless and elaborate.

I glance at the empty two-level theater behind them and wonder if they're going to offer the same kind of shows as Justin did on the *Montaigne Majestic,* seeing as how it doesn't exist anymore—thanks to us.

Rosalie presses one hand to her forehead and curses under her breath. "Oh, Marie, do you mind changing out the Essense canisters for me?"

"Sure," Mama says, without hesitation.

"Thank you," Rosalie replies. "There's a new one in the box by my office door. The shipment came late as hell from the House of Vans. I don't know where Fabiana is or why she's ghosting me, but she's lucky I don't have time to worry with that now."

*Interesting. So ~~Yves isn't~~ I'm not the only one Fabiana disappeared on.*

Mama rubs Rosalie's back. "Don't stress, Rose. I got it. And while I'm in your office, I'm gonna write down the name of that contractor who can come fix the lock on your office window, especially if you're gonna be working late. Right now, anyone could just climb in off the street."

Rosalie clasps her hands in front of her. "You're a godsend, big sis. Thank you." Then she turns and kisses me on the forehead. "Sooo . . . what do you think?"

"It's sick," I tell her. "I can't believe you did all this."

Rosalie beams. "And it's only the beginning."

A server near the bar shouts for Rosalie, and she apologizes before whisking away.

Mama pulls me into a hug and sighs.

"You look tired," I tell her when we part.

She chuckles. "Well, thank you, Clem."

"No, I didn't mean it like that—"

"I know, baby. I was only messing with you. You look tired yourself."

"I am," I admit.

"Calculus woes?"

I nod. *Among other things.*

"Let me know if you need help," Mama says. "I was a whizz at math in school."

"I think I got it, but I'll keep that in mind," I say. "Have you seen Cris?"

Mama frowns slightly and gives the room a quick once-over. "I was about to ask you the same. I haven't spoken with her since we left the park earlier."

"Oh, the festival," I say, suddenly feeling guilty that I forgot all about it. "How'd it go?"

Mama sighs and cuts her eyes at the ceiling. "It was fantastic while it lasted before the Redeemers showed up and got us shut down."

"What?"

Mama nods solemnly.

"That's not okay!" I exclaim. "What are you going to do about them?"

Mama shakes her head. "You sound just like your sister. I'll handle them, okay?"

I half nod. I hate that Mama's reign is tainted with this toxic drama right out the gate. Why do we always have to carry so much? Why can't we just live our lives in peace?

Mama gives me another hug, knocking my anxious mind off course from wandering into another problem that I don't need to own. I already have plenty.

"Do me a favor," she says. "Make sure your sister's okay. She didn't take what happened at the park very well. I seriously do not want y'all getting mixed up in that mess." I open my mouth to respond, but she holds up a finger, quieting me before I can get a word out. "And it's not because I don't think you're mature enough to handle it but because you shouldn't have to. You and Cristina deserve to be kids. I didn't get that, so I will not deprive you of it. Let me deal with this stuff. The only thing you and your sister need to worry about is living your lives."

I nod, even though I haven't enjoyed life very much since my boyfriend was shot in front of me by a Redeemer asshole and died in my arms. I'm glad I have no way of finding out who did it because I'm afraid of what I'd do with that knowledge.

Mama glances up at the ventilation duct directly above us. "Let me go change out those Essense canisters before Rosalie has an aneurysm."

Mama and I part ways, and I weave back through the crowd toward the exit. I don't see Aunt Ursula or LaShawn, which means they must've dipped already. I'll just wait for Cris outside. This party is a bit too overstimulating for me right now anyway, especially once Mama gets that Essense pumping again.

I make it to the front doors without interruption and exit into the vestibule at the same time a man dressed in a fancy tan tuxedo and well-worn brown boots enters. I look up into the familiar white face with the blue-green eyes and dirty-blond hair belonging to Jack Kingston, ex–bar owner and local asshole who enjoyed harassing my aunt Ursula and who also happens to be the father of Zachary Kingston, the self-hating homophobe who catfished and bullied me until I beat his ass. Zac's mom and Jack had a messy divorce; then she took Zac and moved to Huntsville at the end of sophomore year. I hope I never see his dusty ass again.

I've mastered the ability to look past the people around me, seemingly immersed in my own world. I activate my superpower now, pretending to be oblivious to Jack's existence as we pass each other—

And then he puts his fucking hand on my shoulder.

Surprised, I jerk to a stop and glare up at him, but he . . . smiles? Then he winks at me, dips his head, and goes inside.

*What the hell?*

I flee outside to the fresh air. My skin crawls where that man touched my shoulder. That's the same place the Moon King grabbed me. I wish creepy guys would stop putting their hands on me.

The darkness of night engulfs me, and it feels like a balm to my weary soul. The sky is clear, and the Moon is radiant on its throne. I sit to one side of the bottom step of the main entrance and wait for Cris.

The last of the late guests trickle by, pretending not to notice me, which is great because I ignore them too. I don't have the emotional capacity for useless social pleasantry right now.

And where the hell is my sister?

I reach into my pocket for my phone and feel Yves's on top of mine, suddenly remembering I still have it on me. I pull it out and open the text thread with Fabiana.

I love you!

And I'm so proud of you

I know Mama and Daddy are too

Watching from the spiritual realm

I love you too sis

Going out of the country on business for a bit xoxo

Okay. Be safe.

That was the last time ~~we~~ I heard from her. The weekend before Thanksgiving. It's been radio silence ever since.

My thumb hovers over the keyboard. A small voice buried somewhere deep inside my head cries out for me to stop, but my gut goads me on. I type the message.

Hey Fab you ok???

I stare at the SEND button for a long while, but I can't bring myself to press it. The truth is, I'm scared. Actually, "terrified" is probably a better descriptor. Maybe the doomsday clock in my head has already gone off, but I can't hear the alarm buzzing because I've buried my head too deep in the gigantic mound of bullshit that's my present life.

"Whose phone is that?"

Cris's voice jolts me from my thoughts, nearly making me drop Yves's phone on the concrete.

I shove it back in my pocket and glare up at her. "You scared the shit outta me. And hello to you too."

She's wearing a bright red cocktail dress, and her curls are moisturized and thriving. She's pinned them back from her face, which glows in the exterior building lighting. As gorgeous as Cris looks, I can see something else beneath that shimmering surface of perfection. Something not as put together, something a bit ugly and frazzled. Call it intuition, or maybe I just know my twin sister really well. But something's definitely up with her tonight.

Seems I'm not the only one who's had a day.

I stand, and we hug, both melting into the embrace.

"I miss you," I whisper into her curls. They smell like the coconut and avocado oil she uses that I love so much simply for how good it smells.

She chuckles softly. "You just saw me yesterday, weirdo."

I sigh as we part. "I know. I just—"

"It's okay," she says. "It's nice to be missed. I missed you too." She pauses and casts her gaze at the ground. "I really miss having you around full-time at home. It's nice having Aunt Ursula and Rosalie and Jackie and baby Baptiste—especially now that he's sleeping through the night—around, but it's not the same without you. I'm still . . . lonely a lot."

"Even with Aurora in the old Montaigne house?" I ask.

"With as much as we've seen each other, she may as well be in another state," Cris says. "But she has a lot going on, so I get it."

"That's . . . kinda what I wanted to talk to you about," I tell her.

I take Cris by the hand and lead her off to one side of the staircase, where we can talk away from the main thoroughfare, although guests have stopped arriving. And, judging by the noise coming from behind the closed doors, the party's jumping now. Good for Rosalie.

"Is everything okay?" Cris asks, studying me like a detective.

"I have something to tell you that needs to stay strictly between us," I say.

She nods. "I swear."

"And I also need you not to judge me."

Her face pales. "I'd never. We promised. Remember?"

"Right," I say, already wringing my sweaty hands. "Here goes . . ." I blow out a nervous breath, feeling silly for not being able to get the damn words out.

But Cris doesn't heckle me or grow impatient. Instead, she leans against the staircase wall, pulls me beside her, and waits for me to collect my thoughts.

"Last summer," I choke out, "when Yves and I went on that date to the art museum, we didn't break up. Someone shot him in the parking lot. And he died."

Cris claps both hands over her mouth, but the gasp still escapes.

"I don't know who did it," I tell her before she asks. "They were wearing a mask, but they had on a Redeemers tee, and the Redeemers were protesting outside the museum that night." A tear falls from one eye and then the other, tickling my cheeks before I swipe them away. "He died in my arms."

"Oh, God, Clem, I'm so sorry," Cris says. "Why didn't you tell me?" She turns to me for what I assume to be a hug, but I hold up a hand and shake my head.

"I'm not done."

She sucks in a breath, and her eyes slowly widen with realization. "Clem . . ." she whispers, "what'd you do?"

"We brought him back," I say. "He's, uh, not as bad off as Auguste, but he's not exactly *right* either." The words strangle me, filling the wells of my eyes to capacity again. "And I'm scared because now I don't know if I can fix him."

Cris's mouth forms an O, but nothing comes out. Even she can't find the proper words to say—so I stumble on.

"I enrolled him in the HI program at school so he won't fall behind," I say. "I've been tutoring him and doing his coursework and mine."

Cris blinks in disbelief. "Holy shit, Clem. You've been doing all that by yourself?"

I nod shamefully, the pride I once felt for accomplishing such an impossible task now rotted.

"But what about Fabiana?" asks Cris. "There's no way she knows what you've done, and you're still upright, so how in the hell have you been hiding this from her for so long?"

I tell her the whole story about the fake study-abroad program and Fabiana's mysterious absence since before Thanksgiving.

When I finish, Cris nods at my pocket. "Is that his phone?"

"Yeah," I answer. "At first, I thought she was just too busy to check in on Yves, which I took as a blessing, but then I got swamped with other stuff, and days went by, then weeks without a word from her. And, earlier, Rosalie mentioned not having heard from her either. Now I'm worried something might've happened to Fabiana."

"Have you told Yves any of this?" asks Cris.

I shake my head. "He doesn't need that stress, especially considering there's nothing he can do about it in his present state, seeing as how he can't step a foot outside Jean-Louise's house."

"Right," Cris says, looking crestfallen, as if suddenly remembering that Yves is no longer Yves as she remembers him. "How long do you think you can keep this up? Realistically. Auguste has been stuck like that for years now, and Jean-Louise still hasn't figured out a way to restore him."

"Well," I say, "Jean-Louise and I were supposed to be working together on a solution for both Yves and Auguste, but as of this morning, he's effectively bailed on me."

"What?" Cris exclaims. "Why?"

I chew my bottom lip. I knew we'd get to this point of the story eventually. It feels wrong to withhold information from Cris when I'm asking for her help, but I don't want to get sidetracked with the fucking Moon King right now. All I care about is saving Yves.

"I think he's just depressed and frustrated." I shrug. "I dunno."

"Well, I can search the Council Library at St. John's for some answers," Cris says. "The majority of the dark Moon magic texts have been relocated, but there might still be something useful there. I've been through a lot of the archives already, so it shouldn't take too long."

I nod eagerly, energized by the sliver of relief her suggestion brings.

"And, as far as school goes," she continues, "you won't have to shoulder all that alone anymore. I'll help where I can."

"No, you don't have to—"

"I know I don't," she says. "It's my choice. Just accept the help, Clem."

"You're right." I sigh. "I do need help."

"See? That wasn't hard."

"Thank you." I clear my throat. "Well, now that I've divulged my secret, are you finally going to let go of the one you're strangling to death over there?" When she throws me a fake confused look, I add, "And don't pretend like you're not. We shared a womb, sis. I know you better than you know yourself."

She sighs. "I really hate you sometimes."

"Liar," I say. "You love me."

She rolls her eyes and stares up at the sky. "Can I tell you something and you not think differently of me?"

"Are we seriously gonna keep doing this?"

She grins. "Sorry. Guess it's kinda like the standard terms and conditions before every difficult conversation."

"Yeah, click agree, approved, move on," I say, and she cuts her eyes at me, but I motion for her to get on with it. "Stop stalling."

She glances around, making extra sure we're alone, then leans closer and says in a conspiratorial voice, "Tabitha Edgewater is dead."

"Good," I say. "Who cares. She was a bigot and a tyrant. How is *that* your secret?"

"Because it was *me*," she whispers. "I did it."

I crane my head back and blink several times. "Come again?"

"You heard me," she whispers.

"Whoa," I say. "Mama mentioned what happened at the park earlier, but I didn't think you'd go murder that lady, Cris!"

She shushes me and looks around frantically. "Can you lower your voice, please?"

"Sorry!"

"Believe me," she says, "that was *not* my intention."

Cris tells me the story of Tabitha's death; it begins with the sordid details of the earlier events at City Park and ends with Cris confronting Tabitha after following her home. Cris explains she only meant to convince Tabitha to get the Redeemers to back off from harassing gen. I'm not gonna lie, Tabitha's indecent proposal to call off her goons in exchange for access to gen magic took me by surprise—even though it shouldn't have. And I can't believe Tabitha attacked Cris over magic she felt entitled to wield.

I put a hand on my forehead and stare down at my sneakers. This is fucking Alexis Lancaster all over again. How did we get here? Are we doomed to repeat the same bullshit over and over until the world ends?

"I've just been so angry, Clem," says Cris after several quiet moments. "Truly evil people keep doing foul shit to whomever they want, which, mind you, are almost always people of color; and then they get to strut around town as if they own the world without a consequence to be found. Well . . . I've had enough. And even though I'm a bit freaked out that I actually . . . you know . . . I don't have a scrap of remorse for what I did."

I don't know what to say because, to be honest, I'm conflicted myself.

"A Redeemer murdered Yves," I say. "That movement is dangerous and needed to be stopped. Tabitha was indeed a threat to our community, and I'm glad she's dead."

I can't miss the look of relief that dawns on Cris's face. "Me too." Her brow furrows, and she lowers her voice. "Does what I did make me a bad person?"

I shake my head. "I don't believe in 'good' or 'bad' people. We're all only humans who sometimes make questionable choices."

I just wish someone other than Cris had done it because something about Tabitha's demise at my sister's hands, and everything leading up to that moment, makes me *very* uneasy. I'm immediately catapulted back to that day last summer when she stood over Oz, who lay dying on the floor of our foyer, and watched the life slowly fade from him with reserved glee.

And what's even more troubling is that my twin sister and I are so much alike that I'm afraid there might be unspeakable darkness inside me too. She's certainly tapped into hers. And now I'm anxious about who she might become—and where that leaves me.

"Are you not worried about getting caught?" I ask.

She shakes her head. "I was *very* careful. No evidence. No DNA."

I narrow my eyes but don't dispute her. My sister is far better than me at attention to detail, but there's no such thing as a perfect crime.

"Okay," I tell her. "I get it, really, I do, but, Cris, you've gotta be more careful with the"—I lower my voice—"*murder* stuff, *especially* now that the cops have it out for gen too."

She raises a defiant eyebrow. "And what if I told you I didn't care?" Her face changes in the shadow of the staircase, darkening even more, almost to a point where I barely recognize her. "I hope everyone who had a hand in all the dirty dealings against our family gets what they deserve, just like Lenora Savant." She ticks off the names on her fingers. "Dr. Thomas. Eveline Beaumont. And Jack Kingston too. Every one of those motherfuckers needs to understand that each morning they get to open their eyes is a gift from *me*—and I'm suddenly running short on charity."

"You're absolutely right," I say, "but please don't get lost in your anger."

"You have *some* nerve, considering what you just told me *you* did," she snaps at me.

"Okay, but why are you coming for me because I politely asked you to stop murdering people?" I fire back.

She doesn't answer but instead glowers back at me, half her face in shadow, half aglow in the exterior building lights.

"I wasn't trying to do this with you tonight," I say, "but I *saved* a life—you *took* one. It's not the same."

"And you lack the nuance of perspective," she counters.

"All due respect, Cris, but I don't give a fu—"

A dampened, but no less shrill, scream resounds from inside Vice Hall. Cris and I jump and scurry from the shadows to see what's going on.

I climb the staircase into the vestibule and tug on every one of the main doors.

They're all locked.

More shrieks ring out from inside. *What's going on in there?*

"We gotta get inside," Cris says when I meet her back at the bottom of the stairs. "Half our family's in there!"

I snap my fingers. "Follow me."

I lead Cris around the building, and along the way, I tell her about Mama mentioning the broken lock on Rosalie's office window. I step up to the one I assume leads to Rosalie's office and whisper a silent prayer as I lift the pane.

It slides up with ease, and I breathe a sigh of relief.

I climb through into the large dark office. The dense shadows draped across the bulky furniture make them all look like monsters lying in wait. Music blares from beyond the door out in the main room. I can hear faint shouting, like people arguing, but the random screaming seems to have stopped.

I turn back to the window and help Cris through. Once she's inside, she turns on her phone's flashlight and uses it to locate the light switch. The lights blaze on while I slam the window shut, not expecting it to fall so hard.

Cris rounds on me. "Why not just announce on the intercom that we're sneaking into the building, Clem?"

I pull a face but keep my rebuttal to myself.

We exit the office and creep down the short hallway, which bears an overwhelming sweet and citrusy scent. A very light fog hangs in the air, which I notice has a pink tint when the light hits it at certain angles. We step out of the hallway into the main room, and I sweep an arm out to stop Cris from going any farther.

All the guests are sprawled on the floor throughout, some unconscious, others wriggling like maggots, desperately attempting to cling to consciousness but slipping away one by one.

At the other side of the room, Benjamin Beaumont fights with Mama, who struggles to defend herself against the hulking brute. He has hold of both her wrists and slings her around like a child, barely avoiding her kicks. His face is plum red, pulsing veins bulge from his neck and forehead, and his eyes are manic and bloodshot.

"YOU AND YOUR WHOLE GODDAMNED FAMILY ARE TRYING TO RUIN ME! I WON'T HAVE IT! YOU HEAR ME?" Ben bellows in Mama's face.

"Let go of me!" she screams at him.

"I SHOULD'VE TAKEN CARE OF Y'ALL WHEN YOUR SISTER BLACKMAILED ME WITH THAT DAMN VIDEO!"

"I don't know what you're talking about!" Mama cries. "I haven't seen any video!"

Ben lets go of one of Mama's arms to grab her throat in his fist and then tackles her to the floor.

"Mama!" Cris breathes.

"Oh, hell nah!" I shout.

We both take off to help Mama, but a loud hiss resounds from somewhere behind us, and we're swallowed in a suffocating cloud of thick pink smoke.

I'm unconscious before my body hits the floor.

When I open my eyes, I'm still on the floor.

Mama lies to one side of me, Cris on the other, both slowly stirring awake. I push myself upright into a sitting position and try to shake off the remnants of overpowering wooziness. The room spins and tilts slightly, but the effect diminishes with each passing second. I press a hand to my throbbing head as my sister sits up and does the same.

Mama groans and opens her eyes. She grips something in her palm, and I gasp when I realize what it is. Dad's knife. My knife. The familiar initials—NDT—on the handle send my heart on a death drop to my ass.

*Oh, gods. I lost that knife weeks ago. How'd it get here?*

My thoughts are cut off by a heart-wrenching scream from Eveline Beaumont, who drops to her knees and wails in front of the main entrance. Mama and Cris both stare, their mouths hanging open in muted shock.

Ben Beaumont's corpse hangs above the locked entrance doors, his feet dangling a few inches off the floor. His brawny body is held up by two rusted iron stakes driven through the palms of his large hands and into the brick wall just above the entryway.

In shock, I wander a bit closer to get a better look.

The ripped pink tissue along the circumference of the hideous wound on the side of his neck has blossomed like fleshy rose petals, revealing the white of exposed bone deep within. In the shiny surface of the blood pooled below his dangling feet, I see the haunting reflection of his face frozen in a vacant, wide-eyed, gap-mouthed expression.

The killer left a message too.

Written in blood on the door to the left of Ben is the word ROYAL, and REGARDS is on his right. On the floor in front of him is a giant bloody smudge next to the words THE NEW QUEEN.

"Royal regards, the new Queen," I mutter to myself. "What does that even mean?"

Then I gag a little bit when I see *what* the killer wrote their message with . . .

At the base of the "N" in "QUEEN" lies Ben Beaumont's severed tongue.

# SEVEN
## VALENTINA SAVANT

Valentina spent the first twenty minutes after Sofia stormed out doing something she hadn't done in a while, mostly because she found it pitifully inefficient. She cried.

And it was a powerful purge.

Rage. Sadness. Frustration. Shame. Every thorny emotion poured out of her as if tapped from her core by a conjurer.

It felt . . . good.

She hadn't realized she'd been hoarding all those nasty feelings since Granny and Grandpa Felix died nearly nine months ago. No wonder she'd exploded on Sofia. Valentina would have to apologize later. Sofia had only wanted to help, which was more than Valentina could say for literally anyone else.

For nearly two hours, she lay flat on her back on the floor of the closet with the lights off, staring at the chandelier with its shimmering crystals. She shone her phone's flashlight through them, hypnotizing herself with the kaleidoscope of rainbows projected on the ceiling.

Unlike the house she'd shared with her parents, this one contained only good memories for her. And the idea of transforming this place into her own safe haven—something no one else could infest with their bullshit *or* take from her—intrigued her. After all, Granny had left it for Valentina, along with the rest of Granny's money and investments, totaling a sum Valentina had never imagined she'd ever own. Dad was pissed that Granny had left everything to Valentina outright as opposed to putting it in a trust he could steal from. Granny had to have known Valentina was going to have to strike out on her own without Granny around to protect her.

It was a dream. She was on the road to freedom from her miserable parents, and it was really freaking hard to be happy about it.

Granny, alive—sitting next to her, drinking tea, and nosing into her personal life—was worth more than a hundred times all the money in every account that now belonged to Valentina.

But Granny was gone for good, and her soul was lost between realms.

And that was exactly why Valentina would cherish the opportunity to flay Cristina Trudeau alive if she ever got it. And her entire fucking family.

She glanced at the time on her phone. It was already 3:00 A.M.

Valentina got to her feet and stretched.

First things first. She needed to clear out her granny's personal things so she could move into the owner's suite, which was her bedroom now.

*This is my house,* she told herself to assuage the guilt rising inside her like bile as she brought the box of garbage bags back upstairs to begin packing up Granny's belongings.

Valentina decided to donate most of Granny's clothes and shoes to the Temple of Innocent Blood. Eveline would appreciate that. Valentina held back a few vintage jackets, coats, scarves and tignons, and a couple of cardigans for herself.

She picked up a brown cashmere sweater and held it up to her nose, closed her eyes, and inhaled deeply. At once, she felt the phantom warmth of Granny's presence. It smelled of her favorite perfume, the one in the bottle shaped like a dragon; it reminded Valentina of strolling through the botanical gardens on a warm spring afternoon right after the flowers had been watered. She slipped the sweater on and hugged herself. She caught herself smiling but didn't stop. For a brief space in time, she allowed herself to consider the possibility that everything was going to be okay, that she was right where she needed to be.

Valentina had more fun than she wanted to admit going through Granny's extensive shoe closet, which she'd always marveled at from afar since they wore the same size in most styles. Granny loved a label and refused to acknowledge her feet flattening and widening as she aged. Listening to all of Granny's complaining about how tight yet beautiful her shoes were had paid off in a painfully ironic way.

Valentina was sick of those moments.

When the closet was cleared and reorganized, she lugged her suitcases in and began unpacking. She'd been living out of her hastily packed bags for weeks, and there was a noticeable downshift in her anxiety once all her things had found proper places.

By the time the Sun began to pierce the horizon, lack of sleep finally caught up to Valentina. She decided to delay going through Granny's jewelry drawers and cabinets until after she'd had a nap.

She pulled down some fresh bed linens from the hall closet and set to work stripping the bed. However, the fitted sheet caught on one corner of the mattress, and when she yanked it free, she stumbled backward and tripped over her granny's bedside footstool. Valentina's butt smacked onto the floor, and she cursed, glowering at the overturned stool until she noticed something peculiar.

The underside of the seat contained a cleverly hidden compartment. Valentina picked up the stool and studied it, grimacing at the lock set into the wood and painted the same color. She tried to pry the compartment doors open with her fingers, but they wouldn't give. She set the stool on the bare mattress and searched for the key. After twenty minutes of rifling through every drawer, cabinet, and closet on the second level of the house, Valentina took the stool downstairs to the garage. Grandpa Felix had been using one of the five bays as his workshop, though Valentina had never witnessed him see a project all the way through to the end. She set the stool upside down on a workbench beneath a huge shadow board, which housed a vast collection of practically new silver tools that hung on the wall like art. Valentina selected a hatchet.

"Sorry, Granny," she whispered.

Valentina hacked at the small stool, splitting and cracking the precious wood until it lay in pieces—and revealed what it'd been hiding.

A single piece of faded parchment rolled up and tied with a black ribbon.

Valentina picked it up with anxious, unsteady fingers and slipped off the ribbon. Carefully, she unfurled the paper and narrowed her eyes at what was unmistakably her granny's handwriting at the top of the page.

*I'm not taking this secret to my grave.*

Valentina frowned and turned the parchment over and back, studying the blankness of it. "What the actual fuck, Granny?" she grumbled. Her head felt heavy as sleep weighed her down. But she *had* to know.

What was this secret Granny was keeping?

Valentina stuffed the scroll into the pocket of her cardigan, swept the broken stool into the garbage, and retreated to the kitchen. She pulled down a coffee mug from the cupboard and filled it with orange juice. Then she grinned. If Granny were there at that moment, she'd most certainly be reaming Valentina for drinking juice from a mug instead of one of those special little juice glasses she insisted everyone use (which Valentina hated because they didn't hold nearly enough juice).

She glanced at the silver stockpot on the counter and groaned. She needed to bottle that leftover moonglo before it went bad. She'd forgotten that past Valentina had left this job for future Valentina, and the future had become the present. She'd needed quite a bit of moonglo for the summoning spell last night, so she'd made a huge batch in the giant stockpot Granny made greens in every Thanksgiving and Christmas.

But then Valentina got a wild idea.

She took the scroll from her pocket and unrolled it, her eyes shifting between the blank page and the pot of leftover moonglo. She set the scroll on the counter and dashed upstairs to get her empty spray bottle. After nearly tripping on the way back downstairs, she bounded into the kitchen and refilled the bottle with moonglo. Using empty glasses from the cabinet as paperweights, she spread the scroll on the counter, then turned off the lights and drew the curtains, dimming the room a great deal.

She took up the spray bottle and carefully misted the paper, praying this didn't ruin it. In the low light of the room, droplets of moonglo sparkled like tiny cerulean gems falling onto the parchment, where they melted and blended in with the fibers.

She worried it hadn't worked for a moment, but then words appeared in Granny's same dramatic slanted script, as if scrawled by an invisible hand.

Line after line of text appeared, completely filling both sides of the scroll. A secret letter from Granny that wasn't addressed to anyone. Had Granny left this for her?

Valentina turned on the lights, refreshed her mug of juice, slipped on some shoes, and took the scroll outside to the patio. The Sun had risen and not long since burned off the morning fog, but the dew still clung to the world outside. Valentina wandered over to the firepit and the same outdoor couch she'd sat on during so many summer nights and made s'mores with Granny and Grandpa Felix. She flipped the cushion to the dry side and sat, pulling her legs underneath her.

Valentina muttered the date written at the head of the letter aloud. "June nineteenth, 1989." But why did that date feel so familiar? She thought for a moment, then sucked her teeth when she remembered.

That was the day Cris's grandmother, Cristine Dupart, had been accused of murdering the mayor's daughter and slaughtered the mayor and a bunch of other people, which got her family's sovereignty revoked. Granny was Cristine's best friend, and Granny also became Queen after Cristine had disappeared and lost her throne. Granny had never liked talking about that day with Valentina, who'd asked about it more than once. But Granny would always say the memory was traumatic and she preferred not to revisit it. And Valentina had understood that better than most.

Valentina's fingertips quivered with nerves as she traced the text of her granny's journal entry while she read.

*I've known Cristine Dupart since '78 when she was still Cristine Glapion. I was there in '81 when her mama, Angeline Glapion, Queen of the Gen Council, passed and Cristine ascended her throne. And I was one of her bridesmaids in her wedding to Baptiste Dupart the following year.*

*In the years that followed, I got to see a side to the magical community I'd never considered in more than a passing thought. Mama taught me early on that certain stations in life weren't meant for me and that dreaming was a waste of time. So, even when I became best friends with a queen, I never imagined I could be one. All that power and influence. The freedom to exist as I pleased. It was all fantasy to me.*

*Through Cristine, I met Eveline Beaumont, who served as Reverend Mother of the Temple of Innocent Blood—and I felt a connection to Eveline that I'd never had with Cristine. When I heard Eveline's story of how she came to power, I understood why I was so drawn to her. Like me, she'd had one too many people try to dim her light growing up. But unlike me, she fought to change her station and never gave a damn what anyone thought she* <u>*couldn't*</u> *do. Cristine came from parents who loved and nurtured her, and that was why she would never understand women like me and Eveline.*

*However, befriending Eveline wasn't easy, despite my best efforts. That woman maintained a healthy distance from any- and everyone, with the exception of her temple employees and her husband(s). Even the whispers of scandal surrounding Isaac's (her first husband) sudden passing in '86 and her marriage to Isaac's younger brother, Ben, shortly thereafter didn't rattle Eveline's cage. And that was when I realized exactly how much I admired Eveline Beaumont. I always believed Isaac's death and Eveline's subsequent marriage to Ben was a clever power play. I tried baiting her into letting her guard down with me about it once by reassuring her that I thought her strategy was brilliant. She got very offended. I became quite depressed afterward. I felt I'd been cursed to spend my entire life in the shadows of greater women.*

*But two nights ago, everything changed.*

*Eveline showed up at my apartment slightly after midnight. I had no idea she even knew where I lived. I invited her in, and she presented me with a proposition. She explained that she has a plan for power—one that includes me on the Gen Council's throne.*

*I asked, "Why not you?" It was hard (and still is) for me to imagine Eveline passing up the crown, especially in favor of me since*

*I believed she didn't care for me very much. She told me she had set her sights on a different future, and she wanted to give me one that I might not otherwise get. But there's a catch.*

*Eveline wants me to help her cover up a murder. And to do it, I'll have to betray my best friend.*

*I sent Eveline away because I needed time to think.*

*I'm writing this letter now because I've made my decision. I'm afraid of how long I might hate myself for what I'm about to do, but if I'm going to end up hating myself at the end of a measly existence anyway—what do I really have to lose? However history may judge me, I made this choice for me. For my future. And the future of my family.*

*I'm not certain I can trust Eveline Beaumont, so I refuse to take this secret to the next realm with me. <u>Cristine Dupart didn't murder Alexis Lancaster</u>—that was the lie Eveline and I made up together so we could both get what we wanted. Only Eveline Beaumont knows the true identity of Alexis's killer.*

*If you're reading this, that must mean that I'm dead or senile, so do with this information what you will.*

*Lenora Savant*

Valentina swiped the tear that had escaped down her cheek and tucked Granny's letter into her sweater pocket. She had no idea Granny had fought so hard for her own future—and for her family's. Pride ballooned in her chest, though something else, something prickly, threatened to burst it. Eveline was the one who'd decided to steal the throne from Cris's grandmother, but she'd let Valentina's granny take the fall for it solo.

That was an offense Valentina would most definitely *not* forget. Her memory on such matters was long—and sharp. But for now, Valentina needed Eveline.

Before she'd died, Granny had made Valentina promise she would be *better.* But any "immoral" maneuvering Granny might've done didn't faze Valentina because she'd learned fast that people who played by the rules inevitably lost to those who changed the rules as they went. And she either played like them or flipped the board.

It was time for Valentina to put her piece back into play.

First, she needed to assess the playing field, which wouldn't be easy considering she was low on "resources," but she still had one left that was somewhat reliable. Heavy on the "somewhat."

But she had to start somewhere.

Valentina picked up her phone and called Oz Strayer.

# EIGHT
# CRISTINA

Mama's hands are painted in a thick reddish-brown layer of Benjamin Beaumont's blood. So is the knife, the one that belongs to my brother, which lies on the floor by her feet, where she threw it after regaining consciousness and realizing she was holding the murder weapon.

Mama swears she didn't kill Ben.

I believe her; however, other than me and Clem, I'm not sure anyone else does based on the judgmental stares we get from the other party guests, who're also gradually waking up.

Mama would *never* murder someone like this. Not like I have.

But this wasn't me either.

It feels like something darker—more sinister. Most of the traumatized guests turn their eyes away from the corpse, but I study it, quickly trying to piece together what could've happened here. I narrow my eyes at the rusted stakes that anchor Ben's body to the wall by his hands.

*Where in the infinite realms did* those *come from?*

It's a marvel someone was strong enough to lift Ben's hulking frame high enough to hang him on the wall like a gigantic ornament. Ben was a large man, about six-five and around 250 pounds if I had to guess. Mama's barely five-seven and less than half his weight. There's no way she could've done that. Not alone. And not even with magic—as far as I know.

I scan the room but don't see anyone who immediately stands out as a potential suspect. But someone's murdered the mayor and tried to make it look like Mama was the killer. This rings way too familiar to thirty-one years ago, when my grandmother was accused of murdering the mayor's daughter.

But I'll be damned if I allow history to repeat itself on my watch.

Justin and Rosalie push through the crowd of gawkers and stand Eveline up, then whisk her to Rosalie's office so she can collect herself without everyone ogling and whispering.

Mama pulls my arm so hard, she almost dislocates it. I start to yelp, but she shushes me before I can make a sound. She snatches Clem too and leads us out of earshot of everyone else, then leans close, her brown-eyed stare intense as it shifts between me and my brother.

"Clement, baby, did you bring that knife here tonight?" Mama asks. He hesitates, and panicked terror glistens in his eyes. Mama adds, "It's okay, baby, you're not in trouble, but it's important that you be honest with me right now—no matter what."

He shakes his head. "I didn't, Mama. I swear."

"When's the last time you remember having it?" Mama asks.

He wrings his hands, and I scoot closer to him so our shoulders touch. I feel his weight press against me and the shuddering breath he releases before he launches into his breathless explanation. "I had it at Jean-Louise's a few weeks ago, but then I lost it after I left it outside to charge in the full Moon, but I didn't think anything of it because I literally lose it all the time, and then it usually turns up eventually; but I had no way of knowing it would end up at a freaking *murder* scene—"

Mama shushes him. "We don't have time for that. If anyone asks, the knife is mine—"

"But—" Clem and I protest at the same time.

"*Shh!*" Mama presses a finger to her lips. "You are my *children*, and I will not let you get mixed up in this mess—it could ruin your lives. Do not go against me. Not tonight. We need to stick together now more than ever."

Clem and I exchange an anxious glance. I lace my fingers through his, and he squeezes my hand. Our family's under attack again. We can't catch a break.

Mama, Clem, and I hug one another—then part to the cynical glares and bustling whispers of the crowd, focused solely on us now in the absence of Eveline's grieving spectacle.

Rosalie emerges from the back office and attempts to cool the crowd, which grows unrulier by the minute. Mumbles sprout from whispers that grow into angry shouts of "let us out of here!" and "I'm going to sue you to the never-realm!"

"How 'bout you pay your back taxes first, Kenny?" Rosalie yells back, eliciting a wave of snickers from the crowd. "The police are on the way," she announces. "Just hold tight—"

The front doors bang open with an echoing boom like a shotgun blast. Screams rip through the crowd, and several people drop to the floor and fling their arms over their heads. The sudden outburst injects a shock of adrenaline straight to my heart, and it races as I flinch back, still clinging to Clem's clammy hand.

Two police officers enter through the doors to the left of Ben's body and prop them open. Detective Jeida Sommers steps through next, with several more cops behind her. She's dressed in a plain black pantsuit, and her hair's slicked back in a pristine ponytail that exaggerates the razor-sharp scowl on her face. Except for impeccably drawn eyeliner, she's fresh-faced, which makes her dark-eyed stare even more acute.

She gives the room a quick scan, then whispers instructions to the officers, pointing at Ben's corpse, the crowd, and then—*us*.

Mama pushes me and Clem behind her protectively and squares her shoulders. Strength radiates from her like a furnace. I let go of Clem's hand and take Mama's, and he glances at me, then grabs her other hand. My brother and I stand tall on either side of her.

Rosalie approaches Detective Sommers and introduces herself. They have a quick, clipped exchange, and then Sommers steps to one side and addresses the room.

"All right, folks!" Sommers shouts, then waits a moment for everyone to quiet. "The better you cooperate with me and my colleagues tonight, the quicker we can get you out of here and back to your homes. Detective Scott and Officer Calhoun"—she gestures to a copper-skinned Black man with a low-cut fade wearing a midnight-blue shirt, whom I assume to be Scott, and then to the uniformed white cop next to him, Calhoun—"will take your statements and see to those who need medical attention."

She breaks away from them and signals to a uniformed Black cop and Rosalie to follow her. Time crawls as Sommers stalks over, her eyes raking over each of us as if analyzing the purity of our souls. I don't know her, but I don't like this woman.

Sommers's eyes linger on me a moment, then shift to Mama. "Marie Trudeau," she says. "I hate that we're meeting under these circumstances." She stares at the blood on Mama's hands and dress.

"Likewise," Mama replies coldly.

Sommers nods at me and Clem. "Are these your kids?"

Mama tugs us closer. "Yes. Cristina and Clement."

"I need to interview you all about what happened here this evening," Sommers says, and turns to me and Clem.

Clem and I nod. I don't know if my nerves can survive any more of this day straight from the darkest pit of the never-realm.

Sommers turns to Rosalie and asks, "Is there a place we can go for privacy? Your office, maybe?"

"Uh, well, Eveline Beaumont's in there with Justin right now, and the rest of the more private spaces are under construction and not safe for people to be in," Rosalie says. "But she'd calmed down considerably last I left, so maybe we can talk there."

"It'll be quick," says Sommers, gesturing for Rosalie to lead the way.

Mama, Clem, and I follow them down the short hallway. At the end there's an exit, a restroom, and a door Rosalie opens, leading to her stately office. The uniformed officer, who didn't bother to introduce himself, holds the door as we file inside. On the way in, I sneak a glance at his badge, which reads DUNCAN.

Eveline's seated on the couch with a wet towel draped across the back of her neck, and Justin's leaning his scant hips against the wet bar, his arms crossed over his chest. Rosalie introduces them to Detective Sommers, and Officer Duncan records everyone's name in his notepad.

Mama, Clem, and I take up three chairs at the round table in the corner of the room, the partly open window Clem and I climbed through earlier between us and Rosalie's desk, where she sits for the interview.

Detective Sommers closes the office door and stands in front of it, which sends a spark of unease shooting across my shoulders. From where he sits on the other side of Mama, I notice Clem's leg jackhammering underneath the table. I want to get up and sit beside him, but I'm paralyzed beneath Sommers's heated gaze.

"Mrs. Beaumont, how about we start with you," Sommers says. "Tell me what happened tonight."

"Well, first, my husband and I were poisoned," Eveline sneers, and cuts her eyes at Rosalie, who remains silent and puts her hands in her lap.

*Poison? What the heck was going on while Clem and I were outside?*

"We were drinking the house cocktails," Eveline continues. "Ben had the Pleasure, and I had the Ambition. I noticed an off-putting bitter taste in mine at first, though I wrote it off as an inexperienced bartender or a lacking recipe," she recounts with a pronounced wrinkle of her nose.

Rosalie rolls her eyes, which Sommers catches. That woman's eyes scroll the room like camera lenses.

"But moments after I finished mine," Eveline says, "I started feeling dizzy. And Ben was sweating way more than normal, and he'd turned red in the face. I was worried he was about to have a heart attack, especially considering that's what killed his brother, Isaac."

"Your first husband?" asks Sommers.

Officer Duncan's head pops up from his notes, and his eyes dart back and forth between Eveline's shocked face and Sommers. I'm as aghast as he is at the news.

Sommers sighs, clasping her hands in front of her. "It shouldn't come as a surprise given my position in the bureau, but I've done extensive background research on every member of the Generational Magic Council. That was my first order of business when I got to town." She brushes off the sleeves of her blazer and says, "Please continue, Mrs. Beaumont."

Eveline purses her lips and snatches the towel from her neck. "I told Ben I thought someone might've put something in our drinks. He immediately wanted to confront Rosalie about it, but we didn't have time."

Sommers tilts her head curiously. "Why not?"

"Because that's when that strange gas started pumping out of the overhead piping all over the main room," Eveline says. "I was already feeling a bit light-headed from the flowery mess she had flowing at the start of the party—to be quite honest, it was an assault on my nose that reminded me of shopping at Abercrombie back in the early 2000s. Everyone else thought the bubble gum–colored clouds coming out of those vents were part of the 'experience'"—she makes air quotes, and Rosalie bristles in her seat, fighting to keep quiet—"until people started dropping like flies. Out cold. It was utterly terrifying."

Sommers turns to Rosalie. "Care to elaborate on your unique piping system, Ms. Dupart?"

Rosalie straightens at her desk and hands Sommers a manila file folder with a stack of various papers inside. "The gas I use in my ventilation system is called *Essense*," she says. "A completely legal invention of Fabiana Bordeaux's similar to what she uses in the House of Vans. Vice Hall's recipe is comprised of a unique blend of natural ingredients that Fabiana and I curated together. It's made from one hundred percent certified-vegan, organic, non-GMO, gluten-free, and carbon-neutral products. I sampled it myself before I approved it for public use. The effects are no stronger than a single standard dose of CBD; and it most certainly does *not* put people to sleep. It's also blue—*not* pink." She cuts her eyes at Eveline. "Someone must've switched the gas cylinders at some point in the evening. Perhaps the same person who poisoned your and Ben's drinks, though you're such a delight, I can't imagine why anyone would want to do such a thing."

"Rose," Mama warns under her breath.

I tense because I see Detective Sommers eating all this drama up, already formulating her suspect list in her mind.

"Is there bad blood between you two?" Sommers asks Rosalie, pointing at her and then Eveline.

"I don't think about Eveline Beaumont unless she crosses my line of vision, and even then, it's a toss-up to whether I give a damn or not," Rosalie says.

Justin snickers under his breath, and Eveline grimaces at Rosalie but miraculously stays quiet.

"I'll need you to show us the piping control room when we're finished here," Sommers says, to which Rosalie nods. "Who has access?"

"Me, Justin, and our shift leads," Rosalie replies. "That's it."

"I'll need a list of those employees," Sommers orders, and Justin confirms he'll handle it. "Okay, back to you, Mrs. Beaumont," Sommers says to Eveline. "What happened after you noticed people were passing out from the gas?"

Eveline swallowed hard. "Ben became frantic. He started shouting for Rosalie, but he ran into Justin instead."

"Yeah," Justin says, his face twisted into a frown, "and he assaulted me." He points to the darkening bruise on the left side of his face, which I hadn't noticed until now. "Sucker punched me with a right hook."

"And you two fought?" Sommers asks him.

He shakes his head. "Marie got between us and broke it up before I could swing back."

Sommers's eyes pivot to our side of the room, and she wanders a few steps closer. "And then what happened, Mrs. Trudeau?"

Mama takes a deep breath before she speaks. "Ben turned on me." Mama nods at Eveline. "Eveline tried to stop him, but he wouldn't listen. Then she passed out from the gas, and he went ballistic. I'd wrapped my shawl around my nose and mouth, but that only delayed the effects of the gas, which also had a slow effect on Ben, I'm guessing due to his size. I tried to stay out of his reach, but the fumes were making me sluggish. He kept screaming in my face about some tape."

Sommers narrows her eyes. "What did he mean by that? What tape?"

Mama lifts her hands on either side of her and looks Sommers straight in the eye. "I have no idea, and that's the truth."

Sommers turns to Rosalie. "Do you?"

She shifts in her seat and shakes her head definitively, her brow wrinkled. "No, of course not. Every day I get out of bed, I choose to be different from people like Benjamin Beaumont."

Sommers cocks her head, homing in on Rosalie, which sets my pulse racing. "And what does that mean?"

"Rose . . ." Mama warns again.

Rosalie ignores her. "You said you've done your research, Detective, so let's not pretend you had no idea how corrupt Mayor Beaumont and his political besties are—and have been since as long as they've had power *and* privilege."

"You will not slander my husband's name moments after he was *murdered* in *your* establishment," Eveline snaps, sitting up straighter and glaring at Rosalie. "This is on *your* head."

"That's not fair, Eveline," Mama retorts before Rosalie can. "Let's not forget your husband was choking me"—she lifts her head to reveal the bruises shaped like Ben's wide fingers on her neck—"and would've killed me had the gas not taken both of us out first."

One corner of Eveline's lip curls downward. She scoots to the edge of the couch and leans forward, and when she speaks, her voice is low and steady. "I let you in. I played by your rules. And you murdered my husband. Was this your plan all along, Marie?"

"What are you going on about?" Mama asks, not hiding the irritation in her voice. "I did *not* kill your husband."

"Ben posed the biggest threat to all of you because of his support of the Magical Regulation Bureau." Eveline points a trembling finger at Rosalie and then Mama, though neither of them flinches. "You might've succeeded in taking my husband from me, but you will *never* stop my work."

"Again, Eveline," Mama says with an exasperated sigh, "I didn't murder your husband. And I don't know enough about your little raggedy bureau to hate it because you won't even talk to me about it. Has your brilliant mind ever considered that perhaps one of the plethora of people your husband's crossed in his many years of bad business dealings finally caught up with him?"

"*That* part," Rosalie adds.

Eveline slams a hand on the leather couch, but Clem speaks before she can, surprising everyone—even me.

"*Stop this!*" he shouts, and everyone falls silent. "Mrs. Beaumont, please stop calling my mama a murderer. She didn't do it. I *know* she didn't."

"And how would you know that, Clement?" asks Sommers.

"Cris and I were outside talking when we heard screams coming from inside," Clem explains. "We tried to go back in to see what was going on, but the doors were locked."

"Then how'd you two get inside?" Sommers asks.

I point to the window near Rosalie's desk. "Clem remembered Mama mentioning to Aunt Rosalie that she needed to get her office window's lock repaired, so we pushed it open from the outside and climbed through. We went back out to the main room and found everyone passed out all over the place—except Mama and Ben Beaumont. He was strangling her and screaming in her face."

"And then what happened?" Sommers asks. "Did you two try to defend your mom?"

"We would have," I say, taking the full force of Detective Sommers's stare, "but someone crept up on us both and sprayed us with that pink knockout gas."

"Are you claiming there was another conscious person in the room besides you two kids and your mother and Ben?"

Clem and I both nod.

"But who?" Justin gestures at the door. "All the doors were locked from the inside, so they might still be out there."

"Maybe not," I answer, drawing everyone's attention. "Did you open the office window?"

Justin shakes his head. "I didn't, but we were thankful for the fresh air."

"Well, we shut it when we came in," I say. "I remember fussing at Clem for slamming it closed and making so much noise." I stand up and walk over to examine the window, and my heart skips a beat immediately. Several congealed drops of blood are on the windowsill. "I think the killer might've escaped through the window. There's blood here."

Sommers and Duncan come over, and I step aside so Duncan can flash a few pictures and scribble notes in his pad while Sommers examines the evidence.

A knock at the door gives everyone a start except Sommers. Duncan answers it and retrieves a labeled plastic bag with Clem's bloodied knife inside. He hands it to Sommers, who dangles it in front of her.

"Do any of you recognize this knife?" Sommers asks. "The handle is engraved with the initials 'NDT.'"

My heart plummets. I knew we'd get here eventually, but I'm still gobsmacked into silence.

"It's mine," Mama lies. "It belonged to my late husband, whose father gave it to him. It's a keepsake I like to have near to remind me of him."

Clem lets go of a long shuddering breath on Mama's other side, and it takes every bit of resolve I have remaining not to leap across this table and throw my arms around him. The blame for this isn't his to carry, but he's still going to take it nonetheless.

Sommers sighs and hands the bagged knife back to Duncan. "I advise everyone present to *not* leave New Orleans anytime soon." She nods at Mama and says, "Now might be a good time to secure legal representation."

Officer Duncan takes photos of everyone's injuries (those who have them) and asks a few clarifying questions before we're released to exit through the back door so we won't have to navigate the circus at the main entrance.

Rosalie tells Mama she'll be home as soon as she's able to lock down Vice Hall. Mama, Clem, and I arrived separately, so the drive back home is lonely.

Yet again, our lives have been reduced to pieces on a board. I don't know who's playing what game this time, but I'm ready to break the board over their head.

And if I'm going to have to get justice for my family again—then so be it.

# NINE
# CLEMENT

After we got home from Vice Hall, I couldn't sleep more than a few fleeting minutes at a time.

I forgot to close the curtains last night, so the sunlight bounding through my window is punishment. The golden rays burned away the comfort of darkness and now shine a spotlight on the ugliness of my anxiety, which my medication doesn't even seem to be helping much in these trying days. I pull the covers up to my nose and roll over. I don't want to get out of this bed. It's warm and comfortable. And safe.

I run my hand over the empty side of the bed where Yves once slept beside me all night. The sheets are cool beneath my palm, and I draw my hand back and clutch the blankets tighter around me. My mind staggers backward into a memory, equal parts comforting and harrowing, of Yves and me cuddling, our bodies mashed together, at such peace that we fell asleep in each other's arms, our hearts beating the same rhythm.

We tried that once . . . after . . . It took me a long while to get accustomed to how cool his body felt. I guess it was better than him in a casket underground, unable to ever hug anyone again. But what almost pitched me over the emotional edge was the lagging pace of his heartbeat, once for every four to five of mine.

It hurts to think we might never find our rhythm again.

We haven't made out or done anything sexual since his resurrection—not even heavy petting. He tried to initiate once and only once, a few weeks after his revival. I stopped him, and he immediately became withdrawn, which I realized at once was because he didn't want to disappoint me. I explained to him then that our connection was so much more than physical, and if I couldn't experience an orgasm with both of us whole, happy, and consenting, I didn't want it. And that I was choosing to wait for him.

I'll spend the rest of my life searching for a way to save him if I must.

I only hope my mind and body can endure that long.

Someone taps softly on my closed bedroom door, and I call for them to come inside.

Cris opens the door gingerly and steps in. I slide over and lift the blankets, and she climbs in bed with me.

Her eyes are puffy and pink from fatigue . . . and crying. Her lashes are still wet. She snuggles closer to me until our knees bump against each other and our foreheads almost touch.

"I haven't brushed my teeth yet," I whisper.

She smiles. "I'm used to your dragon breath."

"Girl, fuck you."

We both giggle.

"Mama wants to talk to everyone downstairs," Cris reports. "She sent me up here to get you."

"What time is it?" I groan.

"Seven thirty," she says. "And the drama's already started."

My heart dips. "What's going on?"

"Desiree already has an attitude despite being the reason we're meeting so early, because apparently she had a full day planned already and doesn't have time to spare."

Cris and I roll our eyes at the same time.

Aunt Desiree treats family like an inconvenience, particularly when family doesn't behave the way she expects. I saw firsthand how cold she got with Cris after she turned down that summer program at Howard University that Desiree had been campaigning for Cris to go on last summer—when we thought Mama was dying. I don't get Desiree, and I'm honestly not sure I want to.

I get out of bed with a heavy sigh, then wash my face and brush my teeth before Cris and I head downstairs together.

The kitchen is fragrant with the scents of coffee and bacon. Ursula's decade-old Mr. Coffee coffee maker hisses with steam as it spits out the last dregs into the full pot. Ursula swears by that thing, and I can't lie, the coffee is decent and reliable. A big pot of grits bubbles on the stove beside the frying pan from which Odessa removes the last few strips of bacon. She cuts the eyes off and sets the bacon on the pile atop a paper towel–lined plate. My stomach moans, and I'm salivating before I realize.

Aunt Ursula and Aunt Rosalie are both still in their robes and bonnets. Rosalie forces a smile when she says good morning, and Ursula glances up from her phone to murmur a tepid hello. Both their faces bear the heavy darkness of last night's event. Ursula left LaShawn's and came over late last night, so Mama must've called and told her what happened after we got home.

Mama seems a shadow of herself too, standing in the kitchen in some sweats and an old tee, her hair stuffed into a bonnet as well. Dark circles discolor the once-bright tawny skin beneath her eyes, which are weighted with fatigue.

Everyone, myself included, seems beat down—except Aunt Desiree, who's wearing creased slacks, a blouse, and loafers and somehow has found the time to do a full professional beat on her face before 8:00 A.M. She nods hello to us, then continues pounding out an intense email on her laptop. I cringe for the unlucky person on the receiving end of that message.

"Where's Aunt Jacquelyn?" I ask Cris.

She shrugs and whispers, "That's part of the drama. She hasn't been home in a few days and isn't answering her phone. No one knows where she is. But she texted Mama super early and said she was okay and would be back home this morning."

"That's strange," I mutter.

"Tell me about it."

Mama stirs the grits, while Odessa starts cleaning the dirty cooking dishes, and Rosalie and Ursula make cups of coffee for everyone.

Cris and I hover near the back entrance to the kitchen. I want to eat, but my stomach is too woozy with the anticipation of what's going to happen this morning. And the heat of tension radiating throughout the room already feels on the verge of boiling. It tickles my anxiety, igniting the urge to run.

But I don't. Instead, I hold my position next to my sister, who, in an uncharacteristic turn of events, turns down Rosalie's offer to make her some coffee. I decline too. The last thing I need this morning is caffeine.

"I guess Jackie's not coming," Mama announces with a sigh.

Desiree frowns at her computer screen but doesn't say anything. Odessa folds a dish towel and sets it on the counter before whisking out of the room.

"A couple of months ago, I got an offer from Karmine Delaney to invest in Vice Hall," Rosalie says. "I turned him down, and he seemed offended that I'd say no to him."

"Why did you?" asks Mama.

Rosalie's expression darkens more. "I've heard more than a few whispers linking him to the Divine Knights. I don't know if it's true, but I get bad vibes from that guy. And he's been prowling around town the past few days."

"Was he at the soft launch?" Ursula asks.

Both Mama and Rosalie think for a moment. Mama shrugs and looks at Rosalie.

"He made an appearance," she says. "I think I remember him leaving early, though I could be wrong. I was running around a lot and very preoccupied."

"What if Karmine had beef with the mayor?" Ursula suggests. "He could've ordered a hit on Ben easy if he's running a cartel."

Cris's brow furrows, a telltale sign that her analytic brain just kicked up its processing power a notch. I don't know anything about the Divine Knights or this Karmine dude, and I'm almost afraid to ask my sister why this topic suddenly piques her interest.

"But why frame me?" Mama asks.

Rosalie huffs. "I don't know."

Desiree folds her arms and clears her throat. "Well, since everyone else wants to play daft, I'll address the elephant in the room." She pivots in her seat to face Mama. "Did you do it?"

Mama's eyes narrow. "No."

"Don't be ridiculous, Desiree," Ursula cuts in. "But you know, I wouldn't put it past Eveline to have done it herself. I'd be surprised if it were the first time. I never trusted that woman."

Cris and I share a furtive glance. Could there be some truth to Ursula's suspicion? But why would Eveline kill her own husband? Especially since he was the primary person backing her Magical Regulation Bureau. That doesn't make sense.

Desiree raises a brow. "And the poison?"

"Seriously?" Mama says.

Rosalie scoffs. "Desiree, why are you so comfortable being disrespectful? Especially to Marie, who practically raised us—"

"And what does that have to do with the price of dick in Denmark, darling?" quips Desiree.

Rosalie cocks her head. "I guess you'd know since that was the only way you'd get some before you bamboozled Michael Prince into proposing. How'd you do it? Love spell?" She leans onto the wide counter separating them and smirks. "Be honest, sis. I promise we'll only judge you a tiny bit."

Cris stiffens beside me, and I grab her hand. The kitchen's about to blow.

Mama's brow wrinkles under a severe scowl. "Cut it out! I did *not* poison or kill anyone. Nor did I call you all here to fight with one another!" She shakes her head and stares up at the ceiling. "This family is under attack once again. This time it's me and Rosalie. It could be y'all next. This is very serious."

A chill winds through the room like a long-tailed cat, brushing against everyone and making them tense; all except Desiree, who still manages to look irritated.

"Desiree, you have a bunch of high-power attorney friends," Ursula announces, "why don't you make a referral to one of them for Marie?"

Desiree sighs through her nose and closes her laptop. She turns to Ursula and smooths her hands across the thighs of her slacks, then says, "I'm afraid I can't do that."

Ursula cranes her neck forward. "Say what now?"

Rosalie sets her cup on the counter, her eyes wide with disbelief. Mama just stares at Desiree with an unreadable expression that's somehow still terrifying.

Desiree slides her laptop into her alligator-skin briefcase, avoiding eye contact with anyone. "This is why I didn't want to come over here in the first place. I had a feeling y'all were going to want to hit me up for a favor." She stands up from where she was sitting at the island counter, shaking her head. "I can't be associated with y'all's shenanigans this year. I have plans of my own."

"And what exactly would those plans be, Desiree?" Mama's calm voice makes my spine tingle with terror.

Desiree draws herself up taller, a persistent smile pulling at the corner of her lips that she refuses to share with us. "Now that Ben's dead, I'm going to petition the Supreme Court of Louisiana to approve another election. And this time, I plan to run." She throws a look of gracious pity across the room at Mama. "I'm so sorry, Marie, but I can't take the risk of sullying my reputation before my political career even gets off the ground."

Ursula charges across the kitchen like a linebacker. Desiree stumbles back into the counter barstools, knocking several over with a loud clatter. Cris and I leap into action without thinking, and we each grab one side of our aunt and haul her out of swinging distance from Desiree.

Rosalie sneers at Desiree. "When you don't give a shit who you sacrifice to get ahead in life, don't be surprised if your final destination ends up being the never-realm."

Desiree stares hard at Rosalie. "That a threat?"

"Of course not." Rosalie shakes her head. "I pray you change before that day comes."

Ursula calms enough for Cris and me to let her go, though her chest still heaves with angry breaths that flare her nostrils.

*Mood, Aunt Ursula.* So I guess Desiree doesn't care if Mama goes to prison for the rest of her life and leaves her two teenage kids without a parent to care for them, so long as nothing derails or delays her political aspirations. Good to know.

"I'm not going to let y'all make me feel bad because I want better for myself," Desiree says, pointing a finger at her own chest, her eyes welling with angry tears. "I'm choosing to break the cycle of abuse and drama that you people won't stop spinning until you're all dead or in prison!"

Cris bristles beside me. I feel the same, but I tap her hand with one finger and shake my head furtively, a silent reminder for her not to get mixed up in our aunts' beef. This might be the one time it's best to let the adults handle their own shit.

"Get out," Mama says, still eerily calm, so much so that it takes my brain a few moments to register what she said.

Desiree falls still, blinking confusedly at Mama. "Huh?"

*"Get the fuck out of my house, Desiree!"* Mama shouts.

Desiree shocks back to life and snatches her laptop bag from the counter, her bottom lip trembling despite her glower.

"Go be free," Mama tells her. "I'm unleashing you from the chains of familial obligation. May the gods bless your endeavors—because I will not."

A single tear brims in one of Desiree's eyes, but she wipes it away angrily before it can fall. "This family is toxic," she says coldly.

Rosalie opens her mouth to respond, but Mama holds up a hand, and Rosalie swallows her rebuttal.

"Be careful tapping that well of darkness inside you," Mama warns. "It might be cathartic to draw the vitriol from it that you spew at us, but mind yourself, little sister. Darkness spreads, and it'll consume you too. Be easy now."

Desiree shoulders her bag, her face pale, and leaves without saying goodbye to anyone. But as she steps into the foyer, the front door opens.

Cris and I move closer to peer around the corner, just as Aunt Jacquelyn strides through the door, cradling Baptiste, who's sound asleep in her arms. She's dressed casually in a sweatsuit, with her hair in a low pony beneath an ugly jean bucket hat that needs to be burned at the stake.

Aunt Jackie's light-eyed stare is hardened with determination as she casually greets Desiree, Cris, and then me. But we're all too busy gawking at the person who follows Aunt Jackie in.

At first, I almost don't recognize Gabriela Savant, Valentina's mom, who disappeared the night we ended Valentina's grandmother. Gabriela sticks close to Aunt Jackie. I never imagined I'd see *that* woman in *this* house—not unless she'd come to burn it down. But something's odd about her and the way she's looking around as if she has no idea where she is. Her brown eyes are bright and wonderous, soaking in the grand entrance of our home. Then they fall on me and Cris, and Gabriela lifts a tentative hand and waves.

Cris, stubbornly tight-lipped, frowns at her, but I nod hello.

Desiree shakes her head and leaves, slamming the door. Jacquelyn doubles back to take Gabriela's hand and lead her into the kitchen, where Mama, Rosalie, and Ursula speak in low, inaudible voices to one another. When I turn back, I realize Odessa returned at some point and joined the quiet conversation.

"Gabriela?" Mama screeches, shock all over her face. "Jackie, what is this?"

Cris and I share a furtive *oh, shit* expression.

"I know you fucking lying." Ursula slams her mug down so hard on the countertop that the handle breaks off and coffee sloshes over the slides.

Odessa cries out and rushes over with a towel for Ursula's wet hand, which Odessa checks expeditiously to make sure Ursula didn't slice open. Thank goodness she's uninjured; we don't need an unexpected trip to the ER to add to the chaos of this morning.

Baptiste stirs and whines in Jacquelyn's arms, and she bounces him and caresses his back. Odessa takes him from Jacquelyn and tells her she'll take him upstairs to change him and get him settled, and Jacquelyn seems relieved for the short break.

When Odessa and Baptiste are gone, Jacquelyn's expression sharpens, and she points at Mama and Ursula. "Which one of you was it?"

Mama seems confused. Ursula looks two seconds from breathing fire onto both Jacquelyn and Gabriela. *The answer should be obvious, Aunt Jackie.*

Mama pinches the bridge of her nose and lets out a long, deep breath, then puts a hand on Ursula's forearm, urging her to calm down. "One problem at a time." Mama sighs.

Cris and I both cringe, then nestle closer. That's a tough mantra to live by when the problems keep multiplying.

Mama turns to Ursula and says, "Explain what's going on, please."

"This one"—Ursula flicks her hand toward Gabriela, who flinches back, looking more scared by the minute—"was digging around in our family's business and somehow managed to wander all the way up to Baton Rouge to harass Ms. Eileen about how our mama and daddy bought Whittier Brewery."

Mama shifts her disarming glare to Gabriela. "That true?"

Gabriela shakes her head and stammers, "I—I don't know what she's talking about. I'm just a bartender in Baton Rouge at the Hilton Garden Inn, I swear."

"Jesus H., Ursula," Mama grumbles under her breath. "Did you erase her memories?"

Ursula shrugs one shoulder.

"Ursula!" Mama bellows.

"What else was I supposed to do?" Ursula cries. "In my opinion, she came out better than her in-laws."

"Who?" Gabriela asks, her brow scrunched.

Mama lifts a hand and shakes her head with a *don't even worry about it* look on her face.

Gabriela takes the hint and falls back quiet.

"Yeah, I found her," Jacquelyn says, pride puffing her chest. "The night she disappeared, Arturo told me she was in Baton Rouge, which was also the same night y'all killed Lenora and Felix." She grimaces at the last part as if judging us for what we did.

"How did you find her?" asks Ursula.

"I had Baptiste, so I couldn't do much," Jacquelyn says. "I just drove around looking for her on the streets at first."

"Oh, that's utterly brilliant, Jackie," Ursula replies.

"Well, it worked!" Jacquelyn retorts. "Kinda . . . I asked around when and where I could. Shelters. Jails. Hospitals. And I got a room at the Hilton Garden Inn when I realized it was going to take longer than a day. On the third day, I walked back into the hotel ready to give up, when I passed the bar and happened to look up, and she was there." She gestures toward Gabriela, whose face reads as unquestionably uncomfortable.

Gabriela lifts her hands in mock surrender. "Look, I don't know what's going on here, but I was promised answers about what the hell's happened with my memories. Because I apparently rent a room from a rich old white lady I barely know and have been working as a bartender at that shitty hotel despite not being able to make a decent rum and coke. And for the past nine months, I've been desperately trying to piece together who the hell I am, but my memories are just . . . fog in my head." She takes a long pause for a deep breath, then says, "Every day felt *wrong*. I thought I was losing my mind. And you're telling me now that *you*"—she points at Ursula—"did this to me with magic?"

"Unfortunately, yes," Mama answers before Ursula can.

"And she's gonna fix it," adds Jacquelyn rather confidently.

"The hell if I am," Ursula says. "For what? So she can pick up where she left off harassing our family? Absolutely not." She shakes her head vehemently. "No, ma'am."

"Do it." Cris's voice cuts across the room, and everyone turns to her. "Restore her memories, Aunt Ursula. The Council's ours now. We don't need to be afraid of Gabriela. Valentina needs her mom. Especially right now."

I raise a brow at Cris, but she doesn't meet my suspicious stare. Since when did my sister care so much about her archnemesis's well-being? Maybe she's not gone as dark as I thought.

Gabriela's face blanches, and she covers her trembling lips with one hand. "I have a daughter?"

"Don't worry," Jacquelyn says, returning to Gabriela's side and rubbing her back until Gabriela twists away from her. "They're going to undo it." Jacquelyn cuts her eyes at Ursula and Mama.

Ursula's face remains stern and unmoved. "Okay, Jackie," she says. "But I have one question for you first." Jacquelyn puts her hands on her hips and narrows her eyes at Ursula. "Do you honestly believe returning Arturo Savant's wife is going to make him love you and y'all's Van Kid?"

Gabriela's eyes widen, her hand still covering her mouth. I'd feel sorry for her if she hadn't been part of the plot to usurp our family's throne.

Silence blankets the room. I don't even realize I'm holding my breath at first. Mama and Rosalie both watch Ursula and Jacquelyn, likewise shocked into a stupor.

Aunt Jackie's bright brown cheeks burn crimson, and the anger roiling inside her makes her short body tremble like a shapely kettle about to boil. When she speaks, I'm even more surprised she's not yelling either. "You know what, Ursula? All these years, you believed Celeste conjured your loneliness to avoid facing what you and I both know to be true: You are alone because of your nasty-ass disposition."

Ursula recoils as if her sister's words popped her right on the mouth. After she blinks a few times and collects herself, she says, "I'll have you know that I'm dating someone, thank you very much. And I *didn't* meet him at a brothel."

Jacquelyn sucked her teeth. "Your man a troglodyte too? Maybe both of y'all need to pay a visit to the House of Vans to learn how to loosen up."

Mama snickers and then straightens, catching herself. But Ursula whirls on her, looking offended.

"Ursula, please restore this woman's memories so we can get back to the very big and important problem at hand," Mama tells her.

Gabriela clasps her hands in front of her. The hope on her face bothers me, and I immediately feel guilty for it. I want her uncrossed, but I also want her gone. And I'm not sure if that makes me a bad person or not, so I bury that too.

"There's one major problem with that," Ursula says, which makes me groan, and she cuts her eyes at me. "I don't know how to restore memories."

"You *what?*" Mama says.

"Well, *you're* the Queen!" Ursula retorts, gesturing at Mama. "*You* don't know how to do it?"

"No, Ursula," Mama snaps back, "I never learned how to restore memories because I never planned to tamper with people's minds in the first place!"

Ursula huffs a frustrated breath. "I hate to do this, but I'm going to have to call Black Wolf."

I tense. Mama does too. Before anyone can protest, Ursula hurries from the room.

Black Wolf was kind to me when I met him last summer. But that was also right before I asked him to destroy Jack Kingston's bar. I only pegged Black Wolf for the destructive, vengeful type of god, so I'm having a hard time imagining him in the business of restoring anything.

Ursula returns, breathing hard from her dash upstairs and back, with a black card in her hand. I recognize the glowing blue outline of the wolf's head on one side. She presses the card to her lips and plants a lingering kiss on it.

She lowers the card slowly . . . but nothing happens.

"So what?" I ask. "Do we just wait for him to knock on the front door?"

"You rang?" Black Wolf's voice slices through the nervous air of the kitchen, startling everyone. Cris and I both let out a shriek of surprise. Rosalie gasps, dramatically clutching her chest.

Black Wolf sits backward on the same stool Desiree sat on earlier at the island. His elbows are propped on the counter behind him as if he's always been here. His locs are twisted back into a ponytail, and he's wearing a long-sleeved black linen dress with a split up to his hip and chunky-bottomed black boots. He smells rustic and spicy, like amber, leather, and firewood, something dangerous and forbidden.

He lifts an immaculately arched eyebrow above his mirrored aviators as he glances around the room. His gaze stops on Gabriela, then shoots to Ursula. "Interesting company you keep."

"That's why I summoned you," Ursula says, stepping forward. "I partially erased Gabriela's memories, and I need you to restore them."

Black Wolf sighs and slips off his seat with the grace of a ballerina, then whisks over to Gabriela, so light on his feet despite his clunky shoes that it's as if he's gliding. She winces as the god leans close, his eyes closed and hands clasped behind his back. He takes a long, thorough sniff of her, and his eyes shoot open. He snaps back upright and claps his hands once, making me flinch.

I watch the god curiously, wondering if Black Wolf can restore souls too. But Papa Eshu's warning to Ursula last summer about getting tangled up with Black Wolf replays in my head, and I stash that thought on a dusty high shelf in my mind.

Black Wolf turns back to Ursula. "Couple things, love," he tells her, but she already looks hesitant. "First, I can only partially restore her memories, but don't fret, she'll have all the crucial ones, like her family, hobbies, blah blah blah." He rolls his eyes and his wrist. "Second, it's going to take some time to achieve the full effect. Restoring memories is a slow and tedious process."

Ursula folds her arms across her chest. "How long?"

"Eh, twenty-four hours, give or take," he says. "Last, and this is the important bit, so pay attention: No more freebies. This one's going to cost you."

"Now wait one minute, *glasses*," Ursula says, uncrossing her arms to point at Black Wolf. "I've always paid you well—and you drink bourbon as if I have a free tap in my back office!"

The god chuckles. "Relax, love. You'll find my fee easy and affordable. I do this favor for you today, and you do something small for me later, which I'll specify at a time of my choosing."

Ursula's brows knit. "Something small like *what*?"

"I'll let you know—at—that—time," he says.

My mouth is too dry to speak. Nothing about this feels like a good idea.

"Ursula, you don't have to do this," Mama whispers to her. "We can find another way."

I can feel the intensity of my heartbeat, which only amplifies it more.

Ursula shakes her head. "No, I got it. This was my doing, so I need to handle the consequences." She nods at Black Wolf. "I agree to your terms."

He grins.

"Do *not* fuck me over, Black Wolf," she warns.

His smile droops enough to make me uncomfortable. "I would never."

The god plucks one of his locs from his head and struts over to Gabriela. She watches him curiously as he looks into her eyes and says, "Do you consent?"

She looks nervous but nods.

"It's going to be a tad excruciating at first," he says in a teasing low voice, "but *ohhh*, is it going to be *worth it*." He lifts the severed loc to her ear, and it begins writhing like a worm on a hook. The tail end whips against Gabriela's shoulder, giving her a start, but before she can process what's happening, the other end's already wriggled into her ear canal. She screams and tries to pull it back out, but it slips from her grip and disappears inside her head, which reminds me of someone sucking up a spaghetti noodle.

Gabriela's eyes roll back in her head, and she falls unconscious and collapses into Black Wolf's arms.

He lifts her off her feet and turns to Ursula. "She will wake once her memories are restored. She will be groggy and disoriented, so be patient with her. Uh, where do you want me to put her?"

"This way," Mama says, and leads him upstairs to put Gabriela in one of the spare bedrooms.

"And what's your plan for when Gabriela Savant comes to in the den of the family who recently murdered her in-laws and took her throne?" Ursula asks Jacquelyn. "Or have you not thought that far?"

I watch the battle raging in Aunt Jackie's head, telegraphed through subtle shifts in her expression, between fury at Aunt Ursula for calling her out and panic that her older sister's right.

Before Aunt Jackie can come up with an answer, Cris speaks up.

"I have an idea," she announces.

We all turn to her, but I'm the only one of us who's rightfully worried.

# TEN

## VALENTINA SAVANT

Valentina faced the towering front of her best friend's white plantation-style home and gathered her nerve. She'd waited for the Sun to set and the reporters to retreat to their vans outside the iron gate to the Beaumonts' house.

When she'd called Sofia a couple of hours ago to apologize for kicking off their earlier argument, Sofia broke the news that her dad had been murdered the prior night, probably at the same time they were summoning spirits and fighting. Pain had clung to Sofia's voice like a swarm of leeches. And Valentina was all too familiar with that feeling.

Before leaving home, she had scoured the internet, television, and social media, but everywhere was mum about the details surrounding Mayor Beaumont's murder. All Valentina knew was that it'd happened during a soft opening of Vice Hall, a joint business venture between Rosalie Dupart and Justin Montaigne.

Valentina found it interesting that drama followed Justin to his new operation too. She had had no dealings with Rosalie and thus had no opinion of her, but Valentina had never cared much for Justin. He had a rat face for a reason. And seeing as how people kept dying in his places of business, Valentina wondered if he had anything to do with Ben Beaumont's murder—and her grandparents' too.

She took a deep breath in and blew it out. Then she rang the doorbell. She smiled reverently into the doorbell camera until she heard light footsteps approaching on the other side.

Sofia answered, standing in the shadowy foyer of her home, her hair in a messy ponytail and her eyes red and swollen from crying. Valentina threw her arms around Sofia and felt her friend fall into the embrace—the same way Sofia had done for her after Valentina got the news of her grandparents' deaths.

"I thought you could use someone to talk to," Valentina said when they parted. She frowned at all the flower arrangements sitting on the floor of the foyer. They'd gotten so many that they'd stopped unwrapping them and just sat them aside to suffocate and die.

"Yes, please," Sofia said with a weak smile, and led Valentina inside. "Mom hasn't said much to me aside from explaining what all happened that night. She's been shut up in there ever since." Sofia pointed over her shoulder at the closed door of Eveline's office.

Valentina had been over to Sofia's home loads of times but had only ever been inside that particular room once and only for a few seconds.

Valentina recalled Granny's letter mentioning how secretive and aloof Eveline had been and wondered what secrets Eveline could be hiding in that office.

"Do you think she'd mind if I poked my head in to say hello?" Valentina asked. "I don't want to be rude."

Sofia shrugged one shoulder. "We'll see." She escorted Valentina over to the double French doors and knocked softly on one of the glass panes shrouded by thick curtains on the other side.

Eveline Beaumont parted the doors and stared down at Sofia with unabashed annoyance until she noticed Valentina standing behind her. Eveline's hair was still in the elaborate updo from last night's celebration, though she'd changed into sweats and a tank with a silk house robe drawn tight and tied around her waist. She positioned herself in the doorway in such a way that Valentina couldn't see anything inside the room.

"Hi, Mrs. Beaumont," Valentina said. "I came to sit with Sofia for a while and wanted to offer my condolences. I'm sorry about Mr. Beaumont."

Eveline nodded solemnly. "Thank you, Valentina. You girls let me know if you need anything, okay? And help yourself to some food. There's more than enough for us."

"Yes, ma'am," both Valentina and Sofia said in unison.

Eveline nodded once more and shut her office door.

Sofia and Valentina went to the kitchen, where Valentina gaped at the bounty of fried chicken set out on every counter. Every restaurant was represented, from Popeyes to Henri's, in everything from paper take-out containers to silver catering trays. Once, Valentina had asked Granny why people always sent so much fried chicken whenever someone died. Granny had said it was because it's a delicious, low-cost way to feed a bunch of people, and most folks love it despite the ridiculous stereotype. She'd also taught Valentina that missing out on enjoying something rooted in your own culture based on the irrelevant opinions of ignorant people was what racists wanted—and Granny had claimed that was why she made it her business to enjoy as much fried chicken as her sensitive tummy would allow.

No one had so much as brought Valentina a two-piece and a biscuit when she'd lost both her grandparents.

Valentina hadn't been hungry when she arrived, but the sight of all that food made her stomach rumble with ferocity. She and Sofia made small plates of wings and macaroni and cheese—Valentina passed on the potato salad though. She only ate her granny's potato salad because she didn't trust anyone else with that level of responsibility.

Upstairs in Sofia's room, they both inhaled their food while seated on the floor. Sofia's parents had decorated her bedroom in her favorite color—mint green. The entire space was bright and sickeningly coordinated, much like Sofia's life, which Valentina had always secretly envied. Sofia's room was a stark contrast to the rest of their home, which was dim and bleak with mourning.

"I hadn't felt like eating all day," Sofia said. "I guess having you here settled my nerves a bit. I'm really glad you came over."

"Of course." Valentina set her empty plate aside. "Do you want to talk about it?"

Sofia narrated her mom's harrowing version of her father's murder last night at Vice Hall. It was like some shit out of a slasher movie. Poisoned drinks. Knockout gas. Her mom waking up to find her husband hung on the wall like a deer carcass.

"Fuck . . . Sofia . . . I'm so sorry."

Sofia nodded. "I'm worried about Mom."

That Eveline wasn't handling her husband's brutal murder well despite how "together" she'd presented herself just a few minutes ago didn't surprise Valentina. She was well-versed in stoicism herself.

"I saw her eyeing a bottle of foxglove in her office earlier," Sofia confessed. "She claims she got it as a sleeping draft, but the whole thing gave me a really bad feeling." She chewed her bottom lip, as if debating something internally, then whispered, "She and Dad had been arguing a *lot*. Things got super intense last week. It scared me." She pulled her knees close to her chest. "I've never heard them scream at each other like that before."

"What were they fighting about?" asked Valentina.

"Mom flipped her shit about some tape of Dad with another woman," Sofia said. "Apparently someone blackmailed him with it. Dad kept saying it had something to do with an ongoing feud Mom had with some woman named Fabiana, who owns the House of Vans, where the tape was recorded. The weird thing about it was Mom wasn't as pissed about Dad cheating as she was about him ruining her plans with her Magical Regulation Bureau."

"Hmm . . ." Valentina murmured to herself.

"I *hate* that fucking bureau," Sofia said. "It's *all* she cares about—even more than me and what *I'm* going through right now."

For the whole of their lifelong friendship, Valentina had watched Sofia struggle with competing desires to be her authentic self and earn the validation of her difficult-to-please mom, two goals she could never seem to reconcile. Sofia's deepest fear was that her mom had also rejected her the way the gen gods had shunned her from conjuring. That was why Sofia had gotten so heavily into tarot a few years ago. But that hadn't impressed Eveline.

"Have you tried talking to her about how you're feeling?" Valentina asked.

Sofia scoffed. "The only way for me to get my mom's attention right now would be to walk into that office and hand her evidence that Cris's mom killed my dad."

Valentina narrowed her eyes. "Is that what she thinks happened?"

"Mom believes Rosalie tried to poison her and Dad," Sofia explained, "and she thinks Cris's mom murdered my dad after the poison didn't work, which meant either she was protecting her sister or was in on the whole scheme from the beginning."

"But why would she do that?" asked Valentina.

"Allegedly, to sabotage the bureau." Sofia rolled her eyes.

"No shade, but I've wondered more than once why your mom would start an organization like the MRB when she sits on the Gen Council. Isn't that a *major* conflict of interest?"

Sofia threw up her hands. "I don't know why my parents do *half* the silly shit they do."

*Did.* But Valentina didn't correct her friend because she knew how difficult it was to establish a new baseline after losing someone central to your world, especially in such a horrible way.

"I hate to say this, but I don't think Cris's mom did it," Valentina suggested.

"How would *you* know?" asked Sofia.

"Gut feeling. Cris and her morally superior mother only subscribe to 'justified murder.' The MRB wasn't a big enough reason for them to kill your dad. No one even knows what the bureau does. Besides, Cris's mom is Queen. I highly doubt she or her sisters would screw up conjuring a poison if they'd truly wanted your parents dead." Valentina shook her head. "Nah, I have a hunch something else is going on."

"You're probably right," Sofia said. "We may never know what really happened."

"We could," Valentina said.

"We're not detectives, Val."

"We don't have to be. I *know* Cris. If her mom's implicated in your dad's murder, she will turn New Orleans on its head to clear her mom's name. We don't have to beat her to the answer—we just need to be looking over her shoulder when she figures it out."

"Aside from the fact that neither of us is on good terms with Cris," Sofia reminded Valentina, "going through all that to find out the truth is pointless. If Cris does uncover Dad's killer, she'll take that evidence straight to the cops, who'll then tell my mom what happened."

Valentina squeezed her tongue between her teeth to keep from lashing out. Sofia's lack of awareness when it came to strategic maneuvering made Valentina feel like she was dragging a fussy toddler along on her quest for magical world domination.

"Think one level deeper for a second," Valentina told her. "Cris's mom debowed her way onto the Gen Council last summer when the white witches were already giving the Council heat over your dad running for mayor. Your mom isn't really fucking with Cris's mom *or* the white witches right now. So, if *we* were to present your mom with the evidence that would clear Cris's mom's name before the police got to it, your mom could sabotage Cris's mom's defense and finally be rid of her for good. I believe your mom would really appreciate that. Don't you?"

"But if we did that, an innocent woman would go to jail," Sofia said.

"Did you forget they murdered my grandparents?" Valentina snapped.

Sofia hung her head. "And then what? You become Queen?"

"Would that be such a terrible thing?"

"Well, you and I both know *I'll* never have a place on the Council, so what would I get out of all this?"

"You'll be the best friend of the Queen of the Generational Magic Council of New Orleans. I could give you whatever you wanted."

"Like a seat on the Council?" Sofia asked without hesitation.

Valentina tensed, completely unprepared for that question. "Uh, it's not impossible."

Sofia scoffed quietly. "Whatever," she muttered to the floor. "I don't trade futures. What's in it for me *now*?"

"Your mom's respect," Valentina answered.

Sofia's brows knit as she considered the carrot Valentina dangled in front of her.

Valentina picked up her empty glass and got to her feet. "I'm gonna get a refill. Want anything?"

"No, thanks," Sofia said.

Valentina stepped outside Sofia's bedroom and shut the door behind her. Sofia would need time to think. Eveline had made a similar proposition to Granny over thirty years ago. It was kinda strange how, in some twisted fashion, history was repeating itself.

Downstairs in the kitchen, the slightly parted doors of Eveline's office lured Valentina's attention away from quenching her thirst. She set her cup on the counter, and then went back to Eveline's door. She held her breath for a moment and listened. There was only silence on the other side.

Valentina knocked softly. "Mrs. Beaumont?" she called.

No one answered.

Valentina held her breath and eased the door open, slowly revealing the shocked and angry face of Eveline Beaumont, who sat on a couch opposite the entrance. Her eyes had reddened and the skin around them had puffed up since Valentina spoke with her earlier. At some point, Eveline had also taken her hair down, which hung free on either side of her taut face.

"Little girl!" Eveline sat rigidly on the couch, her legs tucked underneath her, her thighs cloaked in a knitted throw. "I didn't say you could come in here!"

"You didn't say 'go away' either," Valentina said, absorbing the sharp sting of Eveline's rebuff. Eveline's eyes widened with incredulity when Valentina stepped all the way inside and shut the door. "I need to talk to you, and it'll be worth your while. I promise."

Eveline frowned. "What do you want?"

"You should know that Madeline DeLacorte is planning to petition MASC to reseat the entire Gen Council. And what happened at Vice Hall last night might make her argument more convincing." Valentina stood firm under Eveline's harsh gaze despite wanting to run to her car and not look back.

"And how in the world would you know that?" Eveline asked, more irritated than impressed.

"Oz Strayer told me," Valentina replied, to which Eveline rolled her eyes. "Apparently, Cris bound him from gen magic, and now he's pissed about it and thinks the whole Council's about to 'get what's coming to them.'" She made air quotes with her fingers, and Eveline scoffed. "Exactly," added Valentina.

"If Madeline has nothing else, she has the audacity," Eveline said, then stared into Valentina's eyes. "Why are you telling me this? You don't have a stake in Council business anymore."

Valentina swallowed her anxiety and spoke around the tremble left behind in her voice. "But I can. I *deserve* to."

Eveline clucked under her breath, which lit a spark of fury inside Valentina. "You're a *teenager*, Valentina. You should be worrying about prom dresses, SATs, and college—not political bullshit."

"My future isn't bullshit," Valentina retorted, her face heating at once for swearing in front of Sofia's mom. "And I'm not just *some teenager*. You certainly didn't feel that way last summer when you let Cris and her family murder my grandparents and steal my granny's and mom's thrones."

Valentina had replayed that day at the Bean in her head a thousand times. The moment when she thought she caught a flash of her granny's name written at the top of a page in Cris's open journal. She'd wondered so many times if her grandparents would've survived if she'd reacted differently that day. There were infinite possibilities, and even though she knew she'd never know which one was the correct answer to her question, she kept evaluating them in her head over and over.

Eveline's expression softened, and she clasped her hands on her lap. "Carrying around all that unchecked anger isn't healthy, Valentina. The situation is way more complicated than you can imagine. Cris and Clem's family had Papa Eshu's blessing last summer. You can't fight the gods."

"Maybe not," Valentina replied, "but *you* can at least give me a seat on the Council so I can have a chance to fight for me—for *us*. I could be your ally."

"All the seats are currently filled," Eveline said.

"Add another. You've done it before."

Eveline sighed hard and closed her eyes.

Valentina was losing her. Granny's letter had mentioned how difficult and closed off Eveline could be with this kind of stuff. But Valentina wasn't willing to give up just yet.

"Madeline DeLacorte wants you removed from the Council," she said. "Aurora Vincent and Justin Montaigne are both in Marie Trudeau's inner circle. And you and Marie"—Valentina paused, letting her voice trail, taking note of the subtle but tense shift in Eveline's poise like an animal sensing prey lurking—"well, let's just say one day, if she decided to change how she felt about you, she'd have the allies to boot you out herself, but who would stand up for you?"

"I think you should get to your point—and quickly," Eveline warned.

Valentina's palms were sweating, but she tucked them in the pocket of her cardigan. "I'm not sure what your endgame is with the Magical Regulation Bureau," she said, "but I know it means a lot to you. You need an ally to watch your back while you work. Let me do that for you."

Eveline relaxed a bit and sat back. "Even if I *were* interested in allying with a *child*, I cannot get over the phantom pain of the massive headaches your grandmother's shenanigans and your mother's complacency brought me over the years—despite their unwavering loyalty."

"I'm not my granny," Valentina said, smothering her outrage at Eveline's slight. "And I'm definitely not my mom. I'm *better*."

Eveline chuckled softly, which made Valentina's skin crawl. After a moment, Eveline clenched her jaw and folded her arms, still studying Valentina.

"I'll think about it," Eveline said. "Now, please, leave me alone. I'd like to come to terms with the gruesome murder of my career and my fucking husband."

Valentina nodded. "Okay," she said. That was better than an outright rejection. "Good night, Mrs. Beaumont."

Valentina left the Reverend Mother alone to mourn—and consider her proposition. Which Valentina hoped Eveline would, because Valentina felt she needed a little insurance in the likely event that Sofia couldn't get her hands on the evidence Cris would need to clear her mom's name—that is, if Sofia even accepted in the first place.

Valentina poured fruit punch into her cup and mused about how Granny had been right about Eveline Beaumont. That woman was made from coldness and cunning. No wonder Sofia struggled so much in that relationship. Maybe no mother was better than a shitty one who appeared perfect on the surface. Although . . . Valentina felt a foreign feeling creeping up her throat.

She wondered where Mom was and if she was okay. Valentina loathed to admit how terrified she was that Mom could possibly meet the same fate as Ben Beaumont—if she hadn't already.

Valentina returned upstairs with her half-empty glass (she'd gotten thirsty on the walk up) and found Sofia sitting in the same spot on her bedroom floor, fussing with her hair.

She smiled up at Valentina as she smoothed her curls into a fresh ponytail.

"I'm in," Sofia said with confidence.

"All right then," Valentina said, surprised at how quickly Sofia had decided. "Let's do this."

# PART II

If you are neutral in situations of injustice, you have chosen the side of the oppressor.

—DESMOND TUTU

# ELEVEN
## CRISTINA

My entire weekend was an unhinged shit circus with no intermissions and no end.

So, yeah . . . I didn't get much sleep.

As a result, I'm a zombie at school on Monday, shambling through the hallways of New Orleans International Magnet High all morning. Ashy face and all. And I do not care, because in the span of one evening, I accidentally killed the head of the Redeemers and my mama was framed for the brutal murder of our city's mayor. My mind was too embattled this morning to worry about skin care—or the lab report on vapor-liquid equilibrium due at the start of third period, which I have not completed. When Mrs. Todd, my chemistry teacher, realizes I've skipped the assignment, she pulls me outside the classroom to the hallway for a private discussion about my "performance."

"The lab report slipped my mind with everything that happened this weekend," I explain. My eyes wander the bright colors of her rainbow sweater to avoid her probing stare. "I'll make it up, I promise."

"We can forget about this one," Mrs. Todd whispers, then winks. "Just between us."

"Thanks," I say, genuinely grateful not to have to take the zero for the assignment, which I was prepared to do. I've never let grades stress me out because I don't believe students should be rated and compared to one another, but I've also grown accustomed to the occasional honor society pin. But lately, spending excess time on academics while my family and I fight for our survival feels a bit facetious.

"I know things happen, and life is tough most times, but I also wanna be straight up with you, Cristina," she says. "Your grades started dropping long before today. You haven't seemed very present in class since the holidays. I was honestly surprised when I heard you weren't on the prom committee. I recall you being excited about your first prom last semester. What happened?"

Something about this line of questioning is making me uncomfortable. Maybe because it's too reminiscent of my family's recent interrogation by Detective Sommers—another person rooting around my personal life for data to form a self-serving conclusion about me. It's violating, which is unfortunately a bit *too* familiar thanks to Oz, whom I, thankfully, have only seen a couple of times today, though each time he made sure to give me a wide berth.

*He had better.*

I just want everyone to leave me alone today.

"Nothing happened," I tell Mrs. Todd. "I promise. Can I go back inside now?"

She acquiesces with a sigh, and I head into the classroom, back to the whispers and stares of the students who've already devoured all the delicious rumors about what happened with my family at Vice Hall this weekend—and the murder my mama's being wrongfully accused of committing.

I glance at the clock to see how much longer I have to sit in this godsforsaken class as I glide to my desk near the back windows. Once there, I block out everything and everyone else for the rest of the period.

I'm used to the cold burn of isolation. I remember it well from right after Valentina made that Instagram post that alienated me from nearly everyone in our grade for most of freshman year. Lately, it's felt like I'm on a reunion tour for every triggering emotion I've ever experienced.

But I don't care about anyone else's opinion of me—in this room or the world at large.

Especially not while the future of my family hangs in the balance yet again.

My day continues its downward spiral promptly at the end of chemistry when I text Aurora about going off campus for lunch and she tells me she's out today for a court hearing. I don't even get to see Clem much because when he's not in class, he's holed up in the library studying.

Clem never misses an honor roll. Not one. Not when Dad died, not when Mama got sick, and not even now, when the rest of his world has sunk underwater. His studies are all that's keeping him grounded in this realm, the one thing he can control that's somewhat reliable and predictable.

I get it.

I don't mention to my brother how much I worry about the way he's dragging the weight of caring for Yves, searching for a way to restore his half-dead(?) boyfriend's soul, *and* managing his and Yves's academic careers simultaneously. And Mama's potential implication in Ben's murder just added another link in his trauma daisy chain.

Instead, I help lighten his assignment load a little. I also give him my old tests from world history last year. We don't have any classes together this year, but we do have the same lunch period. And since Isaiah's been strangely absent from school, Clem spends every lunch hour in the library, studying alone.

Today's library lunch study session is a welcome escape for me from the judgmental gawking of our classmates, which is made twice as good by the cups of gumbo I secure for me and Clem from the food truck that sometimes pulls up outside the school. The first spoonful conjures a smile from my brother, and while we eat, I edit his history essay on the origins of white supremacy around the world. I add some color from my equal parts enlightening and disturbing conversation with Tabitha Edgewater before her fortunate demise.

May she rest in peril.

Aurora, Remi, and I have fifth-period gym together—which Aurora *never* lets us skip, even though for Coach Teague to care, he would have to resuscitate his very last fuck, which died back in 2008 when he lost 90 percent of his retirement after the stock market crashed. I know because he tells anyone who's ever been within earshot of him. Our head football coach turns seventy-five this year and is not shy about letting everyone know that he cares about our school's football teams and *nothing* else. And as long as our varsity and JV teams keep winning championships, the school administration overlooks Coach Teague's blatantly fraudulent and consistent 4.0 average class GPA and 100 percent classroom attendance every semester.

The unanticipated silver lining of Aurora's absence today is I don't have to ask Remi twice about ditching Coach Teague's half-assed lecture about personal nutrition, which he'll undoubtedly exploit as an opportunity to tell us one of his pointless meandering stories about getting food poisoning, which, mind you, are most often the result of bad decision-making on *his* behalf.

Either way, Remi and I are both grateful for the opportunity to disappear from the overbearing weight of obligation and just . . . exist, even if only for a brief fifty minutes.

It's his idea for us to spend our skipped period in the band room, which is typically empty during fifth, as it's the band director's daily planning time.

"How long have you been in band?" I ask as Remi leads me inside the instrument storage room, a long and narrow hallway of floor-to-ceiling cubbies and shelves of various sizes for students to store instruments during the school day.

"I started percussion in eighth grade," he says after we both climb atop a waist-high empty shelf and sit across from each other. "Now I just play quads during marching season because I like performing on the field at halftime and getting into the football games for free."

I chuckle. "Because that five-dollar student entrance fee is so utterly devastating to the son of Michael Prince, who secured a million *plus* dollars to run for office?"

It's Remi's turn to laugh. "Well, Dad reminds me often that that's not his money—or mine. And also, that adversity begets greatness."

I scoff, which refreshes his grin. "I honestly hate that he lost the election. He might've been good for New Orleans."

Remi leans his head against the wall behind him and stares at the white tile ceiling. "I'm not." His golden-brown eyes shift down to me, waiting for my reaction.

"Why not?" I ask.

"I'm worried Dad's burning himself out, trying to save a world that doesn't want to be saved," he admits.

"What do you mean?"

"Look at the election. There were tons of authentic magic users who voted for Ben Beaumont."

I shake my head. "I'll never understand how Republicans can so easily get people to vote against their own self-interests year after year."

"Power," he says matter-of-factly. "Or rather, the illusion of it. Americans love exclusivity, even more when they're the ones doing the excluding. I wish Dad would leave them to it and just focus on his own life for once—and his kid." He frowns and turns away briefly, and I can't help but admire his immaculate temp fade. "But that's Dad. Michael Prince will give his final breath in service of everyone but me."

"I'm sorry," I say, and immediately regret that that's all I have to offer him.

I understand how he feels. His dad effectively abandoned him, which reminds me of Clem.

"Has it always been like that?" I ask. "You don't have to share if you're not up for it."

"It's fine." He shrugs one shoulder. "I feel comfortable talking to you."

"I'm glad," I tell him, smiling, and glance down at my knees, prying my eyes from the face that drags me in like a gator pulling its prey into the swamp. I'm suddenly spun dizzy by Remi's vibrant brown eyes, his vivid beige skin that's beautiful if slightly acne prone, and his lips that are exquisite in form, as if hand molded from clay. I wonder how soft they—

*No. That* cannot *happen.*

But staring at this boy, this gorgeous, kind, thoughtful, gentle person, too long is like looking into the Sun. And I don't need to be doing that right now.

Not after Oz.

I hug my knees to my chest, remembering how I felt the same way about him at first too. And now I wish that story had never been written.

"To answer your question," Remi says, "my dad's always had a distraction. First, it was my mom, and now it's politics."

"Your mom?" I ask.

He takes a deep breath and pulls on one of his loose black curls with one hand. "She was an addict."

"Was? Did she—"

"Nah." He shakes his head. "She left when I was twelve because Dad wouldn't stop trying to force her into rehab." He grimaces at his Jordans and the tiny white scuff on the right one's toe. "He was obsessed with fixing her. I hated him for that for a long time. And then I hated her for giving up on us. I say 'was' when I talk about her so I'm never wrong since I have no idea if she's alive or dead."

"I'm sorry you had to deal with all that," I tell him.

"We all have a cross to bear, right?" He smiles at his own dark joke, flashing the metal of his braces. "My mom is one of mine. But I'm trying to off-load another person-shaped one you might be familiar with."

I roll my eyes. "Desiree."

"The one and only," he says. "I take it you two aren't close."

"You've met her, so I'm sure you can imagine why."

He laughs. "And they're engaged now, which means I get to be stuck with her forever. Hooray."

"Lucky duck," I say.

His eyes hook mine, and I'm trapped there, disarmed and unable to turn away. "Can I tell you something, and you not judge me?" he asks.

"I'd die first," I say without hesitation.

He raises a bushy, overgrown eyebrow. "Well, that's a bit dramatic—"

"Do you wanna tell me or not?"

"Fine," he says, rolling his eyes playfully. "I always hoped my dad would lose the election. Of course, I'd never tell him that. And I haven't mentioned a word of it to anyone else—except you." His admission sends swaths of heat up my neck to my cheeks, but I banish those feelings back to where they came from.

"My dad's not cut out for politics," he continues. "He's too pure, too honest. He believes good always triumphs in the end, no matter what—even after all we've been through. He never had what it took to go up against men like Ben Beaumont and Irving Kingston, who never hesitate to do what it takes to win."

"You can't shine a light without casting a few shadows," I tell Remi.

He throws me a devil-may-care look that makes time stand still and amplifies the sound of my pounding heart. "Let me find out you been dancing with the devil."

It's not hard to look away now. *He has* no *idea.*

*And he never will.*

"Anyways," he goes on, "I spent a lot of dinners alone once Dad's campaign started. He and Desiree practically lived at his headquarters downtown, which was where I had to go most days if I wanted to see him at all. I didn't like it, but I didn't make a fuss because I knew it was important to him.

"But I got worried when I started to notice the telltale signs of stress manifesting on him. The weight gain, the random mood swings, and the dark circles under his eyes that Desiree convinced him to hide with concealer. It was Mom all over again, except this time, he had Desiree in his ear, overwriting anything I told him and constantly pushing him forward. She didn't give a shit about the physical and mental toll that election was taking on him. That's why I never believed she loved my dad."

"Sorry to ruin how this one ends for you," I say, "but Desiree Dupart only cares about herself." He nods his agreement, and I add, "Would you believe she refused to help my mama find a lawyer after what happened at Vice Hall? She'd throw her own sister on the pyre to fuel the flames of her ambition for just one more night."

Remi hangs his head. "That's cold-blooded."

"Yeah," I say. "Watch out for her. Everyone's saying our family's cursed anyway, so you might wanna be careful around me too."

He scoffs. "Oh, *please.* I don't take stock in the bullshit that comes from people who only get their news from podcasts and blogs."

I laugh and watch him lick his lips. Then, when my eyes find his again, I blanch, realizing he caught me staring.

"And even if the curse were real," he adds, smirking now, "getting to know you has most definitely been worth the risk."

The bell rings, and Remi hops off the shelf and extends a hand to help me down.

He shoulders his backpack and, clinging to the straps, asks, "Walk you to sixth?"

"Sure," I say, breathless and powerless to do anything about it.

Maybe Aurora was right. I need to stop skipping gym.

The last two periods of the day seem to drag on forever, which is a special kind of torment while my mind spends that time gallivanting between warm thoughts of Remi, concern for my brother and mother, and trepidation around the yet-undiscovered body of Tabitha Edgewater decaying in her home.

As soon as the final bell rings, I make a beeline for my car. Clem and I used to carpool once upon a time, but since he's been back and forth between home and Jean-Louise's, we both drive alone. Not gonna lie, I miss how he used to get on my nerves on our daily commute, either in the passenger's seat with his nose in a book, ignoring me, or driving like Cruella de Vil—which he hates for me to bring up.

I wonder if we can have a normal life again . . . but was it ever?

I unlock my car, open the driver's side door, and fling my bag onto the empty passenger's seat. I'm about to get in when shouting from the next row nabs my attention.

"Valentina! Hey! I'm *talking* to you!"

I whirl around, my head on a swivel until I see—Sofia? I squint to make sure I'm not mistaking the person presently going off in the student parking lot, drawing stares from the couple of students who've trickled out of the building after them.

Sofia storms down the lot behind Valentina, who flips her braids over one shoulder on the way to her car. I hold my breath, remembering Valentina's assigned spot is on the next row across from mine. Thank goodness the person directly in front of me drives an SUV that blocks me from Valentina's and Sofia's immediate view. I think to just mind my business, get in my car, and leave, but intrigue overrules logic, and I stand behind my open door a little longer, craning my ear toward the mess unfolding across the way.

Valentina's all glower, ignoring Sofia until they're standing in front of Valentina's car, and then she rounds on her. "Congratulations on finally finding your voice, Sofia, but if you raise it at me one more time, all I'm going to have left for you are condolences."

Sofia steps closer to Valentina and says something inaudible—something that widens Valentina's eyes to comical proportions.

I recoil when Valentina slaps Sofia, swinging the girl's head to one side and sending spittle flying.

I yelp with surprise when Sofia rebounds, backhanding Valentina hard enough to knock the girl into the car parked beside hers.

I sigh and close my door. I run over to break up the fight before it gets any worse, drowning out the voice in the back of my head that's screaming at me about how I'm making a mistake by getting involved in their drama.

I snatch Sofia from behind, just in time to save her from a mean right hook that invokes a breathless "oop!" from me. Valentina stumbles forward from the wasted momentum, and Sofia struggles against my embrace. I let her go once she's out of Valentina's reach and I can safely stand between them without danger of getting hit in the crossfire, because if I did, I would wash them both in this parking lot, and no one needs that.

"Okay!" I say, my hands raised on either side of me, ignoring the few onlookers. I need to defuse this quickly before it becomes a show. I've had it with being the main character for today. "I don't know what this is about, but I can promise you, fighting ain't worth it. At least not at school."

"Oh, *please*," Valentina sneers. "I know *you're* not talking—"

I turn my back to Sofia so I can look Valentina properly in her eyes because she needs to see and understand how serious I am. "We used to be *best* friends," I tell her. "And I still don't understand what I did to make you hate me so much."

"You *know* what you did," she snarls, her clenched fists trembling at her sides.

I shake my head. "I didn't take your man, Valentina! Oz was conjuring fucking love spells on me! Are you being willfully ignorant, or does it just come naturally for you?"

Her frown deepens, and she lifts her hand but stops when my eyes narrow.

"I'm not Sofia," I say calmly.

Valentina scoffs. "I don't give a shit about Oz. The problem is—and always has been—*you*." She snatches open her car door. "And I hope your and your mama's souls rot in the never-realm for infinite eternities for what y'all did."

I'm *way* too tired to keep fighting with her. "So, we'll continue this conversation there, then?"

But I'm *never* too tired to be petty.

She scowls at me as she ducks into her car and slams the door. The car's engine starts, and I bolt out of the way, yanking Sofia with me; and just in time because Valentina's car zooms out of the parking space, inches from clipping her friend.

When her taillights round the corner, I turn to Sofia, who's frowning after the car, holding the cheek Valentina struck.

"What the hell was that about?" I ask Sofia.

"Valentina *completely* bailed on prom and left me holding *every* bag," she says. "She dropped out of the prom committee, which meant I got *all* the stuff she'd volunteered to do. And then today she just up and tells me she might not even be going to prom, but it's too late for me to back out now because my mom's already bought my dress and shoes and jewelry and paid the deposit on the limo, which Valentina was supposed to split with me.

"And she wouldn't even tell me why she changed her mind. She said the cards should've told me this was coming, and she called me a charlatan." Sofia stares past me at the school's entrance and the students pouring out and heading for the parking lot.

"I want to say grief makes people do strange things, but Valentina is just toxic," I tell her. "I don't know why you keep hanging around her."

Sofia hugs herself and shrugs one shoulder. "We've known each other our whole lives. It's like you and Clem."

*Nope. I don't have time for this foolishness either.*

"Well, you enjoy that then." I head back to my car, but when I hear footsteps behind me, I glance over my shoulder and find Sofia following me. "Bye, Sofia."

"Where you headed?" she asks, doe-eyed and hopeful as a lost puppy.

"Home," I reply as I open my car door.

"Wanna hang out at the Bean for a bit?"

I frown over the door at her. "We're not friends, Sofia."

She stands back, open-mouthed, stunned silent.

I don't make eye contact when I get in the car or when I drive off and pass her.

She made her choice.

# TWELVE
## CLEMENT

Ayden Holloway is an extremely rare gem of a person, one of the very few who are as kind and generous as prodigious in their talent(s). And I'm fortunate to have come across *two* such people in the sixteen years (almost seventeen soon) that I've been alive.

Ayden reminds me of an older version of Yves in that regard. The thought stings because it reminds me also of how different they are, that Yves might never utilize the full potential of his life like Ayden because he's incomplete and blameless for all of it.

When I DMed Ayden via Instagram Sunday evening to ask if he'd be willing to meet with me for half an hour to answer some burning questions I had about his art and magic, he responded a few hours later with an enthusiastic invite for me to drop by his studio after school. So, naturally, Monday dragged at the speed of a parked car. When the final bell rang, I jetted for mine and cut it across town to the old brick factory building in the South Seventh Ward that's been refurbished and now houses Ayden's studio on the top floor.

I park outside in a sketchy-looking surface lot and follow the instructions on a placard that says to ring the buzzer for elevator access to the businesses located inside. House of Holloway on level three is where I'm headed. It's strange standing in the giant and rickety elevator alone, but it's only a short, jerky ride until the doors open to an expansive and breathtaking space.

Lo-fi hip-hop plays at a soothing level from the overheard speakers that hang like sleeping bats from the metal beams of the industrial loft's ceiling. A row of tall windows makes up the wall directly across from the elevator. The panes are all tilted open, so they pour endless streams of sunlight and fresh air into the studio.

Incense burns from elaborate holders in the most random places around the room. A frog atop a small metal stool holds a burning stick in its mouth like a cigarette. Spread across the tabletop are a bunch of sketch pads, a few small canvases, and a plethora of drawing utensils, which gives me an overwhelming urge to color. The setup reminds me of art in fifth grade with Miss Hill. I used to be hella excited about walking into class every Wednesday, eagerly scanning the tables and the art supplies she'd set out for that day's activity.

I spot another holder on the countertop of the kitchenette to my right. It's a small sculpture of an old fisherman standing on the side of his boat, his hands clasped around the lit incense stick like it's his dick or a fishing rod, depending on how you're looking at it. That one actually makes me chuckle.

Ayden's studio has a distinct smell that's neither good nor bad but no less enticing. The signature fragrance reminds me of creativity and peace. It's as bewitching as Fabiana's Ho-Van Oil. The scent of palo santo is bold from all the burning incense, which was probably lit to mask the lingering odor of the musky, sweet weed he smoked and the Chinese takeout he smashed recently. On the coffee table are his rolling tray, a glass ashtray, and a jungle of dirty napkins and take-out containers. Next to it is a beat-up black leather futon. Both are centered in the studio and sit on the ugliest floral area rug I've ever seen.

But something about this place and all its eccentricities makes me feel as if I've stepped through a portal into a fantasy world—one full of hope, where it's created every day, every hour, with each colored brushstroke and swipe of charcoal. From the moment I step off the elevator, I'm awash with a sense of ease and serenity that I wish more than anything I could bottle and take back with me, just so I can share a taste of it with Yves.

I'd love to hang out here, but I don't want to be weird my first time meeting Ayden in person. I'm just grateful he agreed to meet with me.

Toward the back corner of the room, Ayden paints a gigantic canvas hanging on a portion of blank wall not covered by his other finished artwork on display. I'm not sure I've ever seen a painting in person as big as the one he's working on, which is larger than a projector screen.

It reminds me of how I'd been working Mama hard to convince

her to turn one of the basement rooms into a movie theater. I'd almost worn her down right before she got sick. Sometimes I daydream about going back to those moments in time when my biggest frustration was convincing Mama to let go of the basement room that she'd been in the middle of transforming into a gym with Dad before he died—and ever since has been sitting untouched, collecting dust like a crypt.

A sheet of translucent plastic is stretched across the floor at the base of the canvas as a gigantic spill mat. Various cans and tubes of paint are haphazardly arranged between two ladders, one tall and one short, at either side of the painting. Ayden stands near the top of the tallest ladder with a bucket of white paint and a brush, adding details to the nighttime sky in the background.

On his waist is a dope tool belt with holsters for all his various paintbrushes and palette knives with dramatic tips . . . like little gay trowels. He's wearing an old ratty tank, basketball shorts, and black slides with gray ankle socks. Every portion of his outfit and the dark skin of his thin, sinewy arms is splotched with paint. His locs are tucked up into a bonnet that's somehow avoided the majority of the paint splatters.

"Hey, Mr. Holloway!" I call up to him.

He dapples one more star with one of his dramatic trowels, then turns to smile down at me. "Clement Trudeau, welcome to House of Holloway."

"Thank you," I say, returning his smile.

"Hope you don't mind if I work while we talk," he says. "I'm on deadline."

I ignore how hot this guy looks up there on that ladder, creating, all masterful and godlike, because this is yet another way that he reminds me so much of Yves. And that's who I'm here for.

"This is incredible," I say, stepping up to the edge of the plastic lining the brushed concrete floor to marvel at his work up close.

Central to the piece is a small-framed, bright tawny-skinned child with short, curly auburn hair and downcast, stormy gray-green eyes. They're captivating in a menacing way, penetrating the veil into this world as if *I'm* the person he's so furious with. But as my eyes travel down his figure, I notice the rest of him appears gradually more relaxed and less aggressive, from the slight slouch of his shoulders down to the fluid presentation of the arms, hands, and fingers—a stark contrast to the violence of his gaze. The positioning of his hands gives me the impression of an artist deep in the zone, a god crafting worlds by pulling the various strings like the commander of puppets.

The scene behind him chills my blood. No . . . seriously, it gives me mega goose bumps. The amount of detail Ayden is able to depict in his work is extraordinary. An army of white faces stands at the kid's back—except they all look half dead. Blood runs down their fronts from deep slits in their throats. All their mouths hang open, unhinged and broken midscream. I shudder, imagining how this painting would *sound* if it came to life. The dead (undead?) soldiers are armed with various weapons like knives, pistols, bayonets, and the like. But something else intriguing catches my eye—very slim streams of what reminds me of raw moonlight attached to their limbs, major joints, and heads . . . like marionette strings.

This is the creepiest shit I've ever seen in my life.

It's brilliant.

"What *is* this?" I ask, awestruck. "It's haunting."

Ayden chuckles softly. "Thank you. I call this one *The Boy King.* It's a conversation piece about Caspar Moses, who was a general at the age of eleven and fought in both the War of the Moons and the American Civil War. The gods called him 'Boy King,' but the regular mortal folk here in the natural realm all referred to Caspar as 'Puppet Master.'"

Ayden pauses to mix paint colors on his board and begins adding more depth to the stars. "Caspar was the most dangerous necromancer in the entire history of Moon magic. He had a particularly gruesome trick where he would conjure raw moonbeams to slit his victims' throats and then magically seal their souls inside their dead bodies, leaving them teetering between this realm and the next, shrieking to be let go. He would then attach thin streams of moonbeams to their reanimated bodies and control hundreds of the dead at once. He'd walk on the battlefield alone and instantaneously turn half the enemy's army into zombie-soldier marionettes who then fought for him and him alone.

"What's worst is the ensnared spirits were so traumatized by their deaths that they would howl in agony while they fought, which scared the shit out of the enemy. Once word got out about Caspar, no one wanted to face him in battle. Literal armies would turn tail and run when Caspar and his shrieking undead army approached. But eventually, the Boy King became so powerful that only a god could stop him."

Ayden squints down at the various cans and tubes of paint sitting out across the floor. He points a palette knife at one side of the mess and says, "Do you mind handing me up the tubes of blue lake and ivory black?"

Luckily, I don't have to search too hard to find what he wants because he's helpfully sorted the paints on the floor by container type. I grab the two tubes he requested and hand them up to him, and he salutes me in thanks.

"Baba Eshu slayed Caspar and hid his head," Ayden continues, "not only preventing him from becoming a god in death but also blocking his soul from eternal rest in the spiritual realm, which angered many of the other gods. In the end, Eshu was able to garner favor among the gods and practitioners of Moon magic through pleading with them in warning that if they flirted too closely with the ways of their oppressors, they would be vulnerable to stumbling down that same dark path, and that true vengeance lay in being *better*." There's a noticeable shift in Ayden's tone with that last part, which makes me wonder if he questions that school of thought.

*Same, bro. Same.*

"Then the war took a turn," he explains, "and the Moon magic practitioners started losing ground with the white mages and their vamp allies—vamp communities were divided on the issues and fought on both sides. But Baba Eshu intervened and gave his people the spell that effectively brought the conflict to an end."

"Wow," I mutter. "One spell to end an entire war. What was it?"

"He taught them how to create a passage through time and space to the never-realm. They opened one beneath the safe houses of every prominent white mage and vamp leading the opposition and threatened to send multiple generations of their families straight to hell if they didn't call a truce. Even though the Moon-magic armies were pinned, the white mages and their allies had to stand down. Baba Eshu oversaw the peace talks between leaders from both sides and gave his blessing on the resolution, which became the Treaty of Moons, in hope of fostering peace among the different magical communities of the world."

"I'm not sure I agree with what Eshu did," I say. "If his side was winning, why kill Caspar? Why not just let him wipe out the enemy and end it all without having to give up anything?"

"I'm not sure if that would've been much better, to be honest," Ayden replies. "Someone wielding that kind of power can be terrifying, even when it's on your side. Caspar was a severely traumatized child who'd survived unspeakable acts in slavery—things so bad that I won't attempt to translate that pain into art. The gods took advantage of his trauma and turned him into an unfeeling monster before he even hit puberty."

"Sounds to me like the gods were the real villains," I say.

Ayden stops working and pivots slightly to peer at me over his shoulder. I hold his stare, and he smirks and turns back to his painting. *I meant what I said.*

I haven't forgotten how, last year, Papa Eshu admitted unabashedly that he'd been ignoring my many desperate prayers and generous blessings because he was waiting on my sister to regain her faith. Caspar should've killed them all. Maybe that's what Eshu was really afraid of—the Boy King was gaining the power to topple a god.

I'm beginning to think none of the gods can be trusted. Not even Papa Eshu.

"You know so much about the past," I say. "Are you a historian?"

"In a roundabout way," Ayden replies. "My culture and history are both really important to me."

"Are you gen too?" I ask. "Or a vamp?"

He shakes his head. "Neither. I just have a great deal of respect and admiration for our people's magic, and I love learning about it."

"But how can you learn so much about something and never want to try it out?"

"There are many, many different ways to love and experience our world and people," he intones poignantly while leaning across the canvas and balancing on one leg to add depth to a star far out in the dark sky, which looks so tranquil and enchanting compared to the horrors depicted below.

"What do you know about dark Moon magic?" I ask him. "Specifically resurrections?"

Ayden turns a skeptical glance to me before descending the ladder with his painting supplies, which he sets aside before moving the ladder farther down the canvas to continue detailing the sky. I can't help thinking he would've made a really great professor or art teacher.

When he's standing on the same level with me, I realize he's not as tall as he appeared at first, barely a few inches above me.

"Not much," he answers—finally. "Necromancy used to be called 'spirit work' before it was officially cast off from Moon magic in the Treaty of Moons. Any sort of communing with those who passed on, which spanned from divination to literally summoning souls back to this realm to do your bidding, was considered spirit work, and a highly powerful and respected branch of magic in our community. But after the treaty was signed, all the literature about dark Moon magic was relocated to Europe and locked away under the care and supervision of the Arch Vamp Dejoir. The answers you're looking for are probably in those texts."

"*Shit*," I murmur.

Even *if* I were cool enough with the Arch Vamp Dejoir for him to let me peruse the forbidden magical archives, I don't have the time nor the personal funds to go to Europe.

Ayden eyes me suspiciously. "Why do you want to know about resurrections?"

"I'm just curious," I lie. "Whenever adults try to prevent a particular group of people from accessing information, it's typically something we should know."

Ayden nods. "Fair point."

Unfortunately, I'm going to have to add Ayden Holloway to the growing list of people who can't help me solve any of my problems right now.

But maybe he can help with something else that's been plaguing me.

"I went to your exhibition at the museum of magical history last summer and really connected with your Baba collection," I tell him.

"Thank you," he says, his cheeks plumping from his wide grin. "That's very high praise to an artist. That was also one of my favorite projects."

"I can see why. In the first panel, who's the dark-skinned god speaking to Henri Eshu?"

A darkness passes over Ayden's face, taking his smile with it. "An ancient god. One who's been around as long as *the* God themself. Some have even speculated they might be one and the same."

"What's his name?"

"I wish I knew," he says. "Legend says the mortal Eshu claimed to have been visited by the god of justice on that day all those years ago before he incited the riot that freed everyone on his plantation and so many more in the South."

"Was it the Moon King?"

Ayden's brows knit together. "I don't know anything about a Moon King. Who's that?"

I wave it off and chuckle nervously. "Oh, nothing. Something silly I saw on Reddit that I thought might've been real. Never mind."

"Oh, okaaay," Ayden says as if he doesn't believe me.

"What happened to the god of justice?" I ask. "I've never heard of him before."

Ayden shrugs. "No one's certain. I can only assume his legacy got swept up and locked away along with the rest of our past that made light and shadow magic practitioners uncomfortable."

There's something undeniably violent and sinister about stealing history from a group of people and then denying them access to it. What if Ayden hadn't been kind enough to share his gift of knowledge with the world—with me? In this moment, I realize that most often for people of color in this country, ignorance isn't the fault of the person or even those surrounding them because they're all in the same predicament. We all have a common enemy. A single mutual oppressor.

Ayden's phone buzzes with a notification in its holder on his tool belt. "Sorry to have to cut this very stimulating conversation short," he tells me as he swipes and taps buttons mechanically on his phone's screen, "but I have another meeting happening right now."

The elevator rattles and hums to life, and a few moments later, the doors open, and a tall white man steps out. He's dressed in expensive-looking navy trousers, a casual black shirt, and oversized deep-black sunglasses, and he's carrying two canvases wrapped in Kraft paper. He looks like a model for vice and debauchery.

"Ahhh," coos Ayden, "Karmine Delaney, the Vamp Dejoir himself. I never thought I'd have the honor of doing business with you."

"You flatter me, Ayden," Karmine says in his honey-coated baritone voice. He grins widely, showing all his teeth, reminding me of a crocodile. "Who's our guest? A young apprentice?"

"Noo," Ayden says. "This is Clement. He had some questions about magical history, and I couldn't deny an heir to the Gen Council an audience."

I blush, though I'm not fond of the inference that there's a possibility I might sit on the throne one day because that is the absolute *last* thing I would ever want to do. Cris was always the one better suited for that obligation.

Me, on the other hand? I'm a lover, not a ruler.

"Did he now?" Karmine tilts his head with curiosity, and I'm glad I can't see his eyes behind those glasses, which are probably as dark as his short hair and the eight-o'clock shadow that's as much a part of his outfit as the sunglasses. "I met your sister, Cristina, a few days ago at the park," he tells me. "A shame what happened to your mother's festival." He drops his voice and inclines his head toward me, as if there's anyone else listening in on our conversation besides the three of us. "I'm not disappointed that Edgewater woman's been put down."

I'm speechless for a moment too long before stammering, "Y-Yeah, uh, thank you again," I tell Ayden, and glance at Karmine. "And nice meeting you, Mr. Delaney. I'll show myself out."

I flee for the elevator, and Karmine watches me with a focused stare and eager smirk, reminding me of a cat toying with its prey before devouring it in one bite.

I back my car out of my parking spot when my stomach twists with a sickening realization.

I should probably start thinking about how I'm going to break the news to Yves that I won't be able to fully resurrect him—that he's going to be "wrong" forever.

I pull onto the street and release a trembling, tearful breath and drive away.

# THIRTEEN
## VALENTINA SAVANT

The news about Tabitha Edgewater had Valentina shook—and that didn't happen easily or often.

The cursor blinked on the screen of her laptop, waiting for her to finish typing her essay, but her mind had long since wandered off to darker spaces.

Mom was still missing. And a murderer was on the loose.

Valentina had called Mom's phone again after getting home from school. She hadn't done that for months. She'd known what would happen, but she had to check. One more time. The voicemail box was full, and she'd felt silly for trying again.

Valentina sat on the couch in the tearoom with all the plants that reminded her of Granny. She wondered if the florist delivery person would know anything about some of the more finicky plants that had turned sickly colors and were threatening to croak.

Settling into her new home had included stopping in to see Mr. Willie at Inman Florals promptly after school to reinstate weekly fresh flower deliveries to the house, just like Granny had. After that, she'd swung by the grocery store and loaded up on food and supplies to restock the fridge and pantry.

Her stomach grumbled at the thought of food, pulling her out of her thoughts. She sighed at her computer's screen. All that was left was to write the conclusion to her essay about *The Concrete Jungle* for AP English. It hadn't taken her long to throw together four pages on how the assignment was antiquated and how stifling innovation and change indirectly supported white supremacist agendas. She'd probably get a zero, but she had a 100 percent in that class anyway, so she could take a hit for the revolution. One of the unexpected benefits of her high-functioning anxiety and depression was that she always performed best when her world was on fire—and she had the 3.98 GPA to prove it.

The jarring ring of the doorbell made Valentina jump. It was probably Sofia, which reminded Valentina she needed to have a doorbell camera and electric lock installed ASAP. Being alive was far too much responsibility for any one person.

"I thought you said you couldn't come by tonight?" she asked as she opened the door. She froze and sucked in a sharp breath.

"Hey, Valentina."

Cristina Trudeau stood on the porch, silhouetted against the final rose-orange glows of the setting Sun. Her skin shone like an oil painting, and Valentina didn't miss the decorative scarf Cris had pulled her hair back with, the loose ends tied into seven knots. It was a statement. A bold one.

Valentina couldn't deny it though: Cris was practically glowing in heiress-hood. Disgust curled down one corner of Valentina's lips.

*She better fucking enjoy it while it lasts.*

Valentina pulled her granny's brown cardigan tight and tugged lightly on the black pearl necklace that also used to be Granny's. Queenly things that now belonged to Valentina—a queen in her own right. And she didn't give a damn about anyone's opinion of that—or her.

"What do you want?" Valentina said as politely as she could muster, which didn't crack the mask of pity on Cris's face that Valentina wanted to smack off her.

"How you holdin' up?" Cris's brow furrowed slightly, as if she actually gave a damn about how Valentina was "holdin' up" after a tragedy of Cris's own doing.

"The fuck do you think, Cris?" Valentina sneered. "Why are you here?"

"What was that at school earlier between you and Sofia?" Cris asked.

Valentina glowered at Cris. She was like a vulture. She wouldn't leave without a prize clenched in her talons, but for Valentina's plan to work, she'd have to concede.

"Umm . . ." Valentina mimed thinking really hard. "Let's see . . .

My ex-best friend murdered the only people in the world I gave a fuck about, and the *one* good thing I had going for me was also stolen by that same toxic friend, the girl who already had everything but wanted more, and, uh, what else?" She tapped her chin, and Cris grimaced. "Oh, yeah! My mom is missing and might be dead." She narrowed her eyes at Cris. "So, needless to say, I'm not in the mood for prom, which Sofia—another bitch with privilege for brains—can't seem to understand, especially if she went crying to *you*."

Cris sighed. "Okay, Valentina. I didn't come here to fight."

"Then what *did* you come here for?"

Cris clenched her jaw and stared into Valentina's eyes. "To call a truce."

She scowled at Cris. "Why in the infinite realms of the universe would I do that?"

"Because it's pointless for us to keep fighting about all this Council stuff," Cris said. "That was our grandmothers' beef. But that's over now. And we've lost them both. And I lost my dad too. I'm not asking for us to be friends again, but I don't want to be enemies either. And I don't want either of us to lose anyone else, Val. My personal issues with you were never that deep."

Valentina drew herself up taller, her eyes still glued to Cris's. "Then return my granny's head, and I might think about it."

"I can't do that," Cris said. "Besides, I don't know where it is."

"You're a fucking lie!"

"Let that alone, Valentina," Cris warned.

The darkness that overtook her brown eyes unsettled Valentina. She tensed and glanced down at the line of brick dust she'd laid across the threshold of the door after news broke of Tabitha Edgewater's murder.

Cris followed Valentina's gaze, crouched on the other side of the protective line, and dragged one finger through, breaking the barrier, which she wouldn't have been able to do if she'd meant Valentina harm. "I didn't come here to hurt you," Cris said, and waved toward her car, which she'd parked so far down the driveway that Valentina hadn't noticed there was someone waiting in the passenger's seat.

The door swung open, and Gabriela Savant stepped out.

Valentina gasped. "What the fuck is this?"

Cris stepped to one side but didn't respond.

Valentina's mom looked the same as the day she'd left, her skin still light-brown porcelain, her hair still thick and dark with an essence of auburn in the sunlight. She wore jeans and knee-high boots and a light jacket. Valentina smiled at first, but it died a moment later because how dare her mom come back here looking refreshed, as if she just got back from an extended spa vacation after leaving her daughter for dead.

Mom approached gingerly, cautioned by the look on Valentina's face.

Cris turned to Valentina and lowered her voice. "For what it's worth, what went down that night on the *Montaigne Majestic* had nothing to do with what happened to your mom. My aunt Jacquelyn found your mom in Baton Rouge with her memory altered and brought her back to New Orleans."

"What the hell?" exclaimed Valentina.

Cris held up her hand. "She's fine. All the important parts are still there. She's still . . . your mom."

"What happened?" Valentina asked, trying hard not to get choked up, which annoyed her because why was she being emotional about seeing the mom who had abandoned her again?

Cris nodded at Gabriela, who stepped up to the edge of the porch and smiled nervously at Valentina. "She can tell you."

"Hey, Val, baby," Mom said. "I'm so sorry I've been gone so long." She stepped onto the porch and embraced her. "Cris caught me up on everything on the drive over."

Valentina stiffened at first because it felt weird. Not bad, just . . . unusual. It'd been a long time since her mom had hugged her like she meant it. After the strangeness settled in, fear rang the buzzer inside her. She couldn't get used to this. Both her parents had proven long ago they had no interest in parenting.

Only problem was . . . Valentina really, *really* needed a hug.

So she shut her eyes and allowed herself to unwind. She felt her mom release the quaking breath she'd been holding and squeeze her tighter.

When Valentina and her mom parted, Cris nodded at her and said, "Remember, Val. Let's be done." Then she pointed at the broken line of brick dust. "And don't forget to fix that."

The Sun had disappeared from the bruising sky at some point during their conversation, and now crickets chirped their usual nighttime chorus.

Cris went to her car without looking back.

And Valentina hated her even more.

How dare Cris inflict the most intense pain Valentina had ever felt before on her and then *dare* to present her with a flash of hope in the form of her missing mom who'd apparently had her mind altered? It was so fucking arrogant of Cris to believe she could strut around town toying with Valentina's life, with her emotions, unchecked.

They would *never* be done. Not until Valentina was Queen.

"Have you been staying here alone?" asked Mom.

Valentina nodded.

Mom sighed. "We should go inside and talk."

They both turned and stopped when a pair of car headlights swung into the driveway. At first, Valentina thought it was Cris returning to have Valentina sign an official peace treaty, but the growl of the Maserati engine instantaneously sank her heart.

*Dear gods, no. No, no, no.*

Valentina's dad, Arturo Savant, pulled right up to the front of the drive and leapt out of the car, staring wide-eyed at Mom.

"Gabriela?" His voice trembled with disbelief. "Wh-What are you doing here? How long have you been here?" His shock shifted to anger, and he tossed his hands up on either side of him, his bright brown complexion blushing. "Where the *hell* have you been?"

"I just got here," she said. "It wasn't my intention to be gone so long. I'll explain what I can."

Valentina cut her eyes up at her mom, studying her face carefully and waiting for the moment when the barriers would fall to allow Dad full access to wreak havoc again.

Valentina hadn't even gotten five minutes with her mom yet.

Dad rushed onto the porch and bear-hugged Mom, who grunted and pushed him off her. He turned to Valentina next, but she stepped inside the house and ushered them both in, though she wanted nothing more than to slam the door in her dad's face.

"I was just stopping in to check on you," he said, still grinning, his eyes shimmering.

Valentina narrowed her eyes. That sounded like a lie.

Once inside, Dad looked around, taking in every inch of the space with gluttonous eyes, which made Valentina bristle with alarm. She didn't want him there, in her safe space. But she had to play nice for now, at least until she found out what was going on with Mom.

"You've been taking good care of this place, I see," he said. "Keeping it cleaner than you ever did your room at home."

Valentina bit her tongue and disappeared to the kitchen.

She made a pot of tea for everyone and set up three cups on a tray with sugar and milk. For a glimmer in time, she considered putting foxglove in her dad's drink, but then she winced. She was beginning to think like Eveline Beaumont.

But maybe that wasn't such a bad thing.

When Valentina returned to the tearoom, she found Dad sitting in the center of the sofa with a wounded look on his face and Mom in the armchair with a sour look on hers.

Valentina set the tray down on the coffee table. Mom prepared her own cup of tea, dropping two cubes of sugar into it, then stirring before taking a long, savoring sip. She sighed with pleasure and set it back down.

"You make tea as good as your granny," Mom told her. "We didn't get along, but I could never knock her tea-making skills."

Valentina nodded reverently, still standing, opposite her dad, the table between them. She wanted to ask him to move so she could sit closer to Mom without being next to him, but she sat in an armchair opposite her mom instead.

"Are you going to tell us where you've been?" Valentina asked Mom.

Mom let out a long, quiet sigh, then took another drink of tea. "The morning I left, I needed to get away for a while. All the chaos on the Council on top of your drama"—she cut her eyes at Dad, whose shoulders slumped—"was driving me mad. I was only going to Baton

Rouge for a couple days, though I can't remember why. I had a hotel room for one night, and I remember falling asleep late and waking up with a splitting headache nine months later in Marie Trudeau's living room."

"Did they kidnap you?" asked Dad.

Valentina sat up for the answer, ready to jump in her car and drive it straight through the front door of their house if need be.

Mom shook her head. "I . . . don't think so. That's not what they told me."

"But how do you know they're telling the truth?" Valentina asked.

"Because a god was there, Valentina," Mom replied.

"A god?" Valentina said, incredulous. "Which one?"

"Not someone you need to get tangled up with," Mom said, as she placed a hand over her ear and shuddered.

"So, what? They're just chilling at home with real, live gen gods from the spiritual realm?" asked Dad.

Valentina rolled her eyes. "A more productive question would be: *Why* was a god there?"

"He was the one who returned my memories," Mom told them. "He couldn't restore them to exactly the way they were before, and I've lost some, but the most important ones are still there."

*But why were her memories erased in the first place?* The whole debacle reeked of grand-scale deception.

"I honestly can't tell what's changed." Mom shrugged. "Although I do feel lighter, like I have more clarity and . . . perspective." She cut her eyes at Dad, who swallowed hard in the thick quiet that followed.

"I'm just so glad you're back," he said. "I think it's a sign—that we should be a family again."

Valentina bit the inside of her cheek and almost cried out. She glowered over the coffee table at her dad, who threw a quick smile at her and turned his attention back on Mom, who sat unmoving, hands in her lap, studying Dad's face reticently.

"That doesn't sound appealing to me, Arturo," she said after a moment.

Dad slapped his hands on his thighs and huffed. "Come on, Gabriela. Seriously? You're my wife."

"I've not lost all the memories of how you let me alienate myself from my family for you while you cheated and emotionally abused me at your leisure. That was really fucking depressing, and I can't go back to that."

"Should we, uh, be having this conversation in front of Valentina?" Dad asked, skirting his eyes at Valentina, who glowered at him.

Mom shook her head. "We're in *her* house, Arturo. And besides, your bullshit impacted both of us. Valentina deserves to know what's going on."

It was tough for Valentina to stay quiet, but the fact that Mom fought so diligently for her made it possible. *That* was certainly new. Though Valentina had remembered glimmers of Mom standing up to Granny and Dad in the final days leading up to her disappearance. Maybe she'd finally had enough.

"I'm really sorry, Gabriela," Dad said, then looked at Valentina. "I'm sorry, Val. For everything I've done to this family. I—I just—" He stared into his lap. "Losing both my parents so suddenly and then not having my wife to turn to made me realize how much I underappreciated you. I need you, Gabs."

"What've you been up to since I've been gone?" asked Mom.

Dad sat up straight and blinked a few times. "Huh?"

"Simple question," Mom said.

Valentina wondered how he was going to snake his way out of this one because she knew *exactly* where he'd been. At this point, she didn't understand why he didn't officially invest in the House of Vans since he spent so much money there.

"Th-The usual," he sputtered. "Work and stuff. I don't understand this line of questioning."

"I never took fault with the people who work there," Mom said. "They're earning an honest living, and I applaud Fabiana for giving them a safe environment to do it in. But I also pity them for having to appeal to the wounded sexual egos of fractional men like you."

Dad scoffed. "Fractional? I'm fractional?"

Mom nodded and leaned forward. "I might not remember *why* I went to Baton Rouge, but I damn sure remember how I felt while I was there. And it was incredible to be free of you and your goddamned gravitational pull. I danced all night with beautiful men, women, and people who all made me feel like a goddess. And do you know what I did after that?"

The muscles in Dad's jaw tightened. "D-Did you sleep with someone else?" he asked, his voice timid and eyes wavering. "It's okay . . . if, um, if you did. You deserve a hall pass."

Mom laughed. It was sharp and haughty and surprising.

Dad sat back, offended.

"I didn't cheat on you, Arturo," Mom told him. "But I made that decision for me—not you. I spent the night alone. And for the first time in a very, very long while, I fell asleep with a smile on my face—and slept like a baby."

"That's good," Dad said. "I'm glad you're doing better. See . . . I told you our family's worth saving."

He stood, then knelt in front of Mom. She tilted her head and stared into his pitiful eyes. Dad was going to fuck up everything before it even got on the path to being okay again.

And Mom was about to let him do it.

"My parents' deaths were horrible," Dad professed to Mom, "but maybe this is an opportunity for our family to rise from the ashes of our pasts." He reached for Mom's hand, but she shook her head, and he acquiesced. "That's okay, that's okay! We have a huge house now with plenty of space for us all to take the time we need to repair our family."

*No, no, no! Hell no!*

He was talking about *her* house. He wanted to take it from her.

Valentina's safe zone was under attack. And if she didn't do something, she was going to lose it.

"We can go to family therapy, couple's counseling—hell, I'll even go solo-dolo," Dad continued pleading his raggedy case. "I'll do whatever it takes to keep my family."

"And which family would you be talking about?" Valentina asked loudly, drawing the attention of her parents, both of whom seemed to have forgotten she was in the room.

Dad's face cracked and immediately flushed. "Don't," he whispered. "Please. *This*"—he pointed at the floor—"is my *only* family."

Valentina shook her head. "No, I'm pretty sure Jacquelyn Dupart and the baby you two have together might see things a bit differently."

Dad retreated to the couch, where he slumped and hid his face in his hands like the fucking coward that he was. Valentina giggled inside. That's what he got for trying to steal from her. He'd already taken more than enough. Everyone had. But no more.

Mom shook her head. Then she looked up to the ceiling and shook it again. "I *knew* it," she mumbled. "I fucking *knew* it would happen eventually. I mean, it was always a possibility, right? I'd waited for it, even when I didn't want to admit it. It was like a bomb ticking underneath our bed every night, counting down the time until it would finally blow up my entire life. In my darkest moments, while you were out doing your thing, I swore I could *hear* it ticking in our bedroom." She chuckled again and lifted one brow at Dad. "Well . . . *boom*."

"Gabriela," Dad pleaded. "We don't have to blow up our lives. We can work through this."

Mom laughed again. "And what? Invite your mistress and your Van Kid to move in so we can all be one big happy family? You sound ridiculous, and I won't be your clown anymore."

Valentina couldn't help smirking. Arturo glanced at her, and she caught a glint of his ire, which warmed her like a bonfire on a frigid winter night. It was what he deserved.

"I acquiesce, Arturo," Mom said. "Go now. Be free. Fuck whomever you want. Love whomever you please. It no longer concerns me. *You* no longer concern me. I'll be filing for divorce too. I want my life back. I want *a* life. And this one—with you—ain't it."

Arturo jumped to his feet and rounded on Valentina, who stared up at him, still smirking, unfazed. "Well, you got what you wanted. I hope you're happy."

Happy? Not really. Though she did enjoy the savory flavor of vindication on her tongue as she walked her dad out and locked the door behind him.

She'd protected her home from a predator, and it'd felt damn good. That euphoric power was mesmerizing.

And she wanted more.

# FOURTEEN
## CRISTINA

I feel significantly lighter after my earlier encounter with Valentina. I wasn't sure what to expect, especially after watching her and Sofia go feral on each other in the school parking lot earlier. As awful as Valentina can be, I understand what it's like to hurt the way she has. I hope that having her mom back home can give her some peace—and a reason to let go of her twisted vendetta against me.

I waste several hours when I get back home making repeated failed attempts to focus on my homework. Giving homework on Mondays should be against the law.

I pull a black notebook down from the shelf above my desk and open it in front of me. It's the spell book Aurora and I are—or perhaps *were*—making together. We planned to draft all the spells we created in this notebook, and once we decided we'd accumulated enough, we were going to get a nice leather-bound book like the ones in the magic library at St. John's and record each spell by hand with a feather quill. I'd been bookmarking calligraphy TikToks to share with Aurora so we could practice before writing the official book. We were having a lot of fun curating this collection of spells together, but all that came to a halt when life happened for both of us.

I put the journal back on the shelf. I don't want to dwell there either because if I'm not sad at how my friendship with Aurora seems to be smoldering, I'm trying to figure out why the hell I can control light magic when I've never had a minute spark of a desire to be a white mage.

I don't know anything about these new abilities. All I can really do is make flames dance back and forth, which isn't very impressive on its own—or useful. Although the Sun has had an interesting effect on me ever since I learned about my new . . . talents. The golden hours of every day call to me now, and I often find myself wandering toward sunlight to relish in it with an almost feline fervor. I've never been as partial to nighttime as Clem, but this sudden hyperconnection with the Sun feels new and strange.

I've always been so wrapped up with gen magic that I was never even slightly curious about the world of the white mages and warlocks or even vamps. Now that I suddenly have access to it, I'm hesitant to walk through that door. They would never let me have a seat at their table anyway—which is probably best for them, otherwise I might flip that bitch over on top of them all. Besides, enough's already going on right here in my own community that needs my attention.

Like the white people who're preying on us. And the Black folks who enable them.

I don't realize I'm clenching my fists in my lap until my nails bite into the soft skin of my palms. I relax my hands and pick up my phone to text Aurora.

Hey! I missed you today. Wanna hang out?

I can come over and we can watch a movie or just talk

I need to tell you what happened at school today

Heeey!

I would but I need to get caught up on all the work I missed w/court today

No worries. I understand.

What happened?

Nothing to report. Just our lawyers arguing back and forth in front of the judge about if my brother's claims to our dad's estate are legal.

That fucker is saying Dad's letter is counterfeit and that I "coerced" dad into changing his will after he got sick.

Ugh. Fuck Xavier.

Seriously.

I toss my phone onto my desk, feeling frustrated and defeated.

None of the systems we're told were put into place to protect us actually do. Yet we're told to be patient. Don't ever break the rules.

Follow protocols. Don't get upset. Bite your tongue. Being mad is childish. This is just how it goes sometimes. Take the high road. Be better than them. However, lately it's feeling like injustice is set to default.

And I'm running out of cheeks to turn.

My phone buzzes with another text. I smile when I see it's from Clem. When I open the message, my smile vanishes. It's a link to a news article.

**Brutal Murder of Beloved Activist Leader Baffles New Orleans Authorities**

The article is a quick read because very few details were given—not even where the body was found. By the time I reach the end, my heart's still racing—but for a different reason.

The police have no evidence or leads. They can't even determine with a relevant degree of certainty if the murder was magical, which is . . . unexpected.

Another text comes through from Clem.

People are protesting and counter-protesting outside Tabitha's home. It's bananas. All the police are frazzled.

It's all over Twitter.

Cris. Please be careful.

I will.

You ok tho???

Don't change the subject.

I said be careful!

AS IN: STAY YOUR ASS IN THE HOUSE.

I give a thumbs-up tap-back on the last message and turn my phone on Do Not Disturb.

I go over to my window and throw back my curtains, revealing the cloudy nighttime sky beyond. The Moon glows dim in the blue-black sky, muted beneath a thick blanket of gray clouds.

I open the doors to my Juliet balcony and lean against the rail, gripping the iron tight to ground myself in this world. I close my eyes and focus internally on the breath that flows in through my nose and how it fills my chest. Then I blow it out through my mouth, homing in on the thump of my heartbeat that connects to the blood pumping through every part of me, a current of warmth that originates in the center of my chest. Something shifts in my gut, like the click of a key disengaging a lock. The feeling that swirls through my midsection feels like a gust of fresh air that rushes in from the other side of the unlocked door. It intertwines with the warmth of my blood, the magic of my ancestors and the strength of my own soul, centered in my stomach, in everyone's. Every molecule of my physical existence hums with raw magic. I feel as if I could snatch the Moon from the sky and crush it into powder in the palm of my hand if I wanted.

When I open my eyes, I lean my hips against the iron barrier and stretch my arms outside, my hands upturned toward the sky, beseeching. The subdued glow of the Moon brightens until it burns a hole in the clouds, which then part and roll aside, revealing the Moon and Stars beyond, those closest twinkling brighter as well.

With a subtle half twist of my wrist, I unscrew the Moon from where it sits in the sky, turning the tap of its raw moonbeams that spiral down toward me with sparkling eagerness. When I wave my hand, the Moon fades from full to quarter, and the clouds mash back together, blanketing the heavens once more.

The moonlight floats into my room, where I direct it with one hand to swirl in a circle about the size of a Frisbee. It casts an ethereal blue glow onto my desk and the surrounding bookshelves. I throw open one of the drawers of my desk and retrieve the quill pen I bought for Aurora and me to record our spells.

I open the ink cavity and direct the harvested moonlight to condense and fill it, and when I'm done, the pen's translucent inkwell glows bright blue.

Quill in hand, I climb onto my bed and stand at the headboard, in front of a blank space of wall where I used to hang posters of my favorite celebrities until I got tired of worshipping strangers a year ago and pulled them all down. I bite the tip of my tongue as I write, in not-too-shabby calligraphy, a list of names in hauntingly radiant blue ink on my wall. After I finish, I cross the first name off the list and stand back for another look.

~~*Tabitha Edgewater*~~
*Dr. Gregory Thomas*
*Jack Kingston*
*Eveline Beaumont*

I think about adding Oz's and Xavier Vincent's names, but I've already neutralized Oz, and my issue with Xavier is by way of Aurora, so I'll let her handle her family drama.

Besides, I'll have my hands full with this short list of my own.

And what better night than tonight—while the police are busy with the chaos in Tabitha's neighborhood—to cross another name off my list?

A quick google of Dr. Gregory Bartholomew Thomas reveals he's presently serving on the board of his condo building, a small apartment complex originally built in the '40s that was rehabbed and transformed into private condominiums about a decade ago.

I plunder the recycling bins in his condo's mail room until I find a political flyer calling for public support for another mayoral election that must've been mailed to registered voters in the area, which includes Dr. Thomas—and his address. Thankfully, no one walks in on me, though I had a story at the ready just in case. I toss the advert back in the bin and head for Dr. Thomas's apartment.

A foreboding chill lurks in the air, and I zip up my jacket and throw my hood over my head, completely hiding my hair, which I've pulled back into a low ponytail. The clouds are thin over on this side of town, so the Moon appears prominent in the dark sky, as if watching over me. I stick to the cover of shadow, clinging to the straps of my backpack.

Darkness cloaks areas of the neighborhood outside the sparse yellow-orange cones of light beaming from the tall lampposts, some rust covered and leaning. Most of the windows are dark or dimly lit, their curtains drawn or blinds shut. As I'm walking up the path toward Dr. Thomas's unit, a gust of wind brushes through out of nowhere. It hits my face, and chilly, wispy fingers of air slide around the back of my neck, sending an intense shiver down my spine. I stick my hand inside my hood and rub the gooseflesh as I look around. It felt like someone touched me. But I'm definitely alone out here. This reminds me of the strange feeling I got right before I confronted Tabitha Edgewater—and the wind that felt more like a presence than a natural occurrence.

Outside Dr. Thomas's door, I take out a small dropper bottle filled with raw moonlight. I didn't want to risk anyone witnessing me harvesting it on the scene, so I took care of that in advance. I squeeze out two drops that float in the air in front of me and guide them with my hands, almost as if I were an orchestral conductor, and usher them into the top and bottom locks of Dr. Thomas's door. A gentle wave of my hand back and forth thins and spreads the moonbeams across the metal of the dead bolt and latch. Like before, I feel the magic in front of me on a molecular level as the particles then vibrate while encircling the vulnerable pieces of metal securing the door. The magic heats the various parts of the locking mechanism, which, through a little online research, I learned breaks down stainless coatings and makes the metal highly susceptive to corrosion.

While the moonlight does its work, I retrieve a small spray bottle from my backpack, which contains a mixture of Florida water and a few drops of luck oil, borrowed from a batch Clem made last summer. I spray the concoction into the space between the door and the jamb, while the moonbeams continue to heat the metal, and the smell of rust wafts from the lock. I return my stuff to my backpack, put on the latex gloves I brought, and take a deep breath.

*Please, Oberun, let this work.*

I take the door's handle and grip it tight. I shut my eyes, hold my breath—and push.

*SNAP!*

The corroded locking mechanism breaks like a twig, and the door swings open so easily that I almost face-plant on the tile floor of the cramped, unlit foyer. Quickly, I steady myself just in time to stop the door from slamming into the wall inside the unit and push it closed softly behind me. The muted sound of music comes from somewhere inside.

To my immediate left is an open door that leads to the owner's suite. I poke my head inside.

The bedsheets are undone on one side, and a book, *The 48 Laws of Power,* sits on the nightstand in the soft yellow glow of a bedside lamp. The door to the en suite bathroom is open, and steam billows from inside. I hear water splashing in the shower and a man singing along terribly to the Taylor Swift song playing at a moderate level.

I back out into the short hallway and note that on my right is an office, farther down the hallway on the left are a bathroom and a laundry room, and the living room and kitchen are beyond, all sparsely lit. I first duck into the office, which seems to have been converted from a bedroom. A tall bookshelf takes up one wall in front of a wooden L-shaped executive's desk. I wander over and scan the bookshelves but find nothing of note. It's just medical journals and textbooks and a bunch of degrees, awards, and certifications, the most recent from over a decade ago. I shift my focus to the desk, pulling out each drawer and sifting through its contents, though the only notable things I find are half a joint and a Fleshlight, which I do not touch or question.

I'm not sure what I'm even searching for, but it's starting to feel like a waste of time. I stand in front of the accordion doors of the office closet and shove them aside. In front of me stands a five-foot-tall safe with a keypad entry. I frown at it curiously.

*What are you hiding in there, Dr. Thomas?*

I touch my gloved fingertips to the surface of the safe, wishing I could open it with magic. What I conjured on the front door won't work here because safe locks are a lot more complex. I pull my hand away—and something thumps against the door of the safe—from inside.

I jump back and cover my mouth to keep from yelling. My heart races, and my chest heaves with anxious breaths.

*What the hell was that?*

And then the weird sensation returns. The rush of air behind me, the one that still somehow manages to make the back of my neck prickle as if someone were breathing on me. I whirl around but again find the office empty. I creep back to the hallway and listen. The shower's still running in the owner's bathroom. I'm wondering for a frantic moment if there might be someone else in the apartment when a sudden noise behind me sends a jolt of fear zipping through me.

The safe beeps, and the deep *click-clank* of the lock disengaging echoes in the office.

I turn slowly, my heart thumping so hard against my rib cage that I press both hands over it as if to hold it in place. The door of the safe creaks open slowly, and I narrow my eyes, inching closer. I double-check that I'm alone before opening the safe. I'm not sure how it unlocked, but its contents beckon to me.

On one shelf are several folders of Dr. Thomas's personal information. A passport, a birth certificate, and a number of other useless documents. But one of the folders has an official letter from an insurance company addressed to him.

> Dr. Gregory Thomas, MD—
>
> We regret to inform you that we are TERMINATING your policy, number CRP0666, with All Saints Insurance Co., Inc. As stated in your contract, "we can terminate the client's policy at any time if the client files more than TWO claims of significant value in a policy year." As such, your recent claim M094-GH9 for $5,000,000.00 to cover medical malpractice damages and litigation fees has been DENIED.

I replace the letter without reading the rest. *Whoa. So, you're in* debt-*debt, huh? Figures.*

On another shelf are a couple of handguns. The rest of this big-ass safe appears to be empty. I kneel to peer to the back and make sure I'm not missing anything when something else catches my eye.

A small notebook is stuck to the underside of one of the lower shelves. I reach in and pull it down, wincing at the loud sound of Velcro strips separating. I step back from the closet and lean against the edge of Dr. Thomas's desk to examine the journal.

At first, I'm not sure what I'm looking at. There are a bunch of names attached to dates and some weird nomenclature; each line ends in fairly high dollar amounts. The whole thing looks like some sort of accounting record, but the way it's organized is incredibly confusing, which I'm sure is by design.

*J. Will. 1-V, 5-K, 2-P ($17,000)*
*Cortez M. 0.5-V, 1-K ($4,500)*
*X. Carlos. 5-V, 5-K, 5-P ($52,500)*

Similar entries are grouped by month with dollar totals for each, going back as far as two years.

*What does all this mean?*

I flip to another page, which has a corner folded down. It's a list of medical facilities in the area. Hospitals and clinics, many I recognize as being in mostly Black and brown neighborhoods. A string of letters is written next to each entry, different combinations of *V*s, *K*s, and *P*s. I flip between one of the monthly records pages and back to the location list, thinking quickly, until my breath hitches once I realize.

I get it now.

*V* is for Vicodin. *K* is for ketamine. And *P* is for Percocet.

Dr. Thomas is selling drugs. I turn to another earmarked page and see a badly drawn sketch of the New Orleans map. Initials I recognize from the register sit prominently beneath the names of several familiar neighborhoods like Lower Ninth Ward, Seventh Ward, Hollygrove, and Mid-City. Tulane University is even on here. And then the realization punches me square in the chest, knocking the wind out of me.

These are all predominantly Black and brown neighborhoods.

"Hey! What the *fuck* are you doing in my house?"

My head snaps up, and I meet the angry reddened face of Dr.

Thomas, who stands in the doorway of his office in a pair of sweats. His hair's still soggy and dripping onto the shoulders of his old faded FAT TUESDAY tee.

*Well . . . shit.*

# FIFTEEN
## CRISTINA

I didn't even notice the music from the bathroom had stopped.

Recognition blooms on Dr. Thomas's face, and his defensive posture relaxes—but only a little. "Cristina? How'd you get into my apartment?" He glances at the front door, then back at me in disbelief.

His eyes rove over the office and widen when they spot the open safe. I watch the gasp catch in his throat when he realizes I'm holding his secret journal. I'm disappointed he didn't let it out. I wanted to relish in that disheartening breath once he realized he's fucked—the same sound my brother and I made after he told us our mother was dying last summer.

I shut the notebook and brandish it in front of me. "You're not exactly in the position to be asking questions at the moment, Dr. Thomas."

He stiffens and wrinkles his nose. "You little *thief*. How'd you even—You know what? It doesn't matter because I'm calling the police." He turns to leave—I'm assuming to retrieve his phone.

"Please do!" I bluff. "Then we can all chat about your little drug operation. Should we put on a pot of coffee before they get here?"

He returns slowly and steps into the office, pointing a shaky finger at me. "Now hang on one second," he says, a newfound softness to his voice. "You're barking up the wrong tree."

"Oh?" I ask as I remove the bottle of raw moonbeams from my bag. "I think I have you just about figured out."

He scoffs. "I'm not gonna be threatened in my own home by one of *you*—much less a *child*." He clenches his fists and takes an angry step forward, and I turn the bottle upside down, emptying it. A small splatter of moonlight, no larger than the palm of my hand, floats in the air between us. Dr. Thomas stops and staggers backward.

The azure light reflects in his eyes as he stares at me across it. "Did you come here to kill me like y'all thugs did to Lenora and Felix Savant last summer?"

I move the fingers of one hand in the air as if tugging on the strings of a marionette, and the moonbeams respond at once. The splatter of magic breaks apart into miniscule glowing droplets suspended between me and Dr. Thomas. They crackle with raw energy, a sound only I can hear.

"I went back and forth a bunch of times on the way over here," I say. "I almost turned back once, but then I asked myself, 'What would Oberun do?'"

"Who?" Dr. Thomas screws up his face, accentuating the fine lines and wrinkles that'd been hiding in his pasty features.

I trail my fingers through the air in front of me in a delicate dance that the magic mist mimics. It reminds me of hundreds of fireflies waltzing in the air. Dr. Thomas watches the display, quivering slightly.

"That's not for you to know," I say, and cut my eyes up at him. "And don't interrupt my story again."

He bites his bottom lip and half nods.

"I wasn't sure what I was looking for when I came in here," I tell him. "Maybe a reason to do what I came to do." He swallows hard in the harsh quiet, and the shadow of his Adam's apple dips in the blue glow between us. I hold up the journal in my left hand, my right still conducting the moonlight. "Would you agree that this is it? A reason?"

He holds up a hand, tears glistening in his eyes. "It's not what you think. I didn't have any other choice—"

"Stop playing with me," I snap. "I read the letter from your insurance company. You're on the hook for *millions*. I bet your career's on the line too. And instead of owning your shit, what do you do? Peddle drugs—which, fine, I'm not judging that part—but why discriminate? Why not take your trash to the neighborhoods where people who look like you live? Affluent white folks do *way* more drugs than every Black and brown community combined. You could've charged them triple—gods know they most definitely can afford it. But nope. You, like countless other white people before you, drove your trifling ass across the railroad tracks to shit in our backyards—*again*.

"Too many people in this world believe they can do whatever they please without consequence to whomever they deem weaker or inferior. Like helping Lenora Savant attempt to murder my mama. That's nasty work, Dr. Thomas."

I snap my fist closed in front of me, and the moonbeams fall still. It's the doctor's turn to dance now.

He lowers himself gingerly to his knees and holds his hands up in front of him, pleading for mercy. That didn't work for Lenora either.

"Look, I—I'm sorry," he sputters. "For all of it. Your mother. The drugs. I—I'm in a real bad spot, a-and I didn't know what else to do. Clearly, you read the letter, so you know." He gestures toward the open safe, then runs the fingers of the same hand through his wet hair and clutches a fistful angrily. His face burns an even deeper shade of red. "I'm fucking *ruined*. Is that not punishment enough?" He lifts his hands on either side of him, his eyes wavering in the light of my magic. "What do you want from me? I have nothing left to give except my life. And you're not a killer, Cristina. I know you. And I know you've been through a lot—"

"Aht!" I raise an eyebrow. "How dare you." I take a step closer, both fists clenched now, my left hand tight around the empty dropper bottle. It's a wonder it doesn't shatter in my palm. "How *dare* you after what you've done to my family. You were my mama's *doctor*. We all trusted you. You took an oath when you became a medical professional. But it must not apply to Black people, huh?

"The families that were razed and the ones on fire right now because you flooded their neighborhoods with drugs will never be the same. Most people don't recover from that kind of trauma. How many people have died or gone to prison because of you? How many lives were forever scarred because one white man couldn't take accountability for his own bullshit?" He opens his mouth weakly to respond, but I cut him off. "You can't know, so save your lie. So the answer to your question is no, Dr. Thomas, you have *not* suffered enough. Nowhere close, in fact. You could never suffer adequately for all that you've done. But I'm going to try my best."

Dr. Thomas starts to get to his feet. "Wait—"

I lift my hand to my mouth, my palm facing upward, and blow. Like dandelions propelled by a strong summer breeze, the blue mist glides through the air and straight into Dr. Thomas's face. Droplets absorb into his eyes and disappear up his nose and into his mouth when he gasps in surprise. He coughs and gags, trying to spit the magic back out, but he can't. I've got him.

I can already feel the particles traveling inside him like blood cells pumping through his veins. *Yes. That's a* great *idea, actually.*

I flood his heart with moonbeams, replacing the well of blood there and concentrating my power, which I can feel resonating in the fist I hold out in front of me.

Dr. Thomas wheezes, his mouth falling open, and claws his chest. Right over his heart.

I deepen my connection to my magic, tapping into the moonlight's molecules once more, forcing it into a locked, solid state. I've never attempted to do this before, so the strain from focusing on such a microscopic level sends a wave of icy nausea crashing through me. I back into the edge of the desk to steady myself. But I'm done. It's over.

Dr. Thomas stops scratching his chest, and his arms fall limp at his sides.

The tips of his fingers have turned blue from the cold. Frozen veins of the same color dart up beneath his T-shirt and across the pallid skin of his neck like lightning strikes through a white sky. His heart now a solid block of ice in his chest, Dr. Thomas's eyes roll back, and he thunks facedown onto the floor.

In five minutes, he'll be brain-dead.

In eight, the never-realm can have him.

A floorboard creaks inside the closet.

I turn on my heel with a start and squint into the dark corners on either side of the safe.

Something moves in the shadows.

Something . . . hunched and squeezed into the tight corner. Something alive.

"Well. *Done.*" The voice is a bass-filled whisper that's barely audible yet boisterous at the same time, as if spoken inside my own mind.

A familiar sensation ignites along the back of my neck, and I draw my hand up to stroke the goose bumps already there. "Who's there?" I ask, my voice trembling.

When no answer comes, I pull out my phone, switch on the flashlight, and aim the beam into the closet.

Nothing's there but plastic storage bins and old document boxes stacked in the corners.

*But I* know *someone was there. Unless—*

"Oberun?" I whisper.

I'm not sure if I should be hopeful or fearful. What would I even say to the god of justice if he were here right now? *Had* he been here? Did Oberun bless what I did tonight too?

I turn back to Dr. Thomas facedown on the floor, slowly dying in a puddle of his own drool. I drop his ledger onto the ground beside him and step over him on my way out.

Maybe one day people like him will learn to stop fucking with people like me.

Both my mind and body are exhausted by the time I turn onto our street at nearly 2:00 A.M. I open the gate remotely and drive through, yawning, already fighting sleep. But once I'm on our property, I slam the brakes and almost send my heart screaming through the windshield. I blink a few times and rub the drowsiness from my eyes because I can't possibly be seeing what I think I'm seeing.

Flashing blue lights cascade across the front of our house and lawn. They come from the pair of police cars parked out front. I clap my hands over my mouth at the same time as I accidentally bite my tongue so hard that I taste blood.

*Oh, God. They're here for me.*

I've finally gone too far. Got too cocky. Sommers must've linked me to Tabitha somehow. Have they already found Dr. Thomas's body too? No . . . that's not possible . . . Not that fast . . .

Is it?

I creep my car up to the house, my mouth coppery and dry, playing through potential scenarios in my head where I explain to my family how I've been on a righteous murder spree.

*Would my family understand?* Could *they?*

I pull off to one side of our driveway, out of the police's way, and get out. My hands are shaking so bad, I have to shove them in the pockets of my jacket and clutch the lining in my fists lest I get blown away in the blue shitstorm pressing down on us.

I'm only at the bottom of the stairs to the front porch when the door bursts open, spilling the din of radio chatter from the police scanners inside. Time slows to the drumbeat of my heart thumping in my throat as Mama emerges.

She steps onto the porch, dressed in a plain black pencil dress and heeled boots. A bloodred-and-black tignon crown is exquisitely tied on her head, concealing most of her hair except for the few curls that hang from beneath the fabric. The police lights paint her face in a mosaic of vivid blues and foreboding shadows. She looks like the Queen on her way to a MASC meeting—but that's not what this is.

I stop at the edge of the porch and call up to her. "Mama, what's going on? Why are the police here?"

She turns to me, her eyes brimming with tears. "It's gonna be okay, baby. Ursula will update you. We'll get this sorted. Don't worry about me." Her brows knit when I don't immediately confirm that I won't worry.

I can't do that. I can hardly breathe right now. I take my hands from my pockets and hug myself, gripping my arms and pinching handfuls of fabric and skin, trying my damnedest to cling to reality.

Detective Sommers and an officer—the same one who was with her when she questioned us at Vice Hall—step outside next, my irate aunt Ursula tight on their heels.

Mama holds out her wrists, and when the officer puts the cuffs on, Ursula's eyes almost launch from their sockets.

"Are you shitting me right now?" she shouts. "She's going *willingly!*"

Sommers rounds on her. "And I'm going to overlook how you're talking to me right now, but I can make this a family affair if you'd like."

I make eye contact with my aunt and shake my head furtively. Ursula immediately cools, and we watch Sommers escort Mama from the porch and into the back of one of the police cars. My throat tightens, and the air around me thins.

They were never here for me. But I will have no relief tonight.

Not while Mama's being arrested for the murder of Ben Beaumont.

# SIXTEEN
# CLEMENT

"You sure you're okay?"

I pull my car into a parking spot and turn to my sister, who's staring tight-lipped at the steps leading up to the front entrance of the police station. The hefty bags under her eyes are stuffed full of secrets.

She didn't have to ask me twice about ditching school today so we could come see Mama. I was at Jean-Louise's later than usual last night and arrived home right as Cris was calling to tell me the news. None of us was able to get much sleep.

However, current circumstances under consideration, Cris seems *extra* on edge, which is not like her and frankly makes me (more) anxious. I want to be there for her, but she's closing me out. Again.

She nods. "Yeah. Let's go see Mama."

I narrow my eyes at her as she opens the car door and gets out before I can say anything else.

*What are you hiding now?*

The police station's front desk sits behind a plexiglass barrier and is manned by a lone uniformed cop. This place is dull and drab on the inside, which immediately makes me feel like I don't belong here. Cris steps up and informs the person behind the glass that we're here to see our mother, Marie Trudeau.

The guy, who has some gnarly razor bumps under his chin, shakes his head. "I'm under orders that she's to have no visitors. Today's reserved for questioning."

"The *entire* day?" Cris presses.

The cop's lips tighten, and he nods.

"It's fine," I say. "We'll just wait here until she's done."

He cuts his eyes at us but doesn't protest.

Cris and I step out of earshot of him, and she looks about ready to explode.

"This is so unfair," she grumbles.

"I know." I shrug. "But what else can we do?"

I sit on the bench across from the front desk and the locked door that leads to the rest of the station—and where our mama's being held captive for a crime she didn't commit. Cris sits beside me, and we watch officers file in and out, all raking their eyes over us as if our existence is a glitch in their matrix.

Cris leans her head on my shoulder and releases a shuddering sigh. I rest against her, and I'm not sure how long we're both asleep before the sharp rapping of someone's knuckles against the plexiglass at the front desk jerks me and Cris out of our exhausted slumber.

"Hughes!" shouts the woman who just knocked on the window. "We're going to grab coffee. Want something?"

Hughes, who I notice is not the same guy from earlier, shakes his head and throws up a hand, head down in whatever's on the desk in front of him.

Cris rouses beside me. "That's the detective who arrested Mama." She's on her feet and storming up to the woman before I register what's happening. "Detective Sommers," Cris calls out to the woman, who spins around with an unfriendly expression and narrows her eyes at my sister. "How much longer are we going to have to wait to see our mother?"

Sommers huffs an annoyed breath through her nose and frowns at me too as I approach. "We are holding your mother for questioning. She is the prime suspect in a very high-profile murder investigation."

"And you're going to get coffee," I say. "Clearly, y'all are on break, so why can't we see her? That's our *mother* you have locked up back there, and we've been here *all morning.* Please."

"Okay, fine," she says. "But you only have until I'm back."

Detective Sommers gets Hughes to unlock the door leading to the secure portion of the station and escorts us only a few steps down a long hallway to a set of twin interrogation rooms across from a couple bathrooms. The walls inside are the same dingy eggshell color as the rest of the station, and metal blinds of the same color cover the single small window looking out into the corridor. Cris and I sit in two hard metal chairs on one side of a weathered table.

Sommers tells us she'll be back and leaves. My sister and I wait in suffocating quiet for the several dragging minutes it takes for Sommers to return with Mama. The door opens, and the chains of Mama's hand and ankle cuffs clink as she shuffles in and sits in the seat across from us. She's still wearing the dress and tignon they arrested her in. Cris told me all about Mama's grand exit from the estate last night, and I still can't believe how over-the-top it all was.

"You have twenty minutes," Sommers warns. "Someone will be just outside. Knock when you're done if you finish before I'm back—which would be preferable."

Cris and I both glare at Sommers, but she doesn't stick around to catch the silent shade. The metal blinds covering the window rustle with the brief gust of air from her closing the door sharply after her.

"Are you okay?" Cris asks Mama.

"I'm fine," she says, but her tired eyes tell a different story.

"How long can they keep you here?" I ask.

This interrogation room is depressing enough. I'd almost rather wander the Kahlungha than be holed up in this place.

"I honestly don't know," Mama says. "Ursula's found me a reputable attorney, which is a relief, but there's also been a new development that's made this situation a bit stickier for me."

Cris and I share a nervous glance.

"What's happened?" I ask, terrified to know.

"Someone murdered Tabitha Edgewater and left her body on the steps of the Temple of Innocent Blood the other night," Mama informs us. "They drew the word 'hypocrite' on the ground in blood beside her body with her severed tongue—just like with Ben. And now Sommers is speculating that Fabiana and I are attempting to start a magic cartel in response to Eveline's Magical Regulation Bureau and the Redeemers."

Cris shifts nervously beside me, quiet, her face taut.

I narrow my eyes at her, thinking thoughts that I'm ashamed to admit aloud. Cris already admitted to me that she killed that woman, but she *never* mentioned putting Tabitha's dead body on display out front of the Temple of Innocent Blood. Cutting out someone's tongue and writing messages in blood is grotesque and egregious—and definitively not my sister's style, no matter how out of pocket she can get. Except . . . she's surprised me before.

I hope to the gods that this tangled dread in my stomach with her at the center is a mistake, a simple misunderstanding, a silly misjudgment. But a distant voice in the back of my mind whispers that it's not.

"That's ridiculous," Cris says.

"Tell me about it," Mama replies. "And then that silly woman went as far as to accuse me of allying with the Divine Knights! Imagine that. Your mama. A mob boss."

She shakes her head and lowers her gaze to the table.

I turn to Cris, but she won't look at me, her head downcast too. She's wringing her hands in her lap, which only I can see. Mama could very well go down for Cris's mistake, and I'm honestly not sure how I feel about that.

But I'm not going to snitch on her. I promised to keep her secret. Besides, coming clean now wouldn't make sense. It's much too late. That would only endanger them both.

Mama sighs hard and lifts her head. Every time the metal chains shift when she moves, it makes my skin crawl. I loathe the idea of my mama in chains—at the mercy of people who don't know or care about her—because of something she didn't do.

But what can *I* do?

"Sommers is hunting for Fabiana," Mama says, "which also complicates things. They seem to think Fabiana was my accomplice and fled through Rosalie's office window after she and I murdered Ben together. Sommers has been trying to get warrants to search Fabiana's apartment and the House of Vans, but apparently Fabiana has her own legal team that've been giving the detectives hell."

I wipe my clammy palms on my jeans. Fabiana couldn't have had anything to do with Ben's murder. She's been gone since November . . . unless she lied, and killing Ben and poisoning Eveline were part of her plan all along.

But it doesn't make sense that Fabiana would commit murder at the soft launch of the business she'd invested in with Rosalie. Even though they weren't dating, Fabiana would've never left Rosalie holding the bag like that. At the very least, Fabiana seems much too shrewd of a businesswoman for those kinds of shenanigans.

But now I'm worried that something else—something *bad*—might've happened to Yves's sister.

And—thanks to me—he has no idea.

"I know you and Yves broke up," Mama says to me, "but have you talked to him at all recently?"

The question is about as unnerving as dozens of tiny sharp pins raking down my bare spine at once. I tense and shake my head quickly.

"He's in Paris doing a study-abroad program," I tell her. "I haven't spoken to him. I didn't want to mention any of what's been going on because I didn't want him to be worried while he was so far from home."

"That makes sense," Mama says. "At least until we have more information. I'm just glad he's safe halfway across the world from all this drama."

I look away. "Yeah."

"Your aunt Ursula will be here soon," Mama tells us. "I need to give her the Queen's Regard so she can take over as Regent until I'm out of here."

"What?" Cris says, snapping to attention. "Why?"

Mama stares at her, confused. "Who else do I have?"

"Me!" Cris jabs her chest with her thumb.

Mama's eyes narrow, and she thinks for a few moments. I don't meet her eyes during that stretch of time because I don't want her to ask me to weigh in. If she did, I'd have to admit out loud that I'm not sure giving Cris the crown right now is the best idea. And I don't want to be the asshole who says it first. So I don't.

"I don't mean any disrespect," Cris continues, "but Aunt Ursula on the throne makes me nervous. She's a bit of a hothead."

*And you murdered someone, miss mamas!*

I grip the edge of my seat and stare at the table to keep from glowering at Cris. Hypocrisy aside, she's supposed to be helping *me* find out how to restore Yves's soul. I know this is important to her, but what about me? Does that make me a jerk?

"Being Queen isn't like being class president," Mama tells her. "As Regent, you'd be responsible for governing our entire magical community, and most importantly, overseeing the one in your own backyard. It's not something I think anyone can manage effectively at your age."

"But this is my life," Cris pleads. "It's my future. And it's your legacy. Mine too. This is what I fought so hard for last summer, Mama. Let me stand up for you and our family. You never got to do that for Grandma Cristine, so let me do it for you now."

Mama sucks in a sharp breath and squeezes her eyes shut, but a single tear still escapes. "But who's there for you?" The chains clink as she lifts her hands to wipe her cheek. "I keep failing y'all, no matter how hard I try—"

"You haven't failed us, Mama," I tell her.

She smiles weakly and wipes another tear away. "Oh, Clem. How can I be there for y'all when I'm a prisoner?" The chains shift again as she hides her hands in her lap.

"As long as there's breath in your body, right?" I raise my brows.

Mama's face warms, like the first moments of sunrise on a frigid winter morning. She straightens in her seat and turns to Cris. "Okay, listen to me. All you need to do is hold down the throne until I'm out of here, which hopefully won't be long, according to my new attorney. She'll be working day and night on it—to the detriment of my bank account.

"Meanwhile, your job is to keep the Council running smoothly and delay all that you can. Don't worry about things piling up. I'll address it later." She pauses and leans into the hardened stare she gives Cris, which makes even me sit up at full attention. Cris tenses beside me too. "And if things get out of hand—*ask—Ursula—for—help*. She's one of the few people we can trust. Don't let your pride cost you your birthright, Cristina."

Cris nods. "Yes, ma'am."

"And if I think, for one second, that things have gotten out of control on your watch," Mama adds, "I *will* instate Ursula as Regent—with or without your blessing."

"Okay," Cris says meekly. "I understand."

"How were you planning to do the Queen's Regard ritual here?" I ask. "You don't have any conjuring supplies."

"Over time, the Council did away with a lot of the historical pomp and circumstance around instating a new person to the throne," Mama explains. "And not long before the War of the Moons, the Queen's Regard ritual was created to be done on the fly with only the bodies of the ordained present, which became a necessity when our community was constantly under siege."

Maybe I'm hypersensitive right now because I've been feeling extra hopeless about my and Yves's predicaments, but realizing in this moment exactly how racism, violence, and injustice have shaped our customs makes me afraid I'm doomed to remain trapped in a state of powerlessness forever. No matter what we do, no matter how much we rebuild, rebirth, or reform, the shadows of our community's collective trauma persist, regardless of how much light we shine on them.

Mama glances over her shoulder through the window, making sure we're not being watched, then reaches across the table. Her chains clatter against the tabletop as she wriggles her fingers for us to take her hands. The three of us hold hands, creating a small conjuring circle. Mama's hands are cold to the touch and feel dryer and rougher than normal, while Cris's are clammy, most likely from nerves.

"The Queen's Regard is a simple ritual consisting of three promises," Mama says. "Now, let's begin." She clears her throat, takes a deep breath, and intones, "Baba Eshu! Ancestors! Hear my plea! Your Queen invokes you to bear witness to the Queen's Regard and bless our rite."

I flinch, not expecting the volume of her voice. I look away when I notice the face of the cop standing guard outside peering through the window to glimpse what we're up to in here. Mama makes eye contact with me and squeezes my hand; the expression on her face tells me to ignore them and focus on our ritual.

Mama nods at Cris and says, "Now I need you to close your eyes and repeat after me for this last part."

"Yes, ma'am," Cris agrees.

Mama turns to me next. "You can close your eyes too and let the magic and our ancestors' power flow through you. The more gen present, the stronger the connection to and the flow from the spiritual realm."

"Okay," I say, somewhat breathless with anticipation.

I close my eyes. And instead of the usual muted darkness, I'm met with bright flashes of colors that shift and change like a kaleidoscope. It throws me off at first, but I'm too drunk on the connection to drag myself out of it.

In the quiet of the room, I feel the vibrations of Mama's strong soothing voice like a warm balm rubbed across my chest, right over my heart. And Cris's vibrations follow, quick and sharp and just as passionate. I don't know if it's them or the magic, but I've never felt so in tune with the people and the atmosphere around me before.

"I swear to uphold my duties as Queen Regent of the Generational Magic Council of New Orleans with respect and honor to myself, my communities, my ancestors, and the gods," Mama says, and Cris repeats quietly after.

"I pledge to be just and fair in the governing and leadership of the magical community at large.

"I vow to protect the sanctity and legacies of both my community and our power—until I join with the ancestors."

As Cris and Mama recite the Queen's Regard together, the heat of our connection intensifies. At first, I thought it was just the natural warmth of our hands touching, but this feels familiar, almost as if raw moonbeams were pumping through the veins in our hands instead of blood.

A silhouette forms in the center of my mind's eye. By the time I realize it's a person, it changes again and again, going from rapid to speeds that are almost dizzying. I make out women, men, and others from many generations back. Leaders wearing tignons or other elaborate crowns, past magical rulers before the Gen Council even existed, back to the beginning of our time, of our culture, before we even came to this place. Pressure builds behind my eyes, and the air in the room chills.

I gasp when Mama and Cris pull their hands from mine at the same time, severing my connection to them and the spiritual realm.

Our hands separate with a powerful static shock, and the sudden absence of the connection is overwhelming. Instinctively, I reach for my sister's hand, yearning to feel that power once more, but draw back before she notices. She's wavering in her seat, inebriated on the experience herself.

"It's done," Mama says with a heavy sigh. "You are now Queen Regent." She purses her lips and gives Cris a stern warning stare. "Cristina, please do not make me regret this decision."

"I won't, Mama," Cris says. "I promise."

I hope to the gods she can keep her word.

# SEVENTEEN
## CLEMENT

Cris and I say our goodbyes to Mama and leave the police station. Stepping out of the building into the bright sunlight feels like emerging from confinement in a dungeon. I've always preferred night, but now I greedily soak up the Sun's warmth and inhale deep, gulping breaths of the fresh afternoon air.

And I immediately feel guilty when I remember we had to leave Mama behind.

We get inside my car just as Detective Sommers's black Dodge Charger swerves into the parking lot and into a space across from us. Cris glowers at the detective, and I can feel fury simmering on the other side of Cris's hard stare.

I want to ignore what's happening right in front of my face—but my mind won't let me have peace until I know the truth.

"Cris . . . did you lie to me about what really happened with Tabitha Edgewater?"

Cris faces me, still frowning. "No. I swear. And before you accuse me, I didn't put her body on the steps of Eveline's temple either. I left her in her home."

I let go of the breath I'd had in a headlock and hang my head with relief. And then a new gust of anxiety whips up inside my chest.

"Then we could have an even bigger problem," I tell her. "Someone out there might know what you did. And there's a good chance it could be the same person who murdered Ben."

Cris sinks in her seat and puts her hands over her face. "Oh, gods."

"You heard what Mama told us," I say. "They're trying to pin *your* shit on her too."

Cris fastens her seat belt and remains silent.

"I get it, sis. I do." I lean over, and she lays her head on my shoulder, and the burst of curls from her ponytail tickles my ear and neck.

"But you gotta cool it with the extracurricular activities, if you know what I mean. We don't need any more surprises. Not right now."

She pushes away from me. "Stop lecturing me, Clem."

"You've been acting weird all morning," I say. "Is something else going on with you?"

She hugs herself and shakes her head. "No. Can we go, please?"

My sister's keeping something from me. Again. I can't be mad. I'm guilty too. I wonder, if I told her the truth about the Moon King, would that be enough for her to confide in me too?

But I've not seen nor heard anything of the stalker god since Jean-Louise told me about their encounter. Maybe the Moon King moved on and found better, more interesting people to haunt. What use would I be to him anyway? I can't even save my own fucking boyfriend.

Maybe it's time for me to accept my fate, to do the one thing I've been avoiding this entire time.

"Before you get too consumed by your queenly duties," I say, "would you mind helping me with one last thing?"

Cris straightens in her seat, welcome to the change of subject, but then her face twists. "What do you mean *one last thing*?"

"Let's be real," I tell her. "You're not going to have time to help me with Yves now that you're Queen Regent on top of everything else you already have going on. You heard Mama. That's a *serious* undertaking. I'm not gonna be unrealistic and get my feelings hurt and then end up resenting you when you inevitably get wrapped up in your life."

"You don't know that," she counters. "Do you think I'd abandon you?" I don't answer, and she nudges my arm a little too hard to be playful. "Answer me, Clem!"

"I dunno," I mutter.

I stare down at my sneakers and my ankles, which were apparently too skinny for me to be any good at basketball; the only reason I tried out for JV was because a couple of guys on the team had crushes on me.

Guess I've always been a fool.

Cris unlatches her seat belt and turns sideways so she faces me. "Look at me."

I stare into the same brown eyes as mine, at the familiar perfect thick eyebrows, and the face, so similar to mine, where I've found comfort my entire life.

"I would *never*," she tells me.

I nod. "Okay."

She sits back with a heavy sigh. "Now, what do you need help with?"

"I need to find Fabiana."

"Yeah. Tracking her down could help Mama's case."

"Not just that. I'm going to tell her the truth. About Yves."

"What?" Cris exclaims. "Why now?"

"I can't keep going like this. All the sneaking around and lying and double coursework is *killing* me. Fabiana knows a ton of people in dark places. Since Jean-Louise flaked, maybe she's the best person to help me restore Yves's soul."

"Is he still icing you out?" Cris asks.

I huff a frustrated sigh and stare out the window. "Yep."

"What's his deal? Have you tried talking to him again?"

"I can't worry about Jean-Louise," I tell her, hardening my voice to frighten her away from the topic of Jean-Louise and the Moon King. "I'm tapped on ideas. Can you just come with me to her apartment, please? I wanna check it out before the police get their warrant and ransack it. There might be a clue as to where she's gone."

"Okay," Cris says. "Whatever you need."

I drive us straight to the French Quarter, where Cris and I both chuckle at the pitifully conspicuous undercover cop watching the entrance to the House of Vans from across the street, clearly waiting for Fabiana to show up.

I lead my sister to the elevator toward the back of the building that goes straight to the House of Vans's top floor—Fabiana's swanky penthouse apartment—which I access using Yves's keys, which I swiped from him last night.

After a short ride up, the doors open, and my sister gasps with awe at the sick collection of art displayed on either side of the narrow hallway with the white marble floors and polished concrete walls and ceiling. People of all genders watch us approach the front door with confident and alluring expressions, each painting ensnaring Cris one by one. Not long ago, I had the same reaction my first time here. It's hard for me to look at Yves's work now, knowing he'll never paint again as long as he's in his present predicament.

These small random moments pinch my heart throughout every day, reminding me of Yves's terrible fate and my inability to do anything to change it. I felt so powerful the night Jean-Louise and I brought Yves back. Maybe that's why I thought the ritual would somehow work for me in a way it hadn't for Jean-Louise and Auguste.

I have to tell Fabiana the truth. If I've failed Yves, then I need to take responsibility for what I've done—and any suffering that comes along with it.

Otherwise, I'll be doomed to my own partial life, just like Yves.

I lead my sister to the end of the corridor up to a single dark-stained wooden door with an oversize knocker, beside which someone's taped a handwritten note. I have to lean in close and squint to read the shit handwriting.

> *Your unit's mailbox is overflowing. Please come pick up your mail ASAP.*
>
> *—property mgmt.*

"How long did you say she's been gone?" asks Cris.

"Since about mid-November," I say. "And if that's true, there's no way she could've had anything to do with Ben's murder."

"Yeah," Cris says. "The police got this all wrong. As usual."

I unlock the apartment door with Yves's keys. I still haven't told him his sister's missing, but with the murder investigation going on, I'm not sure how long I can keep that secret from him—especially since he's picked up a new habit of reading the daily newspaper, obsessed with soaking up every tidbit of information about what's going on in the world outside Jean-Louise's house. I got him a subscription to the *Herald* to feed his habit, though he only wants to read physical media. A side effect of their resurrections was that, for whatever reason, both Yves and Auguste have become averse to tech.

Everything inside Fabiana's apartment appears to be in order—just as I remember it: The large comfy sectional in the sunken family room and the cloud-white faux rug at its feet. The elaborate bar that splits the spacious dining area in two, where Fabiana sat perched on a barstool when I first met her. I can still smell the ripe cherry scent of her bewitching Ho-Van Oil. It's as if remnants of it linger in the thick stale air.

The entire apartment is dark and stifling hot. Cris flicks the light switch next to the door a couple of times, but nothing happens.

"The utilities must be shut off," I say.

"It takes a few months of nonpayment for that to happen," Cris says.

I count quickly in my head. "She's been gone almost five."

Cris's brow furrows, and she rotates in place, scanning the room carefully for clues. "We're missing something."

"You don't think she's de—"

"Don't," Cris says. "We don't know that." She snaps her fingers in front of me. "Stay focused. Does anything look different or out of place from when you were last here?"

"Uh . . ." I lift the tail of my shirt up to wipe the sweat from my forehead before taking a second glance around.

The only spaces not visible from where we're standing between the family room and the dining area are the bedrooms and bathrooms. I've only been here a couple of times, and I wasn't paying much attention to the background with Yves and his eccentric sister in the foreground.

I shake my head. "This is almost exactly how I remember it."

"You mentioned she texted you about going on a trip?"

"Yeah."

"Which is her bedroom?" She points at both closed doors on opposite ends of the apartment.

I gesture at Fabiana's room, and Cris heads in that direction. "I'm going to see if her luggage is gone," she announces.

"Oh," I mutter. "Good idea."

"Can you check Yves's bedroom?"

I choke on my next breath but manage a grunt of acceptance.

With every step I take toward his door, pressure builds behind my eyes and in my chest, and I pray the various dams I've built up inside me hold fast. I dunno if I can do this today.

I don't want to do this today.

I take a deep breath and open the door to Yves's room. A wave of hot air hits me in the face as I step inside. His room looks as if he's just gone to school for the day and will be back any moment. Shoes and clothes litter the floor, most left by me. The last time I was here was to quickly grab some personal belongings for him to take to Jean-Louise's. I could barely see what to take because I couldn't stop crying.

The easel with the outline of the self-portrait he'd been working on just before is still up. That's what broke me last time. It beckoned to me, and I couldn't resist, even though I knew it was going to hurt me deep. It was only a light pencil sketch, yet somehow, it already had the audacity to be breathtaking. My mind was incapable of imagining how the finished piece might look. But what tore my heart open was how authentically Yves had captured himself. As I stared at it, I got different impressions of the expression on his face in the portrait. First, it was pondering, then sad, and finally, curious. It was everything all at once. All things I've known and loved about Yves. But the one constant, the tip of the blade that pierced my chest and exposed my beating heart, was the staggeringly accurate depiction of his own enchanting dark eyes that once were portals to other realms. Looking at them in that picture, I couldn't help but recall holding him in my arms as he lay dying and watching those portals close right in front of me. And being helpless to do a damn thing about it.

I keep my distance from the canvas and stare at the tangled mess of sheets on the bed. I wander over and sit on the edge. I run my hands through the sheets, then pull one of the pillows to my face and take a deep yearning breath in, inhaling the spice-and-cedar scent of him that I miss so gotdamn much.

Now he smells of nothing. Always nothing. No matter what. His skin won't hold the fragrance of colognes or oils anymore—another minor aspect of his humanity lost. I never thought I'd miss his normal body odor. The sweaty, chalky scent of his dick at the end of a long day when he pulls off his underwear and presses his groin against mine. And the weight of him—whole and naked bearing down on me—

"Clem?"

I jump to my feet, my heart flailing in surprise. "Huh?"

Cris starts to say something but stops and looks at me and then quickly around the room, pausing briefly on Yves's self-portrait before landing on me again.

"You okay?" she asks.

I nod. "Yeah."

She gestures at the picture hanging on the wall above Yves's bed. "That one's gorgeous."

It's the painting he did of us last summer, the one where we're both nude and he's lying on a cloud, pulling me up from the chaos of the world below my dangling feet. Admiring it now makes my throat go dry, and the boiling air in here becomes too thick to breathe.

"It is," I say as I leave Yves's bedroom, sliding past my sister. "There's nothing in here."

Cris follows me back out into the main area but doesn't say anything else. This whole stuffy apartment is suffocating me. I'm beginning to think this was a waste of time when I glance at the kitchen and notice something odd. A few small appliances lie on their sides as if knocked over. A butcher's block is likewise overturned, knives spilled across the counter. I walk through and examine it all closely, but there's no sign of a struggle or blood or anything else of note.

The door of the walk-in pantry at the back of the kitchen is open, so I peek inside but don't find anything interesting. I turn back, and something on the floor catches my eyes. Hidden in shadow beneath the lip of the cabinet overhang are the shards of a broken vial in a small pool of a clear oily liquid.

I kneel to examine it but bolt back up when the overwhelming scent of Ho-Van hits my nose. I stagger backward from the sudden rush of blood to my head and the magically ensnaring fragrance of ripened cherries.

"What's wrong?" asks Cris, watching me from the edge of the kitchen.

I shake off the bewitching influence of Fabiana's signature oil. That shit should be illegal. "It's a broken bottle of Ho-Van Oil. I think something might've happened in here."

"It does look like there could've been a struggle. Though it must have been quick because it's hardly noticeable."

"Right."

"Fabiana's luggage is still in her closet," she reports. "I don't imagine she'd go on a months-long trip without it. Unless she has multiple sets."

"What if she was abducted?"

"Hmm . . . That's not impossible. But who would kidnap her? And why?"

I shrug and stifle a groan. I hate how nothing ever leads to a definitive answer but instead branches into a bunch more questions that I can't answer either.

"I don't think we're gonna find anything else here," I say. "But I have one more stop to make."

"Where?" asks Cris.

"It'll be quick," I tell her. "It's right downstairs."

I pull open one of the tall front doors of the House of Vans, and Cris and I slip inside. I glance over my shoulder just as the door closes and catch a glimpse of the undercover cop watching. The lobby beyond is dark, the ceiling and walls painted black, and the concrete floor blends with the rest of the shadows, which are barely kept at bay by the flickering flame of a lone candle atop the deserted front desk.

The air is rife with the intoxicating scent of ripe cherries. I glance up at the maze of ductwork and piping snaking overhead, pumping out a gaseous derivative of Fabiana's signature oil. After breathing it for only a few moments, I feel lighter on my feet and a tad giddy. I turn to Cris to see if it's affected her too, but she only frowns.

"I don't like this place," she grumbles. "It's giving me a headache. Reminds me of Bath & Body Works."

"Okay," I say. "We'll be quick."

The muted sound of music, which I recognize as a song by the Weeknd, comes from the other side of a set of heavy dark drapes concealing what lies beyond the arched entrance across the lobby, above which is a lighted sign that reads ECSTASY AWAITS.

I part the drapes and slip through, then hold them open for Cris to follow. Once on the other side, I stop, not realizing my mouth's agape until Cris tells me to close it.

The House of Vans is an alternate reality.

I can see how someone might lose themself in here. I'm not sure what I was expecting, maybe a high-end spa with stripper poles and thin waterfalls cascading from an accent wall in the back, a heavily made-up front attendant handing out little cups of tea and espresso and condoms for clients. I dunno. But certainly not *this*. I'm sweating again, and I'm suddenly extra self-conscious.

Low red lighting paints everything in bloody swatches as if we're underground at the chillest rave ever. Covering every external window are thick drapes, which have been bolted to the walls on either side. I guess this place never gets natural light. Prominent in the center of the main room is a soaking pool filled with all sorts of people, all mixed together in naked utopia. Curling tendrils of steam rise from the water and snake through the tight sweaty spaces between bodies. A few folks lean against the outer walls, relaxing with their arms spread and resting on the lip of the pool.

Cris glances at the time on her phone and then at me. "It's the middle of the day, and this place is packed."

"Must be nice," I mutter.

The main floor is open to the second and third levels in a way that reminds me of a fancy hotel we stayed in once on a family trip. Each floor is serviced by the same piping system steadily pumping every square foot of this place with the tantalizing fragrance of Ho-Van. Endless silk ropes are attached to the three-story ceiling; some dangle over the pool, others over another expansive sunken portion of the floor filled with cushions, pillows, and patrons—those engaging in couple, group, or solo activities as well as others just soaking up the ambiance. Scantily clad people hang from several of the silk ropes and perform the most sensual and erotic acrobatic dance I've ever seen. It's as bewitching as the tainted air in this place.

At the back of the room, grand staircases on either side of an elevator lead up to the second and third levels, whose corridors are open with intricate iron lattice railings. Each floor holds what must be dozens of rooms hidden behind the same dark drapes all over this place. People prance back and forth throughout and from room to room, making it hard to tell employee from patron.

To my surprise, the House of Vans appears to be operating well despite Fabiana being gone for so long, but then again, I'm not sure exactly what a normal day is like in here.

"So," Cris says with an overwhelmed sigh, "where do we start?"

"UH-*UH*!" The shrill voice clips across the air behind us, making me jump.

Cris and I whirl around, and she grabs my hand, seeming just as shocked as I am that we're the people this person's shouting at.

*Dear gods. Why can nothing be easy?*

"Who let you children in here?" they ask as they storm over, pointing the tablet they hold in one hand at us.

Notwithstanding that they look as if they want to throw us out by the scruff of our necks, they carry themself with the elegance and opulence of an esteemed East Asian drag queen who takes their job and station *very* seriously. They're wearing dangling gold earrings; the right one helpfully reads THEY, and the left, THEM. As "together" as they appear, they do have an air of frantic energy about them. The screen of the tablet they point at us lights up constantly with new notifications, and the *two* phones they hold in their other hand both begin vibrating with incoming calls, one after the other. They pause to glower at each device and silence them one by one.

They're wearing a golden-stoned dress and matching heels that perfectly complement the shimmering gold dusted on their prominent cheekbones. I'm intrigued that their elaborate eye makeup, while over-the-top for a Tuesday afternoon, is still not dramatic enough to detract from their naturally narrow brown eyes, which are draped in luxuriously thick long lashes like the finest faux-fur coats.

"Absolutely *no* minors are allowed in this building," they say in a squeaky, exasperated voice.

"We didn't know," I say, raising my hands. "There was no one at the front desk when we came in."

"WHAT?" they exclaim, peering around us as if they can see through the thick velvet curtain. Then their lips prune as they shift all the devices in their hands to hammer out an angry text on their phone. "If Fabiana knew anyone could just waltz in here off the street, she'd murder me with her bare hands! I swear, I'm going to filet Tommie for this."

A woman in skinny jeans and a black tank that reads HOV in plain block lettering walks up and interrupts the person scolding us. "We're out of Tru Reserve, Colby. I thought you said the delivery was coming this morning?"

Colby's shoulders slump, and they close their eyes and take a long, deep breath. "It's late again," they inform the woman.

"But the customers are getting pissy," she insists.

"Then give them something *else* until I can get the time to visit the distribution warehouse myself." Colby tucks the tablet in their armpit and raises their brows at the employee, who leaves, grumbling under her breath.

"We're friends of Yves," I tell Colby, and their expression lightens. "He sent us by to pick up something from his sister's offi—"

One of Colby's phones rings again, and they hold up a finger and roll their eyes at the same time they answer the call on speaker.

"I'm off today," announces the droll voice on the other line.

"Then who's supposed to work the front desk, Tommie?" asks Colby. "You know we can't leave the front door unsecured."

"Look, I told Fabiana *last fall* that I needed Tuesdays off starting this month, and she said she was hiring more people to cover it. I'll be in tomorrow for my regularly scheduled shift."

"Tommie, wait—" Colby glowers at the phone and shakes their

head. "Fuck me," they sigh, and close their eyes a moment before jerking back to attention as if suddenly remembering Cris and I are standing in front of them.

I guess things aren't going as well at the House of Vans as it may seem on the surface. Relatable.

"Y'all wouldn't happen to know where Fabiana is right now, would you?" Colby asks, their eyes wet with desperation.

"We were just about to ask you the same," I tell them.

Colby shakes their head. "She left me hanging right before Thanksgiving with only some bullshit text about going out of town. I had to coordinate the *entire* staff holiday dinner on my own. Christmas too. I couldn't just cancel it. That wouldn't've been right—not with how everyone looks forward to it every year."

"Do you remember specifically what the text said?" asks Cris.

"It was very vague," they reply. "Something about some last-minute international trip. She hasn't answered any of my calls, and whenever I text to ask when she's coming back, she only responds with 'soon'"—Colby makes air quotes and rolls their eyes—"but it's been *months*."

"When was the last time she responded to you?" I ask.

Colby checks their phone and replies, "The day after the mayor was murdered."

"Can we see?" asks Cris.

Colby eyes us suspiciously and pauses for a too-long moment before handing Cris their phone.

She and I huddle together to read the text thread.

Fabiana! Where ARE you??

You need to come back ASAP.

The fucking mayor is DEAD. Nite-Lite got to Vice Hall somehow. And the police are watching us now

The lawyers are on it but they don't kno how much longer they can hold off the cops

wtf is happening I can't do this by myself

BE BACK SOON!

"Do you think it's really her you've been talking to?" I ask after Cris hands Colby's phone back over.

A familiar shadow, cast by guilt, slinks across Colby's face as they turn their gaze to the floor. "I—I don't know. I've certainly wondered. But I felt silly going to the police, considering . . ." They gesture at our surroundings. "Not to mention Fabiana is a well-known member of the unofficial ACAB club, so even if I *did* have the time to report her missing and deal with the cops, I doubt they'd truly give a shit. Women and girls of color, especially Black women, go missing *way* too often—more than a hundred thousand this year, to be exact. But no one who can do anything about it seems to care. And this is for girls who didn't have a bone-deep vendetta against the police."

I've never seen someone look both so divine and defeated at the same time.

"What's keeping you here?" I ask. "Why not find another job?"

Colby's pristine thin brows scrunch together. "The House of Vans saved my life. Being a Vanguard is more than a job, it's an honor—for many of us. This place is our home. Choice is a privilege many of us didn't have until Fabiana gave it to us. And if the House of Vans ceased to exist, the most vulnerable among us might be tempted to turn toward other institutions that prey on the powerless behind closed doors."

"Like where?" I ask.

"Too many to name, but I'll always start with the Temple of Innocent Blood," Colby sneers. "More than a few of us fled that place, Fabiana included. She took us all in and made us Vanguard." They pause and look off to one side as if contemplating whether to tell us more when something across the room grabs their attention.

The elevator doors slide open, and three uniformed employees exit, each steering a separate gurney that carries an unconscious person wrapped in a red satin bedsheet. I gasp, thinking they might be dead at first, until they draw close enough for me to hear two of the three people snoring.

"Shit," Colby says under their breath, shaking their head and turning back to us. "Three aggros in one morning—which means three rounds of paperwork, out-counseling, *and* system updates. *Yay me.* Thank the gods for Nite-Lite though. I can't imagine having to wrestle with these grown folks in the midst of everything else I have to wrangle around here." Before either of us can say anything, they add, "I need to get back to work. Fab's office is on the third floor, first door on the right after you exit the elevator. And be quick about it. I don't need any more problems." They start to walk away but double back and add, "Oh, and if you hear from Fabiana, please tell her I said to bring her raggedy ass back home ASAP." They give us one last warning glare and hurry off to tug on the reins of what appears to be delicately controlled chaos.

Cris tugs me by my hand toward the elevator. She presses the button for the third floor, and after the doors close, she says, "I hate to admit this out loud, but I think you were right. Someone might've kidnapped Fabiana."

I nod and pinch the bridge of my nose. "What the hell is going on around here?"

Cris sighs as the elevator dings and the doors open. "Hopefully, we'll find out soon."

I use Yves's keys to unlock Fabiana's office, and Cris and I go inside and shut the door behind us.

I'm not gonna lie, the sight of this place catches me by surprise. The decor is bold and undeniably masculine, with dark-stained bulky furniture and bookshelves, a gigantic soft leather executive chair that resembles a throne, and a leather couch across from a standing humidor stocked with cigars. Next to it are several other cases that display small personal collections of fancy wines and spirits. The space reeks of power, almost overwhelmingly so, as if possessed by the spirit of Victor Newman (whom I only know because Aunt Ursula is *obsessed* with him). Knowing what I do about Fabiana, there's a story here, and I'm almost terrified to find out what it is.

Fabiana also has one of those cool clear dry-erase boards on rolling wheels, like the crews always have in those heist movies, which, admittedly, is kinda dope. But what's even more interesting is the information written on it.

Project Nite-Lite

3 FORMULATIONS: (1) OIL (2) SPRAY (3) GAS

DEVELOPMENT PROCESS

A. FORMULATION: (1), (2), (3)
B. TESTING: (1), (2), (3)
C. REFINE & RETEST: (1), (2)
D. FINAL APPROVAL: (1)

"Cris, come take a look at this," I call to my sister, who's consumed with plundering the drawers of Fabiana's desk. "Fabiana was tracking the development of something called 'Nite-Lite.'"

"And Colby's text mentioned Nite-Lite making it to Vice Hall," Cris recalls, frowning as she ponders. "That must've been the knockout gas that put everyone to sleep right before Ben was murdered."

"But why would Fabiana be making something like this?"

Cris's jaw clenches as she thinks. "Remember those three people who got wheeled out on stretchers?" When I nod, she says, "Colby called them 'aggros,' which is another word for 'aggressive'; something I only know from hearing Valentina talk about online gaming."

"Makes sense," I say. "So, let's say someone kidnapped Fabiana from her apartment last November—that means she couldn't have been involved in Ben's murder. And if that's the case, how'd the killer get ahold of Nite-Lite, especially considering the gas looks as if it was still in development?" I gesture to the notes on the dry-erase board.

"Maybe one of the Vanguard is the killer?" Cris wonders aloud. "Or maybe they're working with the killer?"

I take a frustrated deep breath and shrug. This is giving me a headache. "I don't know." I stare into my sister's eyes, and the doubt I see there staggers me. "What am I gonna do, Cris? I *gotta* find Yves's sister—"

"Clem—"

"In the middle of this complete drama shitstorm that's taken over my life, I now have to solve a kidnapping . . ." My mind wanders into the dark place I've barely been avoiding. Lately my anxiety has felt like wandering down a long, scary hallway with doors on either side, behind which lie my most carnal fears. Sometimes random doors open when I walk by them, and whatever's inside claws me to pieces, but then I just pull myself back together and keep wandering. And in this hellish hallway inside my head, there's one door I've been avoiding because I know exactly what's on the other side of it.

Fabiana's dead body.

Mutilated. Murdered. Just like Ben Beaumont.

And how could I explain that to Yves?

I meet my sister's eyes again. This time she looks at me with concern, which frustrates me even more, because what good is that to me right now?

"What if she's dead?" I ask. She tries to pull me into a hug, but I twist out of her grasp. "I don't need hugs right now."

She frowns. "Okay. I understand."

No, she doesn't. Nobody understands what I'm going through but me.

"I think we've found everything worth finding," I say. "We should get going."

"Okay," Cris agrees quietly.

We leave and ride in tense silence all the way home.

I'm *so* fucked.

# EIGHTEEN

## VALENTINA SAVANT

Everyone in NOLA knew Queenie's had the best-quality hair and products of any beauty supply store in town—*and* it was Black owned, which was why people drove from all over the city to shop there and also why Valentina didn't gripe about the lengthy car ride with her mom that kicked off her Saturday morning.

She could've done without the awkwardness though. She'd only had her mom back a couple of days, but they'd spent the whole of that time fumbling around how to reforge some semblance of a mother-daughter relationship that had never quite been there in the first place.

"It feels weird going to get our hair braided like it's a regular day when there might be a serial killer stalking these streets," Mom said.

Valentina stared out the passenger window at the sleepy neighborhood of colorful paneled cottages, some with overturned bicycles in the front yards, empty porch swings, or semi-barren flower beds anxiously anticipating the spring growing season.

"There's a rumor going around that Dr. Thomas sold drugs to Black and brown communities to cover debts from a bunch of malpractice lawsuits," Valentina said.

She wondered if Granny had known about Dr. Thomas's secret side hustle before she'd colluded with him to put Cris's mom down. And furthermore, if she had, would it have made a difference to Valentina? Maybe Granny had just seen the evil doctor as a means to an end, the same way white people saw poor folks of color every day, the same way Dr. Thomas saw the communities where he'd peddled drugs.

Valentina was glad that bastard was dead. She'd first heard about it on an IG gossip blog called "The Shade Tree" and then had gone to the *Herald* to cross-check facts.

"And Tabitha Edgewater was . . . well . . . we all know what she was," she added.

"I'm not disappointed they're dead, to be honest," Mom said. "Don't repeat that."

Warm relief unfurled inside Valentina. At least some familiar parts of Mom had remained intact despite her memory hijinks. That'd always been one of the very few viewpoints Valentina shared with her mom—sometimes violence *was* the answer.

However, the idea of tearing down her emotional fortifications to reconnect with Mom terrified Valentina more than the worst crone she could imagine summoning from the never-realm. Having no one to hurt her and nothing to lose was a competitive advantage she'd intended to exploit for the entirety of her rise *and* reign. But this newest development significantly complicated her plans, and that made her anxious as fuck.

"Between Tabitha Edgewater and Lenora Savant, being Queen was a constant migraine," Mom said.

Valentina sucked a sharp breath in at the ill mention of Granny. But she held back her instinct to rip into Mom for the slight. She had a feeling there might be a larger battle brewing under the surface somewhere between them, and she needed to save her spoons for *that* one. Mom had gotten comfortable around Valentina again, which meant it was coming soon.

"I've thought about that time a lot since I've been back," Mom said, and let go of a heavy, pensive sigh, which drew a curious look from Valentina. "I'm disappointed in myself for letting Lenora and Arturo consume me and not using my time as Queen to create a legacy of my own. I've wondered if maybe I shouldn't have let the throne go so easily."

Valentina's heartbeat intensified. She wondered if Mom could hear it in the quiet car.

*There it is.* The encroaching conflict Valentina had sensed, which she also intended to stomp out before it got started.

The throne was *hers* and hers alone.

Mom pulled into the parking lot of Queenie's, which was nearly full despite the store opening only twenty minutes ago. Valentina got out and zipped her jacket up against the extra-crispy chill in the morning air. She despised the cusp of spring every year when it could be fifty degrees at 7:00 A.M. but eighty by 3:00 P.M.

Inside the store, customers milled about the aisles, perusing towering shelves of every hair and beauty product any person might need at any stage in life. Valentina and Mom had been going there since Valentina was a kid, and it'd always been a wonder to behold. It comforted her to see a Black woman like Miss Queenie dominating in her field. Shopping there felt like strolling through the streets of a friendly neighboring kingdom.

Valentina and Mom stopped in front of a massive wall display of packaged hair. Mom, with Valentina's input, picked out auburn hair for long goddess locs, which Valentina thought would be pretty against the soft copper undertones of Mom's golden-brown skin.

Valentina asked a salesperson to pull down a package of hair the deep red of freshly drawn blood. She smiled when she held it in her hands. It was perfect.

Then she looked up and met Mom's frown.

"That's a bit *bold* for you, isn't it?" asked Mom. "You look so good with black hair. Maybe do just a *couple* of the red braids, you know, like highlights?"

The salesperson took a step back and froze, their eyes flitting between Valentina and her mom.

Valentina stared down at the hair in her hands, imagining it'd been dyed in the blood of every motherfucker who'd ever done her dirty. And, like Granny, Valentina chose to fight for the future she deserved.

She stared into her mother's dark-brown eyes. She didn't have to look up far since they were almost the same height.

"I turned seventeen while you were gone," she told Mom in a soft voice that only the two of them could hear.

The salesperson inched closer.

Mom tensed as if she wanted to respond, but Valentina beat her to it. "I learned how to survive on my own. But it didn't just happen during the nine months you were gone. You left me a *long* time before that. And now I don't need you. You're here purely because I *want* you to be."

Mom took a deep breath in and blew it out through her nose. "Okay."

Valentina turned and smiled at the salesperson. "Sorry," she told them. "I'll take two more of these, and I think we're ready to check out."

"All good," they said.

Mom chewed her lip and fidgeted for the whole of the long drive back across town to the salon for their hair appointments but said nothing. To save them both from death by awkward silence, Valentina turned on the Keyshia Cole Pandora station she'd curated specifically for car rides with Mom, who was a major R & B fan (though Valentina's musical tastes had always been more fluid). She hadn't done it out of love. It was a means of survival to avoid dangerous stretches of silence that could lead to attempted heartfelt conversations.

Mom had booked them both appointments with her favorite stylist duo, Mercedes and Tito. Mercedes was shaped like an exaggerated hourglass due to the breast enhancements and BBL she loved to brag about, which Valentina thought made her look a bit too much like a cartoon character. The makeup Mercedes caked on didn't help that image either. But Mom loved Mercedes's work, and Valentina had to admit, as annoying as Mercedes could be, she had no match behind the styling chair.

However, Valentina preferred Tito. He was trans, tall, and gorgeous with soft brown skin the color of wet sand and long silky black hair that was all his—and which Valentina had envied since the first day she'd witnessed it. Tito had been keeping Valentina's hair and brows snatched since she was old enough to care about that stuff. He was also one of the most stable and normal adults in Valentina's life.

"I bet Tee can come up with a sickening look with those pretty red braids for prom," Mercedes announced. "Unless you want something fresh, though it'd be a shame to take them down so soon, seeing as how prom's just around the corner. You should send us a picture of your dress so we can come up with a style for you. Do you have one yet? A dress?"

"I'm not going to prom," Valentina said, and braced for the imminent onslaught that always followed whenever a teenager decided to do something outside the realm of adult expectations.

She caught Tito's subtle flinch at the news in the slight tug of the hair he was braiding. He cleared his throat and apologized under his breath.

Mercedes stopped working on Mom's head and turned to Valentina, one hand on her hip and an extra-wide colored-in brow raised. "What you say now? You were so excited about it this time last year. What happened?" She frowned with concern that annoyed the shit out of Valentina.

"Kids are different nowadays, 'Cedes," Tito said. "They don't always like the same stuff we did when we was their age. And stop harassing my client, heffa."

Valentina squeezed her eyes shut. It wasn't that she wasn't *interested* in prom; she didn't have the luxury of worrying about something as inconsequential as a silly dance when she spent every day fighting tooth and nail for her future. She'd have plenty of time to parade around in gorgeous ball gowns when she was Queen.

"But it's *junior* prom!" exclaimed Mercedes, finally returning to work on Mama's head. "And I can't believe you won't talk her out of this, Gabriela! You know how important these memories are for kids." Mercedes shook her head. "She's going to regret this later. And that'd be a shame too. Pretty girl like that missing out on her first prom."

Valentina narrowed her eyes at the woman.

"That's her choice, Mercedes," said Mom, her voice boldened in a way Valentina had scarcely heard before. "And she's made it, so let's leave her alone about it."

Tito snickered quietly, and Mercedes looked affronted until Mom baited her into another topic with the promise of gossip, which Mercedes leapt at without hesitation.

Mom's words had introduced Valentina to a feeling she'd never felt before . . . Was it . . . security? That unnerved her.

Valentina couldn't afford to get too comfortable. That type of vulnerability, that softened exterior, was precisely what could make her susceptible to rot.

After four solid hours of sitting with their scalps being yanked and pulled, Gabriela and Valentina both returned to the car complaining of throbbing heads. Valentina was more than grateful for the ibuprofen Mom produced from her purse and the bottled waters they'd gotten from the salon's minifridge on their way out.

"The first day's always the *worst*," Mom said as she backed the car out of their parking spot.

"Beauty is pain," Valentina quipped, which drew a chuckle from Mom. "At least we look good."

"You're absolutely right."

At the end of the lot, Mom stopped to glance in her mirror and check out her elegant goddess braids that she'd pulled to one side so they covered almost her entire front.

Valentina's bloodred braids were parted and hung over each shoulder. She smiled, admiring the color. Mom was right. They *were* a bold choice, but they were indisputably *her*.

"Thanks for having my back earlier—about prom," Valentina told Mom.

Mom smiled and nodded. "Of course, Val. And I'm sorry about before. Your feelings are valid, even the ones about me. I do have a lot to make up for. But I'd like to try, if that's okay with you."

Valentina stuck her hands in the pocket of her hoodie and stared at her feet. She could think of a dozen reasons why letting Mom back in was a terrible idea, but she couldn't ignore that she was fucking exhausted. And alone. Very much alone. Trusting someone who'd already done so much wrong and giving them another opportunity to hurt her again seemed so very illogical, yet the massive risk still tempted her in a way that was beyond her control.

"Okay," Valentina muttered unenthusiastically, which didn't miss Mom, who accepted it nonetheless.

Valentina prayed she wasn't making a mistake.

When Mom pulled the car into the driveway of Valentina's grandiose home, she cut the engine and asked Valentina to wait a moment.

"I never had a good relationship with my mother." Mom frowned as if it physically hurt to dredge up that part of her past. "My family sheltered me so much that by the time I was your age, I had no idea who the hell I was. I met your dad one spring when he was in California on business, and we fell in love. My mom and sister forbade me from following Arturo back to New Orleans, but I went anyway." Mom sighed and hung her head. "They were so mean to me after that. We fought whenever we talked, so I just stopped calling. The last time I visited was when you were only two years old, when my mother died. But your aunt Giselle and I got into a big fight after the funeral. She said some very cruel things to me. I did the same to her and left. We haven't spoken since."

Mom hardly ever spoke about her family, and Valentina had long since given up hope that she would ever meet them. All she knew was Mom's mom was a librarian and originally from Puerto Rico, where she'd met Mom's dad, who was a Black man, during his brief stint in the U.S. military. They'd had two kids together: Mom's older sister, Giselle, and Mom. But Mom's dad had died when she was very young, so she had no memories of him.

"I gave up my whole life for your dad," Mom said, "so I felt like I had to make things work with him, or else I'd have to crawl back to Giselle and Mami and admit that they'd been right all along—and I couldn't do that." She shook her head. "Not after how nasty they'd been to me."

Hearing Mom's truth transformed the image of her in Valentina's mind. Mom wasn't weak and pathetic like Valentina had thought before. Mom had been alone, exactly like Valentina, and had been fighting to take up space in the world—just like Valentina.

They had a lot more in common than she'd thought.

Maybe they *both* could be the forces in the magical community that no one had ever given them the chance to be. At the very least, Valentina was in no position to turn down potential allies in her fight for the crown.

After a short stretch of silence, Mom said, "You should meet your family in California."

"How do you know they're still there?" Valentina asked.

Mom giggled softly. "Giselle and I hate follow each other on Facebook. We don't interact, but we both know the other is watching."

Valentina knit her brows, considering how so many adults never seemed to outgrow that "high school behavior" they loved throwing in teenagers' faces with the caveat that it "wouldn't fly in the real world."

"Giselle has two daughters who are only a few years older than you. They're both in college, I believe," Mom said. "Y'all should know one another."

"Sure, I guess," Valentina said.

Expanding her family at a time when she'd never felt lonelier should've thrilled her, but what unsettled her was her egregious lack of connection with her Puerto Rican heritage.

*Will they think I'm Latina enough?* She was too embarrassed to ask Mom.

While Mom's FaceTime dialed, Valentina trembled nervously in the passenger seat. Maybe Aunt Giselle wouldn't pick up, considering she and Mom weren't on speaking terms.

Valentina's pulse bolted when Giselle answered.

"Giselle," Mom said, sounding surprised too. "Hey, sis. You look good."

Valentina peered at her mom's phone. Giselle sat on one end of a couch beside a brightly lit window, which washed out her bright olive-toned skin onscreen and added a serene halo around her thick auburn hair that she'd brushed straight back into a rushed ponytail. She resembled a heavier, slightly more wizened version of Mom, with a taut, no-nonsense face that gave the impression she'd seen some things and feared little to nothing and no one.

"It's been fifteen years, Gabriela," said Giselle, disbelief and suspicion intertwined in her voice. "Why are you calling out the blue? Has something happened?" Mom hesitated so long, staring at her sister's face on the screen, that Giselle said, "Hello? You still there, Gabs?"

Mom jerked out of whatever thought held her captive. "Yeah, sorry, I, uh . . ." She glanced at me and half smiled, then turned back to the phone. "I'm sorry, Giselle. For abandoning you and Mami. I know it's been a long time and a lot of terrible stuff has been said on both sides, but I'd like us to try and move past it—if you're up for it."

Giselle narrowed her eyes as she considered Mom's request. "Are you sure everything's okay?"

"Yes, Gigi!" Mom cried.

Hearing Mom and her sister use old nicknames for each other settled Valentina's nerves as much as it seemed to have had the same effect for both Mom and Giselle, who loosened up considerably in the moments that followed.

"Our issues won't be resolved with one impromptu FaceTime," said Giselle, "but it's a start."

Mom nodded and blinked away the tears gathering in her eyes. "Okay."

"I wish you wouldn't have left so abruptly after Mami's funeral," Giselle told her. "The kids from the library unveiled a mural they'd made for her. Me and Hector and the girls went to see it afterward. You would've liked it. Although the bastards painted over it when they renovated the building three years ago. I'm glad I kept the pictures though. I'll send them to you."

"I'd like that," Mom said. "How are the girls?"

Giselle's face softened, and her mouth turned up in a sweet grin. "They're both at UCLA and doing extremely well. Julia turns twenty-one next month, and she's majoring in biology. Ana's twentieth birthday was this past February, and she's majoring in film and cinema"—Giselle lowered her voice—"and she gets real huffy if you don't say the 'and cinema' part."

She and Mom chuckled together. Valentina couldn't help cracking a smile too.

"You wanna say hi to Valentina?" asked Mom.

"Ooh! Of course!" The excitement in Giselle's voice sounded genuine, and Valentina considered her internal bullshit detector to be state-of-the-art.

Mom handed the phone to her.

Valentina smiled and waved at Aunt Giselle, whose dark-brown eyes, the same as Mom's, glistened on the screen.

"*Ohh*, you're all grown up now," Giselle exclaimed. "And your braids are stunning, mi'ja, but still not as gorgeous as you."

"Thanks," Valentina said, her voice trailing at the end, not sure what exactly to call her aunt.

"You can call me 'Tía Giselle' or just 'Gigi' or plain old 'Tía' works too," Giselle told her.

"I like that, Tía." Valentina's cheeks ached, and she realized she'd been smiling the whole time. But she couldn't stop. She didn't want to. And that was rare.

"You're seventeen now, right?" asked Tía Giselle.

"Yes," Valentina replied. "My birthday was this past January."

"That's right," Giselle cooed. "You're not far behind Julia and Ana. You should come visit sometime. I can show you all the pictures of your abuelos."

"I'd love that," Valentina said.

She'd cherished her granny and grandpa Felix so much that she hadn't taken the time to consider that she'd had an abuela and abuelo too. But now she had none.

"Your cousins are both here wearing out my washing machine and refrigerator. You want to say hello?"

"Yes, please, if they're not too busy."

Giselle side-eyed the camera. Valentina flinched when Giselle turned and shouted Julia's and Ana's names, which rattled the speakers of Mom's phone.

Mom patted Valentina lovingly on the knee and whispered, "I'll give you some privacy. I'll be inside."

Valentina nodded, and Mom left her alone in the car.

Onscreen, two girls entered the room and stuck their faces into the video frame. "Hiii!" they sang in unison, and one of them waved.

"Hey," Valentina said, waving too.

"That's your cousin Valentina from New Orleans," Giselle told them. "Here, y'all chat for a sec." She handed them the phone.

"I'm Julia," said the one with shoulder-length turquoise hair and large black-framed glasses that made her look like a hip scientist, which Valentina guessed was fitting since Julia was studying biology.

Julia also shared the same tawny skin and cool undertones as her sister.

"I like your hair," Valentina told her.

"Thanks!" Julia said. "Mami hates it." Both sisters snickered together, and so did Valentina.

"I'm Ana." Ana smiled wide, shutting her eyes briefly, as if the warmth of the Sun had just hit her face after emerging from a cold dark place. Ana was fat and strikingly gorgeous. Valentina had found herself staring at Ana more than once, but at least that wasn't weird on FaceTime. Ana also had voluminous curly black hair that Valentina could tell Ana was really proud of because she wore it like a crown, and it looked twice as good.

"It's really good to meet y'all," Valentina said. "I wish we could've met sooner."

"Yeah," Julia said. "Me too."

Ana nodded.

This moment felt like uncovering several puzzle pieces that'd been missing from Valentina's life ever since she'd begun trying to piece them all back together. But there were still so many more she had yet to find—if she ever would.

"Y'all should come visit NOLA sometime," Valentina offered. "You can stay with me. I have *plenty* of room."

Both girls' faces lit up.

"That'd be dope," Julia said.

"It would," Ana agreed.

"And you have to come out to Cali," suggested Julia. "Ana and I are putting together a festival at our school that's gonna be game-changing. I wish you could be there. We even got permission to host it on the main lawn outside the SAC."

When Valentina made a confused face, Ana explained, "Student Activity Center."

"Ohhh," Valentina said. "That sounds really cool."

She was genuinely intrigued by her cousins and their work, though her heart lurched from the tiniest pinprick of jealousy.

Both girls were so damn confident in who they were. Valentina wondered how different her life might've been if she'd grown up like

Julia and Ana had. Would she be planning festivals instead of plotting revenge?

"We're calling it Latine Fest right now, but the name might change," Julia said.

"It's definitely changing," quipped Ana.

Julia cut her eyes at Ana. "If you have a better name, I wish you'd tell me already."

"What's the festival about?" Valentina asked, defusing the argument brewing onscreen.

Ana cleared her throat. "We came up with this festival to create a space for Latine folks whose families are from all over the diaspora to come together and celebrate our cultures. It's for *us*, but other people are welcome to come and hang too."

"It's gonna be a blast," interjected Julia, apparently not liking to be left out of the conversation for too long. "We've got a few local musicians lined up to play, several dozen small businesses to set up booths, and a bunch of food trucks. We even got Mami to convince one of her friends who's a dance instructor to bring some folks in from her studio to teach salsa lessons on the lawn."

"Epic," mused Valentina, impressed.

But all the talk about community and Latine heritage made her feel hollowed out all over again. Those were the two things she'd felt closed off from most of her life.

"I feel like such a charlatan." She laughed uncomfortably, but Julia and Ana didn't join; instead they looked at her curiously. "I, uh, don't even speak Spanish." Valentina's cheeks grew hot with her admission.

"That's okay!" Julia said at once. "Ana's not that good either."

Ana shot her sister a dirty look and backhanded her arm.

"What?" Julia exclaimed. "You're not!"

"Neither are *you*!" Ana cried.

"True," Julia countered, "but I'm still better than you."

Ana rolled her eyes, and Valentina laughed.

Julia's brow furrowed with intrigue at Valentina. "But *you* know magic. That's cool. And a part of our culture that we never got to experience."

Valentina felt herself blushing again. "Yeah, I'm pretty good at gen magic. Maybe if we hung out, y'all could help me with Spanish, and I could teach y'all some gen magic."

"Looove that," Ana said, smiling.

Julia nodded. "Please, let's make it happen. But we gotta go, cuz. It was good chatting with you." Ana nodded with enthusiastic agreement. "Keep in touch."

"Likewise," said Valentina.

They exchanged numbers, and Valentina ended the video call. She sat in the car for a moment despite how stuffy it'd gotten inside since Mom had gotten out.

Many years ago, Valentina had resigned herself to the idea she'd never get to know the Afro-Latine side of her family, the one that possessed a portion of her identity that would forever remain a mystery. She should've felt overjoyed, but finding additional pieces of herself gave Valentina an even clearer perspective of just how much more she'd lost than she'd originally known.

She went inside to find Mom.

They had a *lot* to talk about.

# NINETEEN
## ZACHARY KINGSTON

Zac Kingston was a prisoner.

He'd been confined to his best friend's pool house since the end of June, during which time he'd gotten pretty good at ducking Oz's family.

But his mind was in a different sort of captivity. A maddening one, where time passed while simultaneously standing still. Where days, weeks—months, even—went by while he waited for something that seemed as if it'd never come. Day after day, he spent hours wondering when the cops would kick down the front door and drag him from one prison to the next.

Amid all that, his mind was also trapped in a loop of the past, from just before, during, and after he'd pulled the trigger that night nine months ago. He relived those moments time and time again, wishing he'd done things differently last summer.

He spent the first half of every day scouring the news, expecting to find the official announcement that a manhunt had been initiated for the local murderer—aka him. But not a single soul mentioned the Black teenager who'd been shot in the parking lot around the corner from the art museum. It was as if it'd never happened. As if Zac had done nothing at all.

And that felt like fire ants crawling underneath his skin.

"I've tried *everything*," Oz grumbled, then sipped one of the beers he'd stolen from his dad's basement stash for them. "How could she take my magic like that? It's so fucking *un*fair!"

It was late on a Saturday night, and Zac and Oz were lounging on the couch in the pool house, pounding beers and watching music videos while Zac lamented silently and Oz complained loudly. This had become their Saturday-night ritual, which was the only dose of socialization Zac got somewhat regularly.

It was driving him mad.

Zac grunted his disapproval for Oz's benefit and took another sip of the bitter beer, then frowned at the label. It wasn't the kind he was used to drinking with Dad. He pretended to enjoy it anyway.

"Look at my fucking face, bro!" Oz slammed his empty bottle on the table, where it fell over, clinking against the others. He pointed at the long, thin pink scratches raked across his face and forearms. He resembled a pale, fleshy scratching post.

Zac had watched the whole incident go down.

Oz had refused to believe his ex's binding spell had actually worked, so he'd tested conjurings, crossings, blessings, rituals, oils, and anything else at his disposal. But gen magic didn't respond to him anymore. He'd gotten angry with Zac after he'd asked Zac to try and Zac had refused.

He'd *never* played around with magic. And he'd always despised it.

Especially *that* kind.

Oz's final attempt at gen magic had been the same love spell he'd used on Cris. He tested it on the neighbor's cat, a feral short-haired gray beast that'd always hated Oz ever since the first time it'd peered over the wooden fence and hissed at him. After a solid week of candle burnings, chanting, and stealing stray cat toys and collecting cat hair, Oz lured Duchess Nibblesworth into their yard through a hole in the fence. When Duchess let Oz pick her up, Zac thought the spell had worked after all.

But then . . . Duchess Nibblesworth had fucked Oz up.

*Really* bad.

Oz was pissed at Zac for not helping him, but Zac didn't wanna cross Duchess. Afterward, Zac had slathered Neosporin all over Oz's face and arms, and Oz hadn't said a single word the rest of the night.

Oz popped the top on another beer. "Cris is such a fucking hypocrite. She and her whole self-righteous family think they have the right to decide who has access to magic and who doesn't. What she did to me should be illegal." He took a long gulp and burped so loud, it vibrated the couch cushions. "Aunt Maddie is fed up with them strutting around New Orleans like they run this city too. I hope she drowns them all like sewer rats."

Zac agreed. He wanted that entire family to suffer.

Especially Clement Trudeau.

Not a single, solitary second had passed since that night last June when Zac didn't regret shooting Yves Bordeaux and *not* Clem. Zac wished he could go back and get it right this time. Then at least this prison, this hell, would've been worth it.

"I can't prove it," Zac said, "but I *know* they had something to do with my dad's bar exploding too. He'd already thought that Ursula woman had been putting roots on his business."

Oz huffed, popped the top on another beer, and handed it to Zac. "We've been over this before, bro. That's *not* the same."

Zac snatched the beer and set it on the coffee table. He hadn't finished the first nasty one yet. "How so?" he asked, his cheeks heating with mingled rage and humiliation.

Oz rolled his eyes. "Dude, that wasn't magic. Your dad just has bad luck. Get over it already!"

"And maybe you just suck at magic," Zac replied.

"Cris *literally* broke into my house in the middle of the night and *stole* my goddamned magic! It's *not* the same!"

Zac squeezed the long neck of the beer bottle clamped tightly between his thighs so hard that he imagined it snapping in his hand. Maybe he'd use the sharp ends to add a little more flair to Duchess Nibblesworth's handiwork.

"You're totally killing my buzz right now." Oz took out his phone and started tapping out a text. "I'm gonna see if I can bum some weed off Benji. We both need to relax."

"I think I need a friend who gives a shit about someone other than himself," Zac muttered.

Oz pocketed his phone and leaned forward, propping his elbows on his knees and clasping his hands reverently in front of him.

Zac's heart sank on instinct.

"Seriously," pleaded Oz, "you've *gotta* let this shit go. You've been camping out here since summer, bro. This was supposed to be temporary. What are you even doing right now?"

Zac shrugged. He honestly had no idea.

Oz shook his head. "I'm sorry, but you gotta leave, man. Benji's moving in here tomorrow afternoon so he can start 'practicing his independence' or whatever"—Oz rolled his eyes—"as a reward for getting into fucking Cambridge."

"Tomorrow?" Zac sat up, his eyes wide with alarm. "That's in a couple hours. Where am I supposed to go?"

"I dunno," Oz said. "You've had damn near nine months to figure that shit out."

"Can't I just hide out in your room?"

"No way. My parents would have way too many questions that would all eventually lead you back to your dad." Oz spread his hands in front of him. "Dude, just *go home* and *talk to him*. Why are you being so weird about it?"

Zac yanked the bottle from between his legs, smashed it on the edge of the coffee table, and launched to his feet. What remained of the beer exploded and dribbled down his arm and the furniture. His chest heaved with intense breaths that pumped white-hot heat through him.

Oz leapt back, clambering until he backflipped over the couch's arm. He crashed to the floor in a flash of flailing limbs and curses, then jumped back to his feet. Hands raised in front of him, he slowly backed away from Zac.

"What the fuck is wrong with you?" Oz cried.

"You're just like everyone else." Zac tossed the broken bottle aside and left.

Oz was right. It was past time Zac went back home.

Zac pulled into the driveway of the yellow-paneled cottage where he'd grown up at exactly 2:12 A.M. and found every light on inside the house.

Dad's SUV was parked in its usual spot at the head of the driveway underneath the carport, so he was home. But what was going on? Dad wasn't usually up past midnight unless he was working at the bar—and those days had come to an end.

Zac got out of his old pickup truck and gingerly made his way to the front door. He stuck the key in the lock, and the door crept ajar. Carefully, he pushed it open all the way and stepped inside.

The front room was completely disheveled. Not like the last time Zac had come home at the start of last summer. This was different.

It seemed as if there'd been some sort of struggle.

Zac closed the door softly behind him and locked it, then surveyed the room. Tables lay on their sides. Mail, couch cushions, and other random items were strewn around the room. It was like a miniature tornado had whipped through.

Dad's laptop sat on the floor in two smashed halves. The television remained whole and mounted on the wall.

This wasn't a robbery.

"Dad?" Zac called out. Fear flooded his throat, making him sound squeaky and insecure. If a killer was lurking somewhere, the weakness in his voice would lure them straight to him.

Zac noticed a trail of soiled clothing stretched from the edge of the family room into the kitchen. He picked up each piece, which had begun to stink with the foul odors of sweat and . . . decay.

*Dad's tuxedo.*

Zac held up the white button-up shirt and gawked at the ridiculous amount of blood that'd turned black, staining the whole front.

*Is that . . . Dad's blood?*

"Dad?" Zac called out again, his voice louder, more urgent, matching the heightened pace of his thumping heart.

The house responded with silence.

But Zac felt another presence, a warm static sensation at the back of his neck.

He whipped around, quickly scanning his brightly lit surroundings. He was alone.

Gooseflesh prickled his skin.

For a split second, Zac thought something supernatural might be going on. He'd never believed in that shit before. The worst monster anyone could imagine still couldn't hurt him. Not like real, live people had. They were the real monsters.

Cautiously, Zac searched the small cottage, but Dad was nowhere to be found. All Zac had been able to locate was Dad's cell phone, which had died. He plugged it in and waited a few minutes for it to power back on.

There were a bunch of missed calls from Eveline Beaumont and a few others from unknown numbers. The notifications dated all the way back to Sunday.

Six days.

All that blood.

*Is Dad hurt? Or worse . . . dead?*

But where the hell *was* Dad? Zac had checked every room. Every closet. Every corner. Even underneath the beds.

Except the basement.

Zac stood in front of the door, which had been bolted shut from the outside. There was no way Dad could be down there.

But Zac still had to check.

He ignored the anxious lump in his throat as he unlocked the basement door and swung it open. He stared down the dark flight of rickety wooden stairs into a sea of blackness. A cold draft wandered up from below. It brought something more along with it.

Whispers.

The small hairs on the back of Zac's neck rose. He flipped the light switch, but the light was busted. Of course it was.

He fumbled for his phone in his pocket and turned on the flashlight. He shone the light down the stairs, illuminating dust motes that floated in the dank air like gray snowflakes.

"Dad?"

The whispers from somewhere below intensified to a frantic low mumble.

Someone was definitely down there.

"Dad!" Zac called again.

The muttering continued, unbroken by Zac's cry. A masculine voice echoed from somewhere toward the back of the basement.

Zac held his breath and descended.

Every creak of the old wooden stairs sent a chill zipping down the center of his back. At the bottom, his sneakers crunched on brittle shards of broken glass. He swung his phone's light to his feet, which stood on the remains of the exploded light bulb from the fixture above.

*What the hell happened down here?*

Dad had never gotten around to finishing the basement. The forest of bare wooden frames that made up the floor's layout threw shadows when hit with Zac's phone light, which made him shiver from head to foot. He walked in the direction of the incoherent mumbling, shielding his nose with one arm from the encroaching stench of excrement. The talking ceased as he stepped into one of the rooms at the far end of the basement, which they'd once used for storage. All that remained were a few moldy boxes stacked haphazardly around the room.

Something shifted in the dark. Zac sucked in a sharp breath and swung his light into the corner. A ghost of a man squatted there, his back to Zac, naked but for a pair of soiled, dingy boxers, hugging himself and still shivering.

"Dad?" Zac said, still unsure if what he saw was real.

Jack Kingston turned slowly, both cheeks caked with dried blood. He threw up an arm, shielding his eyes from Zac's bright light. Zac turned it away and ran to his dad. The man smelled like a rotting corpse, but Zac didn't care. At least Dad was okay.

But was he . . . really?

Zac stood back and shone the light over Dad's body, examining him for injuries. At the crown of Dad's head, Zac found a gash, which was about the width of two fingers. The skin around it had swollen and turned yellow.

*Shit. It might be infected.*

The rest of Dad's injuries were superficial scrapes or bruises that'd almost healed on their own. But that didn't add up. There'd been way too much blood on Dad's clothes and person to have come from that single cut on his head.

Dad recoiled from the light and started muttering nonsense again. Zac got closer and knelt beside him, then leaned in until he could just make out what his dad whispered.

"He'll be back," Dad repeated over and over, panic increasing every few rounds.

"Huh?" Zac asked. "Who'll be back? What happened to you?"

"He'll be back. He'll be back. He—"

"Whose blood is that all over you, Dad?" Zac asked.

"He'll be back. He—"

Zac backhanded his dad hard across the mouth. Dad's teeth cut into Zac's knuckles, which stung as Dad fell backward against a tower of boxes, toppling them to the ground. He cried out with a frustrated growl, righted himself, and leapt on top of Zac, pinning him to the ground.

"Dad!" Zac shouted. "It's me! Zac! What the fuck are you doing?"

"You have to *leave*," Dad shouted, spraying Zac's face with putrid spittle. "You hear me, son? Leave now! Before it's too goddamned late!"

"Too late for what?" Tears streamed from Zac's eyes. "Dad, *please*!"

Dad stared into Zac's eyes and gritted his teeth as he pressed Zac's wrists into the harsh concrete with crushing pressure.

"Okay!" Zac cried. "Get off! You're hurting me!"

Dad snapped back to what was left of his senses and fell backward.

Zac sat bolt upright, scuttled backward, and massaged his bruised and scraped wrists.

Dad knelt and put both hands on either side of his head. Silent now, he rocked back and forth, shaking his head, refusing to look at Zac.

The fear that'd built inside Zac like a snowbank transformed to guilt—and buried him.

Last June, Dad had all but thrown Zac out, demanding he go back to Huntsville and lie low after what he'd done. But Zac should've never left Dad. If Zac would've stayed, he could've stopped whatever had happened to Dad.

Zac crawled over to his dad cautiously, so as not to startle him again, and put his arms around him. "It's okay, Dad," Zac whispered in his ear. "I'm back now. I'm not leaving you again."

Dad hugged Zac. Squeezed him tight.

Zac let his tears flow. He'd made the right decision. He only wished he'd made it sooner. Dad needed him now more than ever.

They needed each other.

Dad sat back and grabbed Zac's face with both hands and leaned close. When he spoke, his voice was a foreboding hoarse whisper that sent an icy shock down Zac's spine.

"We're both going to die."

# PART III

It is certain, in any case, that ignorance, allied with power, is the most ferocious enemy justice can have.

—JAMES BALDWIN

The New Orleans Herald

# MULTIPLE MURDERS TURN UP HEAT ON MAGICAL CRIME INVESTIGATIONS

**By Sharita L. Green, academic fellow**

Just before daybreak on Saturday morning, the opening shift manager of the Bleaker Street YMCA received the shock of a lifetime when he discovered the deceased body of Dr. Gregory Thomas, a beloved medical professional in the local community for more than fifteen years. Overnight, someone had arranged Dr. Thomas's corpse in a sitting position with his back against the front doors, over which they'd written the words CORRUPT, ABUSER, HYPOCRITE, and DEALER in the victim's blood. Investigators are remaining tight-lipped about other evidence found at the scene of the crime and have declined to comment to the *Herald* on the investigation and whether these murders are connected to the brutal slaying of New Orleans's 61st mayor, Benjamin Beaumont.

The death of Dr. Thomas marks the third murder of a prominent member of the New Orleans community in a matter of weeks, the first being Mayor Beaumont, who was stabbed to death at a private party at Vice Hall; and the second, Tabitha Edgewater, leader of the Redeemer movement. Investigators have been unable to identify a murder weapon, which suggests some sort of magic might've been at play.

After last Friday night's arrest of the Queen of the Generational Magic Council of New Orleans, Marie Trudeau, in connection to the murder of Mayor Benjamin Beaumont, Detective Jeida Sommers was promoted to senior lead investigator for the Detective Bureau of the New Orleans Police Department. In an interview with the *Herald*, Sommers claimed they had no evidence to link Queen Trudeau to the murders of Edgewater and Thomas, "[but] the investigation is far from over."

We reached out to Marie Trudeau, who is presently being detained at Orleans Parish Prison, but the Queen and her attorney denied our interview request; however, they both staunchly proclaim that "[Marie] is innocent of any and all *from p.1*

crime(s) related to the murder of Mayor Beaumont."

Sommers states, "My department is working to confirm suspicions of magical assault as the cause of death for both Edgewater and Thomas." When asked if she was worried that she might be dealing with a serial killer, Sommers declined to comment.

At the close of our interview, Sommers revealed that in tandem with the investigation, her department is consulting with Eveline Beaumont's Magical Regulation Bureau on a policy plan to significantly reduce—and hopefully, eradicate—magical crime in the local community; an ambitious undertaking, but one they hope can become the blueprint for the potential national adoption of magical law enforcement.

However, their grand project might be at risk now that notable government officials are calling for another election in the wake of Benjamin Beaumont's untimely death, the result of which will determine the fate of the newly formed Magical Regulation Bureau, which has lost its staunchest supporter.

# TWENTY
## CRISTINA

That *Herald* article haunts me like a ghoul in the night all week long.

It's just like Tabitha. Someone *moved* Dr. Thomas's body—and went through great trouble to put it on display for everyone to see. Someone who must know I'm the one who killed him.

But who? And for what reason?

The words they wrote about him weren't untrue, which also suggests they must've known about his ledger too, of which there was no mention in the article.

*Figures*.

It all feels surreal. Almost impossible. But no . . . this is really happening.

Clem was right. I hate admitting that, and I can't even talk to him about it because he's already made clear how he feels about my "justice list."

Maybe I shouldn't have killed Dr. Thomas. I'm not so certain anymore. But whether he deserved it or not, I've unknowingly set something in motion that could be my and my family's undoing. After we worked so hard to clear my grandmother's name and retake our stolen throne, we stand to lose it all over again—because of me.

And someone out there knows my secret. With my *and* Mama's freedom at risk, I can never let it get out. But who the hell is it?

Apparently, everyone at school read the *Herald* article too because I become the "main character" once again. I quickly master the art of tuning out whispers, and ignoring gawking stares. My presence at school since last week has been APO™, or attendance purposes only, and all my brain power's been diverted to either coming up with a way to clear Mama's name or worrying about if and when the cops will come for me too.

Over the weekend, I plundered the archives of the Gen Council

Library but most of the substantial books and documents about necromancy have been removed and secured in another facility that remains secret—enough so that I can't ask too many questions without raising suspicions, and I won't dare risk outing Clem.

The dejection on his face after I told him I was unable to find anything to help him almost broke me. And I don't know what else to do.

This entire week has been hell—for both of us—but I've made it to Friday, and now my primary goal is to push through the rest of today so Clem and I can go see Mama at the jail after school.

However, the one bright spot in my dreadful week has been skipping gym class with Remi Prince every day, which inadvertently became a ritual for us. Aurora's been taking advantage of Coach Teague's leniency and cutting regularly too to get caught up on life. Her absence created this vacuum in my and Remi's worlds that kinda sucked us together.

That's why, despite having my own mountain of homework to do, I opt to hang out in the band room with him during gym again. Except today the band director tells us we can't keep squatting in here every day or he'll get in trouble, so our daily refuge now comes with the stipulation that we complete a tedious project while here. Today's task is photocopying and sorting all the music selections for the spring concerts, which I'm taking care of while Remi plunders the instrument storage rooms to pull down all the various percussion instruments they'll need for the production.

Once he's done, he helps me sort the music into labeled folders for all the band members. We sit on the floor next to each other, dozens of organized stacks of papers in front of him, and a few more before me, and several boxes of brand-new music folders staged behind us. I'm proud of the quick assembly process I've set up. It's actually quite calming to focus on something easy and low stakes instead of mud wrestling life-altering trauma to the death. And an unexpected bonus is I get to do it with Remi.

Since we've been hanging out this year, I've been slowly getting to know him better. He has a gentleness and charisma to him that somehow make me feel like I'm sliding between toasty-warm satin sheets on a pillow-top mattress whenever he's around. And he does it so effortlessly. It's just who he is—which is refreshing, considering my history. Even thinking this makes me nervous, but Remi feels safe. I mean, I'm still getting acquainted with him—the *real* him—but the person he's been so far has felt genuine, even the "ugly" parts he's shown me.

Though I'm not sure he'd stick around if I showed him mine.

"You and your dad know a private investigator, right?" I ask him, while adjusting a leaning tower of clarinet folders. "The one who helped Aurora last summer?"

He nods, and his expression darkens. "Yeah, but she's in L.A. now."

"Oh." I sigh, defeat weighing heavy on my shoulders as I sit back on my heels. "I was going to ask about possibly hiring her to help us find Fabiana Bordeaux."

Remi tucks a thin stack of papers into the folder he's holding. "Even if she were still investigating, she wouldn't touch anything related to Ben Beaumont ever again."

"Why not?"

"He and his sleazy lawyers tanked her after he found out she was digging up dirt on him for my dad's campaign—by Desiree's request, which should come as no surprise—"

"It doesn't," I say.

"Desiree also thinks one of Eveline's spies tipped Ben off about what the PI had done."

I raise a brow. "Spies?"

"Same thing I said when I first heard it." He closes the folder in his hands and writes TRUMPET 1 with a black marker on the front and sets it next to one of the stacks beside me.

I pick it up and hand it back to him. "No, no. Woodwinds are here," I explain, "and brass instruments are over there—next to you." I point, and he glances at the neatly organized folders laid out across the floor.

He blinks and studies the arrangement for a moment, and then realization dawns on his face, lighting the thousand-watt smile he flashes at me. "Ah, I see. I love how logical and organized you are."

Heat blossoms in my cheeks. I stare down at my work, doing a terrible job of hiding my slight smile. I hate that he so easily disarms me when it feels so dangerous to let my guard down.

Trusting again feels . . . strange . . . and hard. And scary.

I often fight between anger at myself for letting Oz continue to take from me in his absence and immobilizing anxiety over making myself vulnerable again for fear that I'll just be abused again by someone new.

"Anyways," Remi says, drawing me back to our conversation, "yeah, Desiree claims Eveline's been exploiting her power as Reverend Mother of the Temple of Innocent Blood for decades, taking in people in need and grooming them into faithful spies that she plants in organizations throughout the city. Apparently, no one knows how deep and how wide Eveline Beaumont's spy network stretches." Remi snickers. "It's like some shit from a James Bond movie."

I chuckle at first, which ends on a sour note. Eveline's name is on my list. Lenora Savant was a monster in her own right, but Eveline is a completely different kind of dangerous. The quiet, insidious type that you don't suspect until they've already got a hand around your throat and a knife in your belly.

Remi may joke, but I appreciate the heads-up. I need to be more careful around Eveline.

"Does your dad have any idea what she's planning to do with this Magical Regulation Bureau?" I ask him.

"He and Desiree were talking about that a few nights ago," Remi tells me. "They'd heard a rumor going around about 'registration,' and Dad flipped when Desiree told him about it."

I catch myself wrinkling the paper I'm holding in my fist, so I set it aside. "Registration? As in 'registered magic user'?" When he nods, I say, "But that doesn't make sense. Why would Eveline want that? She's on the Gen Council."

Remi shrugs. "These people are all like comic book villains, Cris. *Now* can you see why my dad isn't cut out for that shit? He's so hellbent on fighting fair. Even after Ben Beaumont took everything from Yasmeen—the private investigator who'd been working for Dad—

all because she got caught digging up some *major* dirt on Ben. And despite all that, Dad *still* refused to use what Yas found." He shakes his head.

"What was it?"

"Some compromising video of him," he says, and makes a show of adding "allegedly" onto the end. "I never saw it. Desiree and Dad had a big fight when Dad deleted the only copy."

"Of course, Desiree would be pissed about deleting that advantage," I tell him.

Remi lets out a long, tired breath.

We work quietly until the bell rings, just managing to finish getting all the music into folders and the folders all properly sorted and stacked.

"Thanks for your help," Remi says once we're done.

"Thanks for the sanctuary," I reply, and we both grin.

"I, uh, wanted to ask you something," he says. I don't miss the small quiver of uncertainty in his voice.

"Okaaay," I say.

I don't know why I'm nervous too. Remi often brings butterflies to my stomach whenever he comes around, but I've gotten used to ignoring them, mostly. But now they're a storm of fluttering wings inside me. And I cannot have that.

"I was wondering if you'd like to go to prom with me," he says. "I know it's kinda late and all, and as far as prom-posals go, this one kinda sucks, but—"

"Oh, uh, I'm so sorry," I say. "But I hadn't planned on—"

"It's okay," he says. "Really! You don't have to explain."

I want to trust Remi. So bad. But I can't. I'm just not there yet. And I don't know if I'll ever be. Besides, I could be going to prison for multiple homicides soon, and I'm not sure if Remi's the type to hold me down while I serve multiple life sentences.

But I did what I did because that is what queens do. Right or wrong, I eliminated two incredibly violent threats to my community—the most sacred thing we have. And it's the Queen's responsibility to protect that at all costs.

"I appreciate you asking," I tell him. "Honestly, I do. But I have a lot of really personal stuff going on right now." I gather my things and shoulder my backpack.

He shifts his hands in his pockets, and his gaze softens even more. "I understand that more than you know. I'm gonna leave Mr. Brinson a note about the folders so he'll know what's going on," Remi tells me. "You good to walk to sixth on your own?"

I suck my teeth. "So you're ditching me now because I turned down your last-minute prom-posal?"

His eyes widen, and his cheeks flush. "Oh, no, no, I would never—here, I'll walk you." He pats his pockets and looks around, though I'm not sure for what. "I didn't think you'd . . . Shoot . . . I was only—" He frowns at me when I laugh. "What's so funny?"

"I was kidding," I say, still chuckling. "You're so—" I stop myself before the word "cute" spills out of my mouth.

He shakes his head, grinning again, and runs a nervous hand through his curls. "Why doth the lady torment me so?"

"Maybe the lady doth enjoy it."

We stare at each other for a moment of awkward silence and then burst into teary guffaws at the same time.

The bell rings.

I say goodbye to Remi and turn to leave but double back after a few steps. "Remi?"

He's still standing in front of the rows of stacked folders, and his eyebrows shoot up, hopeful. "Yes?"

"Have you ever done magic before? Of any kind?"

"No." He shakes his head. "Magic has a price, and it can be kinda steep sometimes. I've seen what that kind of power has cost other people, and I don't want it."

I smile at him. "Have a good weekend, Remi."

Clem and I pull up at the same time outside Orleans Parish Prison, a group of sterile-looking gray stone buildings surrounded by uninviting fencing crowned in razor wire. Walking through all the security checkpoints leading up to the front entrance is discomforting, and when we finally step through, it's as if we've passed through a portal into another realm of security badges, bolted doors, plexiglass, and hard, distant stares.

I worry about Mama being holed up in a place like this. I'm shivering, and I'm not sure if it's because of the frigid temperature inside the building or the general cold atmosphere of this prison. I don't know if I could survive very long in here.

I look at Clem, and his expression says what we both know.

We *gotta* get Mama out of here. ASAP.

The check-in process involves a lot of waiting and paperwork and questioning stares from officials before we're led through a maze of secure doors and corridors to a small conference room with no windows. One side of a gray-topped table presses against one wall with two well-worn gray cloth chairs on one side and a single on the other. I hate being here. It's as if the color scheme of this place was intentionally chosen to depress the people contained here and break them down faster and more efficiently.

Clem and I sit beside each other in the creaky chairs, and our officer escort informs us she'll be back shortly with our mother.

My brother stares down in silence at the gray tabletop in front of us. His expression and posture slumps from the weight of all the endless drama bearing down on him. An overwhelming sadness surrounds him, a fog of depression that seems to be growing thicker every day that passes while Mama's trapped in this concrete prison and Yves's soul remains irrevocably broken. I want to comfort him, but I don't know what to say, so I slide my chair closer to his and put an arm around him.

Clem lets go of a shaky breath and leans on me. We hug for a moment, and I swear I can feel us sharing some of our strength. Genuine human connections can be magical like that sometimes.

The door clicks open again, and the officer from earlier leads Mama inside the room and says she'll be right outside and for us to knock when we're done. Once the door shuts, Clem and I launch up from our seats and throw our arms around Mama.

She squeezes us both extra tight and stands back, smiling with wet eyes as she looks us over from head to foot. I'm surprised she's in good spirits considering she's been locked up in this drab place for four days now. She's wearing a loose-fitting tan jumpsuit, and her lengthy curls are slicked back into a neat ponytail. It's a stark contrast to her appearance the night she was arrested. A bit of my worry recedes now that I've seen she's faring okay—at least physically.

She sits on one side of the table, and Clem and I return to our seats across from her.

"How you holdin' up, Mama?" I ask.

"I'm fine," she says. "Better than I expected, actually. The other inmates have been very kind to me." She smiles again. "I hadn't considered the Queen's influence stretched to this place, but it makes sense. I've had no shortage of people looking out for me, which has been heartwarming despite how nervous it makes some of the guards who've noticed. So many folks here were outside under my mama's reign and have fond memories of her. They were happy to hear our family's back ruling the Gen Council and also pissed that I'm being accused of Ben Beaumont's murder."

Mama's words hit me with an invisible force that sits me back in my chair. I, like her, have been so wrapped up in the community work we were doing *outside* that I forgot the people contained here are part of our community too. But they never forgot about us. An echo of guilt rings deep within me. Once we get Mama out of here, we should seriously talk about what we can do to extend our outreach to the incarcerated too.

"But that's no mind," Mama says. "The lawyer Ursula hooked me up with is stellar. We're hopeful I'll be cleared and out of here sooner rather than later. Most of the evidence against me is circumstantial."

"What do they have on you?" Clem asks, his leg jackhammering beneath the table.

"Well . . . the most damning thing is your dad's knife," she tells us.

Clem blanches. "I'm so sorry, Mama. I swear I don't know how that knife got there. I didn't even have it on me. I hadn't seen it in weeks. I—"

"Shh, baby, it's *okay*," Mama tells him. "We'll deal with the knife, but there's still the matter of the poison in Ben's and Eveline's drinks.

Ms. Mattie Belle's granddaughter, Trina, confirmed to the police that I gave her a vial of foxglove at the start of the party."

"The elixir you make and bless monthly for Ms. Mattie's arthritis?" I ask.

Mama nods. "I usually deliver it to her personally, but I didn't have time this month because I was so busy with the festival and helping Rosalie set up for her soft launch. When I texted Ms. Mattie my apology, she told me Trina was coming to the party and to give it to her there."

I narrow my eyes. "Then how convenient for Eveline's and Ben's drinks to have been poisoned with foxglove."

Mama blows out a long, tired breath. "Every night since I've been here, I've lain awake in the dark, pondering who could be targeting me this time and why."

"Who do you think it could be?" I ask.

"I'm not sure," she says. "But something struck me as odd about this *poison* foolishness. It has Lenora's stank *all* over it."

Clem's brow wrinkles. "But she's dead."

My heart plummets. I know where this is going before Mama can say it.

"Mm-hmm," she says. "But what if we've been confusing someone else's funk for Lenora's all along?"

"Eveline," I say.

Mama nods, frowning. "I can't prove it, but my gut tells me she was up to something capricious that night. And I think something went wrong, and the situation got away from her—and then Ben died. I have no idea who killed him or why, but it wasn't me."

Eveline *fucking* Beaumont.

I *knew* she couldn't be trusted. I should've asked Clem to have his undead army tear her apart too that night on the *Majestic*.

Or maybe I'll just do it myself.

"But gut feelings won't get me out of here," Mama says. "The police also have my fingerprints on the canisters of knockout gas that were hooked into the ventilation system."

I shake my head, anger simmering inside me. If this is truly a setup, it makes sense that Eveline would be behind it because only she would (and could) put together such an elaborate scheme. But why though?

My mind sifts through the memories of our confrontation of both Lenora and Eveline aboard the *Montaigne Majestic* last summer and how Eveline felt slighted by what we'd done. I wonder if this is her idea of a repercussion.

"They're running a test of the prints from the scene," Mama tells us. "The place was a mess of blood and DNA."

"So, what's your lawyer's strategy?" asks Clem.

"They're trying to find Fabiana Bordeaux to help fill in some of the gaps in the story," she says. "But she's disappeared. They can't even locate Yves." She looks to Clem and asks, "Have you two talked since last time I asked?"

His entire body goes rigid before he shakes his head. I take his hand under the table and squeeze it.

"We've been looking for her too," I tell her. "We went by her apartment a few days ago. It looked like she's been gone since before the holidays. She also abandoned the House of Vans."

"Yeah, something about her disappearance feels off," Clem adds. "Fabiana is mysterious, but she'd never leave her employees hanging like that."

A shadow looms on Mama's face. "Look, all this is *my* burden, not *yours*. Let me and my lawyers do the worrying and investigating. You two have enough on your plates between school and prom." She hangs her head. "I'm not sure I'll be out by then—"

"Don't worry," I say. "I'm not going."

"Me neither," says Clem.

Mama's head pops back up. "Why not? It's not because of me, is it?"

Both Clem and I shake our heads. "We're just not feeling it this year," I answer for the both of us. "Maybe next year."

"Okay," Mama says. "As long as it's a decision you're making for *you* and not someone else."

Clem and I nod.

Even if Mama wasn't fighting for her innocence right now, junior prom would not be seeing me or Clem. We've unfortunately got other far more dire things on our minds. Although, more than once, I have imagined an alternate reality where we'd get to go to prom—Clem with Yves, me with Remi—and Mama and Daddy would see us off, and then we'd all have a fun, normal night together with no drama, no fights, and *no* murder.

Maybe next lifetime.

Clem and I look up into the face of the guard when she appears in the window behind Mama. She taps her watch, and I nod.

"Stay strong, my babies, and keep praying for Eshu's blessing," she tells us as she stands up and hugs us one last time.

I hold Clem's hand in the hallway. It's clammy but familiar. He walks close beside me, our shoulders almost touching. Neither of us says a word as we exit through all the secured checkpoints to the front lobby.

Once we're back outside, we stop to take in the fresh air. I didn't realize how stifling the prison was until we'd left it. I tilt my head back, and the Sun's rays on my face feel like bathing in a hot spring. Beside me, my brother frowns at a crack in the pavement as if he's trying to figure out how to dive into it and vanish.

"You okay?" I ask him.

He shakes his head. "I'm so tired, Cris."

"I know." I hug him again, my arms on his shoulders, his stubbly cheek grating against mine. "But you're not alone anymore. I'm here."

"You're here," he says with a heavy sigh. "Thank you."

I squeeze him once more. When we part, I'm startled to notice a woman watching us from a few paces away. Detective Sommers.

She's wearing another one of her boring "detective suits," and her hair's brushed behind her ears, which heightens her surveilling gaze.

"Hello, Cristina, Clement," she says, nodding at each of us. "How are you two? Come to see your mother?"

"You don't care," I tell her.

Clem elbows me, but I ignore him.

Sommers raises one of her thick eyebrows at me. "Excuse me?"

Clem tugs gently on my arm, pulling me in the direction of the parking lot, but I stand firm.

"You don't care," I repeat, "about me, my brother, my mama, or

Black people at all, for that matter. Because if you did, you wouldn't be part of the organization that's unfairly prosecuting gen. You've turned your back on your community to join the bastards who plant evidence and shoot unarmed people." Disgust curls one side of my mouth downward. "You're no better than them."

Clem grips my arm harder, but I won't be moved. Sommers seems unaffected by my words, which makes me even angrier.

When she speaks, her voice is gentle, even—and infuriating. "My younger brother, Darien, was about your age when he died. He'd moved in with me because he didn't get along with our mom and stepdad. I hadn't been on the force very long at that time, but I was working on a case against a shadow magic cartel called the Divine Knights. They did some pretty nasty business in Miami for nearly two decades. Hundreds of unsolved murders were linked directly to that organization."

I cross my arms and glower at her.

*Congratulations, or I'm sorry that happened or whatever, but I'm not going through this emotional journey with you today, lady.* Call me callous, but I don't give a damn about her tragic backstory.

"I didn't know Darien had gotten spun up with them until he moved in with me," Sommers says. "And shortly after, little, seemingly insignificant stuff started happening, like my investigation folders mysteriously moving from where I'd last left them or my work laptop being locked after too many failed login attempts. I was willfully naïve, right up until I ran into my brother during a raid of the Divine Knight's central Miami operation.

"My partner and I fought our way to the roof of one of their warehouses. And there we cornered Victor Delaney, the leader of the Miami arm of the Divine Knights, along with his faithful apprentice—my little brother."

Pain glistens in Sommers's eyes, but I'm not moved. I'm not going to feel sorry for her while she's actively working to orphan me and my brother.

"I pleaded with Darien to walk away from those fools and let me help him," Sommers says. "But I was too late. He'd already been indoctrinated to the Divine Knights *and* Victor. My little brother was drunk on the illusions of power Victor gave him, because Darien had felt powerless his entire life. Victor saw that and used it to manipulate and abuse my little brother for his own ends.

"Darien begged Victor to give him the spark and turn him into a vamp right there in front of me. Victor hesitated until I screamed for Darien to get away from him. And that's when Victor did it. I think out of spite because he had to have known what would happen. Darien was too young to handle the full force of shadow magic. The spark set him on fire, and he burned from the inside out. I stood on that roof that night and watched my baby brother, the same one I'd helped raise, burn like a bonfire until he was nothing but a pile of ashes. It took only *seconds*, but it felt like hours. Victor spit on my brother's remains and then laughed in my face. So I shot him in his."

My face twists into a grimace. "And you're proud of that?"

Clem groans beside me.

Sommers scoffs under her breath. "I didn't want anyone to die that night, but that's what happens when magic users are allowed to exploit your powers without inhibition. I'm trying to save lives in this city by getting dangerous magic criminals off the streets."

"My mama is *not* a murderer," I tell her.

"Well, I don't know your mama," Sommers retorts, "and my job is to conduct a thorough investigation to find out the truth. That's all I owe you."

I clench my jaw and shake my head. I know getting into it with this woman is not a smart idea, but trying to reason with her is as frustrating as attempting a logical conversation with Oz—and thank the gods I've been freed from that burden.

"Bye, Detective," Clem says, dragging me away from Sommers and toward the parking lot. Once we're out of earshot, he whispers, "Yo, you've *gotta* chill, Cris!"

My face heats with rage. Why am I always the one who has to temper myself to deal with everyone else's bullshit? I tighten my jaw harder and stare straight ahead.

"You're not wrong," he tells me. "This whole situation is unbelievably *fucked*, but antagonizing the detective who's investigating Mama isn't gonna help her—in fact, it might have the opposite effect."

I take a deep, measured breath in and blow it out. "I know. I'm sorry. I'm just tired too."

"I know," he says. "But we got each other, right?"

"Right," I say. "Let's go home."

As I leave the parking lot, I ponder adding Detective Jeida Sommers to my justice list. If she wants to find a murderer so bad, maybe I'll give her exactly what she's looking for.

# TWENTY-ONE
## CLEMENT

Maybe I need to practice letting go.

I've been fighting so hard to hold on to everything and everyone. Yves. Me. Us. School. Family. Friends. But what if I just let go, let it all slip from my hands?

What then?

My phone rings on the floor beside where I'm sitting. It's Isaiah. A jolt of excitement sparks inside me—I answer the call.

"Hey," Isaiah says, his voice so heavy with melancholy, it's almost unrecognizable. "You busy?"

I shut my textbook and glance over at Yves, whose head is presently craned over his own math book and the handwritten notes I made for him. I stare at the crown of his head and the hair frozen at the length it was when he died. He doesn't look up for me to tell him I'm stepping out, so I get up and slip into the hallway without disturbing him.

"No," I say softly, shutting the door behind me. "You okay?"

"Loaded question," Isaiah replies. "But not really, if I'm being completely honest."

"Is that why you haven't been at school?"

"Yeah. Last weekend, Mom told me she's letting Dad move me to Chicago full-time. The next morning, she came in my room and asked if I was going to school, and I said no. And I said no every day until she stopped asking. It only took three."

"What?" I exclaim. "Why's she letting him take you to Chicago?"

He scoffs. "Because her side of the family is full of super-conservative religious hypocrites who claim I make them uncomfortable, and my mom is tired of them making slick comments about how I walk or talk or that I sometimes paint my nails and wear eyeliner. They don't like that I'm gay and that my mom's 'accepting' of it. And instead of standing up for me, she's shipping me to Chicago so she won't have to deal with her family's judgment anymore."

"I'm sorry," I offer, even though I know it won't change a damn thing.

"You know what's most frustrating about this shit? I played Dad's stupid game. I was his perfectly behaved 'straight' son all fucking summer, and it *still* wasn't enough. It's never enough. I'm never gonna *be* enough." Isaiah lets out a shuddering breath before the line falls silent.

"Fuck," I mutter. "I wish there were something I could do."

"I appreciate that, friend. You have your own stuff going on. I'll survive. I only have two more years before I can leave and never look back."

"I read in a book once that sometimes we have to pretend if we want to survive, and that's okay so long as we don't lose ourselves in the act," I tell him. "No matter what happens, Iz, remember who you are."

Isaiah sniffs. "Thanks, Clem. I love you."

"Love you too. Can I make a good-luck gris for you? I can bring it by tonight."

"Yeah," he says. "I'd like that. Maybe it'll help me out the way yours did for you last summer."

I chuckle uncomfortably. "You never know."

We hang up, and a pang of anxiety hits me in the chest because I just assigned myself yet another obligation. But it's for Isaiah—so it's worth it. At least this is one of the few situations I can actually affect, even if only in a minor way. It's something.

When I step back inside Yves's room, he looks up at me, expressionless, though I've been around him consistently enough to pick up on what he wants or needs without him having to verbalize it. I'm wrong a lot, but at least I'm trying.

I give him a thumbs-up. "I'm okay."

He returns to reading, and I sit on the floor facing him so our knees touch, the bare skin of mine pressed against the soft cotton of his sweats.

I suck in a big breath and blow it out slowly. Yves closes his book and sets it aside. When he looks at me, his eyes twitch with the slightest hint of a frown not fully realized.

"I lied to you," I tell him. "I'm not okay."

He stares into my eyes, silently urging me to go on.

"Isaiah's leaving for Chicago this weekend," I say. "I'm less sad about him moving than I am pissed about him being trapped with his homophobic dad who's salivating at the opportunity to traumatize his gay son full-time now."

Yves turns his empty gaze down to the floor. I feel bad sharing something so heavy with him when he's . . . in this state, but I feel like I'm going to explode if I don't talk to someone.

"And I'm tired and grumpy all the time," I continue, unable to stop now that I've gotten going. "And all the homework and quizzes and tests and projects and papers and other shit just never fucking end. It's like I'm sinking in quicksand."

He takes both my hands in his chilly ones and holds them tight. I glance at them, then at him. And I know it's time.

"There's something else I have to tell you," I say, trying very hard to ignore the way his fingers flinch against mine.

I've already told Yves about Ben's murder and how Mama's the prime suspect, but I omitted Fabiana's involvement in the whole thing. But I can't carry that deceit anymore. It's too heavy, and if I don't off-load some of this weight, it's going to crush me.

"Your sister is missing," I tell Yves, and he draws his hands back into his lap, which hurts like a slap to my naked heart, but I barrel on because I must. "And we, I mean, I, uh, I'm trying to find her, but I don't really know what I'm doing."

And then I tell him the truth. About everything.

I start with how I've been lying to Fabiana since November, and he puts a comforting hand on my knee. Of course, he knew. He might've seen the texts early on. In a twisted way, I kinda hoped he'd find them so I wouldn't have to explain to him myself how I was willfully deceiving the only person in the world who loves him more than me.

I catch Yves up on our visit with Mama in jail that led to the trip to his home, how we found the smashed bottle of Ho-Van Oil, and our subsequent trip to the House of Vans and conversation with Colby about Nite-Lite.

"I'm just so frustrated," I say through gritted teeth. "I can't make sense of anything, yet everything is riding on this."

My breath catches, and it feels as if my throat's constricted to a hair's breadth.

"Everything's a mess," I say. "I don't know what to do or if I'm going to be able to save you, and I feel like a villain for what I did to you. I was so stupid for not telling Fabiana the truth from the beginning because maybe she could've helped us, but now it's too late, and she's gone, and I don't know where she is, and—"

My pulse heightens until I can feel my heart pounding painfully in my chest, engorged with anxiety. And suddenly, it's boiling hot in the room, which triggers the cool beads of sweat that brim on the crown of my forehead. I wipe them off with the back of my hand and look up as Yves gets up.

He puts one hand on my shoulder and gently lays me back until my back rests on the floor. I stare up at Jean-Louise's popcorn ceiling and the dust motes trapped between the crags of ugly off-white paint. Yves places my hands on my chest and holds them there.

He hovers over me for a second, and his empty dark eyes find mine. The dense nothingness of them makes me uncomfortable, but I don't look away. This is what I chose. This was the only alternative to never seeing him again, letting some mortician sew his beautiful eyes and lips closed and pump him full of embalming fluid before lowering him into the ground to be forgotten.

But these new dead eyes are like black holes that I fear are going to suck me in if I get too close. Except I already feel lost forever, so what do I have to lose?

Yves gives the top of my hands a soft pat, then stands and leaves the room. He's gone for several minutes, during which time I lie still, focusing on the rise and fall of my chest, taking shallow breaths at first, until I start counting. By the time I reach ten, the room has cooled, the air's no longer suffocating, and I don't feel like I'm being dragged to the never-realm by my throat.

*I fucking* hate *panic attacks.*

I rise to a sitting position at the same time Yves returns, leaving the door propped open. He's carrying a large book with a blue cover that's most definitely not one of our schoolbooks. It's old and thin, with an embossed image on the front that I think is a sun at first, until Yves sits beside me, and upon closer inspection, I realize it's a moon with rays of moonlight spiraling out from it. The title of the book is *Practical Applications of Moonlight as an Advanced Medium for Moon Magic*.

"What's this?" I ask, though I know he can't answer. "I thought Jean-Louise took the all the magic books to the storage shed out back."

Yves opens the book and flips to a page, then hands it to me. I skim the text and pictures, which look very old and were hand drawn in black ink. The section talks about using moonlight as a "means to reveal things hidden in plain sight in the natural realm." I read that last part aloud and look up at Yves curiously. "But what does that mean?"

My eyes shift over Yves's shoulder to Jean-Louise, who stands in the open doorway like a ghost. I didn't even hear him open his bedroom door across the hall. His eyes narrow at us as he storms up, snatches the book from my hands, and slams it shut.

"I said *no* magic!" he shouts at me.

"We weren't doing magic," I tell him. "We were *reading*. And why are you yelling?"

"Did you think I was fucking around when I warned you about the Moon King?" he asks, the deep lines in his furrowed brow intensifying with fury. "This is *serious*, Clement. You boys don't get to keep hitting the reset button when you get a game over."

"Don't patronize me, *Jean-Louise*," I tell him. "That's *not* what's going on, but you might know if you came out of your musty-ass room once in a while."

"Watch it," he warns. "If you can't follow my rules, you won't be welcome here anymore."

I look at Yves, who watches both me and Jean-Louise, silent and expressionless, just like Auguste Dupre, the prisoner Jean-Louise keeps locked up down the hall because he's too busy sulking to do what it takes to save him. But I don't say that—as badly as I want to—because I don't need him banning me from this place.

At least not yet.

"Fine," I tell him.

I lean over, kiss Yves on his cool forehead, and whisper, "See you later," as I get up and brush past Jean-Louise.

I need to go home and make Isaiah's gris anyway so I can give it to him before his parents take him away from me too.

# TWENTY-TWO

## CLEMENT

Saying goodbye to Isaiah gutted me. And that pain is what led me to what I'm about to do now.

The whole drive home from Isaiah's house, I couldn't stop thinking that both that good-luck gris that I made from one of Dad's old purple Crown Royal bags and I are useless and pathetic. It just feels so trivial compared to what Isaiah's up against now. But I didn't know what else to do.

Existing in a constant state of powerlessness is so gotdamn exhausting.

It's twenty minutes to midnight, and the crickets chirp from where they sit hidden in the thick grass on either side of the narrow paved road cutting through our estate. The sky is clear, so the Moon shines extra bright tonight, providing ample lighting for the ritual.

The candles and other magical items shift in the reusable shopping bag I clutch in one hand as I walk toward the giant willow, one of many on our expansive estate, at the crossroads that leads to the other areas of our property.

At the intersection, I remove four silver candles from my bag and set one on each paved corner of the crossroads. I walk around and light them, repeating a line of the incantation aloud after each is lit. "Four pathways. Four beginnings. Four ends. Four realms connected to one another."

Then I exchange my lighter with another of Dad's purple Crown Royal bags, which, believe it or not, come in handy quite often. I've already filled it with offerings.

A pack of cinnamon gum.

A mini bottle of Tru Reserve that I nicked from Aunt Rosalie's purse.

A cigar that I likewise borrowed from Jean-Louise's house.

And a small plastic baggie filled with those coffee beans that Cris and Odessa are obsessed with.

I toss the offering bag into the middle of the crossroads and step back until my shoulder blades press against the wide trunk of the steady centuries-old willow behind me.

I need answers, so I'm going straight to the top.

"I summon you, Papa Eshu." I don't shout because I don't need to. However, my voice is bold and unmistakable. "Accept my offering and my audience. I beseech you, Guardian of the Crossroads."

And then I wait, listening to the nocturnal orchestra of crickets, frogs, and other creatures cloaked in the surrounding flora. Even the fireflies have come out to sway in the already-humid early spring air, blinking in and out of view with brilliant sunset-orange light. I'm lost in the beauty of it when the sound of a shoe crunching on blades of grass interrupts my experience like a record scratch.

I don't move.

The shadow of someone stretches into my peripheral as they step from behind the tree. I clench my jaw to hide how my heart races once I realize the summoning worked.

Papa Eshu's come to see me.

He walks past me with his onyx cane and the same pronounced limp without acknowledging my presence. He's dressed in an all-black suit with a black top hat, like a fashionable grim reaper—which I find particularly unsettling. But I'm not going to let him rattle me.

He steps to the center of the crossroads and takes his time stooping to pick up the offering. When he stands again, he turns and approaches, his head down, completely focused on rifling through the bag's contents. He stops a few paces in front of me, then removes the cigar and the coffee beans and makes an exaggerated show of inspecting and sniffing them for quality. Once he's done, he pulls the drawstring taut and pockets the bag.

"Thank you for the generous gifts," Papa Eshu says, finally lifting his enchanting dark eyes to mine. The glowing full moon on his wrist, the Mark of the Gods, flashes as he readjusts his stance to lean on his ornate cane. "What is the meaning of this summons, child of the Moon?"

"I need your help," I say.

Eshu's brows pinch together. "With what, exactly?"

I take a deep breath to still my wavering nerves. "Last summer, someone murdered Yves Bordeaux. I–I didn't know what to do, so I led a necromancy ritual that brought him back to life, but his soul was fractured in the process, and part of it has already transitioned to the spiritual realm." Papa Eshu listens patiently and without reaction, which puts me a bit more at ease with opening up. "Except he's different now . . . with only part of his soul. I don't know how to make him whole again, and I was hoping you could help."

Eshu's brow relaxes, and he purses his lips. "Oh, Clement," he says in a tone that twists my stomach into knots. "Death is hard, even for us gods. That's just the way things go sometimes. You attempted to change fate, and now you must live with the consequences of that choice. I cannot help you restore Yves's soul, as decommissioned Moon magic like what you've done is no longer my jurisdiction—and should be outside of yours as well. I'd advise you not to dabble in such dark arts."

I cross my arms, a feeble attempt at trying to contain the frustrated rage swelling inside my chest. "You *can't* help, or you *won't*?"

Eshu sighs, and his shoulders slump, which feels more like condescension than empathy. "My hands are tied, Clem. Truly, I am sorry."

I scoff under my breath and fight the urge to roll my eyes at the second-most-powerful god next to *the* God. *I call bullshit.* Rules are only a convenient excuse for people in power to say no to whomever they want whenever they want without feeling guilty.

I guess I'm truly on my own. Even faith in the fucking gods is pointless.

Eshu pulls a black metallic pocket watch from inside his coat and checks the time, grimaces, and tucks it away again. "Unfortunately, I need to get going. Was that all?"

I shake my head. "One last question." I push off the tree so I stand full height in front of Eshu, and I stare up into his dark eyes. "Who is the Moon King?"

He stiffens and grips his cane so hard that thick veins plump beneath the dark-brown skin of his hands. "How do you know that name?" he asks, a sliver above a whisper.

"Who is he?"

"Why are you asking me this?"

"Tell me who he is first," I demand.

Eshu pulls himself up taller. "I won't be manipulated, especially not by a child."

"Then you're free to go," I tell him. "You can't help me anyway. The *least* you could give me right now is information."

Eshu shuts his eyes long enough to release a deep breath. Then he leans on his cane and says, "The Moon King is an extremely dangerous ancient god who committed many atrocious acts against humanity in the name of what he called 'blood justice.' When his morally depraved ideals spread to the spiritual realm, he began amassing followers in support of his rise to supreme power among the gods."

"Hang on," I say. "Where was God during all this?"

"In the end," Eshu answers, looking uncomfortable, "it was I who stood up to the Moon King and ended his reign of terror before it began."

I'm annoyed that he blatantly ignored my question, but curiosity gets the best of me, and I ask, "How?" anyway.

"I imprisoned him in another realm from which he can never escape," Eshu says.

I swallow hard, and Eshu keys in on the dip of my throat and narrows his eyes.

"Now," he says, "why are you asking me about the Moon King?"

"My grandma and Jean-Louise both mentioned him to me," I tell Eshu. "But no one knows exactly who he is."

He tilts his head. "And what business does Jean-Louise Petit have with the Moon King?"

I shrug. He can figure anything else out on his own since that's what he's making me do. Not gonna lie, transference of frustration is one of my most prized superpowers.

"Okay then," Eshu says. "I'll be on my way now."

I nod. "Thanks for the audience, Papa Eshu."

He stares at me curiously before disappearing around the other side of the tree.

The brief serotonin boost from unnerving Papa Eshu doesn't last long because I'm back at square one.

As I collect the final candle, the sound of a car's engine starting back up at the house catches my attention. I step back from the road and watch as Aunt Rosalie's car backs out of the driveway and starts down the path toward the main road.

When she gets to the crossroads, she stops, lowers her window, and turns down the volume of the jazz music bumping inside her car. "Hey, babe, what are you doing out here this late?"

I shoulder my shopping bag. "Wasting time. You?"

She chuckles. "I'm wired for some reason, so I'm heading to the office to do some work. I've gotta figure out how to revamp my business in the face of recent scandal."

"Yikes," I say.

"Tell me about it," she says, then pauses to study my face. "Everything okay?"

I nod and wander closer to her car. "Have you heard anything from Fabiana?"

Rosalie looks away and mumbles, "Nope. Nothing."

"Why aren't you trying harder to find her, seeing as how y'all were *entangled?*"

She turns back to me. "Well, for starters, in case you've forgotten, the mayor was murdered at my soft opening, so I've been pretty swamped with shoveling that gigantic mound of shit, and second"—she continues without stopping to breathe—"Fabiana and I were *not* entangled. What we 'had' was off and on—mostly *off*. We were business partners. Dassit."

I lift both hands in mock surrender. "Okay, it was only a question."

She sighs deeply. "Sorry, kid. I guess you're right. I am kinda messed up over her sudden disappearance, but in the short time I've dealt with her, I've learned that when it comes to the enigma that is Fabiana Bordeaux, I'm better served by tending to my own needs." She taps one finger on the bottom of her steering wheel and stares ahead as a smile plays at her lips. "Though she definitely knew how to tend to certain things—"

"Aunt Rose—"

She laughs. "Fabiana is truly one of the most brilliant women, in every aspect—including sex—I've ever met. Did you know that the Ho-Van Oil she created glows in moonlight?" When I shake my head, she nods. "Yep. I didn't either, until she pulled out a bottle one night when we were together. We drew all over each other's bodies with that intoxicating oil and made love by the light of the Moon, high off the fragrance and the experience, our bodies lit up with our secret art. I'll remember that for the rest of my life."

"That sounds sickeningly romantic," I tell her, setting aside my disgust at imagining my aunt having sex.

"I am honestly worried about her," Rosalie admits. "It's unlike Fabiana to be out of contact for so long."

"Did she have any enemies?" I ask.

Rosalie scoffs. "A list of that woman's friends would be much shorter. Though I do wonder if Ben Beaumont might've had anything to do with her disappearance."

"Why do you think that?"

"There's a tape of Ben in a compromising position at the House of Vans," Rosalie says, "which I may or may not have used to grease the runway a bit when it came to getting my regulatory permits and certifications pushed through for Vice Hall." My brow furrows, but before I can respond, she says, "And don't look at me like that. You're too young to understand right now, but sometimes the only way to win against a corrupt system is to use their own tactics against them. Ends justifies the means and all that shit."

"I guess," I say meekly.

"You want me to drive you back up to the house?" she asks.

I shake my head. "Nah, I'm good, thanks. I wanna walk."

"'Kay," she says. "See you tomorrow."

She drives away, and I watch the lights of her car turn onto the main road outside the gates and disappear into the night.

I walk back to the house alone, taking my time with the crickets and the fireflies to allow my thoughts to linger on the interesting tidbits of my conversation with Aunt Rosalie.

The more information I find out about the twisted web of lies and treachery among the adults in this town, the less confidence I have that the police will find Ben's true killer.

I'm still having a hard time believing Aunt Rosalie blackmailed the mayor into helping her get her business off the ground. *Good for her.* That sounds like a trick she might've borrowed from Aunt Ursula's bag.

But one thing sticks out in my mind: I had no idea Ho-Van Oil glows in moonlight.

And then I recall the book Yves showed me earlier, specifically, the entry about using moonbeams as a sort of magical blacklight to reveal "things hidden"—and the realization stops me in my tracks.

I have an idea.

# TWENTY-THREE
## VALENTINA SAVANT

Valentina used Granny's old IG page to identify the fancy dessert stand she'd need to set up the freshly made beignets from the Bean she'd had delivered first thing this morning. Granny had curated her page around what she'd called "Black NOLA Cottage Core." Valentina studied several of the posts to emulate Granny's most decadent tea and snack settings.

She wiped the copper stand down with a soft cloth until it shone under the bright kitchen lights. She draped some of the fancy cream lace doilies she'd found in one of the many kitchen drawers on the stand and arranged a few beignets on each level. Before delivering the desserts to the sitting room, she gave the beignets a fresh dusting of powdered sugar.

Xavier sat in the center of the couch, listening intently to Mom, who sat in an armchair beside him and explained where she'd been for the past nine months. Xavier was a short Latino man with midnight-black hair and a beard that was as full as his ego.

As Valentina set the tray on the coffee table between them, the decorative auto-mister perched on the shelf above Xavier made a soft mechanical squelch as it sprayed a mist of invisible moonglo droplets onto him. It was a special moonglo Valentina had crafted especially for this meeting. She'd even tested it with Mom last night. And that'd been an interesting experiment for more than one reason.

The angry whistle of the boiling teakettle summoned Valentina back to the kitchen, and she whisked away, unnoticed by Mom and Xavier, who were still catching up.

Valentina checked IG once more and pulled down the appropriate sugar and cream containers and the decorated cups, then set up the tea tray. She placed bags of hibiscus and ginger tea in each cup and set the kettle on a crochet pad in the tray's center.

She carried the tea into the sitting room and placed it next to the three-tiered dessert stand, of which Xavier had already cleared one level on his own while Mom talked.

"That's a wild story, Gabi," said Xavier. "I'm glad you're back safe and sound."

Mom nodded her thanks.

"You said you lost some parts of your memory?" he asked. "Do you know what specifically is missing? You seem fairly normal to me—no offense."

"I honestly don't know," Mom said. "It feels like I've lost the parts of me that made me afraid to love myself."

Xavier stared at her curiously, as if struggling to compute what she'd just told him.

"Tea, Xavier?" asked Valentina, throwing him a lifeline.

"Oh, yes, please," he said. "Extra cream, no sugar."

She picked up the kettle and poured steaming water into each cup, then took up her own. "You can help yourself."

She plunked a cube of sugar into her tea and doused it in cream, then sat in the armchair directly across from her mom, who smirked and leaned forward to prepare her own tea.

Xavier looked mildly put out, yet he somehow found the wherewithal to stumble through making his own damn drink.

Valentina sipped hers, relishing the pleasant floral scent. It smelled the same as when she'd first pulled the bags out of the old tin that'd once belonged to Granny, the contents of which had considerably thinned since coming into Valentina's possession. She made a mental note to hit up her granny's favorite tea shop in the Quarter to re-up whenever she got a break from world domination and high school.

"Mmm . . . this is good." Xavier slurped his tea and nodded at Mom.

"Yes, it is," Mom said, and smiled at Valentina. "Thank you, baby."

"You're both welcome," Valentina said.

Xavier cradled the cup in his lap, turned to Mom, and immediately launched into his long list of personal issues, as if she and he were the only people present. Mom glanced at Valentina, but Valentina's calm expression gave Mom the okay to play along.

Valentina would rein Xavier in soon enough. For now, she'd let him spill what he knew. It might prove useful.

"Everything's gone to shit since you left, Gabi," he complained, shaking his head. "I've effectively been closed off from any sort of future. I'm still just a senior director at Savant Capital. I thought I'd get bumped up to partner after Felix died, but he left that nitwit Arturo in charge of the firm, and Arturo hasn't been to the office a single day since it was handed to him."

One thing about Valentina's dad was that he didn't discriminate when it came to spreading his bullshit around. He gave everyone an equal opportunity to suffer for his benefit.

"And now that Ben's dead," Xavier continued, "his interests have been passed on to Eveline, who's apparently decided to remain silent while the other partners circle the blood in the water—most of which is *mine*." He drained his cup and set it on the table.

"And I'm suing my fucking sister because my dad thought it'd be cute to cut me out of my inheritance." He snickered under his breath. "But that's not even the worst of it. I got the fucking cops breathing down my neck because I got tangled up with Karmine Delaney."

Mom sat up, a concerned look on her face. "The Vamp Dejoir?"

"The one and only," Xavier said.

Valentina hadn't ever heard of this Karmine guy, but he must've been somewhat unsavory to elicit that peculiar reaction from Mom.

"He was in Miami last I heard," Mom said. "How'd you two get involved?"

"I've been working with him under the table for a few years now," Xavier admitted. "It was lucrative, and Karmine treated me well, so I kept it going. Mostly laundering money and assisting with setting up supply lanes in preparation to expand an arm of the Divine Knights into Louisiana. He actually caught wind of Rosalie's plans with Vice Hall and asked to partner with her, but she turned him down flat."

Mom glanced at Valentina and then back at Xavier and asked the question Valentina had also been wondering. "Do you think Karmine might've had something to do with Ben's murder?"

Xavier shrugged. "He certainly could have, though I'm not sure how that would've benefitted him."

"Well, the mayor being drugged and murdered on opening night isn't the best way to kick-start a business," Valentina interjected, drawing a pointed look from Xavier. "It could've been sabotage."

"Certainly can't rule it out," said Mom.

Xavier rolled his eyes. "I don't give a fuck about Ben's murder. I'm talking about *me*." He poked his chest with his thumb. "Karmine is getting antsy because he wasn't expecting Detective Sommers to come here and turn up the heat on magical crime just as he's getting a solid foothold in this city.

"They have history, you see. Sommers rode the Divine Knights' asses for years back in Miami. She shaved them down to barely a skeleton crew. That's why Karmine wanted to shift his Miami base of operation to New Orleans. But now Sommers suspects I'm working with him and is threatening me with RICO charges if I don't roll on Karmine. This is so serious. I'm fucking worried, Gabi."

The familiar feeling of anxiety sent a jolt to Valentina's heart. Had she made a mistake inviting Xavier to their inner circle? This mess with Karmine and Detective Sommers might make him too much of a liability. But she desperately needed allies.

Mom sighed hard and sat back. "That's a lot, Zay."

He frowned, deep-set lines crowning his forehead. "No shit. Is that *all* you have to say?"

"And what is it you're expecting from me?" Mom asked. "I could've warned you not to get involved with a man like Karmine."

Xavier scoffed. "I might not have been in this predicament if you hadn't left me for dead."

"Excuse me?" Mom said, calmer than Valentina felt.

"Because you were MIA, Marie and my brat kid sister were able to boot us off the Council," Xavier said. "You left me alone for the jackals to feed on me. If we were still on the Council, I'd have the power of MASC to protect me from Karmine *and* the police. But now, thanks to *you*, I'm a regular nobody again, waiting for my next round of grandiose fucking."

"You should watch how you speak to my mother in *my* house," Valentina warned Xavier, who turned to her with a start. "She survived a very traumatic ordeal. She didn't choose to lose nine months of her life. And you will have some fucking compassion when you address her."

Xavier turned a stunned expression to Mom, who said, "She's right. And if you'd shut up talking about yourself for a moment, we could explain to you how we might *all* improve our stations."

He huffed a shoulder-shrugging sigh and gave in. "Okay, fine."

Mom nodded at Valentina.

"I have a plan to take back the Council," she announced.

Xavier's nose wrinkled. "What is this? I don't have time for high school games." He stood up and waved his hand in Valentina's direction, the whole while speaking to Mom as if Valentina were a toddler. "I already have my hands full with my sister's hormonal teenage bullshit."

Mom raised a brow at Valentina.

It was time.

Valentina rose carefully from her seat, drawing Xavier's attention as she moved closer.

He tensed and took a step away from her, a skeptical frown wrinkling his brow. "What are you doing?"

She lifted one hand in front of her and curled her fingers into a tight fist, calling to the moonglo that had settled in Xavier's throat and lungs over the course of his visit. She felt her magic inside him, like static crackling on her fingertips and zipping along the small hills of her knuckles. She bit her lips and savored the feeling. It was delicious.

Xavier clawed at his chest and dropped to his knees. "Gods! It itches! Wh-What the hell are you doing to me?"

Valentina squeezed harder, digging her nails into the soft skin of her palm.

Xavier gasped and turned his desperate blushing face to Mom, who maintained calm composure from where she sat as if perched on a throne of her own.

They were indeed in Valentina's throne room, and *she* was holding court today.

"Gabriela," cried Xavier through garbled breaths. "H-Help . . . me!"

Valentina held her other hand in front of her and made a fist.

Xavier threw his arms and head back as if they were attached to a tether that had suddenly been yanked tight. Slowly, he rose off the floor, his chest protruding as if his lungs wanted to burst through his rib cage and explode like miniature piñatas, releasing the delectable magic inside that belonged to her and only her.

She drew Xavier closer, the toes of his Gucci loafers hovering just above her prized Mashahir rug. She lowered one hand, releasing some of the pressure on Xavier's respiratory system. They needed him alive after all. Significantly more pliant, but alive nonetheless.

The auto-mister squelched again, and Xavier's eyes shot toward the sound and the light mist of moonglo floating down over his empty seat.

"Fuck," he muttered, "I've been breathing that shit in this whole time." His eyes shot back to Valentina and crinkled at the corners as he released a wheezing laugh. "Moonbeams? Seriously? I am the *Gen Priest*. Do you know what that means, girl? I am stronger than you."

Valentina released her magical grip on Xavier, and he slumped to the floor, then jumped back onto his feet and stumbled backward. He glowered at her, his chest heaving. He threw out one hand and waited for the magic inside him to obey his unspoken command . . . but nothing happened.

The auto-mister squelched again, and Xavier's hand shot toward the mist, and he wriggled his fingers expectantly, his face deeply frowned in concentration. He sucked in a sharp breath the moment he realized Valentina had been toying with him.

She clenched both fists in front of her again. Xavier didn't have time to scream. He didn't even get to release the breath he'd sucked in, the same one that caught in his throat as Valentina squeezed it from the inside with the special moonglo she'd curated.

The kind that only obeyed *her*.

Valentina floated Xavier back into his seat on the couch and stood over him. She lowered one hand, and Xavier exhaled and sucked in a fresh breath, moaning with relief. He flinched when she took a step closer and used her magic to tilt his chin up so his dark eyes couldn't escape her.

"You seem to have a bit of a machismo problem," she told him.

"We're not hormonal—we're just sick of your bullshit. And now two women are gonna save your sorry ass from the fate you deserve. But first, you will understand that *I* am the head bitch of this operation, and you *will* respect me, or I'll make Karmine Delaney and Detective Sommers look like the gotdamned Care Bears." She narrowed her eyes. "We good?"

"Y-Yes," Xavier sputtered.

Valentina opened her hand and waved it to one side, evaporating the moonglo inside him. "Please don't make me do that again," she cautioned him, and returned to her seat. "From here on, I'm going to assume we're all on the same page."

Xavier touched a hand to his throat and looked at Mom, who nodded. He turned back to Valentina, frowning still. "But why not your mom? She was Queen before—"

"She's had her chance," Valentina snapped.

She'd rather not revisit the difficult conversation she'd had to have with her mom prior to forming this little alliance. The one where Valentina had to draw a line in the sand to make it indisputably clear that *she* would be Queen. And *no one* was going to take that from her. Not even her mother.

Valentina had no remorse about smothering Mom's dream before it'd taken its first breath inside her head. A little of the light in Mom's eyes had died at the tail end of their talk, after she'd acquiesced to Valentina's terms, which meant Mom would never reclaim her throne or the legacy she'd allowed to slip through her fingers once already, in exchange for the opportunity to forge a relationship with her daughter.

"It's *my* era now," Valentina asserted.

"Queen Mother suits me just fine," Mom added. "Valentina deserves this."

Mom did a good job of cloaking the pain of regret in her voice, but Valentina knew somewhere deep down inside, Mom was still mourning the dream she'd lost, just like Valentina had grieved the life she deserved but would never know.

"You're so much like Lenora, it's kinda scary," Xavier said.

"No," Valentina said. "I'm *better.* And let me tell you why."

Both Mom and Xavier poured themselves fresh cups of tea and settled in to hear Valentina's plan.

"Madeline DeLacorte is gathering allies in preparation to petition MASC to reseat the Gen Council," Valentina said. "And if that's what she wants, we can give it to her. But we need to get Eveline Beaumont on board first."

"Well, good fucking luck," Xavier said. "Eveline's already sided with Marie. She's the one who had me thrown out of the Council Chamber last year."

Valentina shook her head. "Eveline's just trying to keep chaos at bay while she launches her bureau, but Marie's legal troubles and Madeline's constant threats are making that difficult for her. And I'm proposing the three of us present Eveline with an offer she won't be able to refuse."

Xavier's brows rose with heightened interest.

Valentina shared her and Sofia's plan for Sofia to fake ally with Cris to get their hands on the evidence that would clear Marie's name, which they would then offer to Eveline—the chance to get rid of one major obstacle to her career goals.

"And once Queen Marie is taken care of," Valentina continued, "Eveline can offer Madeline the new Council she's been crying about. Of course, we'll reinstate you as Gen Priest, Xavier. And once I'm Queen, you'll have the Gen Council's and MASC's protections again." Valentina dipped her head toward him, and the ghost of a grin twitched his lips at one corner. "It's a win for everyone involved."

"We should consider bringing Eveline into the fold of our alliance at some point," Mom offered. "I have a feeling she's brewing something big with the Magical Regulation Bureau. And I think it'd be smart to have her as an ally as opposed to an enemy once it all goes down."

"I don't know," Xavier said. "I'm not sure I trust that woman. There are rumblings going around town about magical registration. If that goes down, I'm willing to bet Eveline's bureau will be the one to implement it. Something ain't right with all that."

"No worries," Valentina said. "We'll cross that bridge when we get there."

Eveline's intentions with the MRB were part of a riddle that Valentina was determined to solve. The answer could turn out to be the key to reclaiming her power.

Cris Trudeau was a fool for ever counting Valentina Savant out of the game.

# TWENTY-FOUR
## CRISTINA

If I never hear the word "foxglove" again, I'll know I'm in the spiritual realm, but for now, I'm trapped in the never-realm for the entirety of my Sunday morning and afternoon, while Ms. Mattie Belle oversees the brewing and blessing of her foxglove tincture, which I'm having to remake since the police confiscated the bottle Mama had made for her as evidence in their investigation.

I ask Ms. Mattie why she won't just get Justin to make it for her since I can't seem to get it precisely to her liking, and then she looks at me, her angry brown eyes magnified behind her bifocals, as if I just called her mama out her name or something, and says curtly, "The pier is *too far* for me to drive. Your mama ain't teach you to make foxglove yet, child? It ain't that hard—least I thought it wasn't, but judging by how you struggling today, I'm not so sure anymore."

I want to tell her if it's so damn easy, then she should be able to do it herself, but instead, I smile and tell her I'm trying my best.

Once I'm rid of Ms. Mattie Belle, I set aside what little remains of my evening to get caught up on schoolwork before Mrs. Todd rallies my other teachers to send DCFS to storm our estate. Except I can't muster the energy to complete a single assignment.

Clem told me Isaiah's going to one of those private schools in Chicago where homework is optional. The concept sounds nice, but homework is a far less traumatizing thing to have to deal with than a homophobic parent. When Clem said he'd made a luck gris for Isaiah, I whispered a prayer to Eshu and the other gods to give it an extra boost of power. I really hope Isaiah's okay.

I slam my chemistry textbook closed with an exasperated groan. I'm tapped out. I get up from my desk and fall facedown onto my bed.

Being Queen is far more responsibility than I ever could've imagined. It's so much more than sitting on a grand throne and strutting around in glamorous gowns and crowns and using magical prowess to get whatever you want (ahem, Lenora and Valentina). Every day is an epic fight for your life and the lives of the people in your community, people who look to their Queen for guidance and protection. And there are a million different ways to do that with ten times as many outcomes—and none are easy. This is why not everyone's cut out to be Queen.

I've begun to wonder if even I have what it takes.

I'm about to blow my evening plans and text Remi to see if he wants to hang out (as friends, obvi) when my phone vibrates with a text from Eveline Beaumont.

EMERGENCY COUNCIL MEETING TONIGHT AT 9 PM. PLEASE BE ON TIME.

I'm annoyed instantly, and the caps lock doesn't help.

Hello Eveline. It's a school night and I have a bunch of homework. Can it wait until tomorrow?

IT ABSOLUTELY CANNOT

Okay but what is this even about???

IF YOU ARE UNABLE TO FULFILL YOUR DUTIES, YOU CAN ELECT A PROXY OR I CAN LOOK INTO OTHER OPTIONS

Fine. I'll be there at 9

OK

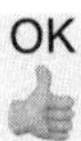

I roll my eyes and text my brother immediately.

Hey Clem

Sorry to be dramatic at the 11th hour but I really need your help tonight

PLSSS

Hey! I got you. What's up?

* * *

I only have a little over two hours to get ready for this emergency meeting, so I plunder Mama's closet in a mad dash to find something proper to wear. My heart's already thrumming against my rib cage, and it almost explodes when Odessa's low, earthy voice comes from behind me.

"Cristina . . . what's the matter?" When I turn around, Odessa's eyes shift from the pile of dresses in my arm to meet mine. "I can feel your frantic energy from all the way downstairs."

"Oh, I'm fine," I tell her. "It's fine. Everything's okay. I just, um, Eveline called this silly emergency meeting last minute, and I'm trying to find something to wear and—" One of the dresses slips from the top of the pile, and I drop the entire load I'm holding when I attempt to catch it. Odessa tries to intercept them, but when we both fail, I release a frustrated sigh that feels as if it's been pinned inside me for ages.

Odessa takes my hands in her strong wrinkled brown ones and tugs me close. "Why didn't you ask me to help you, child?"

"I, well, you already had so much on you with Mama gone—"

She tuts under her breath and pulls me so hard into her arms that my feet almost leave the floor. It's ridiculous how strong Odessa is even at her age. She puts her arms around me and cups the back of my head, and for that moment, I feel weightless. My guard falls away, and the tears waste no time pushing to the forefront, and within seconds, I'm full-on sobbing in Odessa's arms. She just rubs my back and hugs me while I expel all the emotions that I hadn't even realized I'd been shoving aside.

"Listen to me, baby," she says, still hanging on to me. "This is the most important thing I will ever say to you, so if you forget everything else, always cling to this: Life will forever be a challenge, but whenever it feels too hard, too rough, too unkind, remember, you're never alone. Cristina Serafine Trudeau, you are the descendent of Queens, and that means that even when it seems you're standing all alone, you have a long line of ancestors at your back."

She rears back and wipes my face with the tail of her apron, then smiles at me with the strength of the Moon and Sun, the warmth of which burns away some of the cold dejection that settled inside me like a layer of winter frost.

"You've done your grandma proud too, and that means the world to me," she tells me. "And you will continue building on her and your mama's legacy—with your own. And I'm incredibly proud of you."

I smile for a sliver of a moment before that internal freeze returns. Would Grandma Cristine and Odessa still be proud of me if they knew the truth of what I've done?

As if she read my mind, Odessa tilts her head and says, "I *said* what I said."

The way she looks at me and the firm tone of her voice makes me wonder if Odessa knows more than she's letting on. But that can't be. She couldn't know I was the one who killed Tabitha Edgewater and Dr. Thomas—could she? I'm afraid to delve even a millimeter into that topic with her because I couldn't handle Odessa being disappointed with me. Not now.

"Now," she says, "you have a Council meeting to prepare for. And we can't have the Queen showing up late—or raggedy."

She picks out a lovely taupe-colored sleeveless trumpet gown with two flowing capes over each shoulder. She braids my hair up into a bun and covers it with a masterfully tied seven-knotted tignon the same color as my dress. Clem comes home while I'm dressing and starts thumping and thudding around in his room, so Odessa goes to corral him while I do my makeup.

Since we're short on time, I do a simple beat on my face with a dramatic eye. I'm extra proud of my work when Clem compliments me on sight, which helps calm my nerves a little; except they continue to ratchet up the closer time draws to 9:00 P.M.

Clem's dressed in a white button-up and a black vest, tie, and pants. I can't help but grin when I see him because even when my little brother hardly tries, he's still somehow annoyingly dapper. No wonder Yves fell for him so fast and hard—that boy never stood a chance.

Every thought of Yves stings. I have no idea how Clem's holding up through this. I know more than I deserve about carrying around crushing guilt and grief, and I hate that my brother's suffering similarly. And what's worst is I feel powerless to help him.

Odessa sees Clem and me off, and I drive us to St. John's Cathedral. The closer we get to our destination, the faster my heart beats. I don't know why Eveline had to be so secretive about the agenda for tonight's meeting, but the whole thing makes me uneasy. I get us there quickly, and Clem walks next to me up the sidewalk to the church.

I sigh and stare up at the soaring gray-capped steeples that stand sharp against the purpling cloudless sky lit by the majestic glow of the distant Moon. I wish I were attending my first Council meeting under different circumstances.

"I can tell you're nervous," Clem says.

"You don't know my life," I tell him with an annoyed half smile.

He chuckles under his breath. "You were born for this. You're living the legacy you fought so hard to save last summer. That means something."

"But what if Mama goes to prison? We could lose everything—again. This isn't like last summer. It's an active murder investigation."

"Mama's confident that her lawyers are gonna get her out of this. Maybe we should trust her?"

I cut my eyes up the path ahead to the tall wooden doors of the church instead of at him, because I know he's only trying to help. "Yeah, but waiting around for someone else to solve the problem feels treacherous. Mama could be found guilty of a crime she didn't commit and could go to prison for the rest of her life—or worse."

"I don't even want to think about that," Clem mutters.

"Neither do I." Especially not considering I could very well be joining her for the murders that I actually *did* commit.

I close my eyes for a brief second before climbing the steps to the church's entrance.

The interior is deserted and dimly lit, which makes the stained glass stories depicted on the towering windows appear more like nightmares.

We slip through the secret entrances and follow the same path we first took last summer to descend into the bowels of St. John's Cathedral.

The ancient tunnels cutting through the earth beneath the church have never been particularly inviting, but tonight the passage is extra dank, the cobwebs are extra thick, and it's *extra* dark everywhere down here. I have to turn on my phone's flashlight so Clem and I can see how to get to the Council Chamber.

"Why aren't the wall sconces lit?" Clem asks.

"I'm not sure," I say.

I take his hand, and we trek the remainder of the way to the Council Chamber in anxious silence. I'm sure the lights are just a random coincidence, but for some reason, it doesn't bode well for me tonight.

"You ready?" Clem asks when we reach the double oaken doors leading to the Council Chamber. When I nod, he tells me, "You got this."

"I do," I say, and glance at my watch—9:01. "Let's get this over with."

Clem throws open the doors, and we enter together—and stop short just inside.

The chamber room is blanketed in the deepest, scariest darkness that presses in on us from every angle. At the far end of the room, a pitiful light catches my attention, coming from several candles lit in the candelabra hanging above the central dais.

"What the hell's going on?" whispers Clem.

"I'm not sure," I whisper back.

We stride down the bloodred center aisle, hand in hand between the gargantuan stone columns on either side of us caped in velvety shadows. As we approach, I make out Eveline Beaumont, Justin Montaigne, and Aurora Vincent, each standing in front of their separate thrones.

Eveline wears a sharp pink pencil dress and a heather-gray shawl draped over one shoulder. Justin's in a wrinkled blue suit, the coat of which he's tossed onto the arm of his empty throne. Aurora's in a cloud-white spring dress, and her hair's pushed back behind her ears, where it falls in loose waves down her back. The only makeup she's wearing is a light-pink lip gloss, which makes her face look ethereal in the flickering candlelight.

None of them seems to have put forth as much effort as me to dress for the occasion, as if Council meetings with a proxy Queen don't quite count as the real thing. They couldn't even be bothered to turn on the lights. I feel foolish and small at first, but then I tilt my chin up when I remember this is my first meeting as Queen. I'm done letting people invalidate me.

This is *my* Council Chamber.

Clem and I step onto the dais, and Eveline glances down at her watch, displeasure already pruning her mouth. "This meeting will be quick," she grumbles, "which seems ideal as we have nowhere fitting to sit."

"Huh?" I peer around her at her perfectly good throne. "What's wrong with your seat?"

Justin steps over and runs a finger along the arm of Eveline's throne, then turns the dust-coated pad of his finger to me. Several dust bunnies float to the ground in the low light.

"Okay, but why do you have an attitude about it?" I ask Eveline. "Is this supposed to be my fault?"

"No," Aurora says. "That one's on me."

"You've both shirked your responsibilities to this council *and* your communities," Eveline scolds. "I'll remind you that not only does our staff *not* work for free, but they are also unionized. The reason dust and darkness have taken over our beloved Council Chamber is because the entirety of the Cathedral *and* Council staff are on strike due to nonpayment of wages. I convinced them to do so quietly until our Gen Priestess finally took care of her fiduciary responsibilities."

"I already told you I'm going to the bank to sign the authorization paperwork and transfer authority of the Gen Council's accounts first thing tomorrow morning, Eveline," says Aurora. "It's not an excuse, but these sorts of tasks aren't exactly easy in the middle of my brother waging war on me over our father's estate."

Eveline focuses the whole of her ire onto Aurora, who doesn't flinch. "The *only* reason we even still have a staff is because of their loyalty to your father, a loyalty you have *yet* to earn. Lorenzo's not here to protect you anymore, and I'll see you removed before I let you run this organization into the ground."

"Hey!" I interject, my voice echoing in the cavernous chamber. "Cut Aurora a break. You *know* she's going through a lot right now."

"And *you*." Eveline rounds on me. "You stand to bungle the stability of the entire magical world with your childish ineptitude. Did you honestly think your duties began and ended with a title, a throne, and a pretty tignon? Surely, you knew there was more to being Queen than throwing lavish community events and strutting around"—her eyes trace the length of my dress—"in ill-fitting gowns?"

I throw my hands up on either side of me. "Okay, but nobody told us we were supposed to do all this stuff."

"Ha!" Eveline scoffs. "*Told* you? Are you a queen or a servant?" She steps closer to me and lowers her voice. "You talked big shit to me that night on the *Montaigne Majestic*. And after all that, I must admit"—she pauses to look me over once more, her harsh gaze stripping me bare—"I'm disappointed in the lot of you."

Anger flares my nostrils. But I will not let Eveline intimidate me. I stare into her deep-brown eyes, which look black in the dim light, and call back to her name scrawled at the bottom of my justice list. How satisfying it'll be to cross it off one day.

"Since this council has been turned over to the hands of *children*," Eveline continues berating me, "you've allowed the very fabric of this institution—which we have been delicately weaving for *generations*—to come apart at the seams."

"Eveline," says Justin, holding up a hand. "Take it easy, now. They're just kids. They're under enough pressure as it is."

"I don't need to be babied," I snap at Justin, whose face twists with surprise. "But it would be nice if everyone who has an opinion on what I am or am *not* doing would just tell me what the hell I'm responsible for so I can handle it already."

"Well, you might've been able to get that had you not killed your predecessor," Eveline retorts.

Clem scoffs dramatically, drawing everyone's attention. "Because there would've been a peaceful transition of power, right?" Eveline scowls at him, and he inches forward protectively, his shoulder brushing against mine. "Whether you like it or not, we're here, Eveline. And none of us can accomplish what we want while we're fighting and being disrespectful to one another. And speaking of respect, Cris might be Mama's proxy while Mama's busy clearing her name, but Cris is still your Queen. And that means you should probably show a lot more respect for her." He nods at Aurora and cuts his eyes back to Eveline. "For all of us."

Eveline's frown deepens. "Queens *earn* their respect." Before I can rebut, she points to a giant lumpy sack sitting off to one side of the dais that I hadn't noticed until now. "And she can begin with reading and replying to all the correspondence from her subjects."

"Is that thing full of letters?" I ask, eyeing the oversize sack. "Jesus H., did they send them by raven too?" When Eveline only offers a stern glare in reply, I add, "Those can wait for when Mama returns."

Eveline rolls her eyes. "Fine, but that's not all." She reaches into the interior pocket of her shawl and produces a wax-sealed envelope, which she hands to me.

The golden wax bears the symbol of two hands connecting their outstretched thumbs and pointer fingers, a small flame centered in the open space between.

"What's this?" I ask.

"It arrived this evening. A letter from the Arch Dejoir of the French vamps, who's presently at odds with the Gen Duke of Cairo over some artifact they've been warring over for the better part of a year," Eveline says, rolling her eyes. "Things are apparently heating up over there, and they both would like their Queen's counsel." I start to open the letter, and she says, "Not now! That's not why I called you here."

"Okaaay," I say, making no attempt to hide my irritation.

"Unfortunately, we have even bigger issues at hand," Eveline announces. "Our good friend Madeline DeLacorte has requested an emergency meeting of MASC that's to take place in a week, to give time for the white mage and warlock Cardinals and Vamp Dejoirs to arrive."

"Arrive?" asks Aurora. "This meeting's in person?"

Eveline nods. "It hasn't been confirmed, but I'm fairly certain Madeline intends to petition MASC to reseat the Gen Council after Ben's election and . . . death." She cuts her eyes at me before looking away.

I'm about to say something when the gentle tap of Clem's fingers on my hand stops me. He gives a furtive shake of his head when I glance at him.

*Fine. I'll let her live. Tonight.*

"As interim Queen," Eveline says, eyeing me now, "the duty falls on you to speak on our behalf at the MASC meeting."

My chest tightens, and I struggle to draw the next breath, panic amping up my heart rate. "What am I supposed to say?"

"That is for the Queen to decide," Eveline tells me. "And you only have a week to get it together—or abdicate your throne."

Before I can respond, she descends the dais and heads for the exit. Her phone's flashlight shines a bright beam in front of her as she disappears into the tunnel beyond.

Justin puts a hand on my shoulder, making me jump. When I turn to him, his brown-eyed stare is gentle, pitying even, which annoys the hell out of me.

"You okay?" he asks.

I nod, tight-lipped.

He looks curiously between me, Clem, and Aurora, and when no one offers him a word, he follows Eveline.

Once he's gone, I fall back onto my throne with a huff, then immediately burst into a fit of coughs from the puff of dust that blows up around me.

Clem sneezes and fans the dust motes out of his face.

"Sorry," Aurora says. "Really."

"Girl, you don't have to apologize," I tell her. "We've all fucked up, apparently."

"Very on-brand for me," Clem says and grins. "Welcome to the club. I'm already working on our graphic tees."

I groan, and Aurora laughs so hard, she snorts.

"Thank you for having my back earlier," Aurora tells us. "Both of you. Between trying to get caught up with school and fighting Xavier in court, I feel like I was running a race, tripped and fell, and now I'm being dragged by my ankle and can't get back up."

"Relatable," Clem mutters.

Aurora points at him and winks.

"Any news?" I ask her.

"Yeah," she says, "but nothing good. Xavier's lawyers are ruthless. I'm in danger of losing everything if he doesn't quit. I could very well be unhoused soon—"

"You would *never*," I interrupt.

"Nope," Clem adds.

Aurora smiles and glances down at the floor. "I appreciate that. I'm in a real bind. At this point, Xavier's not even willing to split our father's estate down the middle. He thinks that because he's the male heir that he deserves everything."

Clem rolls his eyes. "Dick ain't *that* good."

"I was never convinced," Aurora says.

It's Clem's turn to wink and point at her. They make me so sick that I can't help but grin.

"But I'm struggling with a huge dilemma right now," she says.

"What's wrong?" I ask.

"Detective Sommers called me this morning—"

I groan. "Aurora, please do not get mixed up with that woman. She's framing my mama for Ben Beaumont's murder."

Aurora held up her hands. "I know, I know," she says. "But hear me out."

"Let her talk, Cris," Clem tells me, and I pipe down, though I don't like where this is going.

"Sommers says she's trying to get Xavier on RICO charges," Aurora reveals. "She thinks he's doing business with the Divine Knights, who she suspects have been trying to set up a new operation in New Orleans. She asked if I'd help her investigation by digging up some dirt on my brother for her."

I slide to the edge of my throne, my eyes instinctively narrowing. "And what did you tell her?"

Aurora shrugs. "I told her I wanted no part in her or my brother's mess."

I sit back and let out the breath I'd been holding, then immediately regret it when I cough again.

"But I dunno," she continues. "If it hadn't been for you, my brother would've let me waste away in Chateau des Saints. He got away with it, and still, he's trying to take everything. Would it be so bad if he were gone? He can't sue me from prison."

"Aurora, you can't," I plead. "Please don't get tangled up with that woman, not after what she's done and what she still plans to do to our community. There has to be another way to deal with your brother."

She buries her face in her hands. "I dunno, Cris. I dunno. I dunno. I—"

I get up and step onto the lower platform in front of my friend and take both her hands in mine. "Listen to me," I tell her. "We're in this together."

Clem wanders and leans on the edge of Aurora's throne, inadvertently knocking loose more dust. He coughs and chokes out, "Yeah, me too."

Aurora laughs and shakes her head.

"Our troubles might be wearing us all thin, but at least we have each other," I tell her. "And we'll get through this too."

We embrace beneath the woeful candlelight, sharing what final dregs of strength remain between the three of us.

My phone vibrates with a call, and I frown at the screen when I see who it is and decline it.

Sofia Beaumont calls again, and I'm about to decline once more when Aurora puts a gentle hand on my arm, stopping me.

"Wait," she says. "Could be fate calling. See what she wants."

With a heavy sigh, I answer the call. "What's up, Sofia?"

# TWENTY-FIVE
## CRISTINA

It's not hard to secure an empty booth at the back of the Bean since I sit down with my hot chocolate just before 7 A.M. the day after the emergency meeting. I decided on the drive over to cut back on caffeine because my nerves are already tattered enough without me being artificially wired too.

I sip my hot chocolate and plunder the million and one potential reasons Sofia Beaumont needed to meet with me so urgently.

My booth has a prime view of the coffee shop's main entrance, so when Sofia strolls in, I notice her before she sees me. I wave her over, and she slides into the other side of the booth. I'm hit with a familiar whiff of her coconut-cream hair conditioner and the sweet, citrusy perfume she loves, which smells good but reminds me too much of air freshener. But that's quintessential Sofia Beaumont—sweet and misplaced.

Today her outfit is all black, from the ankle boots, to the stretch pants and the cute cinched blazer over the satin button-up, to the black snapback with her curly ponytail exploding out the back. It reminds me of Janet Jackson in "Rhythm Nation," which I was forced to know because Mama and Daddy were *serious* Janet and Michael fans. I don't know if Sofia's outfit is intentional or a coincidence, but knowing her, it's probably the latter.

"Thanks for meeting with me," she says, as she rotates the black fanny pack she's wearing around her waist so it rests safely in her lap. I know her coveted tarot cards are inside. They're never far away.

"Sure," I say. "How are you?"

She shrugs. "I'm here."

"Understatement of the century," I say, which conjures a small smile from us both. "We don't have much time before homeroom, sooo, what'd you want to talk about?"

"Your mom's arrest and my dad's murder," she says matter-of-factly, as if we're talking about prom committee.

I listen purely out of respect for my former friend, considering she's grieving. I know firsthand how devastating the death of a dad is. Sofia's good at turning up the sunshine and blinding everyone from what's really going on; but I have an idea of what lies in the darkness just on the other side of that joyful glow. People like Sofia, the ones who corral every iota of darkness behind distracting light, are dangerous. Because when they finally shut that light off, they unleash all the unimaginable things that've been festering for ages in the shadows.

"I'm listening," I tell her.

"I don't believe your mom killed my dad," she says.

"No shit," I say, but hold up a hand in apology when she sighs at me.

Sofia clutches the small bag in her lap and draws her shoulders in, shrinking in the oversize booth. "I get that you don't want to be besties again and might not trust me right now, but I want to try and earn back that trust. You know, I've always admired your strength—in magic and in life. I want you to know I *never* agreed with how Valentina treated you."

I roll my eyes. "If you felt Valentina was wrong, then why'd you never stand up for me?"

She hesitates before saying, "Because I'm weak? I regret it so much. I want to make things right between us."

"Conveniently after you and your bestie fell out? I'm nobody's rebound, friend or other." I sit back and cross my arms, watching the rejection register on Sofia's face.

I start to feel guilty, but then I recall how I felt that night, watching that Instagram video and realizing the two people I trusted most in the world aside from my twin brother had betrayed me.

"I'm not asking us to restart our friendship," Sofia says. "All I want is for us to work together on uncovering the truth about my dad's murder."

I'm not exactly in the position to turn down help right now—not when I'm drowning in obligations and issues. Clem has his hands full. Same deal with Aurora.

"Fine," I tell Sofia, and her eyes light up at once. "But this is *only* a temporary alliance to find out who really killed your dad—something we both have a vested interest in."

Sofia nods. "That's fair."

I lean forward and steel my gaze on the gentle brown of her eyes. I don't miss her subtle recoil. I lower my voice so only she can hear, and I say, "And let me make something perfectly clear with you up front—if you screw me over, I will rip your soul from your body with my bare hands and flush it straight to the never-realm."

Sofia blanches, and her eyes widen.

I sit back and narrow mine at her. I hope she knows I'm deadass. If I might already be going down for multiple murders, what's one more lumped on?

Sofia nods tentatively. "I just want to find out what happened to my dad. I swear."

I lift my hands and say, "Then you have nothing to worry about."

"H-How would you feel if I did a reading for us?" she stammers.

I raise an eyebrow. "You haven't done that already?"

"Not exactly," she says. "I mean, I don't know. I thought the answers would be clearer, better, if we did it together, y'know. Combined our energies?"

I sit with that for a moment before responding, sifting through the memories of all the cool shit I've uncovered while digging through the ancient volumes stored in the Council's library.

"You know what?" I say, and Sofia perks up with surprised intrigue. "That's not a bad idea."

"You serious?" She shakes her head and leans back in her seat. "Wait. Please don't make fun of me, Cris."

"What?" I grimace at her. "Why would I do that?"

The bright brown skin of her cheeks flushes, and that's when I realize. Valentina Savant strikes again.

Valentina should be more careful how she treats people. Monsters aren't born—they're made.

"Look," I tell Sofia, "I'm not Valentina."

"She never respected it—the cards, I mean," Sofia replies.

"Why not?"

"She said it wasn't *real* magic."

I laugh. Sofia makes a face until I say, "That's bullshit. Tarot *is* real magic."

"Huh?"

*I hadn't intended on giving a history lesson before actual school, but we're here, aren't we?*

"Tarot and astrology are both branches of divination," I explain, "and divination is a form of Moon magic. But after the War of the Moons, divination got lumped into the 'taboo' category of magic, along with necromancy. That's the only reason it's not associated with gen magic today."

Sofia's brows lift. "But divination's way more palatable than necromancy," she says, "so how'd it get the official axe too?"

"The War of the Moons wasn't about pleasantries," I explain. "It was about *power*. Light-magic users were terrified that Moon-magic practitioners, primarily Black and brown folks, were doing some truly extraordinary shit with our magic. Divination *and* necromancy were the most dangerous parts of our culture, resources that threatened to upend centuries of carefully crafted systems of oppression that white people had painstakingly built. And they simply couldn't have that.

"Recently, divination has become more widely accepted, but only after white folks turned it into a caricature of what it once was, fooling most of the world into thinking divination is a farce, a hobby at best. And do you know what the shittiest part about the whole thing is?" I pause, and Sofia shakes her head, desperately clinging to my every word. "They did such a good job spinning that narrative and were so insidious with installing it in our communities that now Valentina and people who think like her push the racist agenda on their own. One of the greatest tricks white supremacy ever pulled off was getting people of color to self-police in our own spaces."

Sofia blinks a few times and lets out an impressed breath. "Holy shit, Cris. I had no idea. And Valentina talks about this stuff all the time."

"Well, now you know." I sip my drink, which has effectively transformed into cold chocolate now.

I almost pity Sofia, seeing how Valentina has broken her down over the years, the same way she did to me. I honestly hope Valentina might change for the better now that she has her mom back. But my gut tells me that's incredibly naïve of me.

Reinvigorated, Sofia unzips her bag and takes out the beautiful carved carrying case for her tarot deck. She takes precise care opening it and handling the cards, as if they're the rarest, most precious artifacts in the world. And to her, they are.

She shuffles the deck, the loud flapping of the cards' plastic edges drawing the attention of a lone woman in a nearby booth. Sofia ignores her and asks me, "What do you want to know?"

"But you already know—"

"No," she says. "You need to ask for clarity on a particular situation, and then the ancestors, using the power of the universe, will communicate an answer to you—through the cards, which I'll interpret."

"Oh, okay," I say, and drop my voice so no one overhears. "Got it. Ummm . . . I'd like clarity on the murder of Ben Beaumont—specifically who *really* did it."

Sofia hands the cards to me, and I shuffle them and cut the deck a few times, the same way I do when Clem and I are whooping Ursula's and Rosalie's asses at Spades, which I miss. I hand the deck back to Sofia, and she fans the cards out in her hands and tells me to pick three.

I run one finger along the slick backs of the cards, choose three at random, and place them on the table one by one. Sofia arranges them in a line, giving a soft "hmm" with each one.

The first card is the Fool, which makes me frown.

Next is Justice, but it's reversed. *Interesting.*

And last . . . Death. I know the Death card isn't literal, but it's unnerving nonetheless.

Sofia leans forward, studies the spread, then mutters, "Oh . . . this is intriguing."

"So, are you going to tell me what all this means?"

"I just did a simple past, present, and future spread since we're short on time." She taps the Fool card. "The Fool in the past position represents the innocence and wonder of exploring new opportunities. The Justice card reversed in your present position symbolizes dishonesty and unfairness that's being brought to light, considering the cards on either side of it. And last, the Death card in the future position signifies new beginnings and the end of cycles."

"But what do we do with this information?" I ask her. "How does this help us?"

Sofia's brows knit, and she glowers at the cards. "Hmm . . . the past has already happened, so we shouldn't waste too much time there. I typically like to think of that position as the control sample, y'know, to make sure we're tapped into the right vibrational channel. The future hasn't happened yet, so we can be less concerned about that one, so let's focus on the present." She slides the Justice card up, then spreads the deck again to one side of the table. "Choose one card for a double click on the present. Let's see if we can get more clarity here."

"Okay," I say, and pick another card at random, then hand it to Sofia.

She turns over the Emperor and says, "Oh." When I look at her and raise my brows, she explains, "The Emperor represents authority and ambition." She glances up at me with concerned eyes. "Could my dad's murder have been a power play by someone?"

"That seems likely," I say. "If only the cards revealed names."

I silently recall Aunt Desiree's announcement that she plans to call for an election and run for mayor herself. But she couldn't have done this, especially not considering whoever's responsible is trying to frame Mama, her own sister—or could she?

"Maybe not names but clues nonetheless," Sofia says. "The Justice card reversed might mean the killer is someone who's been wronged or unfairly treated. And the Emperor card implies that whoever this person is, they're very structured and organized, which they'll need to be to ensure they get the justice they've been denied this time—almost as a king would be—particularly one who's preparing for war."

"Does your dad have any enemies who might fit that description?"

Sofia shrugs and looks down. "A lot of people hated Dad, especially after he ran for mayor and tons more after he was elected. I honestly wondered how he even won. I steered clear of all that because I didn't want to know if Dad deserved all that hate or not. So I don't know details. I'm sorry."

"It's fine," I tell her.

I can't blame Sofia for not wanting to see the worst parts of her dad, though if you insist on keeping your eyes shut for too long, life has a way of forcing them open.

She sits back and ponders the spread in front of us. "Let's do a double click for the future position. Select another card, please."

I choose a random card and hand it to her, which she flips over and places underneath the Death card. It's the Tower.

"Holy shit," she mumbles.

"What's it mean?" I ask, leaning forward with barely veiled curiosity.

"The Tower card means a functional shift in our world," she explains. "Coupled with the Death card, that could have major implications on the future of our community."

"Is that good or bad?"

"That depends on what cycles are ending"—she taps the Death card—"and which are beginning"—and then taps the Tower card—"but either way, some *major* shit's about to go down. It's probably already started." She swallows hard and meets my gaze. "You might wanna hold on to your ass for the foreseeable future."

Chills trickle down my back like icy summer rain, which makes me hug myself. Tight. I'm unable to find the proper words to describe how terror, frustration, panic, and exhaustion are all battling one another to consume me. All I can do is heave a profound sigh.

"Okay," Sofia says, confidently charging onward, which is endearing right now because I'm usually the person driving, except I'm all out of gas at the moment. "Let's start with what we know."

I recount my side of the story for her, starting with me and Clem hearing screaming and finding the doors of Vice Hall locked and ending with our interview with Sommers before being released.

"So it makes sense to assume whoever committed the murder either hid among the rest of the guests or could've entered and escaped through Rosalie's office window—which they left open," Sofia says.

"I suggested that to Sommers, but she's too concerned with twisting the story and evidence to fit her idealized version of events." I don't fight the automatic wrinkle of my nose at the mention of that woman. I still can't believe Sommers would stoop so low as to manipulate Aurora into doing her dirty work.

"How likely is it that the murderer could've hidden among the guests?" asks Sofia.

"Not very," I say. "Whoever did it would've been covered in blood, but of the people in the room when everyone woke up, only my mama had blood on her. The real killer definitely fled the scene."

"And that would mean . . ." Sofia taps her chin while she thinks. After a few seconds, her eyebrows shoot up, and she snaps her fingers. "I got it!"

"What?" I ask, cautious because I don't want to slip into a state of relying too much on Sofia. I still don't trust her farther than I can throw her, and I'm not that strong.

"Vice Hall is in a business district, right?" she explains. "What if some of the other businesses had external cameras? They might've caught a glimpse of the killer leaving that night."

"You don't think the police already tried that though?"

She slumps in her seat. "It's better than the nothing we had twenty minutes ago."

"You're right. Let's meet up at Vice Hall this evening after school. I'll text you a time later."

She nods. "Sure."

Sofia takes a picture of the spread with her phone, a customary practice of hers, and then I wait patiently for her to pack up her cards. When she's done, she looks up at me and smiles.

"Can, I, uh . . . tell you something?" she asks.

"Yeah?" I reply.

"You were always going to be a better Queen than Valentina."

I'm not sure how to take those words coming from this particular person at this specific time in my life, so I just say, "Thanks, Sofia."

And we leave the Bean for school.

# TWENTY-SIX

## CLEMENT

The one thing that keeps me motivated throughout the slog of the school day is the promise of going to see Mama with Cris the moment the final bell rings.

Cris insists we drive separately because she's meeting Sofia Beaumont later. My sister claims her ex-bestie is a temporary ally who is only interested in finding her father's real killer, which is their mutual goal. I don't have the time or patience to dig into *that*, and, besides, I'm extra annoyed when she tells me about all that because I intended to ask her to come with me to Fabiana's apartment tonight, but now I suppose I'll have to wait.

I don't make a fuss though since ~~both Yves and I~~ I have homework due in nearly every class tomorrow, though the delay is no less vexing and undoubtedly the most unbearable part of having to depend on someone else. I'm not a fan of trading autonomy for vulnerability, but I'm also fresh out of choices.

As much as I hate to admit it, and as frustrated as I am with Cris, I really need my sister to go back to the apartment with me. I don't think I can go there alone again. I feel stronger and safer with Cris by my side, and no matter how mad we may get at each other, that's always been true. I'd *never* turn my back on her.

Not even when she blatantly lies to my face about murdering our enemies in cold blood.

Yeah . . . I saw *that* article the other day when I brought Yves's morning newspaper up to him. And once I read it, Cris's strange behavior the day Mama had been arrested suddenly made sense. I'm not as mad about her dishonesty as I am worried about the darkness inside her.

Lenora and Felix Savant, Tabitha Edgewater, and Dr. Thomas were all undeniably vile people who got what they deserved, and I'll never feel sorry for any of them. But what concerns me about Cris is the possibility of that unchecked rage transforming her into someone I can no longer recognize and connect with, someone far darker and more villainous than the best friend with whom I've shared every second of my existence. That's a type of abandonment I don't want to *ever* think about again.

So I kick those distressing thoughts into the shadiest, cobwebbiest corner of my mind and focus solely on navigating the various security checkpoints at Orleans Parish Prison with Cris, who, thankfully, does all the talking to check us in at the front desk.

A guard takes us along the same path to the same tiny visitation room we were in last time. Cris and I sit in the same creaky chairs on the opposite side of the same gray table. This is becoming way too familiar, which disconcerts me. The only thing new is the overpowering scent of bleach wafting up from the floors and table, which still bear wet streaks from a recent cleaning.

It's not long at all before the door opens again and Mama walks inside wearing her usual brown jumpsuit. She looks good, healthy, albeit a bit slimmer, which worries me that she's not eating. I don't know if it's the food or the stress or both. I wish I could take her away from here. She doesn't deserve this.

She smiles when she sees us, and her eyes glisten in the sterile white light of the meeting room, but I sense something more behind the happiness on display, which I clock at once as a façade meant to hide the intense sadness sitting just on the other side.

"My babies!" Mama exclaims, spreading her arms as she rushes up and crushes us both in her embrace before Cris or I can stand to greet her properly. "No, no, sit," she says after releasing us, and takes her seat on the other side of the table. "How are y'all?"

Cris and I share a quick glance, and I lie first. "We're good, Mama. How about you?"

"Still fine, baby," she says. "My attorney, Namina Falana, says all the evidence against me is circumstantial. She's putting a ton of heat on Sommers and thinks she'll have me out of here soon."

One of the many, many knots in my chest unravels at the news. It's a promise, and I know how unreliable those can be, but I've been without hope for so long that I'll devour whatever crumb I can get my hands on.

"That's good," Cris says.

Mama nods, still smiling. "Gods willing, I'll be back home where I belong in no time." She turns to Cris and asks, "How's Council business?"

It's my sister's turn to fidget. I squeeze her hand underneath the table, and she calms a bit.

"Madeline DeLacorte's called an emergency meeting of MASC," Cris tells her. "She wants them to vote to reseat the entire Gen Council."

All the happiness bleeds from Mama's face at once. "She *what?*" She draws a deep breath in and pinches the bridge of her nose, then blows it out again with a soft chuckle. "That woman truly is a gift each and every day of her miserable life." She takes a moment to collect her thoughts and says, "Okay, we're obviously gonna have to call in Ursula for help with this."

"What?" Cris exclaims. "Why?"

Mama looks at her curiously. "Surely, you don't think I expect you to deal with the Magical and Spiritual Coalition on your own? Cristina, please be serious. Holding down Council duties is one thing, but this problem is out of your league."

"No disrespect, Mama, but I disagree," Cris replies. "I meant what I said when I took the Queen's Regard. I should be the one to speak for the throne that we wouldn't have if I hadn't fought so hard to reclaim it for us."

Mama sits back and clenches her jaw tight, studying Cris for several tense quiet moments.

"Okay," Mama says. "This isn't as daunting as it may seem. Your strategy should be to buy us time."

Cris nods. "Okay. Got it."

"And then once I'm out of here, which will be very soon," Mama says, "I'll handle Madeline DeLacorte, personally.

"I'll give you a quick rundown of everyone on the board of MASC and how best to approach each of them," Mama tells Cris. "But first, there's something else I need to tell you two."

I sit up, anxiety stiffening my spine.

"This is going to be your last visit to this place," Mama tells us, a boldness in her tone that communicates this decree is not up for debate.

I glance at Cris, who's visibly fighting to keep quiet.

"All this"—Mama gestures around the room—"is traumatic. And I don't want this foolishness to rob you of your childhood. This is my bullshit, and it's my duty now to get out of it and back to you." Resolve hardens her stare, which shifts between me and my sister. "I swear. Nothing is going to stop me from coming back home to my babies."

Her words, another promise, fade to nothing as the temperature in the room nose-dives, and a muted buzzing fills my head.

Mama's cutting me off too.

# TWENTY-SEVEN
## CRISTINA

There are a lot of Black-owned businesses in Vice Hall's neighborhood, and my and Sofia's plan relies on the strength of our assumption that most of the business owners support Mama as Queen of the Gen Council and, as such, would surely be interested in helping her find justice.

I hope.

The Sun starts its disrespectfully early creep down beyond the horizon, which reminds me of how much I loathe daylight savings as Sofia and I wander the blocks surrounding Vice Hall. The encroaching night makes it more difficult to spot cameras as we scour corners of buildings, peep under awnings, and survey parking lots and alleyways.

It's not until our second canvas of the area that I notice the small one-way street nearby that leads to a surface parking lot for customers of the shops on this block. Clem mentioned parking here the night of the soft launch.

The alley cuts through to the next street over, splitting the lot in two uneven sides. Several dumpsters sit at the bottoms of ramps that lead to the docks and back doors of several businesses, one of which is a bakery whose sign proclaims the name Yay! Beignets! And then I spot the camera perched above the back entrance to the bakery.

"Up there," I tell Sofia, and point to it.

She glances up and grins.

I lead the way around front and inside the brightly lit bakery. It's decorated in pastel pinks and yellows and smells of fresh bread and sugar, nauseatingly so, and yet, my mouth still waters at the endless treasure trove of beignets on display. They sell so many that they have an entire glass case dedicated specifically to them.

A stocky aggressively balding older Black man with a salt-and-pepper handlebar mustache and beady dark eyes greets us from behind the counter.

"How can I help you?" he deadpans, his face unfriendly. My eyes find the badge clipped to his chest with his name, LANCE, spelled out in block lettering above his title: GENERAL MANAGER.

Sofia jabs me conspicuously with her elbow, which Lance of course notices. He frowns when I step up to the counter.

"Do you own the security camera overlooking the parking lot out back?" I ask.

His expression softens a little, and he nods. "Yeah. Had to install it myself because customers kept complaining 'bout these knucklehead kids who wouldn't stop breaking into cars back there. What is it? They get you too?"

"About three weeks ago," I tell him. "The night of that big party a few doors down at Vice Hall."

His eyes narrow, and he looks us both over long and hard. "Funny you should ask," he says, not unsuspiciously, "the police came by asking for my camera footage from that exact same date. A lot of stuff happened that night, but I don't remember no car break-ins."

"Was there anything . . . strange on the footage from that night?" I ask him.

He shakes his head. "Something happened with my cloud storage, and the files for the entire day *and* night were all corrupted. Couldn't help you if I wanted. Sorry, girls. Wanna buy some beignets?"

Sofia purchases a dozen, which she asks Lance to split into separate boxes so I can take some home. My first thought is I can't wait to share them with Clem. I wish I could deliver them to him now at Jean-Louise's, instead of waiting for him to find them on his bed after he wanders in at some ungodly hour. But he'd never allow it. I once mentioned coming over to help them study, and Clem almost had a panic attack. He didn't have to say it, but I know he doesn't want me to see Yves in the same state as Auguste. He doesn't want me to witness what he's done. I get it—and I respect it.

I wish we could both be more vulnerable with each other about our individual darknesses. It's annoyingly ironic that I'm the closest

I've ever been to my twin brother, yet this is the furthest I've ever felt from him.

"Can we just go look back there one more time?" Sofia asks once we leave the bakery. "We might've missed something. Maybe someone else has another camera hidden somewhere since robberies have been an issue back there."

"Won't hurt," I say, and we walk back around to the rear of the building.

The Sun has left this part of the world, darkening the canvas of the sky that's awash with dense clouds blotting out the Moon and most of the Stars. Pitiful streetlamps on either side of the lot buzz to life, though they aren't too effective at fighting back the night's hoard of shadows.

We stand in the partially empty parking lot, our heads craned upward, scanning for additional cameras, and neither of us notices the pile of clothing shift next to the dumpsters at first.

Sofia leaps behind me and grabs hold of my arms.

"*Really?*" I snatch out of her grasp. "That's a person, not the boogeyman."

"Oh," Sofia whispers behind me, and I roll my eyes.

The unhoused person sits up, watching us curiously. Their hair is long and knotted, which makes my scalp ache when I notice. Grime smears their chestnut skin in some places, and their eyes are similarly dimmed—the pain trapped there is tough to stare at for too long. It reminds me of the terrifying image of Aurora trapped inside the reflection of her own eyes.

I wave at the person. "Hi. We didn't mean to disturb you."

They don't say anything at first. Then they stand up and stuff their belongings into their sleeping bag and gather the bundle in their arms.

"I wait here for the bakery to close sometimes," they say in a low, almost bashful, voice. "And sometimes, the nice people who work here give me the food they were going to throw away." Their face contorts into a disgusted grimace. "Except the manager. He's an asshole."

"What are your pronouns?" I ask.

"She."

"And what's your name?"

She looks surprised at first. "Emma," she tells us.

"I'm Cristina." I point to Sofia. "And this is Sofia."

Emma gives us a slight nod. "I heard you say you were trying to find out what happened the night of that party at Vice Hall—the one where the mayor was murdered."

"We are," I tell her. "Did you see something that night?"

"Many strange things happened that evening," Emma says, a chill in her voice that conjures goose bumps on my arms like a draft of cold air. "Gods walking among men." She drops her head and murmurs, "In them."

"Can you be more specific?" Sofia asks.

"Can you spare some money?" Emma retorts.

*Shit.* I pat my pockets instinctively, though I know I don't have any cash on me.

"Why can't you just tell us?" asks Sofia. "Why the quid pro quo? We need *help*."

I glower at her. "Are you being for real right now, Sofia?"

She grimaces back. "What?"

As kindhearted as Sofia can be, she hasn't always been the most considerate of unhoused people. I honestly blame her parents for how they raised her. Once, we were riding in Valentina's car, and when we passed a small camp of unhoused folks, Sofia mused aloud, "Why are they always walking around with coats on in the summertime?" Valentina rolled her eyes and didn't answer. Once I realized Sofia was serious, I replied, "Yeah, I don't know why they just don't leave them in their closets at home." It took her a good minute to comprehend that I was *not* on her side in that argument, and then she didn't speak to me again for the rest of the drive.

But before I can say anything else to Sofia or Emma, the back door of Yay! Beignets! slams open, and Lance, the general manager, emerges with a heaping black trash bag in each hand. He frowns at me and Sofia, but when he sees Emma, he loses it.

Lance slams the bags into the dumpster so hard that one of them hits the rim and falls to the side. "HEY!" he bellows, both startling and confusing me, because why the hell is this dude yelling at us?

"GET OUTTA HERE!" He makes sweeping shooing motions with his hands toward Emma, which sours my stomach on the spot.

She clutches her belongings and scurries away, ignoring my desperate pleas for her to come back.

I round on Lance. "Why'd you do that?"

"Thought I told you girls it wasn't safe back here!" He scowls past us at Emma's back as she disappears at the opposite end of the alley. "That homeless woman is dangerous."

"Unhoused," I correct him.

"Wha?" he says, his mouth hanging open, one thick graying eyebrow raised.

*"Unhoused,"* I repeat.

"What's the difference?" he asks, visibly annoyed now.

"Google it," I tell him. "And she's not dangerous."

He huffs. "The man she attacked a while back might disagree."

I don't believe him for a second. "Emma doesn't seem the type to attack someone unprovoked," I say.

Lance tilts his head down, peering over an imaginary set of glasses at me. "You know her?"

"No," Sofia answers, having suddenly found her voice again.

I shoot her a mean side-eye.

"I saw her assault a man with my own eyes," Lance tells us. "Probably would've killed him had I not intervened. I was staying late, finishing up the evening paperwork, and I came outside to have a smoke. That's when I saw them." He points to the far end of the parking lot beneath the sickly yellow glow of the streetlamp. "He was lying on the ground, kicking and screaming, and she was on her knees over top of him. I ran over and pulled her off, and she crawled away, blabbering about demons or something."

"Demons?" I ask. "Do you remember her exact words?"

Lance tosses his hands up in exasperation. "I dunno," he replies, dragging out the response. "She was probably high out of her mind. Half the stuff these ho—" He pauses when one of my brows shoot up. "—unhoused people say when they're geeked up doesn't make sense."

"She was lucid and coherent to me just now," I say. "Everyone in her situation isn't a drug addict. And even if she *were*, that doesn't mean she's not deserving of respect."

Lance huffs an annoyed breath. "Yeah, okay, but like I said, the guy was beat up pretty bad. Covered in blood. Really bad gash on his head. I helped him up and was about to call the police, but he stumbled away from me and then just took off running."

"Where'd he go?" I ask.

Lance shrugs. "I hope he's okay."

"What'd he look like?" asks Sofia.

Lance runs a hand over the shiny bald center of his head. "White guy. Dirty-blond hair. Maybe in his thirties or forties?"

"You just described a quarter of the men in New Orleans," I say with a defeated sigh.

"He was dressed in a fancy tuxedo," Lance adds. "I assumed he'd been to that party."

"At Vice Hall?" I ask.

"I dunno," he says gruffly. "Didn't think to ask."

Emma was right—Lance *is* an asshole. "Did you get his name?"

He shakes his head. "Look, I already told you this alley is dangerous." He points at us. "Stay from back here, especially after dark. Now, I've warned you. Anything happens to you out here—that's on *you*."

"Well, thanks," I tell him.

He half nods and heads back inside, glancing back at us one final time before vanishing and letting the door thwack shut after him.

"Do you think it's a lead?" asks Sofia.

"A piss-poor one if it is," I say. "We've scoured this area thoroughly. I don't think we're gonna find anything else here tonight."

Sofia sighs with disappointment.

"I think we should call it a night anyway," I tell her. "I have homework that I need to get started on."

"Yeah, me too. So what do we do now?"

"I'm not sure. I'll let you know if I think of something."

"'Kay. I'll do the same."

Along the short walk back to our cars, my phone goes off with three rapid-fire text messages. I pull it out of my back pocket, and the moment I see Eveline Beaumont's name in my notifications, I want to hurl this annoying metal box into the Mississippi.

I open the text thread with dread.

URGENT NEWS
MASC MEETING HAS BEEN MOVED UP
NOW HAPPENING TOMORROW NIGHT AT 9 PM.
COUNCIL CHAMBER.
DO NOT BE LATE.

I take a long, deep breath and shove my phone back into my back pocket.

*Great. This is exactly what I needed tonight—it's right up there with an extra booty hole on my elbow.*

"Everything okay?" asks Sofia.

"Splendid," I reply with a forced smile.

My phone buzzes. Dear gods, drag me to the never-realm. It's Eveline. Again.

ARE YOU GETTING THESE??????????

I hammer out a quick response.

Yes. I'll be there. Thanks for the heads up.

I stare at the screen, anticipating her reply, but I don't even get the three dots that mean she's typing.

Unfortunately, I don't have time to be properly annoyed with Eveline's terrible text etiquette because I now have barely twenty-four hours to convince an international board of magical leaders that my family should remain in power.

No pressure.

# TWENTY-EIGHT
## ZACHARY KINGSTON

Something was really, *really* wrong with Zac Kingston's dad.

After Zac had found him a disheveled and unhinged mess, cowering in the basement, he'd hauled Dad back upstairs, washed him off, cleaned and bandaged his wound, and put him to bed.

Dad had been in bed ever since.

And the whole time, Zac waited. For whoever (or whatever) had hurt Dad to return, like Dad had warned. Zac slept on the couch every night with Dad's shotgun cradled in his lap, ready to blast the head off whoever or whatever was threatening to take his dad away from him.

But no one and nothing ever came.

And with every day that passed, Zac wondered exactly how not okay Dad was—and by extension, Zac too. He was losing his grip on reality, shut in the house with his father, who'd also stopped speaking. Zac thought to call for help once, but when he considered all the questions other people would have and the judgments and consequences that would follow the answers, he killed that idea. So he took care of Dad on his own because no one else could or would.

Dad's PTSD and depression were eternal parting gifts from his military service. And everyone made him a leper for it. It didn't matter to them that he'd gotten that way from putting his brain and body through a meat grinder for the same lazy fucks who sat at home and got fat off the government.

Zac hated them all. Every-fucking-body.

Dad had been wrong that night in the basement. They were not going to die. Zac was going to see to it that they both stayed alive as long as possible.

He was proud of himself after scavenging the expired amoxicillin pills from the bathroom, which staved off his dad's infection. Although he worried that maybe Dad should've gotten stitches. Dad's head wound was healing into an ugly keloidal lump on the crown of his face, which was once handsome but now was gaunt and haunted.

At least he was alive.

But keeping him that way was more difficult than Zac had thought it would be.

Zac had to hit Dad to get him to eat the first day. He hated doing it, but it had been for Dad's own good. After that, simply the threat of violence was enough to get Dad to obey.

Dad ate every meal and set the dishes on the empty side of the bed—where Mom used to sleep—and he kept his back turned whenever Zac came in to pick up the dishes. It'd been a blunt, painful sting the first couple of times, but Zac took it all in stride.

At least Dad was still there.

Even though he only got out of bed to use the bathroom attached to his bedroom.

Zac hadn't ventured back to the basement and was okay with never going down there again. The thought of cleaning up Dad's filth was almost as bad as his nightmares.

Almost.

The dreams were consistent. And relentless. They'd started the first night he'd come back. And they were all the same. A deep and raspy voice . . . masculine . . . and . . . old—but not like a grandpa old, *ancient* old—would ask Zac if he wanted to know what his dad had been up to.

Every time, Zac would search for the voice in his dream. It always sounded close, as if the person stood behind him, whispering into both his ears at the same time.

Almost like . . . it was in his own head.

But no matter how Zac answered, even when he refused, the voice *always* showed him . . . what Dad had been up to.

There was always a door. It was different every time but always there. And behind the door was a room, which also changed; but what happened *inside* those rooms was always horrific and always involved his dad committing unspeakable acts.

Once, Zac opened the door and found Dad sitting naked in the center of a white-tiled floor in a puddle of his own blood. His lips, chin, and chest were drenched in it. He smacked and growled as he shoved his foot farther into his mouth and tore off pieces of tendon and flesh, chewing greedily. He'd already eaten his way nearly to the ankle.

Zac vomited when he woke up.

In another nightmare, Zac opened the door to his childhood bedroom, where a preteen version of him slept peacefully—until Dad crawled from underneath the bed like a ghoul. Zac stood in the doorway and watched his dad strangle the younger version of himself to death.

He didn't want to remember the ones Mom was in. No, he couldn't. They were too much.

He wondered often how fucked his mind must be to come up with such twisted shit.

Because sleep tortured him, Zac learned to survive on as little of it as possible. Besides, he needed to be alert so he could look after his dad.

Dad had seemed fine, outside of sad and frustrated, when Zac left last summer, but the swiftness of Dad's descent into near madness worried Zac. He didn't know if he'd ever get the truth out of his dad about what had *really* happened to him.

Zac hadn't realized he'd fallen asleep until the sound of the front door creaking open jerked him out of his slumber. He sat bolt upright on the couch and aimed the gun at the door—at his dad, who stood like a sentry, staring at him over one shoulder.

Zac thought he was dreaming again at first. He sat the shotgun down and rubbed his eyes. "Dad? Where are you going?"

Dad had thrown on a ratty old leather jacket over a gray tee, jeans, and a pair of worn work boots. Shadows exaggerated his sunken eyes and cheeks, making him appear ghastly and skeletal, as if something had begun sucking the life out of him again.

Dad turned and left.

Zac sprinted over to the front window and watched Dad back his SUV out of the driveway. Before Dad pulled away, he made eye contact with Zac, who stared at him from the window.

"What the fuck?" muttered Zac as his dad drove away.

He threw on some sneakers, grabbed his keys, and bolted outside to his truck.

Dad wasn't driving fast, so he wasn't hard to tail. That was strange. It was almost as if he wanted Zac to follow him. Still, Zac kept his distance and hoped Dad wouldn't pick out his white pickup from the other cars in the city traffic, which thinned as they headed west past the suburbs to a rural area where trees and swampland ruled either side of the highway.

They drove until the Sun nearly set. Then Zac turned a sharp curve and had to slam the brakes so as not to pass Dad's SUV, which was pulled over on the side of the road to the right.

Zac parked behind him and got out in time to see Dad step into the forest.

Zac followed.

The Sun still lit the wood, so it wasn't difficult keeping up with Dad without being seen or heard. After a short straight walk through the trees, Zac emerged onto a dirt path.

He trailed Dad deeper into the forest and surrounding swamp while the Sun sank lower in the sky. As he walked, Zac wondered where the hell Dad was going and if it had anything to do with how weird he'd been acting.

The path ended at a small empty clearing. Dad stepped onto the edge of grassy nothingness and stared up at the darkening sky.

Zac hid behind a tree at the edge of the path and craned his neck up too, trying to find what Dad was staring at, but all he saw was the faint twinkle of Stars in the bruised sky above the treetops. Somewhere behind them, the Sun finally slipped below the horizon.

An invisible fog evaporated from the clearing, unveiling a small one-room cabin. Zac put a hand over his mouth to keep from gasping aloud. None of this made sense. That was most definitely a *magic* cabin, but Dad had never done magic before. Zac knew members of the Gen Council sometimes hired Dad for freelance work—but never magic.

Zac crept out of his hiding spot and watched as Dad approached the cabin and unlocked the door with a key he drew from his back pocket. He pushed the door open wide, exposing the dimly lit room beyond.

Every breath evacuated from Zac's lungs.

He stumbled backward and tripped over his own feet. His ass smacked the ground hard, sending a shock of pain vibrating up his tailbone. He pushed to his feet and took off back down the path in the direction he'd come from.

He didn't wait to see what Dad would do next.

He didn't want to know what Dad had been up to in that cabin.

Zac gnawed the inside of his cheek raw on the drive home.

His world had spun out of control, and he couldn't fix it.

# TWENTY-NINE
## CRISTINA

My brother puts his hands on my shoulders, stares into my eyes, the same as his mottled-brown ones, and says, "You've never let a bitch intimidate you before, and today's not the day to start. You got this, sis."

I hug him. And he squeezes me back. We stand like that for a moment in front of the doors to St. John's Cathedral. Concealed within the surrounding shrubbery, crickets chirp and frogs croak in a nighttime song that feels like a prelude to spring—as opposed to the opening credits of my undoing, which is what tonight feels like.

With such short notice, I didn't have time to shop for a dress appropriate for the occasion, so I reprised my look from the night of our final show aboard the *Montaigne Majestic* last summer. Rosalie was able to recreate my makeup and the lavish bun with the curly tendrils framing my face. And this time, I'm wearing a knotted tignon crown the same midnight blue as my gown.

Clem opens the door, and I head inside first. Aurora, Justin, and Eveline are awaiting on the sanctuary pews. Everyone sits alone, distant from one another, and turns to face me as I walk in. They're all dressed plainly, Justin and Eveline in normal business casual, and Aurora and Clem in the same street clothes they wore to school today, which makes me feel out of place in this gown.

Eveline glances at her watch, all business as usual, and purses her lips. "Are you prepared?"

"I'm ready," I tell her. *No thanks to you.*

I clasp my hands in front of me to hide how they quiver. I'm scared out of my mind and second-guessing everything I thought I wanted before because maybe this *is* too much responsibility for me right now. But I bite down on those feelings and swallow them.

Justin wanders forward and smiles warmly. "You can do this."

Eveline turns a cold stare on me and says, "And don't fuck it up."

I'm about to respond when Aurora pulls me away, and she, Clem, and I huddle near the entrance to the cathedral's basement.

"I handled my shit," Aurora says. "Everyone got paid with interest, and the union's happy again, so the lights are all on down there. I already checked."

"Thanks," I say, clutching a hand over my chest. "My nerves are too frazzled to walk through that dark-ass tunnel alone tonight."

"You're never alone, remember?" Aurora tells me.

I nod. "Right."

"As if I wouldn't walk you anyway," Clem says. "Stop being dramatic. We'll be here when you come back up."

"Okay." I take a deep breath, open the doors, and descend the candlelit staircase into the depths of St. John's Cathedral.

The old dusty tunnel makes me sneeze at first, but I pick up my skirt and hurry quickly through the passageways to the Council Chamber. I occupy the time by running through the canned speech I put together about the importance of my foremothers' legacies, all the positive things Mama did for the community and still has left to do to continue our family's work, and how that all only begins shaping what my own legacy will be, who I will become—what kind of Queen I will be. I only figured out what to say after several panicked hours of scribbling stilted lines in a composition notebook through a dozen false starts until I decided to go with an argument centered around my and my family's passion, which is our legacy, both collective and individual.

I also sift through the copious mental notes on the five members of the Magical and Spiritual Coalition, which I got in great detail from Mama. Thank the gods for her. Especially considering Eveline couldn't be bothered to help, and Justin is generally useless unless his arm's being twisted—and I have neither the time, patience, nor muscle.

I take one last slow, deep breath in and blow it out. Then I swing the doors wide open and enter the Council Chamber.

I stride down the red marble main aisle, a one-girl parade—a Queen. The starry fabric of my dress twinkles and glimmers in the bright light produced by the rows of golden candelabra dangling from the ceiling like miniature suns. I'm terrified, but I hold my head high the entire way.

I'm doing this for Grandma Cristine.

I'm doing this for Mama.

I'm fighting for our legacy. For *my* legacy.

It's not until I'm nearly at the end of the room where the main dais resides that I realize the space has been rearranged. The red stone path ends in a circle at the highest tier of the platform, a detail I hadn't noticed before due to the placement of the thrones. Now the circular portion of red floor has been repurposed as what appears to be an impromptu stage, with six thrones arranged in a ring around the perimeter.

And it's intimidating as hell.

A chilling silence blankets the room as I approach. Every face—every *white* face—turns to me. Every light-colored eye watches me, scrutinizing my dress, my shoes, my hair, my lips, my skin . . . but I won't be rattled. I am a Queen. And this is *my* kingdom. And I will end every person in this room before I let them colonize it.

I step onto the first level of the platform and am close enough to see that each throne sits on an elaborate tapestry at the end of which is a symbol representing the member's magical affiliation: A full Moon for generational magic, which is on the rug beneath Mama's throne, the only empty seat on the dais. A blazing Sun for light magic, and a solar eclipse for shadow magic.

But I notice something else that immediately sets my pulse racing anew.

Of the six tapestries ringing this circle, there is only *one* Moon. Only *one* person who looks like me and practices like me represents me here—and that person is *me*. That feels unfair. And then it hits me like a dropkick to the chest.

This was by design.

I step onto center stage, the middle of the red stone circle, at the same time questioning if MASC has always been a system to keep us gen in check. Does the Queen truly lead this organization, or is our power here only an illusion?

Which begs another, more troubling, question: What is tonight *really* about?

Despite feeling ambushed and woefully unprepared, I hold my head high, clasp my hands in front of me, and turn slowly in place, locking eyes with every person assembled here to pass judgment on me and my family tonight.

Starting clockwise from my empty throne is none other than Madeline DeLacorte. Her fiery-red hair and pearlescent skin practically shimmer in the light reflected from her tiara, which is studded with green gemstones. Hidden beneath a layer of foundation are the rust-colored freckles on her nose and cheeks that run in that family. Her rapist nephew, Oz Strayer, has the same ones. I knew his aunt would be here tonight, but that doesn't make seeing Madeline's smug face any easier.

She's wearing a hunter-green gown with gold chains crisscrossing the breast and held in place by emerald stone clasps perched on her shoulders—which immediately snatch my attention like a doorknob snagging a belt loop.

Those emeralds are charged with light magic.

I can feel it pulsing inside those stones, calling out to me—a telepathic whisper only I hear, a tug on my consciousness only I can feel. I wiggle my fingers at my side and feel the connection to Madeline's magic, which flows through the air in an invisible rivulet like a stream of water. I massage the coolness of it for a moment I spend contemplating why exactly Madeline might wear a dress with charged stones to a place where she knows all magic is nullified.

*What are you* really *up to, white lady?*

I wrap my fingers around the streaming connection to the magic trapped inside Madeline's stones that won't stop pining for me—and then I give it a little *tug*. Not enough to steal it away. But just slight enough that Madeline flinches forward a shade, then quickly dispels the unintentional look of shock on her face. But it's too late.

I saw it. I'm already tasting it. Already enjoying it.

Madeline narrows her eyes at me suspiciously, but I turn to the person on her left and tilt my head in greeting to Steven Grant III, U.S. Cardinal Warlock based in Louisville, Kentucky. His deep-set eyes, bulbous nose, and slivers of pink skin passing off as lips are as cartoonish and unserious as he is. He's dressed in a designer suit made of blue jeans with silver-studded snakeskin boots, but his crown gags me for a second. He's wearing a cowboy hat covered with glittering crystals. That thing must weigh five pounds. Yikes.

Mama's advice on this guy was clear and succinct: "That man is a slave to Madeline's will in exchange for access to her magic and her body, and she's only ever given him one. And yet he would still light himself on fire if she told him to. You will never get his support. He's not to be trusted."

*Understood, Mama.*

Next, I rotate to face the woman on Steven's left, who's far more intriguing than him. Winnie Houghton, the Arch Cardinal Mage from Ireland, who governs all light magic in Europe—meaning there are zero warlock leaders in power on her watch. Not only that, but she's the first trans Cardinal Mage in Europe's centuries-long history.

Winnie has a plush, round face and piercing bright blue-gray eyes. Her stares are quite conspicuous; when she's watching you with those eyes, you know it. She studies me now, devoid of emotion, as if I'm something mysterious for her to decode, something small enough for her to conquer. Her long auburn hair is loose and curled, tumbling over her sizeable bust, which she displays prominently and proudly in her low-cut gown that bears a thigh slit up one side, exposing one voluptuous half leg that's been oiled and glittered for the gods.

Winnie the wild card. She's generally kind but also capable of being twice as mean and is most definitely *not* easily controlled. Fat and trans and proud of both, Winnie is not the typical Cardinal Mage that Bethesda and Madeline DeLacorte were used to, so much so that they actively fought Winnie's bid to become Arch Cardinal even though she had proper succession rights. In fact, had it not been for the support of the man sitting on her left tonight, Winnie might have had her legacy stripped from her, the same way Madeline wants to do to me and my mama tonight.

Next I pivot to the Arch Vamp Dejoir, Raphael Beauregard, a highly refined statuesque man. Literally. His face is wizened and static as if chiseled from stone, and his cold-eyed stare is petrifying. But Mama claims he's mostly harmless until presented with a reason not to be—and honestly? Mood. He kinda reminds me of an uncle who scares the shit out of everyone but who's also the best guy you'll ever meet. He's demisexual and writes short stories and poetry about love and magic. I googled him last night, and a quote of his stuck to the walls of my mind: "The intrinsic euphoria of delving into the complexities of the human mind far exceeds the limited depth and brevity of an orgasm; however, marry the two, and one may temporarily experience what it is like to be a god."

Raphael's wearing a sleek crystal crown with purple amethyst adornments and an exquisitely tailored plum suit with a ruffled black blouse underneath, the lengthy laced sleeves of which pour out from the ends of his jacket sleeves. His wintry silver eyes are rimmed in stark black outlines that call extra attention to his transfixing gaze. I have to yank my mind from his mental clutches, which startles me at first. I don't know much about shadow magic, but something about the vamps and their power makes me extremely uncomfortable. I'm not sure what that something is yet—or if I really want to know at all.

And finally, Mr. Tall and Dark himself, Karmine Delaney, U.S. Vamp Dejoir headquartered in L.A., who sits between Raphael and my empty throne. Karmine's dressed in all black tonight, from his studded crown to his velvet suit, sheer lace top, and high-heeled Chelsea boots. He looks like an expensive shadow.

Mama's briefing on him replays in my head: "That man is highly intoxicating and incredibly dangerous. Raphael keeps him in check mostly, but the best policy regarding Karmine is to stay neutral and distant."

He watches me now with a coy half smile, as if he's sitting courtside at a basketball game. White people sure do love treating the life-altering decisions they get to make about Black folks' lives like trivial games. It's going to be hard for me to keep neutral around people like him.

I stand in front of my throne and speak loudly and clearly—and with authority. "I am Cristina Trudeau, Queen Regent of the Generational Magic Council of New Orleans and Interim Chair of the Magical and Spiritual Coalition, and I am speaking on behalf of my mother, Queen Marie Trudeau." I scan the faces ringing the dais in front of me. "Shall I begin?"

Both Winnie and Steven make confused faces.

Madeline chuckles softly, and her saccharine voice twists my stomach. "You appear to be mistaken as to the purpose of this meeting."

I narrow my eyes at her suspiciously. *The fuck is she talking about?*

Madeline sits back in her throne and steeples her fingers, sizing me up for a moment with a frigid stare. "The fate of the Gen Council has already been decided." She waves her hand dismissively and adds, "This is just a formality, really, so you can set your affairs in order."

"Excuse me?" I snap at her. "I am the Chair of this council! How could you have come to a decision without my input? Without my vote?"

I look at the riveted white faces encircling me, watching me react like a caged animal at a zoo. And then I finally catch up to what's really going on, and the fire that ignites inside me burns all the oxygen from my lungs, flaring my nostrils. I struggle to breathe. I ball my clammy hands into fists at my side to ground myself. I'm just as angry with myself for not catching on sooner.

There are six thrones here for the six people present, which would've presented a challenge when it came time to vote for the fate of the Gen Council. Except I was never meant to have a vote—or a say. Our fate was sealed before the meeting was even set.

I've been playing a rigged game.

MASC is nothing more than another oppressive system created to keep people of color compliant. My stomach churns, as if I found out a group of kids had been pissing in the pool I'd just been swimming in. I'm so mad, I could fight.

How could I have been so naïve?

Systems created by corrupt leaders cannot be reformed. But they can't be ignored either because they won't allow us to exist in peace and harmony without their interference. It's stifling . . . and suffocating . . . and . . . hopeless. And I've had it.

I'm slowly coming to realize how I want to define my legacy as Queen. I have no desire to fix oppressive systems like MASC and Eveline's MRB.

I'm going to blow them all the fuck up.

"I'm afraid things have gotten too far out of control on your council's watch." Madeline's soft, condescending voice drags me back out of my head. "It pains me to do this, especially to another woman, but it's for your own good, hon. The persistent blunders of the members of your council, Queen included, have now put the livelihood of this board and our respective communities at risk."

"Blunders? What are you talking about, Madeline?" I ask bluntly. "Speak in facts, please."

She nods. "Very well then. Has the Gen Council's Reverend Mother of the Temple of Innocent Blood launched a government bureau to regulate magic under your leadership?"

"Well . . . yes," I reply, "but that was already underway long before we took—"

Madeline holds up a hand. "And is your mother presently imprisoned for the murder of Benjamin Beaumont, mayor of New Orleans and husband of the aforementioned Reverend Mother? Can you even fathom the depth of the mess you all have wrought?"

"My mama didn't kill anyone," I announce, not just to Madeline but the whole damn room.

"And what of the deaths of Tabitha Edgewater and Gregory Thomas?" continues Madeline. "There's a magical serial killer on the loose, and I'm willing to bet they're from *your* camp." She points and narrows her eyes at me as if she knows something.

But she doesn't. She can't. She's just trying to shake me.

And damn her because it almost works.

"My mama had nothing to do with their murders either," I tell her.

Madeline sighs and folds her hands in her lap. "Being as young as you are, I understand you lack the capacity to understand the gravity of the situation we're in right now, so allow me to break it down for you. The first white mage in recorded history was Agnes Simpson of Scotland, our founding sister, to whom I owe the meaning of my existence. But in 1590, witch hunters on the order of King James VI, raided Agnes's coven and brutally slayed most of her sister mages.

Agnes and a few others barely managed to escape. She was never heard from again, or rather, the Agnes Simpson from North Berwick, Scotland, was never seen or heard from again.

"But the bigot king was not satiated. He and the nonmagical public launched an official assault on white mages throughout Europe, which drove most of my sisters into hiding, those who weren't brutally murdered—or worse. These witch hunts bled across continents and generations, even sparking the Salem Witch Trials here in America." Madeline leans back and crosses her legs, resting her arms on the sides of her throne. "So I trust you understand now why I cannot allow that to happen again. Not on my watch."

I scoff. "I don't need a history lesson, Madeline, especially not from you, of all people. But I'll do you a solid and not be as long-winded with my response."

Karmine snickers, which draws a wrathful glower from Madeline and Raphael. I don't miss Winnie's brief flash of a smile. My original plan's out the window, and I don't care who I piss off tonight. I will not let this white woman disrespect me in *my* house.

"I'm well aware of the danger of history repeating," I continue, feeling a fresh surge of adrenaline after having effectively needled Madeline. "I'm trying to stop my mama's defamation, similar to what happened to my grandmother thirty years ago. And just like my grandmother, my mama is a light in our magical community that someone's been desperately trying to put out. You're right about one thing, Madeline: We cannot afford to repeat the mistakes of our pasts. But our joint futures rely on us ending our present infighting and combining our efforts against our *common enemy*—unfair magical regulation.

"And while we are on the subject, let me be frank. Eveline Beaumont is no friend of mine, and neither is her Magical Regulation Bureau; however, we cannot help you resolve those issues if you remove us from power. Reseating the entire Gen Council is not the way. I hear you, Madeline, and I understand where you're coming from; but we deserve a chance to fight for the safety and protection of our communities too." Although I doubt these people genuinely give a damn about *my* community.

Madeline sucks her teeth. "Nice try, sugafoot, but like I said before, the decision's already been made."

"*Wait.*" Winnie's thick Irish accent cuts across the space, immediately casting a sour expression on Madeline's sharp face. Winnie holds up a finger and says, "The Queen Regent makes a convincing argument. Magical regulation would be disastrous for all of us." She glances at Raphael and Karmine, who both nod. "MASC was founded to promote peace and magical cooperation among the different factions of our world, not to further alienate one another—especially not someone who's barely had a chance to prove herself. Something to which I can personally relate."

"Are you fucking kidding me right now, Winnie?" Madeline growls, her teeth clenched. "What are you doing?"

Winnie sighs hard. "Changing my mind, Madeline. It's not a novel concept."

"Uh, she's not the only one." Raphael raises one of his heavily ringed fingers. His voice is as cool and steady as his features and demeanor. If statues could talk, I imagine they'd sound like Raphael Beauregard (at least the French ones). "Karmine and I have, uh, had a sudden change of heart as well, and, if I may"—he chuckles—"and, *of course, I may,* I've come up with a bit of a, uh, compromise." He gestures to me. "You are undoubtedly a wise and impressive Queen Regent." Karmine tilts his head in agreement, smiling wide. "Eveline Beaumont and the Magical Regulation Bureau are indeed all our problems, but immaterial to how we resolve that, we simply cannot have a Queen in power who has murdered a government official—it, uh, sends the wrong message for our cause. Nor can we risk a child on the throne while we weather what could, uh, potentially be a greatly tumultuous time. So here is my proposal—we will give you and your council thirty days to prove your Queen's innocence in the case of Ben Beaumont's murder; and if you fail to do so, the next meeting of this board will be to determine who will succeed you on the Gen Council, which will be effective at once."

Madeline scoots to the edge of her throne and snarls, "Hey! I don't agree to that!"

Steven hesitates, captive in the drama of it all, until a sharp glare from Madeline reactivates him like a shitty sleeper agent. "N-Neither do I. We already voted."

Raphael scratches his nose and laughs, both delicately. "It doesn't matter. Winnie, Karmine, and I make up the majority." He pulls his immaculate sleeve back to check his watch. "It's time to wrap this up. I have an early morning flight to Cairo." He looks me in the eye and nods. "Perhaps we, uh, we'll discuss that in thirty days. Or perhaps not. We will see, yeah?" He doesn't wait for me to respond before rising from his throne, dipping his head in goodbye to the others, and leaving.

As if tethered to Raphael, Karmine repeats the farewell gestures and follows the Arch Vamp Dejoir.

After Winnie leaves, Madeline stands slowly, glowering at me with barely restrained abhorrence bristling in her eyes. She can go on hating me until it burns a hole through her chest.

She steps casually toward me and stops, her shoulder nearly touching mine, and says real low, so only I hear, "I don't know who you think you are, but be careful wandering too far in worlds you're not familiar with. You might not make it back home." She sniffs and adjusts one of the emerald clasps on her shoulder, then descends the dais.

I frown at the back of her narrow head as Steven whisks by me in a whiff of cool perfumed air and trails Madeline, his ridiculous cowboy hat crown sparkling like a disco ball beneath the candelabra.

Once they're gone, I'm left alone standing atop the dais. I stagger backward and collapse onto my throne. I have to clasp my hands over my mouth to keep from letting rip the mighty scream that's been building inside me since the moment I stepped into the Council Chamber. Instead, I opt for several long, deep breaths in and out until my nerves settle.

I can't believe it. I did it.

A thirty-day stay of execution is not the outcome I wanted, but it's better than the fate Madeline had planned for us.

I stood up to MASC. Tonight was intended to be a setup—a

slaughter, really—but Madeline DeLacorte made a grave mistake in underestimating me. Tonight I fought for myself and my mama and my grandmother. I stood up for us and our community.

Because that's what Queens do.

# THIRTY
## CLEMENT

When Cris reveals that Madeline DeLacorte colluded with the remaining MASC board members behind our backs to ram through her agenda to reseat the Gen Council, I'm pissed too but not surprised. Hindsight may be twenty-twenty, but my present sight has always peeped the monsters behind the masks worn by Oz and his entire creepy-ass family, especially his aunt Madeline.

I'm more concerned about that woman ending up on Cris's vengeance list. Nobody can help her then. Not even me. Because once my sister's made up her mind about something—even murder—she becomes a freight train barreling toward its final destination. As scary as that can be, I respect that so much about Cris.

"I'm worried," I tell her. "Thirty days isn't very long. What if Mama can't get out by then?"

"I'm not giving up that easy," Cris says. "We won't let them take the Gen Council from us."

"Right," I sigh, yearning to believe her. "How about we start by going back to Fabiana's apartment? There's something I need to do."

She checks the time on her phone and frowns at me. "Now? It's after ten."

"It's the perfect time, actually."

I drive us to the Quarter, and along the way, Cris and I share our mutual outrage over the audacity of the all-white MASC organization that seems as if it were created only to keep melanated people in line, which is their twisted version of "peace"—or "magical cooperation." Having to swallow this knowledge without being able to do anything about it makes me want to gag. And the worst part is, I can never *un*know it, which means I have to live with my new tainted reality, wherein even while ruling the Gen Council, we're still not truly free.

The darker side of me is not-so-quietly rooting for Cris to blow all this shit up. And I'll bring the matches.

"You think they got that search warrant yet?" I ask her as we pass the ridiculously conspicuous undercover cop on the way to the rear of the House of Vans.

"It's been a hot minute," Cris says, "so, probably, yeah."

I hold my breath on the ride up, silently praying the cops haven't destroyed the place so much that I won't be able to get what I need.

Cris and I both release an audible gasp when the elevator doors open.

I want to fall to my knees, but Cris steadies me when I waver.

Yves's gorgeous artwork, the entire hallway collection, lies strewn across the floor, canvases ripped and torn, frames broken, hefty boot prints across the faces of some. The few that were granted the privilege of maintaining their stations on the wall have been knocked askew and likewise defaced.

Cris stoops to pick up one of the ruined paintings. "What the hell?" she murmurs, and leans it against the wall. "I'm so sorry, Clem."

I turn away and continue down the short hallway because I don't know what else to say. Nothing seems appropriate. All this destruction feels particularly cruel and malicious. And now I'm terrified to find what's waiting for me behind the front door, which I have to uncover from a web of yellow police tape.

"I just hope inside isn't a mess," I say as I remove Yves's keys from my pocket and unlock the front door.

"What exactly are we looking for?" asks Cris.

"I think Fabiana might've left a message here," I tell her. "Something only someone who knew her intimately would find."

Cris raises a brow at me. "And *you* knew her 'intimately'?"

I scoff. "Of course not. But Aunt Rosalie did."

"I remember you telling me about that last summer."

"Well, I'll spare you the gritty details, but the other night, Aunt Rosalie told me that Ho-Van Oil glows in moonlight."

Realization dawns in Cris's eyes. "Brilliant."

I nod and push the door open. It's dark and uncomfortably hot inside. I start sweating not long after stepping into the room. The power's still out, so both Cris and I turn on our phones' flashlights and shine them around the apartment.

Only one word can describe the inside of Fabiana and Yves's home: calamity. It's as if someone shook the place up like a snow globe. Drawers upended, lying atop their contents. Furniture overturned and slashed or broken. Cushions taken from the couch and sliced open and tossed aside, their cottony entrails leaking.

Without a word, I beeline for Yves's room. Cris doesn't try to stop me.

I throw open the door of his bedroom. A muted whimper falls past my lips as I shine the light around, surveying the damage.

They destroyed Yves's painting—the one of us in space. Now it lies on the bare mattress of his bed, the frame broken and the canvas ravaged. *What was the reason?*

My vision blurs, and I swipe the beginnings of tears from my eyes. I scan the rest of the room, ignoring the carnage, until I spot the overturned easel hiding beneath sheets that were tossed from the bed. I rip them aside and lift the easel. Beneath it, the canvas lies facedown on the floor.

My hands can't move fast enough. I pick it up and turn it around. I cry out in pained relief and hug it to my chest. It's still intact. They didn't fuck it up.

"You okay?" Cris asks softly from where she stands in the doorway.

"Look!" I show her the sketch, and her face lights up. "I'm gonna take it with me."

She nods. "Yves would like that."

I stand with the canvas safely tucked under one arm, and we head back out to the main area.

"I'm guessing the cops didn't find anything when they searched this place, or else Mama would've told us," Cris says.

"There was nothing to find because they were looking for evidence that Fabiana orchestrated Ben's murder, which I'm betting she had nothing to do with."

"I believe you're right. And there's still the mystery of the bloody guy in the tux who Emma had a run-in with the night of the party."

Cris already shared the details of her investigation with Sofia the other night when they met Emma, the unhoused woman who claimed to have seen someone acting strange the night of Ben's murder, in the same surface lot where I and other party guests had parked. Unfortunately, we don't have anything else to go on, and the bakery store manager chased Emma off before Cris could ask any more questions.

I go to the kitchen and set the canvas on the counter, then locate the spot where the smashed bottle of Ho-Van Oil remains—to my surprise—among the rest of the mess.

"So what's the deal?" Cris asks, standing beside me.

"First, I'm gonna need a little raw moonlight," I tell her. "You're faster since you can conjure it without the full ritual now."

"You can too," she tells me. "I'll show you. It's not very hard."

She takes me over to a door off the kitchen and dining area that leads to a patio and pulls it open, unveiling the dark sky outside, shrouded in thick gray clouds that nearly mute all the light of the Moon. The Quarter has an eerie quiet aura to it tonight, as if the volume was turned down on the usual din that consists of music blaring, people shouting, and the occasional car horn. The balcony overlooks a sequestered side street, which helpfully keeps us out of sight from anyone else, particularly Officer Obvious out front.

Cris steps outside, tugs me out too, and stands behind me. "Put your hands on your stomach," she instructs, her voice gentle over my right shoulder.

I do as she says, and she reaches her left hand around and rests it on top of mine, then puts her right on my shoulder. She pulls back softly, urging me to stand taller and straighter.

*Right. Gen magic requires confidence.*

"Even when we're not conjuring," she tells me, "we have a constant connection with the spiritual realm thanks to our lineage, which is tethered to our souls here"—she pats the hand that rests on top of mine over my belly—"in our gut."

"Why there?" I ask.

"Did you ever wonder why your stomach is often the first place you feel an intense emotion?" I nod, and she says, "Your gut is a thriving ecosystem that helps regulate your entire body—it's the throne of your soul."

"Makes sense," I say. "I mean, whenever I'm anxious, I usually feel it there first. But with all that going on in there"—I shift my hands against my tummy—"how am I supposed to know what's what?"

"I'll show you how to sense your tether," she says. "Close your eyes and focus on the warmth inside you, the center—the sun—of your body's ecosystem."

I shut my eyes and concentrate, though, I can't lie, it feels silly at first. I really hate that about gen magic, how mastery requires such high levels of faith in a person's own skill *and* the gods at the same damn time.

"Once you connect to your center, you can entreat with the gods—"

"Any specific one?" I ask, my eyes still tightly shut.

"Nah," she replies. "Anyone will do."

*Good.* I'm not interested in calling on Papa Eshu for help again after our last encounter.

I nod and immediately feel Cris's hand slide off mine. I take a deep breath in through my nose and blow it out slowly from my mouth. I concentrate on the warmth in my belly, on my core, which starts churning at once—and reminds me a little too much of anxiety. But I think of Yves and push past my nerves, and the sensation vanishes as quickly as it came.

I've lost the connection to my core.

I huff a frustrated breath and let my arms fall to my sides. I open my eyes and glance up at the sky and half Moon above. It appears larger tonight, or maybe I'm just bugging, I don't know. It feels inhumane to be denied this skill when I'm—as Papa Eshu called me—a child of the Moon. Nighttime is my zhuzh. Always has been. The Moon has brought me more consistent comfort and peace than the whole of every story I've temporarily escaped into, of which there were many. I try not to linger on how much I miss reading for pleasure, or else it'll make me really sad, and I don't need that right now.

"Focus," Cris insists. "Try again. You got this."

I wiggle my arms and shoulders and exhale deeply. "Right. Okay." I put both hands on my stomach and hesitate as doubt snakes through my center like a snake slithering through water.

"The first couple of times, you have to concentrate really hard to hold the connection," Cris tells me. "But it gets easier with practice. I swear. It's like learning a new language."

"Okay," I say.

I can do this.

I am a son of the Moon.

I am the descendant of Queens and Kings.

I fucking got this.

I shut my eyes and put both hands back on my stomach.

This time, instead of thinking about Yves, I picture Mama and Cris and my aunts—Ursula, Rosalie, Desiree, and Jacquelyn.

And then Grandma Cristine and Grandpa Baptiste.

And Great-Grandma Angeline Glapion, our grand matriarch who wrote the spell book we still use three generations later. The visions of my grandparents, especially my great-grandma, are fuzzy, because I only got to meet them through grainy photographs from decades ago.

I clench my stomach muscles beneath my hands and recall moments from my past where I've shared magic with my family. Making good-luck gris with Mama during finals freshman year. Perusing only the best gen magic supply stores all over the city with Aunt Ursula. And flipping through the pages of Grandma Angeline's spell book, captivated by the expansive world inside.

"You're doing it," Cris whispers. "It's working." She taps my shoulder. "Look."

I open my eyes, and my mouth falls agape. The Moon beams in the sky, filling out completely and building to a throbbing pulse, begging to be tapped. The clouds surrounding the Moon melt away like cotton candy doused with water.

"Now that you've connected with your tether," Cris instructs, "feel the flow of energy between realms and trace the line straight to the heavens where it connects with the Moon, your conduit, and hold tight to it."

"This is sooo wild," I mutter.

It's as if I can actually *feel* an invisible rope of warm air that connects me to the entire freaking *Moon*!

"You're doing great," Cris tells me, and lifts my right hand from my stomach and prompts me to reach out toward the sky. "You still feel it?"

"Mm-hmm."

"Feel along the length of your tether until you find the Moon at the end," she says. "Then grab hold of it and give it a little twist, just like turning on a faucet." She demonstrates, then gives my shoulder a hearty pat and says, "Go for it."

This feels really strange but exhilarating at the same time. My fingers trace the rope of warm air, which grows hotter and more pronounced the closer I draw to the Moon, until I happen upon a massive warmth as if I suddenly stuck my hand into a hot bath.

"Gods . . ." I utter, breathless. "I can feel the magic pulsing . . . like a heartbeat."

I unscrew the Moon, mimicking the motion Cris made. It's awkward at first because it reminds me of those silly perspective vacation photos everyone takes of pretending to hold up the Leaning Tower of Pisa or touching the tip of the glass pyramid at the Louvre.

But either way—it *works*.

*Ho-ly shit.* This is so freaking cool.

Thin streams of moonlight trickle down from the Moon. Tendrils of blue light spiral through the sky toward the balcony where we stand. I start to freak out as they draw nearer because we don't have a vessel to put them in.

Cris reaches up and closes the Moon's magical tap with one hand.

"Thanks," I mumble. "Uhhh . . . What do I do now? How do I hold on to it?"

"Don't panic," she tells me.

*Easier said than done.*

"You can feel the moonbeams, even if you're not touching them, and command them without speaking," she continues. "Just as you felt your tether to the spiritual realm at your center, you'll want to make a similar connection here."

I sense the moonbeams nearing. It's like at the beach when the undertow tugs at your ankles right before a big wave hits you. And just like at the beach, I cannot control the water.

The moonlight corkscrews through the air at increasing speeds, heading straight for me. I struggle to get a grip on it, the warmth of the connection is familiar, but the sudden slipperiness is new. The magic hurtles toward me, crashes into my chest, and bursts into a million azure sparks of light that scatter in the air before us.

Cris waves one hand gingerly in front of her, and the moonlight melds together into one softball-sized orb of glowing baby-blue light.

"Sorry," I mutter.

"You did amazing for your first time," she tells me. "Better than me even. It took Aurora a few days and like a dozen attempts before I could do what you just did."

Cris directs the sphere of moonlight into the apartment. "Don't worry," she says. "I know you'll get it. Just keep practicing. That's what I did."

"Sure," I say. "Aurora taught you a bunch of stuff, huh?"

Cris nods, then gets a distant look on her face—one I haven't seen in a long time. But as fast as it appears, she snaps out of it. "Not all the credit's hers," she tells me. "I learned a lot from the Council's library too. It's so strange to me that Valentina had access to all that information and still struggled as much as she did with gen magic."

"Maybe she just sucked at it in general?" I suggest.

Cris's brow furrows. "I dunno. But either way, there's so much more you can do with raw moonlight aside from using it as a catalyst for conjuring."

"Like what?"

I miss witnessing my sister get this geeked about magic. It reminds me of a time in our lives when things were much simpler. Happier. Fuller.

"You know how moonlight's kinda viscous and warm?"

I nod.

"Well, you can alter its physical state to transform it into almost anything at your will," she explains.

"So kinda like the T-1000 from those old *Terminator* movies?" I ask.

She groans. "Not exactly, but you get the idea. Watch me."

She holds out her hand, and the ball of moonlight spins above her palm, gradually increasing in velocity until it glows orange like molten lava. When I reach for it, she slaps my hand away.

I glower at her. "Ow! What the—"

"Don't touch that if you want to keep that hand," she warns. "It'll burn right through you."

"Whoa," I murmur. "Is that how you—"

"Yeah," she says abruptly. "I can freeze it too."

He brows pinch as she concentrates, glowering at the orb of orange light, which stills at once and cools, dissipating the heat haze wavering the air around it. The moonbeams return to their usual blue hue but continue lightening until they become nearly white—like a sphere of solid ice. I reach for it again, but I yank my hand back when Cris practically growls at me.

"What is your obsession with touching everything?" she asks.

I shrug. "Habit?"

She rolls her eyes. "Anyway, when you master accessing your tether to the flow of magic from the spiritual realm, you'll be able to delve deeper into that connection, which will allow you to manipulate raw moonlight on a molecular level."

"Okay, but I'd be remiss if I didn't call you out for how you totally sound like a Marvel villain right now," I tell her.

"Clem—"

"Joking! Sheesh!"

She cuts her eyes at me, but I don't miss the slight smile playing at her lips. I hate that if both our lives were simpler, we could have more time for moments like this.

"Anyway," she says, "that's the end of the lesson. If you want, I can grab you some books from the Council Library that helped me."

"Uh, I'm good," I say. "I have plenty to read already."

Navigating the mess with my phone's flashlight, I kneel in the kitchen beside the broken bottle of Ho-Van Oil. Cris helpfully thaws the moonlight so it glows once more, so bright that we're able to turn off our phones' flashlights. Thank goodness, because my battery's almost dead.

"Over here," I say, pocketing my phone and then sweeping aside some of the clutter on the floor. I gesture for Cris to bring the light closer.

She maneuvers the moonlight back and forth, which reminds me of a crime scene investigator waving around a black light on one of those police television shows.

And then we both see it at the same time.

A large splatter of Ho-Van Oil glows sea green on the floor in the moonlight. It's since dried, but a frantic path of various finger- and handprints trail toward the front door and thin into nothing. This can't be it. There *has* to be something here.

"Look." Cris kneels beside me and points at a spot of the glowing oil stain on the floor that I hadn't noticed before. "What's that?"

My breath catches. I *knew* it.

I was fucking right.

Scribbled hastily beside the splatter are the letters *J* and *K*.

*Fabiana, you genius.*

"JK," I mutter, and turn to Cris. "What could it mean, though?"

"We can probably rule out 'just kidding,'" she says, and then has the nerve to look put out when I scowl at her. "So jokes are only okay when they're yours?"

"Mine are funny," I grumble. "See how that works?"

She flips me off, and we both grin.

Cris takes a picture of what we found with her phone. A few moments later, mine chimes with a new message notification after she shares the pic with me.

"Thanks," I tell her.

We both stand in the kitchen for several silent moments more, ogling the coded message on the floor of Fabiana's kitchen until frustration rises in my chest like the ocean at high tide.

"I'm stuck again," I say. "I have no clue what this is supposed to mean." I stare at my sister through a wavering pane of tears. "What am I supposed to do now?"

She doesn't say anything at first, and it's as if I'm slipping into a cold bath of despair. I'm afraid if I don't do something, if I keep standing here clueless, I'm going to drown.

"Fuck!" I kick a saucepan across the room.

My outburst makes my sister flinch, and I immediately feel like an asshole for it because I don't ever want her to be afraid of me—but then she puts two firm and comforting hands on my shoulders, looks me in the eyes, and says, "For starters, we're going home now to get some rest. We're not going to figure anything out while we're exhausted. We can talk again tomorrow when we're fresh."

I raise a brow. "You forgot what tomorrow is?"

"No," she says confidently. "It's Saturday."

"Yeah—and it's also prom."

She tenses and looks away.

Yeah, she forgot. Can't blame her though.

But I haven't.

I glance at the canvas of Yves's self-portrait on the kitchen counter. Everything is so bleak right now that it seems ludicrous to waste a single thought on prom. Although I have an idea that might lift both Yves's and my spirits if I can pull it off.

"We've got all we need for now," I tell my sister as I grab the painting and tuck it under one arm. "Let's get out of here."

# THIRTY-ONE

## VALENTINA SAVANT

Valentina pulled up to the front of the prom venue, which was lavishly decorated with lush green palms and an army of soft fairy lights. On the sidewalk at the base of front steps was a wildflower wall that spelled out NOLA MAGNET HIGH PROM.

Sofia Beaumont sat on the bottom step with her gorgeous sage-green tulle dress bunched around her as if she'd transfigured herself into a sad mossy hill. The arms of the dress were sheer and embroidered with elaborate flowers and vines in cream, jade, and lilac. Her waist was even belted with a decorative jade sash tied in a decadent bow. She had curled and pinned her hair, and she wore a simple tiara that would've been lost in all her hair had it not been for the bright golden gems that somehow shone even in the absence of light, which gave the impression she wore a crown of fireflies. Sofia looked like a fairy princess.

Valentina looked down at the ratty sweats and T-shirt she wore and sighed, feeling FOMO's fingers squeezing her shoulders. She shook it off. The night wouldn't have ended much differently if she'd gone. She didn't regret her decision to stay home.

Sofia's face brightened the moment Valentina pulled up to the curb. Sofia leapt up, a little too excitedly, and nearly face-planted in her heels—but recovered. She opened the passenger door, hiked up her skirt, and hopped into Valentina's Jeep. Sofia slammed the door with an angry sigh and stared straight ahead.

"Girl, you all right?" asked Valentina.

Sofia rolled her eyes. "Sorry. I'm just very irritated."

Valentina winced. "It was that bad?"

"I must've misinterpreted my spread this morning," Sofia said, and shook her head. "I hardly *ever* do that. The cards predicted I'd have a good night. That's why I went even though my gut told me not to."

She touched the fingertips of one hand to her temple dramatically. Valentina fought to suppress a laugh. Sofia stayed doing the absolute most. "I dunno what's going on with me. I feel so off."

"I thought that was status quo for you, but okay," Valentina mumbled as she drove them away from the prom venue, hoping some distance might help calm Sofia a little. "But how was it?" Valentina asked. "Really."

Sofia gave her a knowing side-eye. "Corny and lonely. The DJ was a crabby older guy who only played clean versions of songs and refused to take requests." She fished her weed vape pen from her purse, digging around the box of tarot cards that never left her side. She took a long drag, shutting her eyes, and blew it out. Valentina lowered her window to let the smoke out. "Sorry," Sofia muttered. "And I got the munchies while I was there, but the food was gross, and the punch tasted like syrup." She made a fake retching sound, and Valentina laughed.

"I knew the prom committee was doomed when Cris didn't join after I dropped," Valentina said. "I want to throw her in front of a bus, but she and I were the only people capable of saving prom."

"Imagine what you two could accomplish if you'd only work together," Sofia said, and turned quickly to the window, narrowly avoiding Valentina's pointed glower.

Since Sofia's dad had died recently in a very gruesome manner and she'd just had a shitty first prom experience, Valentina chose to ignore Sofia's comment.

"I hope you at least got some dope-ass pics of you in that dress," Valentina said.

Sofia scoffed and turned to her with one eyebrow raised. "Oh, I was gonna do that anyway 'cause that's just how I am."

They both guffawed. Damn, it felt good.

After they arrived at Valentina's house, she gave Sofia a pair of comfy sweats and a tee to change into and hung up her stunning fairy-princess gown in the closet. While Sofia dressed, Valentina went downstairs and joined Mom in the kitchen.

Gabriela had already laid out all the ingredients to make almojábanas on the large center island. To one side, a weathered notebook lay open. Valentina walked over and studied the recipe written on the tarnished page in the unfamiliar curly handwriting. Had Mom always had this? Valentina wondered why she hadn't seen it before.

"That's your abuela's recipe book," Mom told her when she caught her staring. "Well, it used to be your abuela's. It's mine now." A shadow passed through Mama's eyes that Valentina didn't miss. "And I'll pass it to you one day . . . if you want it. No pressure. It's just that—"

"Did Abuela Juliana give that to you?" asked Valentina.

Mom shook her head. "I stole it when I left back in '99."

Valentina's brows shot up with surprise. "Really?"

"I was pissed at Mami and Giselle," Mom said. "They were both so fucking mean to me about Arturo. I don't remember what they said, only that it filled me with rage. Maybe that's one of the memories I lost for good, and if so, good riddance." She sighed and shook off the heavy thought that had hold of her. "Right after Mami's funeral, Giselle had the nerve to demand that I give her the recipe book, which she felt she deserved since she had to console Mami after she had to try to recreate it from memory. When I refused, Giselle called me an evil selfish bitch."

Valentina released the breath she'd been holding. "And what did you say?"

"I said 'fuck you,' and I left," Mom said. "I wanted to tell her that it wasn't fair to me that *she* got to have Mami all her life. Giselle was Mami's *treasure,* the smart child who became 'her backbone after Papi died.'" She rolled her eyes. "A weathered recipe book hardly compared to having a real mami—a real family who gave a damn about you."

Mom had some nerve, considering Valentina had the same beef with her. But she didn't want to dig into that, especially not with Sofia there.

"Why didn't you tell her how you felt?" Valentina asked.

"I don't know," Mom said, the lull of contemplation rolling into her eyes like fog right before she dropped her gaze. "I—I just couldn't. It wasn't about the recipe book though. I hadn't even looked at it since before you were born. I would've given it to her if she hadn't been so disrespectful about it. The whole exchange reminded me why I left California in the first place. It wasn't just for your dad. I needed to escape."

Relatable. It was really beginning to weird Valentina out how much she and her mom actually had in common.

"So I held on to the recipe book all these years out of spite," Mom admitted with a sly smile. "If you decide that you'd like it one day, you won't have to steal it. I'll proudly give it to you." Her eyes shone in the light, electrified by the anxiety she must've felt at laying her feelings bare in front of Valentina to either coddle or crush to death. "I'd really like to do that for you," Mom said.

Valentina glanced at the small notebook with the soft-green cover that'd started to curl and fade around the edges. She felt guilty taking that part of her abuela from Julia and Ana, but it was all Valentina had that was a tangible link to the heritage she'd been unfairly shut out from—which Julia and Ana had always had.

Valentina shuddered. *Dear gods. I'm turning into my mother.*

Mom's expression shifted until Valentina smiled and said, "I'd like that too."

"Hi, Mrs. Savant," sang Sofia sweetly as she entered the kitchen, just in time to save Valentina from diving too deep into a sentimental moment with Mom—something she wasn't quite ready for yet.

"It's Ms. *Rosier* now," Mom corrected, stepping around Valentina to give Sofia a long, swaying hug. "I'm taking my family name back." Mom stepped back and rubbed Sofia's arms in that loving *mom* way that Valentina rarely got, the sting of which she couldn't ignore no matter how hard she tried. "You doing okay?"

"I am," Sofia said. "Thank you for letting me hang out."

Mom chuckled and returned to her station at the counter. "My mami never did this kind of stuff with me and my friends, so I'm looking forward to having fun with y'all tonight."

Valentina wanted to remind her mom that neither did hers, but she also wanted to have fun sans drama, so she kept that to herself.

"What are we making?" Sofia asked as she eyed the flour, butter, oil, and other ingredients set out on the counter.

"Almojábanas," Mom said. "They're fritters made with rice flour and little bite-sized pieces of heaven. I'm going to dust off my abuela's recipe. Have y'all ever had them?"

Valentina and Sofia shook their heads, both looking intrigued.

"I'm not sure I know how to make them better than my abuela, but I guess we'll see," Mom said.

While they cooked, Mom told stories about growing up in California, which began with the one about how Abuela Juliana once stopped talking to both Mom and Giselle for a week after Mom admitted aloud that a batch of almojábanas Giselle had been practicing for *months* to learn to make tasted better than their mom's.

After the almojábanas cooled, Valentina, Sofia, and Mom did an official tasting—that didn't go so well for Mom, who professed at once that making almojábanas was a delicate process, and she might've let them stay in the oil a tad too long. Having learned her lesson from Mom's story, Valentina didn't speak ill of the almojábanas, which actually weren't too bad when Valentina drowned them in melted guava paste. Maybe Mom would redeem herself someday in the future. Or maybe Valentina would even give it a try.

Mom had insisted on watching her favorite movie: *The Players Club*. Valentina had already seen it a couple of times (and loved it), but this would be a brand-new experience for Sofia, who admitted that her mom would flip if she knew Sofia was watching this movie. Mom promised not to snitch if Sofia and Valentina didn't. With their pact firmly in place, they cozied up on the massive sectional in the family room with a tray of extra-greasy almojábanas and laughed as Mom and Valentina recited their favorite lines along with the movie.

Mom yawned as soon as the credits rolled and disappeared to her bedroom, leaving Valentina and Sofia downstairs alone.

Sofia spent a few minutes giving Valentina the play-by-play of the short time she'd spent at prom before she'd decided to send out a distress signal. They laughed and gossiped until they both grew tired and went upstairs to climb into Valentina's bed together, which they always did when sleeping over at each other's houses, even though they hadn't slept over in a while.

For several harrowing moments, Valentina lay completely still, wondering if in an alternate universe, she'd have had this night with Cris instead of Sofia. The thought was troubling for too many reasons. Valentina was annoyed at Sofia for even planting that seed in the first place, but it was short-lived.

Valentina was glad for Sofia's friendship. She wasn't perfect, but she was there, which might not have meant a lot to most but was everything to Valentina.

She looked over Sofia, whose back was turned, rising and falling with short, relaxed breaths. "Sof?" Valentina called softly. "You sleep?"

"On the way," Sofia mumbled through her grogginess. "'Sup?"

"Remember we talked about me being Queen?"

"Yeah . . ."

"I'm forming an alliance to take back the Gen Council, and I want you to be part of it."

Sofia sighed. "I'm shunned. What would even be the point?"

"That doesn't mean you can't be part of the community."

Sofia lay still.

"I've also been thinking of a backup plan in case we can't reseat the Council as planned. Maybe your mom would pass her seat to me so she could get Madeline DeLacorte off her back, and that way she could focus on her bureau. How do you think she'd respond to that?" After several extended moments of silence, Valentina turned on her side and stared at the back of Sofia's head. "Sof?"

"I dunno," Sofia grumbled.

Valentina sighed and tugged the blanket up higher on her friend and turned over, nestling in herself. Despite the plush physical comfort of her bed, her mind remained troubled.

Tonight had been the one night she'd promised herself that she wouldn't worry about that stuff, but Valentina had no idea how *not* to be concerned about her survival. Sofia's espionage mission hadn't turned up anything useful, and Madeline had already gone forward with her petition to MASC to reseat the Gen Council, which meant outsiders would have the power to choose the next Queen, and Valentina wasn't confident they'd choose her.

It took much longer than usual for Valentina to fall asleep, her brain unable to relax with the insatiable beast that was anxious paranoia pounding the front doors of her mind, demanding to be let in.

Yet again, Valentina Savant found her future in jeopardy.

# THIRTY-TWO

## CRISTINA

Dad's bread pudding makes everything better. I can't prepare it as well as Mama, but I'm using my Saturday night to try my best. Odessa offered to help, but this is something I need to do on my own. Preparing this dish is the only situation where I can control the outcome—with my own two hands—and I just need to dive headfirst into this low-stakes task and disappear for several hours.

However, Remi Prince was never part of my original plan.

Yet here he is, standing next to me in the kitchen, flashing his luminous metal smile, the one that burns away the fog of sadness within me like the rising Sun. He texted earlier to ask if I wanted to hang, so I invited him over to cook with me. He's skipping prom too, as are my only other friends right now—Aurora, who's busy surviving (as usual), and Clem, who's at Jean-Louise's with Yves (also as usual).

But this isn't a substitute prom date for me and Remi. We're just keeping each other company tonight, and as such, we're both in sweats and tees, a nonnegotiable condition of hanging out alone like this, so that we wouldn't make it weird. Not long after he rang my doorbell and I let him inside, I grew tired of denying how I've come to long for the gentle comfort and joy I get whenever I'm around him. But I'm terrified of letting go, falling under the spell of another boy. I cannot do that again.

But how am I supposed to know if Remi's safe? The constant back-and-forth is driving me mad. But then his disorienting eyes grip mine, and he licks his pink lips and smiles again, and the tension leaves my body, my muscles slacken, and I lean even further into his world. But then internal alarms blare, and I'm rushed back outside, where I begin questioning if he's safe all over again. And I don't know how to break that cycle. It's like a recurring nightmare that I can't prevent from coming every time I close my eyes.

But for now, one night only at least, I want to forget about all that and just enjoy my *friend*'s company.

Odessa's insistence on supporting my baking endeavors tonight wouldn't be thwarted no matter how hard I tried, so despite my turning down every offer of help, she still set out all the ingredients, dishes, and utensils I'd need so I wouldn't have to search for them, which I ended up really appreciating.

I'm not doing this just for me though. I want to get this right for Odessa too. Bread pudding is her favorite dessert. Whenever Dad made it, I'd often find Odessa sitting at the kitchen counter late at night, relishing a small piece with a golf ball–sized scoop of butter-pecan ice cream. It might seem childish or silly, but she's given us all so much over the years that I want to give her something back. And right now, this bread pudding is the best gift I have.

Remi turns his phone on Do Not Disturb and puts it in his pocket before washing his hands. Then he studiously watches me pour all the ingredients into a large mixing bowl. The way he devotes the whole of himself to spending time with me and the genuine way he engages with me are so endearing that it's almost intoxicating. And that's also stress inducing. Even the thought of potentially falling victim to another love spell makes me feel like my lungs are shrinking and my throat's closing until I slowly suffocate and die.

I'm absentmindedly following the recipe, measuring and dumping cups of milk into the mixture one by one, until Remi places a gentle hand on my wrist, stopping me after the third.

"You're using fresh bread, so you wanna cut the milk a bit unless you want bread soup instead of pudding," he explains.

I set the milk and measuring cup aside. "I didn't know you knew how to cook. You've been keeping secrets from me, Remi Prince." I tut under my breath. "And I thought I could trust you."

The words taste sour, which I hadn't anticipated. There's truth in jest. Or am I searching for reasons not to trust Remi?

He chuckles. "It never came up. I've known you for what? Like five minutes?"

My eyebrows shoot up in surprise. "Oh, yeah? Don't be rude."

He laughs. "Well, the purpose of spending time with friends is to get to know them better. That's what we're doing, right?"

"And who said we were friends?"

"If I'm not a friend, that means I'm an enemy or a stranger, and I don't imagine you'd welcome either of them into your home *and* cook for them . . . unless . . ." His jaw drops with dramatic surprise, and he says in a ridiculously exaggerated New Orleans accent, "Oh, my God. I declare, Cristina Trudeau, are you trying to poison me?"

I laugh so hard that I snort, which makes Remi laugh too.

"I needed that laugh," I tell him.

"Happy to provide," he says. "I learned how to cook at a young age to help out my parents. Some days, when things got really bad between them, if I didn't cook, they wouldn't eat." He casts his gaze down at the countertop and shrugs. "The more I did it, the better I got at it."

I nudge him gently with my elbow, the same way I do all the time to Clem. "I'm glad you're here to help me then, because I don't care very much for bread soup."

He winks and points two cheesy finger guns at me, which makes me giggle once more. He greases the baking dish with butter while I assemble the ingredients for the Tru Reserve glaze.

"You got any maple syrup?" he asks me.

"Yeah," I reply. "I think so. Why?"

"Add a quarter cup to the glaze. Trust me. The richness it'll bring to it will change your life. You won't go back."

While I finish the glaze, Remi pours the bread pudding mixture into the baking dish and places it in the oven to cook, making sure to enlighten me to why it cooks better in the bottom third of the oven. He's so nurturing and loves explaining things, which he says is "the joy of sharing knowledge." It's really cute though—like I'm hanging out with a future professor.

"You graduate this year," I say. "What's next for you?"

"I'm going to Tulane to study math."

I pull a face before I can stop it. "Math? Why math?"

"Because it's reliable. In the math world, the rules don't change, and the goalposts don't move. Two plus two is always four in any place at any time and in any language. The answers there are never subject to opinion or emotion." His cheeks flush, and he stares down and shrugs. "I dunno, maybe my love of math is a trauma response, but numbers can't hurt me . . . or poison me." He lifts his head and grins at me.

We laugh again. A real, deep belly laugh. The kind that rattles your soul and wakes you up.

Talking to Remi feels like bathing in moonlight.

"What about you?" he asks me.

"I've been thinking about Tulane too," I say. "They have a degree for magical-history studies that seems interesting."

"Magical history?" He feigns falling asleep until I poke him in the side of his head. "What in the world will you do with that?"

"Knowledge is power. I am to be Queen, and I don't intend to half-ass it."

"I know. And I adore that about you."

It's my turn to smile. It feels good to be seen.

Once the glaze is finished, we both sample it, and Remi was right. The maple syrup adds a decadence to the glaze that makes it irresistible. Remi turns to face me, cheesing so hard that I shove him playfully. "Stop being a weirdo," I say.

"Then I'd be boring," he retorts.

Ugh. He's right. "Carry on then, weirdo."

"Thanks," he says. "Uh, if I can be serious again—"

"No." I shake my head. "Stop it." When he sucks his teeth, I say, "Kidding, of course."

"I'm really grateful to you for rescuing Aurora," he says, a grave seriousness in his voice, a clear distinction from a minute ago. "I hate Xavier for what he did to her. It's so fucked up that he got away with it *and then* turned around and made her life hell. Where's the justice in that?"

"That's the issue," I tell him. "There isn't any. And you're right. It's *very* frustrating."

Remi lowers his voice and averts his eyes. "Would you judge me if I said I'm glad Tabitha Edgewater and Dr. Gregory Thomas are dead?"

*That depends—would you judge me if I told you I'm the one who murdered them?*

"It gives me a glimmer of hope that there's some justice in this world," Remi says.

My heart skips a beat and flutters uncontrollably. I want to tell him that that's not off-putting at all and then leap into his arms, kiss his full pink lips, and then go on a rampage with him—driving across the city and eventually the whole country, literally blowing away the evil people of our world—

"Yikes," he says, wincing. "I guess I must've overshared."

"No!" I say, chasing my silly thoughts away. "I was just thinking about how I agree with you and that you were right about what you said before—about your dad. You can't fight evil if you're not willing to throw a punch. Sometimes violence is the answer."

Remi lifts his head and stares into my eyes. "Sometimes I think I don't fit in anywhere in this world."

"What do you mean?" I ask, genuinely curious.

"Everyone's so fucking cutthroat and selfish. It seems the only way to win is to be like Xavier, and I can't do that."

"That's not true," I say. "We can choose to be better."

"That's what my dad tried. He decided to be good, to fight the good fight. But he got crushed by the villains who run this town and the world at large."

"Yeah, I gotta admit, it's not very inspiring out here."

He scoffs. "Did you know that most of the time Aurora was gone, I was pissed at her?"

I shake my head. "Why?"

"I thought she abandoned me. I wasted months being mad at her because she just up and disappeared. I got desperate and went to Xavier to find out what happened to her. He told me she'd been in an accident and was rehabilitating at a private treatment facility and refused to tell me where."

"What the fuck," I mutter.

"I persuaded my dad's private investigator to help me out, which she did because she'd also been wondering what'd happened to Aurora, who'd disappeared right after they'd uncovered something top secret together. After we found out she was at Chateau des Saints, I tried to see her, but the staff wouldn't let me. And Xavier declined to authorize my visitation. I tried everything. I thought there was nothing else I could do. I gave up, and I just left my friend in that place. And I feel so fucking guilty about it. If it hadn't been for you, Aurora would still be there." He pauses and bites his lips, and his tear-filled eyes ensnare mine. "So thank you, Cris. I'm glad to know you and honored to be your friend. You truly are an extraordinary person and will be an even more incredible Queen."

"Thank you, Remi," I say. "That's very sweet. I'm glad to be your friend too."

While the bread pudding finishes in the oven, Remi invites Odessa to watch a movie with us while we eat and then scours Netflix for a selection. And I cling to the counter to keep from floating away.

The fact Remi lets me exist so comfortably with no pressure to be anything more than what I want to be at any given time makes me want him more. It's like magic, which is anxiety inducing, but this time I know it's not a love spell.

Aurora and I have been working on something we described as a "love spell vaccine" that will hopefully prevent people from going through what I experienced with Oz. I've been happily testing it out on myself; but even so, the painful memories follow me like a phantom tethered to my soul.

But Remi's not Oz. Not even close, thank the gods. He's so much more that it feels foolish to compare the two—which I don't need to do because Remi's my *friend.*

Maybe he could be more, but he's being what he is right now just fine.

And I'm good with that.

# THIRTY-THREE
## CLEMENT

Jean-Louise and I aren't exactly on speaking terms right now, so I muster the courage to ask for assistance from Auguste, who, mind you, I see outside his bedroom as rarely as Jean-Louise. I'm not sure Auguste understands the assignment at first, seeing as how he can't really communicate with us and, as of late, his face seems stuck on one setting: murderous.

But when 8 P.M. arrives on Saturday evening, I send Yves down the hall to Auguste's room on a fool's errand, where, once there, Auguste will give Yves the handwritten note from me instructing him to spend the next hour winding down with Auguste and that I'll swing by to scoop him shortly. I went out super early this morning to gather supplies for tonight, and I also picked up a bunch of local and national newspapers so Yves would have plenty to occupy him while I set everything up.

The moment Yves disappears inside Auguste's room, I bolt downstairs to grab everything from the trunk of my car, then run back up and begin a mad dash, shoving furniture aside to clear a space for us in the center of the small room. Earlier, I made a pit stop by the House of Vans and convinced Colby to sell me a few bottles of Ho-Van Oil, which I emptied into a large mason jar. Using a paintbrush, I paint the back of the door with the translucent oil.

Next, I paint stars on nearly every available surface—the walls, ceiling, and floor too. It's hard to see exactly what I'm drawing, but I'm too committed to the concept to second-guess it now. While I work, thoughts of Ayden Holloway and Yves occupy my mind. I never considered myself an artist, certainly not like them, but I can understand now why they enjoy it so much. Losing myself in the act of creating happens to be a very satisfying distraction from being anxious about the impending doom constantly pressing down on me from every angle. So, yeah, this is kinda fun.

I save a bit of the Ho-Van Oil for a very special project. I sit on the floor and prop the canvas of Yves's self-portrait against the wall in front of me. I pause, homing in on the way my heart flutters apprehensively, which is even more pronounced in the dense quiet surrounding me. I have to hype myself up to make the first brushstroke because I'm terrified of fucking it up. I know it's just a painting—a sketch, really—but it means a lot to me, and I'd very much like *not* to ruin this thing too—if I can help it.

I dip the end of a thin paintbrush in the oil and take a deep breath, then exhale slowly before touching it to the canvas. I work carefully and slowly at re-outlining Yves's sketch with the Ho-Van Oil, hoping on repeat that I'm not completely trashing Yves's artwork.

It takes a little longer than I expected to finish, but when I'm done, I hang it on a blank section of wall near the window. I use temporary plastic hooks to mount it because I don't want the noise of my hammering to summon Jean-Louise from his musty chambers to give me shit.

Another benefit of my restlessness last night is that I practiced tapping the Moon for raw moonlight and testing the limits of my ever-present tether to the spiritual realm. I managed to collect enough moonbeams to fill another large mason jar; and then I spent several hours afterward experimenting with deepening my grasp on my tether and exploiting that connection to manipulate magic on a molecular level like Cris showed me. I broke more than a few jars in the process, but thank goodness we had plenty of spares at home.

I take out the glass vessel of warm moonlight from my bag and clutch it in my hands like a steaming mug of coffee. I wish I could wrap my entire body in this stuff and let the heat seep into my pores. I remove the lid and coax the magic out.

My invisible grip on it slips at first, and I have to use both hands to maintain my hold on the magic. But once I'm back in control, I'm able to shape the moonbeams—partially with my hands, partially through my unspoken will—into a sphere the size of a basketball. I give it a spin, and it keeps spinning where it hovers in the air in front of me. As it turns, it burns brighter, filling the room with a pure soft-blue light that sparkles against the luminescent Ho-Van Oil painted around the room.

I lift my hand, and the magical sphere obeys, rising to just a hair above the ceiling, where it continues to revolve.

The scene around me steals every breath from me. The light turns the oil into glittering sea-green sparkles that make it look as if we're standing in the middle of space. It reminds me of the picture Yves painted of us, the one the police destroyed.

Oh . . . this is *perfect*.

Next, I set up my Bluetooth speaker. This morning, I painstakingly curated a playlist for tonight, which is a perfect mix of slow and up-tempo songs—a holistic vibe from start to finish, including some of our mutual favorites. I queue the first song and put on the navy-blue blazer I brought from home over my white tee. I also brought one for Yves. They were Dad's once. Mom's been saving them for me, so they're a little big, but we needed something special for tonight.

I step out into the hallway and close the door behind me, then head to the end of the hall and find Auguste's bedroom door open. I watch from the doorway as Auguste adjusts the oversize black blazer on Yves's smaller frame.

"It's okay," I say, lifting my arms in the coat that feels more like a bathrobe on me. "Mine's kinda swallowing me too."

Yves turns, and his eyebrows rise slightly. I know he'd be smiling right now if he could. I take his cool hand in mine, thank Auguste for his help, and lead Yves back down the hallway to his room. Once there, I get behind him, cover his eyes with one hand, and open the door with my other. I gently direct him inside and shut the door, then turn him around so he's facing the glowing message on the back of the door.

PROM 2020

WELCOME TO THE DARK SIDE OF THE MOON

CLEM & YVES

Yves cups both hands over his mouth, but I turn him around and direct his attention to the canvas hanging on the wall, the self-portrait sketch that now shimmers, blue green and radiant, in the magical light. Yves wanders over to it and touches the painting's surface with a quivering finger and then turns back to me. I'm afraid he hates it and is pissed at me for ruining it—but then he hugs me.

Yves buries his face in my neck. I'm running hot right now from all the prep, and the cold of him against me is shocking at first, but I don't care. He's as close as possible, and yet somehow, I manage to hold him closer, tighter.

"I know this isn't exactly the prom you had in mind," I whisper. "But I wanted to make sure this day was special for you . . . even though . . ." I choke on the next words. My eyes are wet, distorting the beauty all around me into a candescent seafoam-colored mess.

Yves holds me now. And I let him.

Kehlani serenades us, and we dance under the glittering ball of magic spinning above our heads. When the song finishes, I stand back and snap my fingers. "Oh!" I exclaim. "Almost forgot."

Yves cocks his head and watches as I retrieve the two paper crowns that I got from Aunt Ursula. She keeps a giant box of them at the Wishing Well because she hands them out to customers every year for Mardi Gras. I place the first one on Yves's head and then put on mine too.

"The best thing about hosting our own solo prom is we get to be the undisputed prom kings," I tell him.

Yves reaches a tentative hand up to touch the crown atop his head, then clutches his heart, looking at me through dark and dead wavering eyes. It's unsettling in a simultaneously haunting and heartbreaking way that's hard to stare at directly for too long. I let out a sigh of reprieve when he embraces me again.

"I'm so glad you like it," I whisper in his ear as we dance, and I press his cold body against mine, hoping to share some of my warmth and my life with him even though it's impossible.

We dance until I'm sweaty, but only me, because Yves doesn't sweat anymore. Then we collapse on the floor and stare up at the magnificent stars on the ceiling.

I can't fix everything, but at least I was able to salvage junior prom for us both.

Yves pulls me into his arms so my head rests on his chest, and completely unaware of how exhausted I was until that very moment, I fall asleep at once.

# PART IV

The ultimate measure of a man is not where he stands in moments of comfort and convenience, but where he stands at times of challenge and controversy.

—DR. MARTIN LUTHER KING, JR.

# THIRTY-FOUR
## CLEMENT

I wake up late on Sunday morning, still in Yves's chilly arms, which I've grown accustomed to. At some point in the night, a blanket and throw pillow joined us on the floor of Yves's temporary bedroom at Jean-Louise's. This is undoubtedly the most uncomfortable place I've ever slept, but that was undeniably some of the best and most restful sleep I've had in ages.

Yves untangles himself from me and sits up when I do. He lays his head on my shoulder, and I rub the small of his back.

"I'll never forget last night," I say. "I love you."

He raises his head and faces me. We press our foreheads together, gently, until the tips of our noses touch. I close my eyes and cradle his head in one hand, caressing his earlobe with my thumb.

"I don't want to leave you," I whisper, "but I gotta meet up with Cris. Maybe we'll find some answers today that'll help all of us."

Yves pats my cheek lovingly with his cool palm. I lean into it and shut my eyes, longing silently for his warmth and the familiar scent of cedar and spice that I haven't smelled in forever. I want so badly to make that promise again—the one where I tell him I'll never give up fighting for him, even though I don't know how much longer my body and my brain and my heart can keep all this up. But I can't swear one more time that I'm going to fix this—fix him—when I have no idea how to do that. Those promises don't mean anything anymore. To keep repeating them feels diminishing and cruel.

But last night wasn't just for Yves. It did something for me too. Those moments we shared reminded me why I swore I'd walk between worlds for Yves Bordeaux and why no matter how fucked this situation seems, as long as there's breath in my body, I will not stop searching for a way to make him whole again.

I kiss him on his forehead and leave for home.

* * *

After I get home and shower and dress, I'm in the kitchen getting some juice when I make the mistake of letting Odessa hear my stomach growl, which results in her holding me and Cris both hostage until we "get a hot meal in our bellies." I'm annoyed at first because I'm ready to get to work on piecing my life back together, but the smell of sausages frying and biscuits baking promptly shuts me up.

Cris meets us downstairs just in time for breakfast. She's wearing skinny jeans, a plain tee, and sneakers, and her hair's been moisturized, oiled, and braided back into a neat ponytail. We eat to Odessa's satisfaction, and she releases us to our task by late afternoon.

We take my car because I'm too antsy to let Cris drive us—not that she can't, but being in control helps my anxiety. This part of town isn't particularly busy this time of day on Sunday, so it's not difficult to find a spot in the surface lot at the back of Yay! Beignets! where I also parked the night of Aunt Rosalie's soft launch of Vice Hall. I suggested to Cris that we come back here to try and find Emma again. I'd like to speak with her about what she saw the night of Ben's murder. I have a sneaking suspicion too wild to say aloud, but something in my gut is nudging me in this direction—and interestingly enough, Cris was also thinking the same, so she wasn't hard to convince.

Cris points out Emma's camp, which she tells me has moved since last time, now just outside the line of sight from the dented and scarred metal back door of the bakery. We approach the woman, who sits crisscross applesauce on a swatch of cardboard, busy sorting through several ziplock bags full of toiletries and other personal items. She looks up at us when Cris clears her throat.

"I was worried we might not find you here after last time," she says. "I'm really sorry about what that jerk did to you."

Cris explained to me on the drive over how the manager of the bakery had chased Emma away and then accused her of attacking a stranger. Might just be me, but Emma doesn't exactly give off "feral aggressor" vibes.

She stares at us cynically, her light-brown eyes dancing between me and my sister. Her skin is chestnut brown, and she wears an ivygreen fisherman's beanie at the edge of which I can see her closely shorn hair.

"The assistant manager of the bakery tells me when the general manager's gonna be around now, so I don't have to run into him," Emma tells us.

"Did they give you that stuff too?" Cris asks, pointing to the items spread out in front of Emma.

She frowns. "What do you want now?"

Cris starts to ask another question, but I put a hand on her forearm, stopping her. She turns to me with a confused look, but I nod, and she stands down.

"Do you like coffee, Emma?" I ask.

She shakes her head. "Earl Grey with a little bit of milk and cinnamon like how my mama used to make it," she mutters.

"Would you like one?" I ask.

She nods this time.

"Okay," I tell her. "We'll be right back. Oh, I'm Clem, by the way."

Emma's eyes narrow, and she gives a brisk nod.

Cris and I head around to the front of the shopping plaza to fetch Emma's tea. We pass an ATM along the way, and when I double back to it, Cris glowers at me.

"Clem, what are you doing?" she asks.

"*We* are getting some cash for Emma," I tell her. "I think a hundred from each of us should be enough."

"Okay, but a hundred dollars?" Cris exclaims. "That's going to clean us both out, and it's not like we're getting a regular allowance while Mama's in jail. Maybe we give a bit less since we don't even know if she really knows anything."

"It's not that complicated. We need help, and so does Emma. We have resources that she does not. And even if she can't help us, she's still a *person* who needs assistance—and we have more than enough."

I turn back to the ATM, slide my debit card in, and withdraw five twenty-dollar bills. I step aside and gesture for Cris to take my place.

She sighs and steps up to the machine. "I hate how you so easily make the rest of us look like ignorant jerks," she grumbles, then puts her card in and makes the withdrawal.

"It's a superpower," I say. When she hands me her money, I snatch the bills and add them to the others. "Thank you. Consider this a superhero tax."

She doesn't complain while we grab Emma's tea. I wonder aloud if we should get her some food too, but Cris points out that Emma would probably like to make her own choice of what to eat. After I just read her at the ATM, Cris delights in redemption through explaining to me that taking away someone's autonomy can often be more harmful than helpful. I think about cracking her face by telling her that getting a blueberry muffin or a beignet to go with the lady's tea isn't that deep, but I decide to let my sis be great. All that matters is Emma gets what she wants.

And maybe it is selfish that I'm so motivated to help her right now because I can't seem to help anyone else; and I desperately need to feel good about *something.*

We're back at Emma's camp in less than twenty minutes. I hand the tea to her along with a small plastic ramekin with some extra cinnamon inside.

"Got you some extra," I tell her. "In case I didn't put enough."

She takes a cautious sip and grimaces. "Did you put any at all?"

"Well, that's why I brought you extra." I grin and sit down across from her on the pavement, and she tenses, eyeing me suspiciously. I hand her the two hundred dollars, and her brows shoot up so high, they nearly disappear into her beanie.

She takes the money, though slightly hesitant. "What's this for?"

"For you," I say.

She frowns at me and then at Cris, who sits beside me.

Emma glances at the sky and blinks a few times before tilting her head back down, a smile on her face. "You're the first people to acknowledge my personhood in a very long time," she says. "I can't even remember the last time someone looked me in the eyes, much less with an expression other than pity or contempt. I never imagined I'd end up like this."

"What happened to you?" asks Cris.

Emma casts her gaze down at her weathered hands folded around the paper cup resting on her lap. "There was a time when I was the most skilled and respected diviner in the entire southeast, believe it or not. Back in the late nineties, people would travel from all over—other countries even—to see me, and my mama before me, and her mama before her, and so on. The business that had been in my family for generations was passed down to me, and I let it slip through my fingers.

"Things were going well—too damn well—and then I let some fast-talking funds-management joker invest the bulk of my money under the guise that he was going to help me create 'generational wealth' for me and my descendants." She scoffs so hard that she chokes and coughs. "Then, about thirteen years ago, the stock market crashed. I lost everything, and he disappeared. My family's home and the place where we'd done business for generations went into foreclosure, and as soon as it hit the city's auction block, a local real estate investment firm bought it for mere pennies compared to what it was worth so they could continue gentrifying my neighborhood. They were waiting with their checkbooks open like sharks who'd smelled blood in the water."

"That's awful," I murmur. "I'm so sorry, Emma."

She sips her coffee. "Me too. People like me are sacrificed every day for the sake of capitalistic greed. After I lost my home and my business, I tried to start over, but divining was my only skill, which isn't as marketable or profitable as it once was. If you take nothing else from this conversation, kids, remember that in this country, all it takes is one setback big enough to sweep your legs out from under you; and once you fall, it's near impossible to get back on your feet on your own. And you won't notice until years later when you look up and realize you've grown accustomed to this new lower station and being looked down upon or flat-out ignored by the people who used to be your peers. There's an entire world down here most people never see until they're trapped in it."

Cris and I exchange an unnerving glance, which makes Emma smile, and she says, "But on extremely rare occasions, I'll meet someone like you"—she tilts her head toward me—"and I'm reminded that humanity still exists inside some of us. You have the trappings of a noble king, Clem."

"I, uh . . ." I shake my head. "No . . . I don't think so. That's not really my thing. But I appreciate the compliment."

She tuts under her breath. "And who better to wield absolute power than those who respect it absolutely?"

I think Emma might've broken my brain. Still though . . . ruling's not my thing, and I wish people would leave me alone about it.

"Full transparency, Emma," I say, "my sister and I wanted to ask you again about what happened a few weeks ago that night you had the run-in with the white guy in the bloody tux."

She takes another sip of tea. "Hmm . . . he was acting really strange that night. And I never attacked him. I was only trying to help."

"Neither of us believed that manager from the bakery for a second," Cris says.

Emma nods with an expression of gratitude. "He staggered up from that direction"—she points toward the sidewalk leading up to and through the parking lot—"with blood dripping down the front of his fancy suit. He caught my attention because he was arguing with himself. Then he just started screaming and fell over." She stares off and nods toward the lamppost at one corner of the lot. "Right there, it was. I went over to check if he was okay, and he just started thrashing around and hollering." She shakes her head. "I thought he was high on something."

"Did he tell you his name?" asks Cris.

"Not exactly," Emma replies.

"What do you mean?" I ask, leaning forward.

"In between screaming his head off about demons," Emma says, "he kept saying the name 'Zac' over and over. I asked if that was his name, but he just kept repeating it. But then I noticed he'd gashed his head when he fell off the sidewalk. I was trying to calm him down to keep him from hurting himself again when the bakery manager came running over and accused me of attacking the man. The manager threatened to call the cops, so I took off. I wasn't about to die for a white man I don't even know."

"Do you remember what he looked like?" I ask.

She frowns, flicking the plastic edge of her cup's lid while she thinks. "Tall. Light eyes. Dirty-blond hair. Late thirties to forties, maybe?" She shrugs. "Sorry I couldn't be of more help."

"It's okay," I tell her. "You've helped plenty. Thank you."

"You're welcome," she says as she collects her belongings and gets to her feet. "There are some things I need to go take care of now. Good luck with whatever you two are up to." She starts to walk away but pauses, staring down hard at the cracked pavement. Then she turns to us, an unsettling look of concern on her face. "Word of advice: There are several paths ahead of you both. Be careful which you choose, and be wary of the ones people try to push you down." She rushes off before Cris or I can ask her anything else.

Once Emma's gone, I stand up and help my sister to her feet too. I'm about to comment on what just went down when Cris stares wide-eyed past me at the dark space beneath the nearby dumpster. She freezes, and I hear the gasp catch in her throat.

I turn to find the pair of glowing eyes blinking at us from the dark. When whatever's under there moves in the shadows, my soul almost flees this realm.

Cris latches on to my arm with a crushing grip. "Oh, gods. Tell me you see that."

"Yep," I whisper.

We both squeal when the possum darts from beneath the dumpster, scurries across the lot, and disappears beneath a parked car. It takes us a few moments to catch our breath, but Cris seems way more rattled than me based on how flushed her face has become all of a sudden. She rakes the back of her hand across her forehead, swiping away sweat.

"Everything okay?" I ask her. "You're usually not this jumpy."

She hesitates a moment, then nods. "I'm fine."

"Liar," I grumble under my breath. "Come on, Cris. It's me. What'd you think you saw just now?"

She lets out a sharp breath. "I . . . don't know. I've been seeing weird stuff recently. I mean, it's been a while since it last happened, and I got preoccupied with everything else going on—"

"What exactly have you been seeing?" I ask. My chest feels stretched like an elastic band pulled too close to snapping.

*There's no way.*

It can't be. *Please, gods.* Don't let it be what I'm thinking.

Please don't let the Moon King be hunting my sister instead of me. That's *not* how this was supposed to go. I was trying to protect her by keeping that from her, but now I might've put her in more danger. *Fuck!*

"When I was at Tabitha's," Cris explains, "I heard a voice. And I definitely felt a presence. I—I thought it might've been an ancestor or . . . or maybe Oberun."

"Who?" I ask, twisting my face. "I've never heard that name before."

"Most people haven't. Oberun is an ancient god of justice, older even than Eshu. I learned a little about him from some old books in the Council Library at St. John's."

Cris goes on to give me the abridged version of the sparse history of this Oberun and his absolute disappearance from existence, including the part where she suspects he was the one who blessed her with the snakeskin that she used to bind Oz from gen magic. Though let the record show that I am in perfect alignment with her decision to ban Oz from further appropriating our culture. Ten out of ten.

I shake my head, not bothering to fight the way my posture subconsciously wilts. "I need to tell you something."

"Okay," she says, her voice low and timid.

"Last summer, when I was in that car crash with Aunt Ursula, I was knocked unconscious and accidentally astral projected to the Kahlungha."

"Wait," she says. "Why does that name sound familiar?"

"It's the secret hallway between the natural realm and the spiritual realm," I explain. "The place Auguste was trying to find to enhance his necromancy abilities."

"That doesn't make sense though," Cris says. "If Auguste *died* trying to access that place, how'd *you* end up there by accident?"

"I'm not sure, but the entity I encountered there was the Moon King, and that place was his prison—until a little over a month ago."

"How'd he escape?"

I run through the very brief story of how the Moon King hitched a ride out of the Kahlungha on the back of Jean-Louise's soul—the same as he'd tried to do with me—and then fled to gods know where to do gods know what.

Cris hugs herself. "So, he's out there now, prowling around New Orleans?"

I nod. "And Jean-Louise is *terrified* of the Moon King. He's been shut up in his room ever since it happened. He's effectively abandoned magic *and* me too." I stare into my sister's worried brown eyes and my reflection in them. "I'm scared too, Cris. But I won't leave Yves hanging the way everyone's done to me. It all seems silly anyway because I haven't seen or heard a peep from the Moon King since Jean-Louise's warning."

"This . . . Moon King"—Cris's voice is steady, careful—"is that his real name? Could he go by another?" She swallows hard. "Like Oberun?"

"Cris, I hate to tell you this, but I think the Moon King might've been catfishing you as Oberun this whole time. You've gotta be more careful. He's *really* dangerous."

"Shit," Cris says under her breath.

"But we don't need to get too distracted with the gods and their ancient drama right now. We've got more important shit to deal with—like finding Fabiana so maybe she can help with clearing Mama's name and de-zombifying Yves."

"Yeah," Cris says. "You're right."

I ponder our next move for a moment. "All the clues we've gotten so far don't make sense, but I think it's because we can't see the connection yet."

"Right," she says. "Let's review what we know."

"Fabiana's been missing since November," I say. "There's a high possibility she was kidnapped by someone. She left a cryptic message on the floor of her apartment—the letters *J* and *K* and nothing else."

"And her Nite-Lite gas was used to knock everyone unconscious right before Ben was murdered," Cris adds. "So whoever abducted Fabiana might've also had access to the Nite-Lite formula she developed."

"And a white man dressed in a tuxedo and covered in blood had a run-in with our new friend Emma," I say, "in this same parking lot."

"What if the letters Fabiana drew on her kitchen floor were initials?" Cris asks.

I consider that for a moment, and then realization plunges my heart. *Of course!* A portion of the larger picture comes into focus, and it's so obvious that I feel ridiculous for not having figured it out sooner.

"I *thought* he was acting strange when I ran into him at Vice Hall that night," I say, "but I brushed it off because I had so much other shit going on, but I should've *known*."

"Clem . . ." Cris says, annoyed with me already. "Who are you talking about?"

"Jack Kingston," I tell her. "I think that's who killed Ben Beaumont."

It takes a moment for the pieces to click together in her mind, but when they do, realization brims in her expression too.

"Come on," I tell her. "It'll be dark soon, and we need to go."

"Wait . . . where are we going?"

"To pay Jack Kingston a visit."

# THIRTY-FIVE

## CRISTINA

It's early evening when we pull up to the yellow-paneled cottage belonging to Jack Kingston, and the Sun's already begun preparations to pack up and transition to the other side of the world for the night. I'm grateful Clem already knew where Jack lives because otherwise I have no idea how we would've gotten this man's address. But as it turns out, Clem's been here before.

Way back in sixth grade, he came over here after school one day to work on a science fair project with Zac, his assigned partner. They were a dreadful match. Zac came over to our house once to work on that same project, and he and Clem squabbled nearly the entire time. And when they weren't arguing, Zac was being really weird—lots of quiet staring and scowling. I never understood that boy.

Clem parks the car at the edge of the driveway and glares intensely at the white pickup truck parked at the other end. It looks familiar, but I can't recall why.

"What's wrong?" I ask.

He stares a moment longer then shakes his head. "Nothing. It's just . . . I feel like I've seen that truck somewhere before."

"Me too," I say. "But are you okay? Really?"

He sighs hard and runs a hand down his face. "I'm good. Let's go see Jack." He's out of the car and halfway to the front door before I can unlatch my seat belt.

I get out and catch up with my brother as he pounds on the door. We stand there and wait for several slogging minutes without a single sound of life from the other side.

Clem squints and tries to peer through the tiny gap in the curtains on the other side of the window but can't see anything. "I don't think anyone's home," he says.

"Then whose truck is that?" I point my thumb over my shoulder at the pickup in the driveway.

He shrugs. "I think I know how to break in. Yves showed me last year."

"Clem!" I whisper-shout at him. "Stop that! What if someone's home?"

He ignores me, closely examining the panes of glass in the door.

I'm about to drag his ass back to the car when I feel a draft slide across the back of my neck like clammy fingertips. I jump with a start and turn around as my hand flies up to my neck.

Clem glances over his shoulder at me. "What's wrong?"

I shake my head. "Must've been the wind, I guess."

"Wind?" His brows pinch together. "What wind?"

"Nothing," I say.

"You wouldn't happen to have a screwdriver on you, would you?"

I screw up my face at him. "What? Boy, *no*. Can you stop?"

Desperate to try anything outside of breaking and entering at this point, I turn the doorknob—and the door creaks open.

"No way," Clem gasps.

We exchange a cynical glance. I can see the gooseflesh on his bare arms. He swings the door open, revealing the disaster inside.

The house looks like it's been sacked. Clem holds out an arm protectively, then steps through and gives the front room a quick once-over before gesturing to me that it's safe to come inside too.

The entire living room and what I can see of the kitchen beyond are completely disheveled. It reminds me of those fight scenes from action movies where two people go at it so hard that they completely obliterate their surroundings.

"Were they robbed?" Clem asks in a hushed voice.

"No, this was something else." I point to the cracked flat-screen television on the wall and the broken laptop on the floor.

Clem and I both pull our shirts over our noses to mask the harsh smell. Clem groans, "This place *reeks*," which comes out muffled from beneath his shirt.

I nod, not really wanting to open my mouth. There are so many notes to the pungent stench in the air that it's hard to pick them out; however, I do get very distinct hints of body odor, urine, and mold that are bold enough to make me gag just a little bit.

Clem's hand jackhammers my shoulder. I look to where he's pointing at the barely noticeable rust-colored droplets of blood that trail from the living room and disappear into the next room. We follow them to find a quaint and egregiously unkempt kitchen.

Flies buzz around empty pizza boxes, and the fermented smell of stale beer burns my nose. The dirty dishes have been removed from the sink and piled on the countertop on either side to make room for the giant wad of something that's soaking in murky copper-colored water.

"We can use this to see what's in there." Clem bends down to pick up a long-handled spoon from the floor, but I yank him back up by his arm before he can touch it.

"No!" I tell him. "Don't touch *anything*. We don't know if this place is a crime scene yet."

He side-eyes me. "Know a lot about those?"

"Yeah, I do," I say, glowering at him before directing his attention to the sink—and more specifically, to the mildewed edge of a tan suit jacket's sleeve poking out of the water. "That's a tuxedo. And judging by the color of that funky-ass water, I bet it was covered in blood. It matches what Emma told us. But why would he kill Ben Beaumont? And why kidnap Fabiana?"

"None of this makes sense." Clem huffs. "We're missing something."

"We're missing a lot," I say. "We just need to find the source. If Jack's not here, then where could he be?"

A loud whimper resounds from somewhere in the house, startling us both, and my heart plunges into my stomach when I realize we just assumed no one was here and forgot to check.

*Shit.*

Clem directs me to get behind him, and we follow the faint sound down a short hallway to a bedroom door that's slightly ajar. We lean close and listen to the sound coming from inside.

It's . . . crying?

Clem and I look at each other, and when I nod, he pushes the door open and leads the way inside.

It's a bedroom, but it's so plain that it's painful to look at. There are empty light-colored rectangles on the wall, where I assumed posters once hung. There's a barren desk pressed against the wall but no other furniture aside from a double bed.

Curled into the fetal position atop the unmade mess of the bed is Zachary Kingston. He's almost unrecognizable and stinks like he hasn't bathed in days. His eyes are red and swollen from crying, and snot runs in a stream that cascades over his lips and into his mouth and down his chin. He doesn't notice us at first, until Clem steps into his line of vision, and then Zac shoots upright, suddenly alert.

There's a bloated and charged moment of silence before Zac shrieks and flails in a fit of unnerving terror and screams, "Don't take me, demon!"

Clem and I exchange worried, confused looks.

Zac, shivering like a wet puppy, cocoons himself in a tangle of sheets and continues mumbling about demons.

"Maybe we should've called Aunt Ursula or Jean-Louise for backup," I say.

"Too late," Clem replies, deadpan. "We're already here. Let's see it through."

He approaches the bedside with cautious, measured steps, calling Zac's name, gentle at first, then louder when Zac doesn't respond.

Clem bellows, "*Zac!*" But the boy beneath the sheets doesn't reply. Clem grabs a fistful of the covers and rips them off, exposing Zac again.

He scampers up toward the head of the bed and cowers there, hiding his face in his arms.

I can feel the frustrated energy rolling off Clem in waves, which is unsettling for me, so I can only imagine how disoriented Zac must be right now. But it's not him I'm worried about.

My brother has never struggled to show empathy before. I know he's been depressed and exhausted and a lot of other not-so-good emotions lately, but today he feels closer to the edge than usual—and that troubles me.

I step between Clem and Zac, then put a hand on my brother's chest, which partially snaps him back to the reality of the gentle Clem I've always known.

"Can you get a glass of water for him, please?" I ask.

He cuts his eyes at me. "So, I can touch stuff now?"

I throw him a treacherous glare. "You wanna keep being able to?"

He stomps off and immediately trips over an errant sneaker and curses. Once he's gone, I wander a bit closer to Zac and ask if he minds if I sit. When he ignores my question, I sit anyway.

He cries quietly with his head turned and his face hidden.

"I know you're scared, Zac," I tell him. "Magic and the gods who govern it can be downright terrifying. But it's okay now. You're not alone anymore. You can relax."

He doesn't respond. But his breathing slows enough that he at least doesn't seem to be panicked anymore. Maybe we can have a coherent conversation now.

Clem returns with a glass of water. I take it from him and offer it to Zac.

He takes it in an unsteady hand, examining the trembling surface of the water in the glass and then my face for a long moment before drinking. He's stopped crying at least, but his face is pallid, his cheeks still wet with tears like the boardwalk after a fresh hard rain.

"We didn't come here to hurt you," I tell him.

Zac cuts his eyes at Clem, and my twin glares back at him unflinchingly for a tense second that charges the air in the room. I watch with bated breath, not sure what to do, but then Zac releases a sigh, clenches his jaw, and then drains the glass as if it's his first drink of anything all day.

I take the empty glass from him and set it on the bedside table. "Where's your dad, Zac?"

He shrugs with exhausted nonchalance that's frustrating as fuck. "He's been acting strange for a while now," he murmurs.

"Strange how?" I ask.

"Like he's possessed."

Clem and I lock eyes, and I wonder if we're thinking the same thing. Could the Moon King be possessing Jack Kingston? But why? This whole ordeal just keeps getting messier and more unhinged by the minute. I worry Clem and I are never going to be able to make sense of all this.

"Where's your dad right now?" Clem asks from where he stands a few feet away, his face hardened and stoic, his arms crossed over his chest.

"The cabin in the woods," Zac answers.

"What cabin?" Clem asks. "And when's he coming back?"

Zac's face flushes again. "Look, I *don't know.* He goes there every evening, and before you ask, I don't know for what. And I don't want to."

"Okay," I interject, just as Clem drops his arms in preparation to get out of pocket. "Where's this cabin? Can you give us the address?"

Zac huffs and shakes his head.

Clem takes an angry step forward, his fists balled at his sides, but I hold up a hand, and he stops. I mouth, *Chill.* His frown intensifies, but he falls back and stays quiet.

I turn back to Zac, who's no longer hiding his face but staring at his hands in his lap. His blond hair's greasy and overgrown, and his nails have been gnawed down to nubs, some covered in caked blood. This boy's a mess. What the hell happened to him?

"Look, Zac," I say, my voice as soft and empathetic as I can muster right now. "We believe you about the demon. If your dad's possessed, we might be the only people who can help him. Please. Can you tell us how to get to the cabin where your dad is?"

Zac shakes his head. Clem throws up his hands and slaps them onto his hips, then turns his back on us like a disappointed uncle.

Zac looks into my eyes for the first time. His have dulled considerably despite their light color, making me wonder again what he's been through.

He chews his bottom lip for a second, then says, "I'll take you. But we need to leave now. It'll be hard to see how to get there after sunset."

Clem spins around, suspicion heavy on his face.

I stand and nod at Zac. "Thank you for helping us."

He stares at me curiously, and his left eye twitches with a few uncomfortable ticks before he says, "I'm not helping you."

"What?" Clem growls over my shoulder.

"A demon is eating my dad," Zac says. "And when he's done with him, I hope he eats you next. Both of you. And I want to watch."

A chill skates across my back.

"The fuck did you just say?" Clem starts for him, but I tug him back before he can take a second step.

I narrow my eyes at Zac, but he doesn't flinch. *He meant every sadistic word.*

"Leave it," I tell Clem. "Now's not the time." I turn to Zac and say, "Let's go. Now."

He makes a show of getting out of bed on the opposite side so he doesn't have to walk by us, which, whatever, as long as he gets his ass outside to the car. No wonder he and Clem never got along. Although a part of me—a very tiny, miniscule part—wonders what kind of person Zac could've been had he grown up under different circumstances . . . with different parents.

"I need to pee first," Zac announces, and hurries from the room.

Clem and I hang back in the bedroom. "Should you be going to confront Jack if the Moon King is after you?" I whisper to him. "What if he's there?"

"Seems he's been following you too," Clem says. "The answers to all our problems could be at that cabin. Neither of us can afford *not* to go. Besides, I'm not leaving you alone with *that* creep." He cuts his eyes toward the hallway. "If the Moon King shows up, we'll just have to deal with him."

Clem's "jump right in" attitude is annoying at best, particularly right now, but I don't have a better idea, nor do we have the time to come up with one.

We step into the front room, and Zac pops out of the kitchen pantry, giving me and Clem both a fright.

"You pissing in the pantry now?" Clem asks.

Zac wrinkles his nose at him. "Fuck you. I'm hungry."

"Can we go?" I ask, gesturing toward the front door.

Zac leads the way out, and the three of us head for Clem's car at the end of the driveway. Zac stops at the rear passenger door and tugs on the handle, then frowns up at Clem, visibly annoyed.

Clem holds his key fob in his palm, staring reticently at it. "I thought you moved to Huntsville last year, Zac."

"I came back," Zac says, clipped.

"That your truck over there?" Clem nods in the direction of the white pickup at the other end of the driveway.

Zac glances at it and then back at Clem, frowning harder. "Yeah, *why*?"

Clem tilts his head, his brow furrowed. "How long you been back?"

Zac blanches. His frantic eyes dart between Clem and me. "Why are you grilling me?"

"Yeah, Clem," I say. "What's this about?"

"Answer the question," Clem orders Zac, ignoring me.

Zac lets go of the door handle and steps back.

"Clem!" I whisper. "Drop it!" When he doesn't respond or look at me, I add, "*Please*."

Clem presses the unlocking button on the remote, and the car chirps. He opens the driver's door, gets in, and slams it. Zac glowers from the other side of the car at me as I walk around to the passenger side.

"Please," I repeat for him. "Let's just go."

He hesitates long enough to make me want to grab him by his skinny throat and shove him into the back seat. He drinks in all of me during the anxious moments I spend wondering what we'll do if he refuses to help us. He consumes every bit of it until he's had his fill. And that tiny drop of power he wallows in for that brief slice of time is enough to make one side of his mouth twitch upward and to balloon his chest with pride.

He climbs into the back seat and shuts the door gingerly, then watches me through the window. The way he stares makes my skin crawl.

I massage my throbbing temple with one hand as I open the door and heave a deep irritated sigh. But before I get all the way in the car, I make the mistake of looking back at Jack and Zac's home.

I choke on my next breath.

The dark faceless silhouette of someone stands in the parted curtains at the front door.

Watching.

I gasp aloud and flinch back.

"What's wrong?" Clem asks, leaning across the console to stare up at me from inside the car.

I blink and rub my eyes, but when I look back, the curtains are drawn again, and no one's there. My heart continues in overdrive when I turn back to the car and catch a glimpse of Zac in the back seat, his head tilted down, his overgrown greasy tresses hanging like vines over dull eyes focused on me, and his mouth in a wicked close-lipped thin grin.

"Nothing," I mutter, and slide into my seat and buckle my seat belt. "Just drive. Get us the fuck away from this place."

I lower my window for some fresh air to mask Zac's BO as my brother backs the car out of the driveway.

I don't know what the hell's going on around here, but it's starting to feel like I'm living inside a nightmare that I can't wake up from.

And I desperately need it to be over.

# THIRTY-SIX
## VALENTINA SAVANT

"Sofia Denise Beaumont, where the *hell*—are—you?" Valentina grumbled into the voicemail message. "I can't stall for you much longer. Get your ass over here, or call me back. Now!"

She ended the call and slammed her phone on the counter. It wasn't like Sofia to screen Valentina's calls, not unless they were in a fight, which they weren't—but they damn sure were about to be. Valentina had taken a major risk inviting Sofia into her alliance, and the credibility she'd busted ass to build with Mom, Xavier, and even Eveline was on the line.

Valentina hadn't bothered referencing Granny's IG to set up the tea and snack trays for the meeting this time because she'd finally learned where everything was and had mastered the basics when it came to elegant presentation. Although that particular evening, she lacked the patience to fuss with unnecessary frills and pleasantries while her future staggered along the edge of a cliff.

The kettle whistled from the stove, and Valentina snatched it off the heat and smacked it down onto the tray, which she then gathered and carried to the sitting room where her mom waited patiently with Xavier Vincent, who'd demanded an urgent meeting with the alliance late last night—one Sofia had assured Valentina she'd attend with an update on their espionage plans.

That was the last Valentina had heard from Sofia.

Mom gave Valentina a questioning sidelong glance, and Valentina shook her head. Sofia, who might've held the keys to their uprising, had officially ghosted. Most of all, Valentina hated not knowing if Sofia had betrayed her or was dead or was just incredibly absentminded. None of those options eased Valentina's nerves.

Mom pursed her lips, unspoken concern wrinkling her forehead, which annoyed Valentina until she met Xavier's intense expression of irritation.

He shifted his body with a flighty unease that triggered Valentina's anxiety. She'd barely gotten Xavier on board in the first place, and she was afraid any hiccup would scare him away from their alliance. He'd always been a wild card, but he had access to a network of "darker" resources, which he'd built from so many years under Granny's and Grandpa Felix's tutelage, something Valentina planned to make sufficient use of once she was Queen.

Valentina wondered if Sofia had maybe seen something in the cards that morning that'd told her to flake. Damn those cards, and damn Sofia for putting Valentina in this position. But what if Sofia had seen something bad in the cards and kept it to herself? Maybe she didn't tell Valentina because of how rude she had been to Sofia about tarot in the past. Something had felt *off* in the deepest hollow of Valentina's gut all day. She'd thought it might've been nerves brought on by Xavier's impromptu freak-out, though it felt like something more—and that worried her because the last time she'd felt like this, her grandparents hadn't come home, and now they never would.

Xavier looked at his watch and stared angrily between Valentina and Gabriela. "Look, I don't have a whole lotta time here. What are we waiting for?"

"I know," Valentina told him. "I understand the pressure you're under." He grimaced, but she pressed on. "I'd intended for Sofia to be here so she could download us on what she's found so far through chasing clues about her dad's murder with Cris. I assure you, Xavier, we're close. And when we hand over her husband's killer and the key to putting one of her most dangerous enemies out of commission, Eveline Beaumont will have no choice but to give us the Gen Council."

Xavier raised his hands on either side of him, boiling over with impatience. "Well? What are these 'clues' that are going to magically save all our asses?"

"That's why we're waiting on Sofia—"

"So where is she?" Xavier asks, staring expectantly at me and then Mom.

"She got tied up, but she'll be here soon," Valentina lied.

"When?" pressed Xavier, growing more restive with each passing moment.

"Zay, you have to trust we're working on it," Mom said. "What's really going on with you?"

Mom's words settled him enough that he blew out a long sigh and relaxed his shoulders some, which Valentina realized had been tense the entire time they were speaking.

"Both Karmine Delaney *and* Detective Sommers have been up my ass," Xavier confessed. "I think Karmine might've gotten wind of me talking to Sommers. I've been ducking him, but he'll catch me eventually. And Sommers keeps pressuring me to roll on Karmine or go down with him."

"Maybe you should lie low for a while and let us work," Mom said with a charming, motherly softness to her voice, a power Valentina had only recently discovered her mom possessed.

Xavier threw up his hands again and huffed. "My sister and her bastard lawyer have my balls pressed against the wall. I might not have anywhere to 'lie low' by the end of the week—if Karmine doesn't kill me or Sommers doesn't arrest me first." He buried his face in his hands and mussed his hair, which had become greasy with nervous sweat. "I gotta do something. Tonight."

"And what exactly are you planning to do?" Valentina asked.

"Please don't do anything rash," Mom pleaded. "You can stay here if you need." She looked to Valentina for confirmation, and though Valentina wished Mom would've asked her if it was okay to invite someone to crash in *her house* first, she nodded.

Xavier bolted up from his seat, startling Valentina and Mom. "I knew this was a bad idea from the start. I can't depend on teenagers to save me from the *two* hammers waiting to pound me into dust."

"Just give us a few more days," Valentina said. "Once we have Eveline and the Gen Council and MASC—"

"Time is a luxury I do—not—have!" Xavier shouted, red-faced. He swept the remnants of spittle from his lips with the back of his hand.

"What are you going to do then?" asked Mom.

"I'm thinking about taking Sommers's deal," he said.

Valentina and Mom both scowled at the same time. A wild card, yes, but Valentina had never taken Xavier for a snitch and a rat—an unforgivable offense in her kingdom.

"No, Zay," Mom said, disappointment dragging her words. "You can't."

"What choice do I have?" he cried.

"Not the feds," Mom said. "Go to Karmine. He's not the most levelheaded person to be in business with, but you chose to skip down that path with him. Now let your business partner help you."

Xavier scoffed under his breath. "Neither of you gets it. I only matter to Karmine as long as I'm useful to him. I'm not dodging him because I'm afraid he'll be disappointed in me. If he finds out I've talked to the police, he'll disappear me from this realm *and* the next."

Mom rubbed her hands on her thighs, likely contemplating potential solutions. "What if we went and talked to Eveline together—"

"I already told you I don't trust that damn woman!" Xavier said.

"Why?" asked Valentina. "Seriously. If there's something about Eveline we should know, you need to tell us."

Xavier clenched his jaw, and his stare hardened as his eyes shifted between Valentina and her mom. "I was in my senior year of high school back in 2012 and really proud of pissing off my dad for taking Felix Savant's offer to join his firm as an associate. He said he'd teach me the ropes better than any college would or could—and he did. Him and Lenora both."

Valentina clasped her hands in her lap and squeezed tightly, trying to keep her feelings focused on the external pain of her nails digging into flesh as opposed to the internal acidic prick of jealousy that Xavier had gotten to have experiences with her grandparents that she would never have.

"It was a really cool job, especially for a kid like me," Xavier continued. "But then one day, Felix gave me this super-weird assignment. I had to go meet some shifty-looking guy at one of the investment properties, a warehouse, which so happens to be Vice Hall now. There was a car there that'd been sitting in that empty building for three years. The tires had rotted, and it'd had a ton of body damage, like it'd been in a bad accident. It had to be towed away. When I got back to the office, I asked Felix about it, and he told me not to worry with it.

"That same evening, Ben Beaumont stopped by the office. I remember because I thought it was odd they were meeting so late after hours. Felix and I were preparing the firm for the month's end, which typically meant a late night and early morning. Ben thanked Felix for holding the car for him for so long and helping him get rid of it. But then he'd said something strange, that he'd begged Eveline to 'leave that damned Bordeaux girl alone, but she feels guilty, and now they hate each other.' I don't know what happened exactly, but what I took from that experience is that Eveline and Ben Beaumont were not people I wanted to trust. I learned a lot about how to survive in this type of world while working with Felix and Lenora."

*That damned Bordeaux girl* stuck in Valentina's mind. Bordeaux wasn't a common surname. She only knew one Bordeaux family who might be involved with Eveline Beaumont, and that was Yves and his older sister, Fabiana.

Valentina and Yves had gone to the same school since they were small. She still remembered the whispered rumors among the students *and* teachers about the "poor boy" in their grade whose parents had died in a "tragic car accident."

It was then that Valentina realized perhaps Xavier had served a greater purpose in her pursuit of power. Because he might've just given her a clue to salvage her game—and her future.

"What do you think Ben and Eveline did?" asked Mom.

"I don't give a shit," Xavier replies. "I only shared that story to caution you from getting tangled up with that duplicitous woman. This little alliance game was fun while it lasted, but I gotta get back to the real world now, ladies. Tomorrow morning, Sommers promised that she's going to start her day with a fresh carafe of coffee while she plunders my financial documents—both at work and home. And next up is a search of all the firm's real estate holdings. I don't even know half the shit Felix, Lenora, and Ben have stashed throughout Savant Capital's vacant properties, but it might become my problem. I could lose everything, including my freedom." Xavier turned to

Valentina and gave her a pitying glance that needled her gut. "And that is not something I expect a seventeen-year-old girl to understand, but good luck to you two anyway."

He turned and left.

Mom got up to go after him, but Valentina waved her back into her seat.

"Let him go," Valentina said as the front door slammed after him. "We don't need him anymore—nor Sofia. I have an idea how you and I can still win the day." She stood up and told her mom, "I'm going to see Eveline."

"What are you planning?" asked Mom, standing too.

"I'll tell you when I'm back."

Mom followed Valentina to the garage door, and just before Valentina pulled it open, Mom told her, "I'm proud of you."

Valentina stopped and caught her breath before turning around. Mom had never said that to her before. Valentina had never felt like more than a burden to her parents, and enjoying this moment terrified her.

But she hugged her mom anyway.

It felt . . . nice . . . at first but then quickly became abnormal.

That type of affection with her parents hadn't been part of Valentina's life in a very long time. It would take some getting used to, which was what scared her. That was a lot of work that could potentially end in heartbreak—and she'd already had enough of that to last through this life and the next.

When they parted, Mom said, "You got this."

And she was damn right.

Valentina nodded and left.

# THIRTY-SEVEN
## CRISTINA

Hey. Can we meet??? I need to tell you something

It's urgent

Can't. Busy. TTYL

It's about our investigation. I have info for you.

TRUST

You wanna hear this

I respond to Sofia's text and put my phone away. "Can we take a quick detour to the Bean?" I ask my brother, who's been strangling the steering wheel and grimacing at the road with the intensity of Cruella de Vil since we pulled out of Zac's driveway barely three minutes ago.

He turns his frown on me. "Absolutely the fuck not, Cris. Are you serious right now? You wanna stop off for a latte *now,* when—"

"No, *jerk,*" I tell him. "Sofia wants to meet there. She claims to have something urgent to tell me about the investigation that can't wait."

Clem groans. "Cris. We don't have time for this."

"It's on the way. We're literally on the same street as the Bean right now. You won't even have to turn the car off. Just pull up to the curb, and I'll get out and see what she wants. It'll only take two minutes. Max."

"Fine," he grumbles. "Even though we already don't have time to waste."

"It's almost sunset." Zac's creepy singsong voice from the back seat makes me shudder.

I'm ready to be rid of him. I consider ditching Sofia, but my gut tells me I should at least hear her out. We did start this investigation together. Maybe she knows something that might give us an advantage when we confront Jack.

Sofia's waiting for me outside when we pull up at the Bean. Her hair's a mess of wild auburn curls, and she's wearing jean shorts and a rainbow pin-striped tank and a pair of white Chucks she must've hand painted with rainbow colors to match her top. She has on a different fanny pack today, but I'm sure the same old tarot deck is inside.

I get out and meet her on the sidewalk near the car. Clem tries not to be obvious with his eavesdropping, tapping the steering wheel and looking everywhere but directly at us.

"Hi, Sofia," I say. "What was so important that it couldn't wait until later?"

She glances around and lowers her voice. "Valentina wants back on the Gen Council, Cris. She hasn't let all that shit from last summer go."

Of course, Valentina's plotting despite my bringing her raggedy mama back to her and asking her nicely to leave me the fuck alone. I pause to think before responding to Sofia's intel and lock onto her light-brown eyes, suddenly recalling the fight between her and Valentina in the parking lot of school not too long ago. And now I wonder . . . were they trying to play me all the way back then?

"And how would you know this?" I ask. "Aren't y'all in a fight right now?"

"Because she's been trying to get in good with my mom."

"And what? You're jealous? I don't give a shit about y'all's drama, Sofia. And tell Valentina to leave me and my family *alone*."

"No," Sofia pleads. "That's not what I'm trying to tell you. I"—she heaves a sigh and stares at her colorful sneakers—"I'm tired of Valentina's abuse. She's not a nice person. And you made me feel seen the other day. I meant what I said. You deserve to be Queen. She doesn't."

"Are you spying for Valentina?"

Sofia shakes her head. "No! I mean, um, not anymore. I hadn't told her anything yet anyway."

I take a step closer and glimpse the fear welling in her eyes. "Please tell me you're not trying to play both sides here, Sofia, because you and I both know you're not smart enough for that. And I warned you what would happen if you tried me."

"No," she insists. "I'm trying to *warn* you! I want to help you!"

Clem beeps the horn and yells, "Two minutes are up, hunny! Move your ass!"

I give him a thumbs-up and turn back to Sofia. "Look, this isn't an episode of *Gilmore Girls*. Your dad died, and my mama could go to prison for the rest of her life for it. This is my *life*, Sofia."

Clem honks the horn again. "I swear to the gods, Cris, I *will* leave you!"

"Okay!" I shout back. "I'm coming!"

"Where are y'all going in such a hurry?" asks Sofia.

"None of your business," I tell her at once.

Clem stares deadpan at me and lays on the horn, which draws the attention of nearby people both on the sidewalk and sitting inside the Bean. I pump my hands at him to stop, but he doesn't until I start toward the car.

"Goodbye, Sofia," I tell her over my shoulder.

She sweeps up behind me and peers into the back seat of the car. Zac stares at her, his face flat and expressionless. He waves, and Sofia recoils. "Why are y'all hanging out with *him*?" She turns to me with suspicion in her eyes. "What are y'all up to?"

"I said none of your business," I repeat. "I do not trust you. I barely did before, and I damn sure don't now."

The sound of gravel crunching snags my attention as Clem inches the car forward, glaring at me through the open window.

"I'm coming too!" Sofia demands.

"No, you're not!"

By the time I realize what's happening, Zac's already thrown open the back door of Clem's car and slid over to make room for Sofia, who dives in and slams the door before I can stop her.

"What the fuck, Cris?" Clem says when I get in. "We're not going on a movie date. Why is *she* here?"

I buckle my seat belt and pinch the bridge of my nose.

"Hey! Hi there! Hellooo," says Sofia from the back seat. "Daughter of the dead guy whose murder you're investigating is *right here*. I have as much reason to be here as *him*." She jabs her thumb at Zac, who grins wickedly.

"The Sun is settiiinnng," he sings, which makes my skin writhe.

"EVERYONE, SHUT THE FUCK UP!" I shout. "CLEM, DRIVE! NOW!"

Clem peels away from the curb and heads west of the city at Zac's direction.

We pull off the road and park behind a dark gray SUV.

I turn around and ask Zac, "Is that your dad's car?"

He nods.

"Where are we going?" asks Sofia.

"You'll see," I tell her. "If you're scared, you shouldn't have invited yourself." Her phone lights up in her hand, and she glances down at it.

I check my phone and curse under my breath when I see NO SERVICE in place of my signal bar. I turn to Clem next. "Do you have service?"

He checks his phone and shakes his head.

*Great.*

I turn to the back seat just as Sofia's phone lights up again. "I'm assuming you have service since you're sitting on the hotline back there." Sofia blanches and turns her phone facedown on her lap. "Save your battery in case we need to call for help out there."

"You shouldn't have even brought your phones," Zac mumbles, as he throws open the door and climbs out. "You won't need them." He slams the door and goes up to his dad's SUV and peers into the trunk, then inspects the back and front.

"Anyone inside?" Clem asks as he and the rest of us get out too.

Zac shakes his head.

He leads us on a straight worn trail through thick woods that runs into a narrow dirt path after a short walk. The Sun sets just as we make it into the path, blanketing the forest and surrounding swamp in deep darkness. We stop and gather at the intersection.

"It's getting dark," Clem says. "How do you know where you're going?"

"We won't get lost," Zac says. "It's a straight shot from here."

"And how will we know how to get back?" asks Sofia, hugging herself against the encroaching nighttime chill in the air.

Zac points to a large tree near the trail we took to get to the dirt path, which has an X carved into its trunk, something I hadn't noticed before. Then he directs our attention to a tree on the opposite side of the path with a low-hanging branch that resembles a gnarled hand pointing at the X—and the direction back to the highway.

"If you miss the mark, that tree's always pointing out the way back to the highway," Zac explains. "But you won't need to remember that. We're not coming back."

"What?" Sofia exclaims.

I raise my brows at her. "Well, I bet now you'll think twice before jumping in other people's cars, won't you, Enola Holmes?"

Sofia sulks at the rear of the single-file line. Zac's at the helm, followed by Clem, and then me. I keep expecting to turn and see an empty path behind me, Sofia having fled back to the main road to call a rideshare to come rescue her. But every time I glance over my shoulder, she's there. Looking scared half to death and clinging to that ugly fanny pack. But always there.

The wet foliage and muddy earth are particularly fragrant tonight despite the chill that's crept upon us at dusk. I'm shivering slightly, but not all from the air. It's mostly nerves.

I don't know where we are in the middle of these creepy-ass woods *or* where exactly we're going, and my brother and I are literally sandwiched between a Great Value spy and the most capricious boy I've ever had the displeasure of meeting.

The path ends in an empty clearing of tall grass and weeds but nothing else.

Zac presses his hands to both sides of his head and starts pacing back and forth. "Th-That's not right. Where is it? It's magic, and it only comes after sunset. It's *supposed* to appear at night! It's *night*! Where's the *fucking* cabin?" He rounds on us, his cheeks splotched red and eyes wet. "The demon must've taken him already."

"The who now?" Sofia asks, wide-eyed.

My brother and I share a knowing glance. This is Moon magic. But Jack Kingston doesn't practice magic. It's why he and Aunt Ursula don't get along—because he thinks she used magic to steal his business (when he had one).

So . . . who's *really* behind all this?

I look to the sky. The cloud cover is dense and absolute tonight, as if this part of the world has snuggled beneath a heavy knitted quilt. I lift my hand toward the sky and feel for the phantom warmth of the Moon's light pressing against the backside of the clouds until I find it.

I close my eyes, take a deep breath, and focus. I place my other hand on my stomach, connecting to my core, my link to magic, my ancestors, and the spiritual realm. And then I sense the raw magic of the Moon throbbing behind the clouds. I wave my hand gingerly, and the Moon brightens in response, glowing with a brightness the Sun would envy. It burns a hole through the clouds that roll back on themselves like ocean waves. Bright moonlight beams down, illuminating the clearing—and the cabin appears at once, as if it'd always been there. Well, technically it was.

But who could've done this? This is no simple conjuring. This level of magic requires real skill. Not many people in New Orleans have that kind of power.

The log cabin before us is small, probably one room, with a single sad mildewed window that's too stained to see inside. The whole building looks old and weathered. The roof's rotting but mostly whole for now. A single solar panel aimed toward the sky sits atop a stake at the back of the cabin. And the dark green paint of the front door has dulled and chipped with age and wear.

*How old is this place?*

"Is your dad in there?" Clem asks Zac.

Zac has calmed despite aggressively chewing on his thumbnail. "Open the door and see."

"Why don't *you* open it?" Clem snaps back.

Zac shakes his head and floats to the back of our group.

"I'll do it." Clem huffs.

I inch closer behind him as he approaches the door. Zac and Sofia hang back, peering eagerly around us. Clem turns the knob slowly, then stands back and kicks the door open, flooding the interior with bright moonlight.

And I can't believe what I'm looking at.

A sepia-skinned Black woman in a plain gray sweatsuit lies on a mattress in a far corner of the room. Encircling one of her ankles is the iron cuff of a giant chain, which tethers her to a thick ring bolted to the middle of the floor like a metal umbilical cord.

Clem gasps and stumbles back a half step. "Oh, God," he mutters.

The woman raises her head and stares at us in shocked disbelief.

We found Fabiana Bordeaux.

# THIRTY-EIGHT
## VALENTINA SAVANT

When Valentina pulled into the Beaumonts' driveway, she immediately noticed Sofia's mint-green Prius was gone. However, several lights were on in the front of the house, which Valentina hoped meant Eveline was home.

Valentina hurried up to the front porch and rang the bell.

Eveline Beaumont opened the door and tilted her head curiously, irritation lining her forehead. "Hey, Valentina. I'm afraid Sofia's not home right now."

"I came to see you," Valentina said. "Can we talk? It's important."

Eveline sighed and stood aside to let Valentina in.

The forest of forgotten flowers in the foyer had been cleared since Valentina's last visit, but an air of darkness and mourning still hung thick in the Beaumont home like the lingering scent of frying fish. This place felt cold, so much so that Valentina hugged herself on the short walk with Eveline to the kitchen.

Eveline refilled a wineglass on the counter from an open bottle. "Would you like something to drink?" She took a sip, eyeing Valentina over the rim, and added, "Not this."

"No, thank you," Valentina said.

"Then what'd you want to talk about?"

Valentina ignored the blatant lack of enthusiasm in Eveline's voice. The woman's formerly rich brown skin seemed duller, even in the bright kitchen lighting. Her eyes were wine drunk and tired, and her hair was tied back in a red satin scarf patterned with gold flowers. She wore the same satin robe as before, wrapped and tied tight over her pajamas.

Valentina had seen and experienced grief many times. The devastation she saw on Eveline's person wasn't just that. There was something else there that Valentina also knew well. It was the anguish of having the rug suddenly snatched from beneath you and your world flipped permanently upside down. And the disorientation that followed while you flailed, trying to get back upright so you could attempt to flip your life back right side up again, except you couldn't—because time dragged you by the ankle. It was a fucking exhausting experience.

Perhaps one Valentina could use to her advantage.

"You need to pass your Council seat to me," Valentina said, her eyes locked on Eveline's, her conviction bold and transparent. Eveline frowned and set her wine down, but Valentina didn't give her time to rebut. "That way, you can focus on the Magical Regulation Bureau but still have a hand in Council business—through an allyship with me."

"And why would I give the responsibility of my Temple *and* Council duties to *you* of all people?" Eveline asked.

"You're running low on allies," Valentina said, to which Eveline narrowed her eyes. "How long will you and Marie realistically be cool with each other, especially after your bureau's up and running? And how will you even get it off the ground with Madeline DeLacorte circling like a buzzard? You're surrounded by threats. You need someone you can trust, someone with a level head and an eye for strategy."

"And what makes you think I'd trust you?" Eveline asked. "Notwithstanding the fact you're a *child*."

Valentina ignored the slight and soldiered on. "We have common goals. And you're the type of woman who won't let anyone stop her from getting what she's due. And I respect the hell out of that about you." A smile tugged at Eveline's lips. "And that's why after you got rid of Isaac, you got with his less attractive younger brother, Ben."

Eveline tilted her head. "Tread carefully, little girl."

But Valentina wasn't frightened. She was all the way in her bag, and she wasn't leaving until she got what she wanted. Eveline couldn't cow Valentina the way she'd done Granny all those years ago.

"We don't need to be careful with the truth," Valentina said. "Not when it's *us* talking, Eveline. That's the benefit of allying with me. The Beaumont family had connections very high up in the Louisiana government that branched all the way to Congress—and the White House. I know because I researched. You've been playing the long game. It's quite impressive."

Eveline sipped her wine, the subtle nod to her ego having done its job of cooling her down.

"Rosalie didn't poison your and Ben's drinks that night at Vice Hall," Valentina said. "That was part of your plan to take Rosalie down as payback for the compromising video of your husband that she used to blackmail him, which I'm guessing had something to do with Vice Hall. You needed to send a strong message to anyone who might potentially throw a wrench in your plans to start the MRB. I figured that part out when Sofia mentioned seeing you with foxglove."

Eveline sat still as a statue. Valentina could see the gears turning in Eveline's head through her steady, unreadable gaze.

"And the knockout gas that was taken from the House of Vans threw me until earlier tonight," Valentina said. "I didn't understand why you'd include Fabiana in it, unless the compromising video of your husband was leaked from her brothel, but I had the sneaking suspicion it was deeper than that for you—and I was right."

Eveline's entire body tensed. She drained her wineglass, and her jaw clenched while she hastily refilled the glass and took another big swig.

"Who was driving the night you and Ben killed Fabiana and Yves Bordeaux's parents?" Valentina asked. "It was him . . . wasn't it?"

When Eveline spoke, her voice was raspy and tired. "Who've you told?"

Valentina shook her head. "Nobody. I don't judge you for anything you've done. I would've done the same. How do you think I put it all together? I know what it's like to do what you must to survive. And now we're both fighting for survival again. But we can help each other this time. We've come too far to let them win."

Eveline eased herself onto one of the stools at the counter and hung her head, gazing into the half-full wineglass. "Despite everything else, it's been the guilt that I haven't been able to contend with. The notion that maybe if I hadn't been scheming against Rosalie and Fabiana that night that Ben might still be alive." She drained her glass and set it back down on the counter. "I never really believed Marie did it, but I was so angry at her and that whole damned family for barging into my life and threatening to uproot everything it's taken decades to put into place."

"All the more reason to let me help you," Valentina said. "You can't do this alone."

Eveline chuckled and shook her head. "You're very smart, Valentina, but you don't know as much as you think you do about what I've been through." A long stretch of silence passed between them, and Valentina let the conversation breathe for a bit, until Eveline released a heavy sigh and said, "You know, I *begged* him to let me drive that night. One simple decision could've saved so many people so much strife. But that white-man hubris was rooted *deep* inside Ben, worse than his brother. And I'd worked so damn hard to get rid of that buffoon, Isaac, and then to mature Ben into a responsible adult. I couldn't start over." She shook her head and sighed. "I hated every moment of it, but I went along with the cover-up to protect my future.

"I honestly tried to help those kids. I brought them to my temple. Fed them. Clothed them. Housed them. But I couldn't protect them from the truth. The day Fabiana found out, she turned a dark corner once she realized she would never get justice, that Ben would never face a consequence for what he'd stolen from Fabiana and her brother. And that darkness preyed on her until she became a shadow herself."

Valentina knit her brows, confused. "What do you mean?"

"She claims what she's doing at the House of Vans is *philanthropic*, but there are quite more than a few spouses in New Orleans who would gladly see that place shut down for all the grief it's brought into our marriages and our lives."

Long ago, Valentina learned there was a particular nuance to operating efficiently in the world alongside other egotistical humans, which way too many adults either couldn't understand or refused to acknowledge. But that was a battle for another day. So, instead of speaking her mind on the matter, she bit down on her bottom lip and stayed mum, which was the part she hated most about this sort of strategic maneuvering.

No one forced anyone's spouse to visit the House of Vans, Ben included. If there was ever any fault to uncover, it lay, and always had, with the partners who chose to betray their spouses' trust, not with the people who were simply trying to work and mind their business. And Eveline had a lot of nerve to judge Fabiana for how she chose to repair the life Eveline and her husband had blown apart.

"Would you believe that eleven years later, she still won't forgive me?" Eveline said. "And still yet, I tried to save Fabiana. After the mess with the tape last fall, Ben wanted her gone. Permanently. But I still tried. I gave her chance after chance to repent and spend the rest of her time doing something *worthwhile*."

"Like helping you build the Magical Regulation Bureau?" asked Valentina.

Eveline shook her head and fell quiet.

"Everyone's been speculating about what you're really doing with the MRB," Valentina said.

"That's my business, not theirs," Eveline snapped. "They can speculate all they want. Hell, the bureau's on life support now, and whoever's elected mayor might pull the plug for good."

"Then let me handle the Temple of Innocent Blood and Gen Council business for you while you focus on saving your bureau," Valentina said. "Trust me, Eveline."

"And why do I get the feeling there's a catch to this offer?"

"I may be young, but I'm not naïve. I'll support you and the MRB—but I want in."

Eveline sat back on her stool. "But you don't even know what I'm planning."

"I have an idea."

Eveline raised a curious brow.

"Magical registration," Valentina told her. "Once the MRB controls magical law for all branches of magic, you're going to make magic practitioners register themselves *and* their secrets. And then you'll have unmitigated access to every bit of secret knowledge about

Moon magic, light magic, *and* shadow magic. No one would be able to stand against you with that kind of power."

Eveline sat quiet, the stoic expression on her face battling the smug grin that fought to break through. As much as Eveline believed in moving in silence, she couldn't hide that she enjoyed being witnessed.

"There's a reason you won't talk about magical registration publicly," Valentina continued. "It's because you don't want to give your detractors a chance to get ahead of you. Smart. And once you set the playing rules in New Orleans, you'll be able to expand to Louisiana, the South, and eventually nationwide—maybe even the rest of the world. Queen of the Gen Council and Chair of MASC pales in comparison to the empire you're building." Valentina smirked. "I want in."

Eveline folded her hands on the counter in front of her and thought for an insufferably long moment before she lifted her eyes to Valentina's and said, "Fine. You've worn me down. I'll give you *one* chance. But disappoint me and you're done. Cross me—and you're dead. You were right before: I'll do whatever it takes to protect my future, including murdering a kid. Do not fuck with me, Valentina Savant."

Valentina appreciated when people bared their fangs to her face. Existing around people was always more comfortable when she knew what to expect. It was the ones who liked to hide their teeth, like Cristina Trudeau, whom Valentina really took issue with.

Speaking of Cris, Valentina couldn't *wait* to see Cris's face when she sat next to her at the next Council meeting.

Eveline stood up and gestured for Valentina to join her. "Come with me," she said. "If you're going to be taking over as Reverend Mother, I should start getting you caught up on Temple and Council business."

"Can't wait," Valentina said, beaming as she followed Eveline into her office.

Valentina had set out to be Queen but landed a bit short as Reverend Mother of the Temple of Innocent Blood. However, she'd gotten back inside the Gen Council, which was only the beginning. She wasn't finished yet.

Not even close.

And her future had just become even brighter than she could've ever imagined.

# THIRTY-NINE

## CRISTINA

Clem dashes inside the cabin and up to Fabiana's bedside in the left corner of the room.

I follow slowly, taking in the maddeningly simplistic cabin interior.

Rough pale brown planks make up the floor, walls, and ceiling, and a bare light bulb and fixture with a long dingy pull string dangles just above our heads from a fat wire sprouting from the ceiling. It provides a pitiful, somber light to the claustrophobic space. On my right, at the back of the space, is a single discolored toilet, a meager roll of toilet paper sitting atop the tank, the lid of which is askew.

Centered on the wall between the makeshift bed and the toilet is the window I saw from outside, rendered useless by the thick layer of grime coating its surface. Moonlight glows dully from the other side due to the Moon, which still pulses feverishly in the sky. The mattress Fabiana's been lying on is bare and soiled, exposed beneath the blue floral quilt spread haphazardly beneath her.

How long have they had this woman—Yves's sister—chained up here? Was someone trying to frame both Mama *and* Fabiana?

Surely, this couldn't *all* be Jack Kingston. Not on his own.

But who's he working with? What conjurer is responsible for this cabin's magical cloak? Even if Jack were dabbling in gen magic, he couldn't do all *this*. *I* don't even know how.

"I'm fine, I swear," Fabiana says to Clem, who immediately shifts from fussing over her to fumbling with the heavy-looking cuff attached to her ankle. "I've been better, but at least they didn't torture me—technically. Or worse. Though what they did was bad enough."

"What did they do to you?" asks Clem.

"And who is *they*?" I add.

"Jack Kingston kidnapped me," Fabiana reveals. "But he's not working alone. He could never be the brains of an operation like this."

Zac growls under his breath from where he stands with his back pressed into the corner of the room nearest to the door.

Fabiana cuts her eyes at him. "I know someone's helping him," she says. "I just don't know who."

"Did you ever see anyone else besides Jack?" I ask.

"Yes and no," Fabiana says. "Soon as I got here, I started having this really strange recurring dream where the Sun has just risen, and the whole clearing is lit in this really rich orange glow. The front door opens slowly, and I see the silhouette of a person standing there, hidden in shadow from the bright early morning light behind them. But that's all I remember, and then I wake up midmorning, and my head's always foggy. After a while, I realized it wasn't a dream. Someone was fucking with my head, magically erasing my memories daily. I don't know what they want from me, but I just want to get the hell out of here, *please*."

"I'd love that for you too," Clem says, "but we need a key to get this damn cuff off."

"Jack has it," Fabiana tells us. "He keeps it on him. I'm surprised you didn't run into him."

"No, we didn't see him," I say. "His car's still by the road, so he must be around here somewhere."

"But where?" asks Clem. "It's only forest and swampland out here."

"He might be dead." The grave, hopeless tone of Fabiana's voice ices my skin. "He's in bad shape. He comes every so often to tend to me, and each time he looks worse and worse. Today he was damn near a walking corpse. It's like the devil's been whooping his ass—and he deserves every bit of it."

Zac mumbles something inaudible from behind his fist without pausing from going to work on his nails.

"How long have you been here?" I ask Fabiana.

She frowns at the window with the obscured view. "I have no idea. What day is it?"

"April twenty-sixth," Sofia announces helpfully.

Fabiana's face pales. "Oh, God," she breathes. "It's been *months*.

I knew it'd been a while, but I had no idea it's been *that* long." A shadow passes over her face. "My brother. My employees. My business."

"We've been trying to find you," Clem says. "We went by the House of Vans, and Colby was holding it down—not like you, but they were making it work."

Some of the distressed tension eases in Fabiana's neck and shoulders. "And Yves . . . ?"

Clem hesitates before blurting out, "He's okay."

Fabiana lets out a deep sigh of relief. "I'm so glad he wasn't there the night Jack attacked me. Blessings to the spiritual realm for him being away at that study-abroad program." She looks at Clem. "Have you spoken with him?" Clem bristles, and she notices, tensing again. "Does he know I was kidnapped?"

It's hard watching truths and lies battle on my brother's face. I don't know how he's going to tell Fabiana what really happened to Yves, who also made it quite plain from the very beginning—the only person Fabiana Bordeaux cossets more than her employees is her little brother—the same one Clem partially resurrected from the dead and stashed at Jean-Louise's house.

"No, he's—" Clem swallows hard, and I sense him struggling with his lie. "He doesn't know. I didn't want to upset him while he was out of the country until we knew what was going on, especially so close to the end of the semester."

Fabiana half nods, and her lips part, birthing another question. Beads of sweat already crown Clem's forehead and temple.

"What happened the night Jack kidnapped you?" I ask Fabiana.

Clem thanks me with only his eyes, and mine communicate back, *I gotchu.*

Fabiana pulls her knees close to her chest, the rusted iron chain clinking as it snakes with movement, then slides her fingers between the cuff and massages her purple and swollen ankle. "I got home from the office late one night, and the asshole had been hiding in my fucking pantry, waiting for me to come home. He ambushed me in my own kitchen. We fought. I smashed a bottle of Ho-Van Oil upside his head, and he threw me to the floor, but I kicked and struggled long enough to write his initials on the floor in the oil before he caught my feet and dragged me out. It was a long shot, but I hoped Rosalie might see the broken bottle and find my secret message."

Clem shakes his head. "Not Rosalie. Me. But she's the one who told me Ho-Van Oil was luminescent."

"Then thank the gods for you, sweet boy," Fabiana says, smiling. "My brother is fortunate to have found a brilliant mate like you."

"Uh, we should call for help," I announce, and Clem nods, ecstatic for the change of subject. I turn to Sofia and hold out my hand. "Can I borrow your phone?"

"Sure," she says, but the moment she pulls it from her back pocket, it lights up with another call. Her *oh, shit* expression is unmistakable in the bright glow of her phone's screen.

I snatch the phone out of her hands, and Sofia makes a pitiful attempt to grab it back but wilts the second I stare lasers at her. I look at the caller ID, and my heart stammers.

*Valentina Savant.*

"Well, let's see what she wants." I answer the call on speaker.

The connection is riddled with static owing to the single bar of signal. Sofia looks like she wants to melt into a puddle and seep into the cracked floorboards.

"FINALLY!" The voice that blares through the speaker, albeit somewhat garbled, undoubtedly belongs to Valentina. "WHERE"—*static*—"BEEN? WE"—*static*—"MEET WITHOUT YOU. I'M STARTING"—*static*—"YOUR"——*static*—"THIS ALLIANCE!"

I cut my eyes to Sofia, and her face flushes. She trembles under the gaze of every person in the room.

"HELLO?"—*static*—"THERE? HEL—"—*static*.

I end the call. "Well, *that* was interesting."

"It's not what you think," Sofia blurts.

*Sounds familiar.* That's the exact same bullshit Oz tried to feed me after I caught him conjuring love spells on me. Believing that lie even once could be deadly. No . . . this is exactly what I think and precisely what it looks like. I've caught yet another of Valentina's pathetic pawns.

I fling Sofia's phone at her. She fumbles it, and the phone thunks to the floor at her feet. Behind her, Zac eyes it, but no one moves to pick it up.

Sofia stares at me, shaking her head. "Cris . . . *please*."

The drama and tension between me and Sofia enraptures Clem, Fabiana, and Zac, who all watch with bated breath.

"Why do people like you do the foulest shit to other folks but then beg for mercy once it's y'all's turn to finally get tapped back?" I ask Sofia, calmly. Her chin and bottom lip quiver, but she offers no reply. "You played on my sympathy and my kindness," I tell her. "You *and* Valentina. I really tried to be civil with y'all, but that wasn't good enough . . . so maybe you'll understand this."

I go over to the toilet and snatch off the tank lid, underestimating how heavy it is, which makes me stumble backward a half step. The sad roll of toilet paper unfurls across the floor in a trail of white. I regain my footing, readjust my grip on the porcelain lid, and fling it through the window. The glass shatters outward, revealing the dark forest and nighttime sky beyond. Moonlight pours through, illuminating the room even more.

Fabiana scoots farther away from me on her mattress. "Goddamn, girl."

The Moon still burns bright and cerulean in the circular gap in the thick blue-gray clouds. It pulses, nearly bursting with raw magic, heralding the promise of vengeance and justice, begging to be tapped. I reach one hand through the broken window, beneath the Moon, and unscrew it in the sky. A geyser of raw moonlight spirals down in mere seconds. I raise my other hand, my palm facing upward, my fingers pointed toward Sofia, who flinches back.

Moonbeams stream over my flesh, dragging heat across my skin like steaming-hot water from a shower. The magic spirals up my forearm and around my chest; some of it swirls my shoulders, tickling the back of my neck, then rushes down my other arm and over my palm to my fingertips, where it sprays with the intensity of a high-pressure garden house straight into Sofia's open mouth. The force of it lifts her feet from the floor and slams her back against the door of the cabin.

She has no choice but to open her mouth and drink in the moonlight.

"You wanted magic so bad," I sneer, "well, now you can fucking have it!"

The moonbeams flowing into Sofia project an eerie blue glow into the room. The powerful stream of magic swings the hanging light bulb around, which tosses shadows wildly around the room, ramping up the chaos of it all. I've gone too far to stop now.

The back of my neck prickles with the sensation of someone watching me from the other side of the broken window, but I don't break my focus. The rage inside me has finally broken free. Maybe it's time I stopped restraining it. I tried and tried to make peace and move on, but these people refuse to let me have it, so what other choice have they left me?

"Cris!" Clem screams at me. "What the hell are you doing? Stop it! Sofia's your friend!"

"Leave me alone, Clem!" I growl at him. "Maybe if I make an example out of her, the rest of them will finally stop fucking with all of us. They need to be *stopped*."

Zac scurries on his hands and knees across the floor like a rat and quivers behind the toilet.

I ignore him too and close the connection to the Moon. The clouds are nearly all gone, the ones remaining mere translucent sheets stretched across the sky. The tap dries at once, the magic spray dwindling to a rivulet, a trickle, and then nothing. I drop my hands at the same time Sofia falls to the floor and doubles over.

The stripes of her rainbow tank are stretched and distorted due to her bulging stomach, pumped full of magic. Her mouth is coated with azure remnants of it as if she were a messy toddler at lunch. Sofia coughs and spits a blue splatter of moonbeams onto the floor at her feet. When she jabs one finger in her mouth and gags, I throw my hand out and latch on to the warm invisible connection to the magic inside her, and I massage it with my fingers, coaxing it into doing my bidding.

Sofia writhes, scratching feverishly at her neck, her arms, her face, and digging in her scalp—but nothing satiates her, and the fraught expression on her face intensifies when she realizes that nothing will. Not unless I allow it.

"Get it out of me!" she cries as I goad the magic through her veins and arteries and let it soak into her muscle tissue until it's spread completely throughout her body.

When I lift my hand, she also rises into the air, kicking her feet, still clawing angry red welts into her bright brown skin. I flex my fingers and seize control of her limbs.

"Since you insist on being a puppet, you'll be mine before I end you," I tell her as I approach slowly, my hand held aloft, keeping her suspended in the air against the door like a Christmas wreath. I test out my control of the magic inside her and move my fingers as if each were attached to marionette strings that controlled her limbs. "All I asked was for you and Valentina to leave—me—alone."

The gentle weight of a hand on my shoulder snaps me out of my rant, but I don't flinch or relinquish control. Clem presses his forehead against my temple and whispers, "Sis. I know you're pissed. You have every right to be. But if you kill Sofia tonight, you *will* go to prison. And that's exactly what Detective Sommers wants. Do you want to switch places with Mama when we're so close to saving her?"

"Of course not," I mumble, still glowering up at Sofia, who whimpers softly. "I'm not worried about that. I can figure out how to make bodies disappear."

"Okay, but this ain't that deep though." The insistence in his tone and the way he leans back from me feels authoritative, and his attitude is giving *irritated*. "What Sofia did isn't the same as what the others did. Let this shit go. Please. I'm begging you."

"It might not be 'that deep' for you, but it is for me," I tell him. "How many times have I 'let it go' only to be brought right the fuck back here? I told her from day one not to bring that bullshit into my life, and she sat in front of me and told a bold-faced lie. How many times must I go through this with them before they see a consequence?"

Clem grimaces but has no answer.

Fabiana and Zac watch, both rapt silent in their corners, consumed by shock and wonderment—respectively.

"It's time I tried a different resolution," I say.

I clench my fist in front of me, envisioning the molecules of magic inside her transitioning to the solid state—ice—again, just like with Dr. Thomas. Except this time, I'm going to freeze her entire body and drop her into a rip straight to the never-realm.

I start at her extremities. Fingers. Toes. Sofia begs for me to stop, but I ignore her and Clem's whispered pleas. However, another voice echoes in my other ear, one that's strange yet familiar at the same time—and gives me permission to choose violence.

They murmur that murder can be righteous when done in the name of *blood justice* as Sofia shivers from the cold spiraling inside her. The more of her I freeze, the louder the voice of vengeance and rage becomes, drowning out everything else around me until it becomes a gravelly, low chant that I can't discern from sound or thought.

*It's what she deserved.*

*She betrayed you to ally with your enemies.*

*They took your grandparents from you. They murdered your father. Almost killed your mother too.*

*Tsk. Tsk.*

*Pity toppled the compassionate Queen's kingdom.*

*But the vengeful Queen reigned supreme by wielding the Queen's Justice.*

*Be the Queen. Use the power of the gods. Dispatch the Queen's Justice.*

*End her.*

*End her.*

*End—her.*

Sofia gasps and falls silent, gawking down at the veins in her hands that've swollen and turned vibrant blue beneath her bloated appendages.

It's as if my will runs on autopilot now, and for a moment, I feel completely weightless. All the frustration of injustice and unfairness vanishes in the shadow of the rage that grew a little more every time someone slapped us and we had to turn another cheek.

Well . . . my rage and I have both run out of spare cheeks.

Clem grips my shoulders and cries into my face, "Cris, *please*!"

I clench my fist tight. It's time to finish this. I won't be callous and torture her. I'll at least make death quick for her. But Sofia's end doesn't come fast.

Or at all.

The magic inside her warms and dwindles until it evaporates into nothing like fog hit with vivid daylight.

"No," I mutter in disbelief. "No, what is this? What's happening?"

Sofia crashes to the floor in a screaming heap, clutching her left hand to her chest. The tip of one of her pinky fingers has turned black with frostbite. The force of her teeth chattering vibrates her cheeks.

Clem zips to her side to help her up, but once she's on her feet, she shoves him away from her.

I'm still stunned, glancing between my hands and her. I reach out the broken window toward the Moon again, grasping the air hungrily for that familiar connection, but it's gone. The Moon doesn't respond. I put one hand over my stomach, then both, and again—nothing.

My tether to the spiritual realm—to generational magic—is *gone*.

*Oh, God. What happened to my magic?*

Sofia's in my face before I realize what's happening. She slaps me so hard that I stagger to one side. That was unexpected. But maybe it's what I deserve.

The ringing in my ears grounds me in reality again, sobering me from the intoxicating rage that took control of me. And that voice in my head goading me on . . . what the heck *was* that?

Nausea churns my insides like a washing machine once I realize how close I just came to killing someone I considered a friend once. Sofia has her faults, but Clem was right. This is different from Tabitha and Dr. Thomas. This is Sofia, for gods' sakes.

What the hell have I done?

Maybe this is why Oberun's influence was erased from history. I've allowed him—or rather, the idea of him—to lead me astray. And then Clem's warning from earlier slaps my other cheek. Could that have been the voice of the Moon King I heard before at Tabitha's and Dr. Thomas's homes? And just now?

I take a step back and glance around the room, but no ancient gods are here with us, only the concerned stares of four other people that communicate a myriad of emotions, none of them good.

"Sofia . . ." I start, and immediately find the words hard to get out, but I fight through the humiliation and disappointment anyway. "I'm sorry."

My apology feels massively inadequate, though while I regret what I did, I don't take back any of what I said. Murdering Sofia's not the answer, but judging by the fire in her eyes, I've sent a clear message—albeit one that might've somehow cost me my magic.

Sofia's nose wrinkles. "I was wrong before," she sneers. "You and Valentina are exactly alike. And I hate both of you mean bitches. Where is my phone? I'm getting the hell out of this dumbass cabin and these stupid-ass woods." Her voice wavers at the end, and she clamps her mouth shut tight but fails to hide her trembling lip as her eyes well to the brim. She turns in place, searching the floor for her phone until she meets Zac's mischievous stare.

He points to the toilet.

"You put my phone in the fucking toilet?" shrieks Sofia.

Zac sits on the toilet (fully clothed, thank the gods) and grins at Sofia. "I told you already that you don't need phones. No one's going anywhere. We're all dying here tonight. My dad already told me."

"Oh, fuck this," grumbles Sofia. "I'll walk back to sanity and civilization."

She turns and snatches open the front door—and screams. She stumbles backward, trips over her own feet, and falls ass first to the floor.

Sofia scuttles back several feet, terrified as she stares up into the face of Jack Kingston, who stands in the doorway, a gaunt and ominous silhouette against the moonlight.

# FORTY
## CLEMENT

Jack Kingston lumbers into the cabin, leaving the door partially open. He stumbles while stepping around Sofia, falls up against the wall, and slides down to his butt in a pitiful breathless heap.

Sofia gets up and scurries to the other side of the room and presses her back against the wall, watching everything unfold with frightened wide eyes.

Fabiana was telling the truth. Jack looks awful. The man's rail thin despite a conspicuous belly, a stark contrast from how I remember him at the Vice Hall party. The slacks and dress shirt he's wearing are mud stained and torn ragged in some spots as if he was in a fight with someone—or some*thing*. His hair's greasy and brown and slicked back from his splotchy, sweaty face. And the dark circles under his eyes are so prominent that they're downright ghoulish.

"Dad!" Zac cries out. He bolts across the room and drops to his knees at his father's side. When Zac leans in for a hug, Jack palms the boy's face and shoves him.

Zac falls aside, and shock and hurt register briefly on his face, but then he shakes it off and scoots closer to his father, putting his back against the wall next to him. He pulls his knees up to his chest and hides his face behind them, his beady eyes poking out at us over knobby curves of pink flesh.

Jack, his face pinched and eyes shut as if in excruciating pain, reaches into his pocket and removes an iron key. His eyes part slightly, and he holds it out to me.

I snatch it from him, immediately caught off guard by the heavy weight of it. I hurry over to Fabiana, who's already sitting up, her ankle extended, ready to be free again.

When I turn the key in the lock, the resulting *click* is so damn satisfying. I open the manacle carefully and help Fabiana lift her swollen, bruised ankle from the medieval device.

"You think you can walk on it?" I ask her.

She winces and hisses when she tests out putting a little weight on it, then stretches her leg and flexes her foot. "I just need a minute," she says. "Nothing's stopping me from getting the fuck out of this raggedy cabin and back to my brother."

I catch Cris's face snap to me and sense her drawing closer before she takes the first step.

I release a shaky breath. "There's something I need to tell you. It's about Yves."

Fabiana withers. "What? Is something wrong? I thought you said he was okay?"

"Not . . . quite." I look away momentarily to gather my resolve.

She snaps her fingers in my face, regaining my attention. "Hey, what's going on?"

"Last June, Yves and I were leaving the art museum together. It was late at night, and we were in the parking lot alone, and—"

"I need you to get to the point," Fabiana snaps.

Cris appears beside me and puts a hand on my shoulder. She doesn't utter a word. She doesn't need to. Strength radiates from her. My invisible connection with my sister tugs on my heart, much like the tether to the spiritual realm connected to my gut.

"This guy snuck up on us," I say. "I still don't know who it was or why he targeted us, but he, uh . . . he had a gun . . . and . . ." The room becomes stifling hot all of a sudden, but I press on in spite of the tears brimming in my eyes and the pressure building behind them, threatening to burst my damn of emotions. "He shot Yves . . . and he died . . . in my arms . . . and I didn't know what to do, so I took him to Jean-Louise Petit's house, a-and we resurrected him. But his soul is broken, and I don't know how to fix it, and I've been hiding it and trying to do everything on my own, but I need help."

Fabiana sits so rigid and still that I seriously begin to fear she might've either turned to stone or she's on the cusp of an aneurysm. Cris's grip on my shoulder remains firm. I want to reach up and grab her hand, absorb more of her strength, but I hold fast and don't look away from Fabiana. This is part of my penance. As bad as it may be.

She scoots to the edge of the mattress, closer to me, and narrows her eyes. "This whole time, you've been lying to me?"

"Technically, no," I say. "Only from June until November."

Fabiana's glower deepens, and her mouth prunes. "You people," she sneers. "You—*fucking*—people. Y'all won't be satisfied until I've got nothing left. I try *so* hard not to be the villain I could be, but that restraint gets tougher to maintain every day."

"What are you talking about?" I ask, standing up now, because I'm quite confused. "I didn't *take* anything from you."

"Doesn't matter," she quips.

My sister takes a protective half step forward.

"And hear me straight and clear on this, Clement Trudeau," Fabiana says. "Stay away from my brother."

She pushes herself to her feet and starts to walk off but stumbles and cries out in pain. Sofia jumps up and dips underneath Fabiana's arm, draping it across her shoulder and steadying the woman.

I'm too numb to respond. I had a feeling she might not take the news well, but I didn't think she'd respond like this. Fabiana was my final lifeline. And she's abandoned me too. Even the gods won't help me. It's time I accept my shitty fate.

*I'm all out of options, Yves. I'm so sorry.*

*I failed you.*

Fabiana limps toward the door, clinging to Sofia, who walks in ragged step with her. Fabiana stops and points at Jack. "I take it this piece of shit can't make the walk back," she says.

Jack remains seated with his back to the wall, slumped forward, his face frozen in a twisted expression, his eyes shut tight. He's panting and sweating as if stuck in a fever dream.

Sofia peels away from Fabiana and quickly rifles through Jack's pockets until she finds his car keys. They jingle in her hands as she returns to her position as Fabiana's human crutch.

Zac watches them with a contemptuous glare. The eerie shadows cast on him by the still-swaying light amplify the vicious, dogged hatred on his face.

"You two stay here and keep an eye on them," Fabiana says to me and Cris. "I'll send the police back for you." She looks at Clem, and her face twists. "And for your sake, I'm going to try my damnedest to calm down on the walk back to the main road."

The last thing I ever wanted to do was end up on Fabiana Bordeaux's bad side. I was only trying to help.

"Fabiana . . ." Cris steps up in front of me, the back of her shoulder braced against my chest. "You deserve to be angry. But my brother didn't murder yours. Clem loves Yves, and Yves loves him. Right, wrong, or indifferent, Clem did what he did to preserve Yves's life. Be mad, but don't be reckless. That's *my* brother you're speaking to."

So many intense emotions flog me at once that I don't know how to respond to any of this. No matter how cold the world treats me, I'll always find the warmth I need in my sister, even when she's changed so much that I hardly recognize her. And that's why I cannot imagine a life without her in it. No matter what.

Fabiana scoffs. "You are significantly less intimidating without your magic. I said what I said. All you kids are *just* like your parents." Sofia casts her eyes at the floor, and Zac still looks put out. "And you can't even see it. They're raising you all up in their images. Fine, go on and live out your sick fantasies, but leave me and my family out of it."

She turns and hobbles out the door with Sofia and vanishes into the forest.

"Something's not adding up." Cris frowns at me and then rounds on Zac and Jack, the only others left in the room with us.

Jack opens one glassy eye, and Zac continues scowling at us over his dingy kneecaps.

My sister studies them with patent suspicion. "Kidnapping Fabiana. Murdering Ben Beaumont. And framing our mother. Months of coordinated effort just to walk in here now and hand us the key to free Fabiana? The math ain't mathin'. Why would you do that?"

Jack's other eye inches open halfway and twitches. He cocks his head and lets out a gurgling chuckle. "Jack Kingston wouldn't." His voice has become all bass and gravel, which is terrifying in the already-creepy atmosphere of this cabin. "But *I* would."

I move closer to my sister, preparing to grab her and run straight out that door behind Fabiana and Sofia.

Jack jerks forward and groans, clutching his strangely swollen belly. He bares his teeth and rips open the shirt, sending several buttons shooting across the room. Something serpentine moves inside him, pressing against the underside of his pink flesh. His eyes widen with terror.

Zac cries out and reaches for his dad, but Jack knocks him away again.

Cris gasps and grabs my hand. We both take a step back.

"What the hell is this?" I whisper.

Cris squeezes my hand, but she has no idea either.

"Oh, God! Fuck!" Jack screams. "It hurts!"

He gets on his knees and presses his forehead to the dusty cabin floor, sobbing and holding his stomach—and whatever's writhing inside him.

Zac crab walks a few paces away. Tears stream down his cheeks as he watches his father howl in agony, powerless to do a damn thing to stop it.

Jack's back hunches as he dry heaves. The painful-sounding retching turns my own stomach. Cris grimaces beside me and clings tighter to my hand, but neither of us can turn away—not even when the milky-white bile spews from his mouth and spatters onto the floor in front of him.

And it doesn't stop.

More and more sputters from his open gurgling, moaning mouth like a faucet with too much air in the pipeline. But then he gags one final time, and his face and throat redden and then turn purple as something with the girth of a grown man's forearm wriggles up his throat and pokes its serpentine head from Jack's mouth before squelching onto the floor. It's some sort of half snake, half worm alien thingamajiggy that makes my skin crawl—from the inside.

"What the fuck is that?" Cris whisper-shrieks beside me.

"You asking *me*?" I whisper back. "I dunno!"

Jack collapses, out of breath, facedown in a pool of his own cloudy vomit.

Whatever thing Jack just spit up slithers toward the door as its tail splits in half and miniature feet with webbed toes form on the ends. Arms sprout from the upper portion of its body with hands and fingers developing as well. The creature swells in size and darkens in color as it drags and kicks itself across the floor and out the front door, leaving a trail of white ooze behind.

# FORTY-ONE
## CLEMENT

I can't believe I'm standing in a magical cabin in the middle of the woods, debating whether I should follow the nightmarish creature that just exorcised itself from Jack Kingston's body in the most grotesque and nasty way possible. Zac, overwrought with panic, flips his father onto his back and frantically tries to bring him back from his half-conscious dazed state after that taxing and horrific experience.

"I need to see what that was," I tell Cris.

I don't wait for her to try and stop me, nor does she but instead follows close behind as I carefully pull open the front door and step into the chilly night air outside.

The creature, which now resembles a small bald gray-skinned toddler, drags itself several yards away from the cabin. The sight of it is surprisingly not as disgusting as the sound it makes.

Its muscles rip themselves apart beneath its ashen skin, crinkling like tissue paper. Bones snap apart, breaking and mending themselves back together, clacking like knitting needles. White slime oozes from its pores like sweat and steams when it hits the cool air, as the being continues dragging itself through the grass, constantly evolving its now-humanoid form until it's the size of an adult man.

He's on his hands and knees on the ground in front of us, butt-ass naked, his skin darkened to a brilliant purple-tinted ebony, the same color as a starless nighttime sky—like in the Kahlungha.

The Moon beams above us like a beacon, drawing my eyes to it. I've never seen anything like it before. It's engorged overhead as if peering down at us—at the very clearing where we're standing. I've never seen anything like it before. Cris stands silent next to me, gaping up at it too.

The man-being in front of us pushes to his feet and stands up, stretching to his full towering height. The underside of his right wrist, usually where the Mark of the Gods would be emblazoned, is a mess of splotchy scarred skin, as if his mark was clawed off by a feral creature. The sight of him sends shocks of terror zipping through me. I recognize him at once.

The Moon King.

He turns around with clunky, treelike movements and stares down at us with contrasting bright eyes, each a miniature full moon shining down on us like the real one above. His thin lips stretch into a grin that sends hot needle pricks down my back. Several rows of jagged teeth twinkle with starlight as if they were made from the Stars themselves. He flexes his thin fingers at the end of his long, spindly arms.

I never imagined a god would look so monstrous.

"Hello . . . children of the Moon."

The Moon King's voice is low and rumbling and reminds me of the distant sound of rolling thunder. When he speaks, every nocturnal animal that was chittering in the clearing falls quiet at once. I can hear my heartbeat in the heavy silence as I stare into the eyes of the looming god, who tilts his head and stares back. The few fireflies loitering in the clearing grow their ranks and all float up to encircle the Moon King's head in a crown of blinking, dancing light.

Cris sidles close to me and clings to my arm. She's quivering as much as I am.

*Please, don't let us die here tonight,* I pray silently in my head.

"Possession is such nasty work," says the Moon King. "I loathe it."

I'm not sure if we're meant to respond to that, so I don't and neither does Cris. I stare past the Moon King at the path back to the main road and wonder if we'd make it if we ran for it. But then I remember the story of Jean-Louise's previous encounter with the Moon King.

There's no running from a god.

"You're the Moon King," I say, breaking the silence after a few tense moments.

He nods, then turns his overwhelming celestial gaze onto Cris. "But you know me by another name."

She gasps and shakes her head. "No . . . that's not true . . . it can't . . ."

I'm as shook by the reveal as my sister. Here I was the whole time, thinking the Moon King was catfishing her, when he actually was the ancient god of justice she'd been praying to all along.

"*You* are Oberun?" she asks.

The Moon King spreads his hands. "Are you disappointed, daughter of the Moon?"

"Why do you keep calling us that?" I blurt before I can stop myself.

"You don't know?" He stares at us curiously. "The circumstances surrounding your birth make you both substantial conduits for Moon magic. Have you never wondered why you two shared such a strong connection to it?"

Cris and I exchange confused glances. No one has ever said anything of the sort to me, not even Aunt Ursula, and if anyone in our family would've known, it would've been her.

"You two were born one minute after midnight during an Ultra Blood Moon. The flow of energy between the spiritual and natural realms was so strong that night that it pulled the Moon closer to Earth, making it appear *twice* the size of a Super Moon. You children took your first breaths on the most powerful night in history for Moon magic. Your human minds cannot comprehend even a fraction of what we could accomplish together."

I shake my head and touch the shoulder he grabbed during our first encounter, and the icy memory of his grip on me returns. "I thought it was a dream at first, but I always *knew* it'd felt too real."

"You astral projected to the Kahlungha, Clement," confirms the Moon King. "I'd been trapped there alone for centuries. I was no stranger to hallucinations. For so long, I was furious and lonely and morose. And then one day, all those emotions overwhelmed me, and in a fit of rage, I grew myself up as tall as I could go, straight up to the heavens, and I ate the sky, thinking it would help me escape. But it did not. I feared I was doomed to spend eternity alone in my prison—until I saw you. And once I realized you were real, you became my way out of that desolate realm. But I lost you. And I waited for you to return. Or anyone. But only more illusions visited me, crushing what little hope I'd gained from the mere moments I'd known you.

"And then that man appeared—Jean-Louise—and I thought he

was a conjuring of my mind too. Until I smelled you on him, and I knew at once. My time had come."

"Yeah," I say. "You traumatized the shit out of him."

The Moon King stares blankly but doesn't acknowledge my accusation.

"But how'd you get stuck in the Kahlungha?" asks Cris, her voice quivering and unsure, which is rare for her.

The Moon King frowns so deeply that I swear I hear him growl. "Eshu put me there."

"He told me about you," I say, drawing a look of disgust from the old god.

"Mostly lies, I can imagine," the Moon King says. "Did he tell you we were lovers?" The shock must register on my face because his expression lightens. "Ah, see what I mean? Once a liar, always a liar."

"What happened between you two?" I ask, genuinely curious since Eshu was frustratingly closemouthed about everything when we talked.

The Moon King could totally be selling me a fable right now, but what am I supposed to do when he's the only one willing to tell me what the heck is going on?

"I loved Eshu," the Moon King tells us. "And I thought he loved me too, but then he betrayed me and locked me away in that purgatorial realm. We fought each other there, in the Kahlungha. I was far stronger than him, but I lost because I wasn't capable of hurting him the way he so easily did me. He pinned me down and tore my mark from my wrist with his bare teeth like a rabid animal. I broke his leg and cursed the bone so he would have a perpetual reminder of what he did to me. And then he left me there. Without the Mark of the Gods, I was no longer able to walk between worlds—at least not on my own."

"But why would he do that to you?" I ask.

"Because I'm the one who started the War of the Moons," replies the Moon King. "All I wanted was to give power back to our people. Eshu was on my side for a while, until he started disagreeing with my stance on justice more and more. He began preaching tolerance, but I believed that violence was the only answer when dealing with the type of people who were enslaving, raping, torturing, and murdering ours. They might've all been human, but they were the real monsters. It was never me. And they deserved everything we did to them and so much worse. I was well on the way to leading my very own Boy King to victory when Eshu sabotaged me."

"The Boy King," I mutter, recalling Ayden's painting in his studio. "You mean Caspar Moses?"

The Moon King nods. "Eshu tanked our revolution and ended the war in a stalemate that allowed him to maintain peace and spiritual control by convincing our people to cow to their oppressors. It truly hurt me how quickly he forgot that I was the one who rescued him from a slave plantation.

"But Eshu fancies himself more than the Guardian of the Crossroads. He's been hiding a dirty little secret that none of the other gods know but me—a secret *I* told him first. *The* God, the head of the spiritual realm, is missing—and has been for over two millennia. And Eshu grew to fancy the empty throne of God for himself. What he did to end the war was never about violence—it was all about him squashing me before I amassed enough power to take over the one thing he'd grown to covet more than me—the throne of the spiritual realm."

Is every fucking living being in the universe in the throes of an epic power struggle? And why am *I* in it?

"I know I'm not physically appealing," the Moon King waves a hand across his monstrous form, "but Eshu doomed me to transform into this when he left me in the Kahlungha." He casts his eyes downward a moment, long enough for a single tear to fall to the ground like a glittering shooting star. "He never visited. Not even once. And I got to wonder for centuries if he'd ever really loved me, or if I'd been a fool all along."

Odessa always told me there's two sides to every story and the truth usually lies somewhere between. Something about this sudden vulnerability from the Moon King is extremely off-putting. I squeeze Cris's hand and draw an X with my thumb on the side of hers. She does the same back to me.

We can't trust him.

"I've been watching and helping you." He nods at Cris. "It was I who delivered the black mamba snakeskin to you. I was there at Tabitha Edgewater's home when she revealed her true nature to you. And I'm the one who unlocked Dr. Thomas's safe so you could see him for who he really was. And I was the one who moved the bodies so the rest of our community could know the truth too. The only language enemies of our community understand is blood—and that is what we gave them."

"We?" Cris shakes her head. "No, that's not what I was doing."

"Wasn't it?" asks the Moon King, tilting his head. "I only wanted to help you fulfill your legacy, see that you got the blood justice you deserved."

Cris lets go of my hand and hugs herself tight. "No. If I'd known *you* were Oberun, I would've *never* prayed to you. Now I see why you were scrubbed from our history. Eshu was right. You *are* dangerous."

"It was you all along," I interject. "You're the reason why we couldn't make sense of anything that was going on. Why are you doing all this? And if you're on our side, why would you murder Ben and let my mama take the fall for it?"

A bonfire of fury burns inside me. We would've never figured this out on our own. Neither of us stopped to consider how much the gods were meddling or that they were involved at all, especially considering how "hands-off" Papa Eshu claimed to be when I went to him for help.

"That wasn't my original intention, but it served my purpose nonetheless," the Moon King admits. "I caught wind of an elaborate scheme concocted by your own Reverend Mother to frame Fabiana Bordeaux and your aunt Rosalie Dupart for attempted murder via poison—foxglove to be exact."

Cris huffs an angry breath, and I shake my head in disbelief.

"I was there that night," the Moon King says. "In the body of that one." He points at the cabin.

He was possessing Jack that night. It wasn't really Jack who'd smiled at me and grabbed my shoulder in the vestibule at Vice Hall.

It was the Moon King.

I touch my shoulder again, shocked. He's been around all along. All this time. Watching. Meddling.

"The repugnance for me on your faces pierces my heart," the Moon King says. "Ben Beaumont would've killed your mother that night, you know." My heart plunges into an ice bath in my stomach. "I saved her life. His death was a gift of blood justice—from me to all of you. And the message I left in that vile man's blood was intended for your mother. 'Royal Regards *to* the New Queen' is what it was meant to say, but that fool started bucking against my control and smudged part of it right as people started coming to, and we had to get out."

"Yeah, and you left our mama to get the blame for everything," Cris says. "She could go to prison for the rest of her life. So thanks, but no thanks."

The Moon King huffs and spreads his arms. "My children, do you not understand with whom you are speaking? I can give you everything you desire—all you need to do is ask."

"And what's the catch?" I fold my arms over my chest and my thumping heart. "All magic comes at a price."

The Moon King chuckles. "Smart boy. You are right. I can do anything for you; however, I will require something specific from you in return."

"And what would that be?" I ask.

Cris nudges me hard with her elbow, but I ignore her.

"A spiritual war is coming," the Moon King tells us. "Some of the gods are already preparing and amassing allies, even the ones who're pretending they're not. Join me. Become my new boy king, and let's fight for justice together."

A seed of possibility sprouts inside me. I feel it break through the earth of my consciousness and unfurl in the fresh air, flowering into . . . hope.

But I'm nervous.

This feels like a trap. The Moon King speaks to me as if he already knows what I'd ask for.

I shake my head. I won't be manipulated by anyone—human or god.

"Sorry," I tell him. "But I have zero interest in participating in your and Papa Eshu's lovers' quarrel."

Cris takes up my hand again. "Me neither."

"I wasn't talking to you," the Moon King snaps at her, then turns back to me. "I'm not your enemy, Clement. You can trust me. I can prove it."

He stalks past us and over to the cabin, which looks like a playhouse beside his massive frame. He clasps his hands in a giant fist, swings his arms back, and knocks into the side of the building with the same effect as a wrecking ball. The walls and roof splinter, and the whole structure falls apart, leaving Jack and Zachary Kingston huddled and cowering together among the rubble.

They both stare up at the Moon King with wide eyes. Zac screams like a wild boar caught in a hunter's trap when the Moon King lifts him and his father up by the scruffs of their necks. He turns and tosses them in our direction, and they slam hard into the ground and roll in a puff of dust from the debris of the demolished cabin.

Jack groans, lying on his back, rocking side to side but unable to sit upright. Zac collects himself and scrambles to his dad's side, shaking him and calling his name, but Jack only moans in response.

Cris and I cling to each other and take a few steps back. I sneak a look at the path from the woods and am about to tell Cris we should run for it when the Moon King interrupts me.

"Running is pointless," he says, as he stalks back to us and stands over Jack and Zac. "And rude. I'm trying to present you with a gift, Clement Trudeau. Here is your father's killer." He nudges Jack with one of his massive feet. "And if that doesn't sufficiently move you"—he points a long, lanky finger at Zac, who ducks his head between his shoulders like a turtle attempting to escape into its shell—"I present to you your lover's murderer."

"You're lying," I murmur.

The Moon King shakes his head.

"How would you know?" Cris asks.

The Moon King leans down, grabs a handful of Jack's hair, and lifts the man into a sitting position. Jack wails painfully, probably from a back injury. "Tell them what you did," the Moon King orders him.

"I-It's the truth," Jack stammers. "L-Lenora Savant paid me to poison your dad's drink in my bar that night. I needed the money. I'm s-sorry. *Please*."

The Moon King slams the man back down on the ground, and Zac latches back on to his dad.

"His son's a murderer too," the Moon King says. "He's the one who shot Yves Bordeaux in the parking lot last summer—with a bullet that was intended for you, Clement."

I'm snarling before I realize it. I'm so mad, I could rip chunks out of them with my bare teeth just like how Papa Eshu did the Moon King. All along—it was these two. The two most horrendous events of my life, the deaths of my dad and Yves, were all because of these two sorry excuses for humans.

The source of all my pain lies in front of me, and I'm finally presented with an opportunity to strike back for once, to transfer all this hurt and frustration and rage back to them.

Would I regret my revenge more than I've hurt over the years and more than I'll miss for the rest of my life?

"Clem . . ." Cris says in a low voice. "Don't let him goad you. We can't trust him, remember?"

I pull my hand from hers, instantly irritated. "You're one to talk." She rears back in surprise. "Yeah, I know about Dr. Thomas. I asked you to stop after Tabitha, and you lied to me. I knew it was you from the moment I saw the news. At least I'd be killing for a reason."

Cris nor I noticed when Zac snuck the gun out from where he'd been hiding it, tucked into his pants, but when the *click* of it cocking echoes in the silent clearing, we all turn our attention to him.

He aims at my chest. The barrel trembles, and his eyes narrow at me. I push my sister behind me and glower back at Zac. The Moon King was right. It *was* him.

Those eyes. That gun.

This is too familiar to be a coincidence.

"I promise I won't miss this time," Zac says.

And he shoots.

Cris screams.

I don't have time to flinch before something hard, hot, and fast punches me in the chest. I fall backward into my sister's arms, and we tumble over each other. She's still screaming and pawing at my chest in search of the bullet wound.

But she doesn't find one.

"Oh, thank the gods," she breathed. "The spell worked."

And then it makes sense. She had an ulterior motive all along when she was so adamant about doing my laundry ever since I told her about what had happened to Yves. She was conjuring protection on my clothes. And then my heart sinks—because what if she hadn't? Would the Moon King have let Zac murder me?

Why do we accept that the gods can choose to stand idle and watch bad things happen instead of intervening on our behalf? If they'd come to my grandmother's aid sooner on the night that mob lynched her and my grandfather, maybe none of us would've had to endure all the pain and trauma that we have for generations.

I get back to my feet and glare at Zac, my fists clenched at my sides.

He looks surprised at first, then determined as he raises his gun higher.

"Fine then," he says. "Head shot it is."

He shoots again.

# FORTY-TWO
## CRISTINA

The guttural scream that claws its way up my throat nearly scrapes up a pound of flesh along with it. The bright flash of the gun's muzzle stupefies me, petrifying my limbs and preventing me from doing anything other than staring, captive and still and utterly horrified.

I can't look.

I don't want to see my brother dead on the ground, shot to death by the manic boy who also killed my brother's boyfriend and whose father murdered ours. An endless wheel of death spun 'round and 'round by the grief-stricken survivors.

But my brother releases a loud strangled breath that draws my eyes to his, and I gasp too.

Clem's alive.

The bullet hovers, paused in the air midflight, a hair's breadth from piercing Clem's cheek, hardly an inch beneath his left eye. A thin glittery film of moonbeams encases the round, which, I suspect, is how Oberun usurped control of the bullet.

The gun, still aimed at my brother, quivers in Zac's hand. He stands protectively in front of his father, who remains facedown on the ground, moaning and partially conscious—heavy emphasis on the "partial." Zac scowls at Clem.

Oberun steps behind Clem and reaches around to adjust the position of the bullet so it floats between Clem's eyes. Oberun turns his stoic yet ferocious gaze on Zac. "That where you were aiming?"

Zac puts a second hand on his gun, and his knuckles whiten from his grip. He looks foolish brandishing that thing against an ancient god, Oberun—aka the Moon King himself. But I guess when staring down death, even that tiny bit of power, albeit useless, gives him the illusion of security and comfort.

Oberun resembles a hungry nightmare the way he looms over my brother. He has to stoop to put his large spindly hands on Clem's shoulders.

Clem flinches but doesn't move away.

But then Oberun turns to me, and my blood runs frigid. When he speaks, his voice booms, projecting throughout the clearing and bouncing off the surrounding trees. "*That* is why you do not show the enemy compassion or pity." He flicks his wrist at Zac, who still stands like a battle-weary soldier, his gun pointed at my brother. "These emotions are naught but a Trojan horse filled with opponents who, the moment you allow them access, will slaughter you and everyone you love."

I shake my head. "That's not true, Clem. The world isn't black-and-white like that."

Oberun's laugh is deep and grungy, the sound of boulders tumbling down a rocky hill—it's also insulting. "Come talk to me when you are no longer magically impotent. Until then, your opinion is as irrelevant as you."

"Was it you?" I ask, clenching my fists. "Were you the one who took my magic?"

"Me?" he asks, seeming genuinely surprised at my allegation. "Ho, ho . . . nooo," he coos. "I would never do such an ugly thing. Especially not after personally grooming you for so long. I am admittedly annoyed to have lost such a substantial opportunity in you."

*Grooming me?* My trauma with Oz bobs on the surface of the bile rising inside me. Nausea gives way to a quiet anger that clenches my jaw and fists. I want to rip this god limb from limb like how the undead did Lenora last year.

Oberun's monstrous brow furrows. "I, unfortunately, cannot restore your connection to the spiritual realm, which reeks of godly influence, most likely Eshu's, so you're going to have to take that issue up with him."

But that doesn't make sense. Why would Papa Eshu cut off my connection to my magic and the spiritual realm? To stop me from killing Sofia? But why?

"However, since I'm in a giving mood tonight," Oberun tells me, "I will return your precious matriarch to you, which I expect might catalyze the unclogging of your spiritual pipeline. And when that's all fixed, come see me."

I glower at him. I would never ally myself with the likes of him. The way he uses and manipulates people is no better than Valentina or Lenora or Eveline—or apparently even Papa Eshu. I'm still gooped—and high-key pissed—by Oberun's assumption that Eshu took my magic.

Oberun steps from around Clem and kneels in front of him, his jagged teeth much too close to my brother's face for my ease. "I am offering you everything, Clement." He holds out his hand, feigning a gentle, innocent invitation. "Become the Boy King and get what you desire. All you must do is prove that you really want it—that you *deserve* it."

"And if I am to be a king," Clem mutters, "then what will you be?"

"I am God," Oberun intones.

Zac waves his gun between Clem and Oberun. "Me and my dad won't be the only ones dying here tonight." Quick bursts of light from muzzle flashes illuminate the clearing alongside earsplitting pops of gunshots as Zac rapid fires until he empties the clip and the barrel jumps back.

However, with deft reflexes, Oberun flings orbs of moonlight to intercept every bullet. Two rounds stop in the air in front of me, the others suspended before Clem.

Oberun steps toward Zac, closing the distance between them in half a stride. Zac's knees buckle, and he drops to the ground and turns his head away. Oberun snatches the gun from Zac's hand and puts it in his mouth. Oberun's teeth, sharp as diamonds, crunch on the metal, breaking it down to violent morsels and crumbs; he eats Zac's gun as if it were a tea cake. Zac's mouth falls agape, and Oberun slaps the shit out of him.

"Stop doing that," Oberun admonishes Zac, who lies on the ground, holding his face and whimpering like his dad. "You foolish humans and your stupid guns annoy me."

Zac curls up beside his dad and sobs, and Jack groans pathetically, his eyes half-open.

"Can you really do *any*thing?" Clem's voice scythes through the tension in the clearing.

Oberun stretches to his full towering height and turns slowly, revealing a wide sparkling toothy grin that sinks my heart straight to the never-realm.

He nods at Clem.

"Clem!" I cry out to my brother. "You said yourself that Ober—I mean, the Moon King can't be trusted!" I point at the ruins of the cabin. "What I did back there wasn't *all* me. Oberun pushed me to that point. It's been *him* all along."

"No, he didn't, Cris." He shakes his head at me. "That rage was all yours. It was inside you the whole time, before you even met the Moon King. You might not have put it there yourself, but that rage belongs to you all the same. He only helped you uncage it. And like your rage, I have a great deal of pain and sadness built up inside me. And the Moon King can give me some relief." He lowers his head and sniffs. "I'm so tired, sis. Don't you want me to be free too?"

My mouth drops open, but I'm devoid of words. I can't refute a single word he said or what he's asking. I've been raging for weeks now, striking back against my abusers and the villains of my community. But it wasn't all magnanimous. Some of it was self-serving. It felt *good* to reclaim my power and take some of theirs too.

But Clem never had such selfish motives. He's only ever wanted to share the surplus of love penned up inside him that no one seemed to truly appreciate—until he met Yves.

"Clem, please listen to me," I plead. "What the Moon King's offering you is not freedom. You'll become his slave."

"If it's the only way to save Yves, I don't care," Clem says. "Besides, I'm already a slave to all the shit I'm powerless to change. May as well put my exploitation to good use."

"But what about me? Are you just going to leave me?" I'm desperate now.

"Don't do that." The pained look of disappointment on my brother's face breaks my soul at the seams. "I'm not making this decision to hurt you. You know why I'm doing this, so I don't really care if you don't understand."

He's right. Convincing him not to trade his life to save the boy he loves feels abominable of me. And self-serving. I don't want that to become my brand.

I can't lose my brother either.

But I'm not going to change his mind. In this regard, Clem is irrefutably my twin.

He turns to Oberun, carefully studying the divine being from head to foot, but says nothing.

"Confide in me your heart's desire, Clement," Oberun tells him.

Clem's voice is timid and unsure when he asks, "Can you restore Yves Bordeaux's and Auguste Dupre's souls? Parts of them were—"

"Lost to the spiritual realm during subpar resurrection rituals—yes, I'm aware," replies Oberun.

He snaps his fingers, and two balls of grainy golden mist resembling a glowing fog filled with fireflies appear over the open palms of his hands. One is smaller than the other, the difference between a golf ball and a basketball. Oberun glances at each, smug pride radiating in his inhuman smirk. "*Anything*," he croons.

When he lowers his hands, the pieces of Yves's and Auguste's souls remain suspended on either side of him. He then conjures a piece of luminous parchment the color of raw papyrus from thin air.

Jack turns his head, still whimpering quietly, but Zac, Clem, and I stare at the radiant paper as if it were a television screen while bright blue script scrawls across the page from top to bottom and ends with a single underline. For a signature.

Gods. It's a fucking contract.

"Clem! No!" I snarl. "I'm not letting you do this!"

I grab his hand and attempt to physically drag him from this place, but Oberun whips out one of his egregiously long arms and shoves me back with such force that my feet leave the ground for a moment.

"STOP INTERFERING!" Oberun roars.

My back slams into the hard earth, evacuating the air from my lungs. I roll over onto my stomach, then push up onto my hands and knees, gasping for air.

*Fuck . . . that hurt.*

"Ey!" Clem shouts.

I get to my feet, and the cold fingers of shock grip my neck as I watch my brother stand up to the Moon King.

Clem's chest puffs out and heaves, and his nostrils flare. "Hurt my sister and you and your deal can fuck right off."

"Then make your decision while I still have the patience for this bargain," retorts Oberun.

Clem looks up to the Moon and shuts his eyes. He stands there for a moment, his head tilted back, tears squeezing out and streaming into his ears.

"Clem, I'm begging you . . ." It's useless, I know, but I have to try again. "Don't fall for Oberun's tricks. Let us find another way. There has to be another—"

"Shut your mouth, you useless girl!" Oberun flicks his hand at me, and a strip of thin moonlight slaps across my mouth, a magical gag I'm powerless to remove.

Still, I crawl toward my brother, drawing closer on my hands and knees, my cries stifled.

But he won't even look at me.

I assumed he might be meditating on his decision, but when I glance to the sky, the truth gut checks me. He's already made up his mind.

Clem opens his eyes and walks up to Zac with measured, deliberate steps. Clem kneels in front of the boy with the tangled nest of dirty-blond hair and the bloodshot gray-green eyes, who even in his present pitiful state, musters enough hatred to sneer at my brother.

It's difficult to watch, but I can't turn away either. There's a darkness inside me that's cheering Clem on.

"Why'd you do it?" asks Clem with gentle assertiveness.

"Fuck you," Zac snarls. "All of you." He puts a protective hand on his dad's back and glowers at my brother. "This happened to us because of your damned family. Y'all took the bar from us, so I took something from *you*. But it was supposed to have been *you*. It should've been *you*, but I fucked up."

Oberun drifts closer, his eyes widening with intrigue as he observes the exchange. He creeps along the periphery, his long, dark tongue snaking out to lick his lips, relishing the savory conflict.

"I don't feel sorry for you," Clem says, oblivious to the rest of us. "And I don't care what kind of person that makes me because *you* are the monster. *You* are the thug. The criminal. The killer. You murdered the only boy I ever loved over a raggedy-ass dive bar."

Zac's mouth prunes, and his jaw muscles shift as if he's preparing to spit in Clem's face. With electric reflexes, Clem punches Zac in the mouth.

Zac's head snaps back, and he coughs, choking on the wad of saliva and phlegm he'd intended for my brother. Zac spits a bloody glob on the ground instead, then cranes his head upward as Clem stands over him. Clem looks briefly to the sky, then back down at Zac. I glance up too and gasp behind my gag.

About a dozen spears of moonlight revolve in the air above us, inching closer every second.

Zac's lip curls with disgust as he sneers. "You stupid *Bla*—"

A sharpened rod of frozen moonlight impales Zac through the back of his head, cutting off his insult. It pierces his throat and travels through his chin and slams into the ground, kicking up grass and soil from the impact.

Clem's already learned to manipulate magic on a molecular level. But how'd he learn so fast?

Another ice spear slams into Zac's back and exits through his chest in an eruption of blood, viscera, and earth. Zac's body, awkwardly held aloft on two pikes of icy moonlight, seizes in his final moments. He gasps and gurgles, sending blood and saliva trailing down the frozen stake stabbed through him.

Jack wails incoherently from where he lies on the ground, snatching hopelessly at the tail of Zac's T-shirt.

Oberun steps forward and melts the frozen moonbeams with a wave of his hand, then reshapes them into shimmering puppet strings that he attaches to Jack's head and wrists. He jerks the man up into a kneeling position like a human marionette.

Oberun turns to Clem. "And what of this one?"

"Saved him for last," Clem replies, cold and unfeeling, his voice almost completely unfamiliar had I heard it come from anywhere other than my own twin brother's mouth. "I wanted him to watch the person he cares about most in the world be taken from him, so he'll know how it feels . . . right before he dies too. I'm done with him now."

Clem dips his head, and a moonbeam spear hurtles across the clearing and slices horizontally across Jack's throat. His flesh splits and blooms, curling back like flower petals. Blood pours from him, soaking his front and spattering the corpse of his only son. Oberun magically clips Jack's strings, and the man falls over dead across Zac's body.

Oberun produces a quill from nowhere, kneels in front of their corpses, and fills the quill's inkwell with blood. He stands and hands it to Clem, who goes over to the contract, which still hovers in the air, and signs his name on the bottom line. Grinning fiendishly, Oberun pockets the contract and snaps his fingers, and the souls hovering in the clearing like dazed fireflies vanish.

My magical gag disappears too, and I cry out and launch myself at my brother.

We crash into each other, and I feel his weight leaning heavy on me, and I take it. Gods, I wish I could take it all, absorb every bit of his burdens, lift him onto my shoulders and flee this place with him, get him out of these damned woods and back to safety, back home.

Clem leans back from our embrace and presses his forehead against mine. Our tears drip down the fronts of our shirts and mingle on the ground between us.

What a mess we've made.

"I'm sorry, Cris," he murmurs. "I tried my best. I swear. I'm just so damn tired."

"I know, Clem," I tell him. "I know."

"Don't think differently of me, please."

"Never," I whisper. "I love you so much."

"I love you too, sis."

"Hey, listen to me." I grab both sides of his wet face and stare into his wavering eyes. "I'm not letting you go. No matter where he takes you, I will come for you. Just hang on as long as you can. Okay?"

He chokes out, "Okay," and sniffs hard. "I'm really scared, Cris."

"I know," I tell him. "I'm scared too. But we'll get through this, just like we do everything."

"Tell Yves I love him," Clem says. "And tell Mama I'm sorry. And that I love her too."

I nod. "Of course."

He fishes his car keys from his pocket and is about to hand them to me when Oberun grabs Clem by the back of his neck with one of his spidery hands. My brother cries out and reaches for me as he's jerked away, and he and Oberun both disappear. Clem's keys fall to the ground, and I tumble forward.

On my hands and knees in the grassy clearing beside two corpses and a demolished log cabin, I let out a long, ugly, painful sound that's part scream, part howl, and all pain.

When I'm done, I stare at the trampled grass beneath my hands and the weed stalks nestled between my fingers where my brother stood moments ago.

But he's gone now.

It's done. It's all over.

And I'm utterly alone.

I don't want to lift my head. I can't bear to look at the destruction around me or the dark trees or the heavens above. I can't see the world without my brother by my side.

Nor can I fathom making the long lonely trek through the woods back to the car by myself.

# PART V

You can't separate peace from freedom because no one can be at peace unless he has his freedom.

—MALCOLM X

# FORTY-THREE
## CRISTINA

"He's gonna be okay. We can fix this." Aunt Ursula clings to me, which I think is more for her comfort than mine, so I ignore the urge to slide away from her.

I don't want hugs that aren't my brother's. And hugs won't save him from the Moon King.

Ursula didn't take the news about Clem well. After I told her, I had to convince her not to go hunt down Jean-Louise and take his head for unleashing an ancient homicidal god on her nephew, unintentional or not. Once she calmed down, she wept for an uncomfortable while, blaming herself for abandoning Clem between snotty sobs. After I finally got her to collect herself, she called Mama's attorney, Namina Falana, to meet us so I can tell her and Detective Sommers that Jack Kingston was Ben Beaumont's murderer—not my mama.

The police station is cold and devoid of color except for the eggshell-stained tile floors and walls and the occasional flash of a gold badge pinned to black-uniformed officers who travel back and forth between the main entrance and the secured-access door leading to the rest of the station. A single woman runs the front desk of the lobby from behind a plexiglass wall above a rickety-looking metal speaker. I sit beside Ursula on a wooden bench across from the front desk.

"We're gonna get your mama back home," Ursula tells me. "And then the three of us won't sleep until we come up with a plan to get Clem back too. I will throw down with every god in creation to save my nephew if I must."

I nod. I don't know how I'm going to help with that in my current magic-less state, but that's a worry I keep to myself.

When I told Aunt Ursula the story of what happened back at the cabin, I left out the part about me losing my magic in the middle of trying to kill Sofia Beaumont for betraying me. Nor did I share that I'd killed two other people prior to that incident with my ex-friend. I won't be able to hide my present magical affliction or what I did to Sofia for too much longer, but my final encounters with Tabitha Edgewater and Dr. Gregory Thomas are secrets I plan to take with me to the spiritual realm.

Namina called Ursula a few minutes ago to say she was on the way. By the time I downloaded Ursula with all the details of our investigation into Ben Beaumont's murder that ended at that creepy cabin in the woods, it was well past midnight. Now it's almost 2:00 A.M., and I'm delirious with exhaustion but too full of grief and hopelessness to even think about rest. I feel like a zombie with a foot in two worlds, not wholly present in either, floating through both. I can't stop staring blankly through the glass doors leading to the small vestibule and the dark world beyond.

I can't even be happy about uncovering the truth that could potentially clear Mama's name because all I can think about is Clem. Where is he right now? Is he hurt? Is he alone? Will he be okay without his anxiety medication? I let out an anxious breath I'd been strangling, and Ursula's arm tightens around me instantaneously.

Detective Sommers appears on the other side of the entrance, and my heart trips a beat. I don't recognize her at first because she's in a FAMU hooded sweatsuit and her hair's up in a high ponytail. She enters the station and goes straight up to the front desk, where the woman behind the glass slips her a notepad and a pen through the tiny mailbox window in the glass barrier. Sommers opens the pad to a fresh page and comes over to us. Up close, I notice the stubborn sleep lines still lingering on the side of her face. We must've woken her up.

"This is quite the surprise," Sommers says. "What can I do for you at this late hour?"

"You can let my mama out of jail," I blurt before Ursula can say anything.

Sommers's brows pinch together. "And why would I do that?"

"Because Jack Kingston is the person who murdered Ben Beaumont," I tell her. "He also kidnapped Fabiana Bordeaux and was holding her hostage at a cabin in the woods west of town."

Sommers scribbles notes on her pad. "And where is Jack now?"

I'm about to answer, but I pause, realizing if I tell the whole truth, it'll implicate my brother. So I stick to only what Sommers needs to know. "Dead," I reply. "His body's still in the woods."

"I definitely have some questions for you," Sommers tells me. "I'll go find a partner to assist with the interview, and I'll come grab you once I have a private room for us to talk."

"Okay," I say.

Ursula nods, and Sommers gets up and hurries through the secured door.

I wipe my sweaty palms on my pants, but they just keep perspiring. Is Detective Sommers even going to believe me when I explain that an ancient god of justice was possessing Jack Kingston? And more importantly, what the hell am I going to tell her about how Jack and Zac died? If I lie and they figure it out, that might jeopardize Mama's freedom; but if I tell the truth, it'll put Clem directly in Sommers's crosshairs.

I don't know what to do. And I don't have long to figure it out.

"I know this is tough for you right now," Ursula says, "but I'm so damned proud of you." She rubs my back lovingly. "You will be a legendary Queen one day. I know your grandma is watching you from the spiritual realm ten times as proud as I am right now."

I grip my knees and suck in a sharp breath. "Yeah," I mutter.

I wonder how she feels about her granddaughter the murderer who's lost her magic and her twin brother in the same night.

I stare out the glass front doors again, through the vestibule and into the night. Cars pass by sparingly on the road outside, and I focus on the distracting glow of their headlights. In the dark, just outside the cone of dim orange light illuminating the front entrance, something shifts in the shadows.

I squint at it, curious, as the foreboding silhouette of that same something rises gradually from the ground just outside the cone of light. It stretches and blends into the form of a freakishly tall humanoid being.

My back goes rigid, and I gasp, drawing Ursula's attention.

"Noo . . ." I mumble. "He's back. Did he come for me too?"

And I'm powerless to defend myself right now.

Ursula takes her arm from around me and pivots to look at me. "Who?"

"Oberun," I reply, barely above a whisper, watching him stalk toward the entrance?"

*"Who?"*

"The fucking Moon King!" I shout, and point toward the entrance.

She turns to the vestibule and leaps back, throwing a protective arm across me. "OH, SHIT!"

The Moon King stoops, bending his lengthy joints and contorting his otherworldly figure to fit through the low doors. His long arms drape after him, dragging the corpses of Jack and Zachary Kingston into the station.

Ursula and I stand and back up against the wall farthest from the entrance, and she stands partially in front of me, shielding me with her body, which is useless, but I let her do it anyway since it makes her feel better. If the Moon King wants me, he'll have me, and there's nothing she can do to stop that. I don't consider running or hiding. All that's on my mind at the moment is my brother and what the Moon King's done with him.

Once inside, the Moon King holds the bodies up by the backs of their necks like newborn pups, except their heads loll, their skin already pallid from the early stages of decomposition. "Where do you want these?" Though calm, his voice thunders, rattling the plexiglass around the desk.

The attendant cowers in the corner behind the desk, her hands clasped in front of her, staring at the god with terrified wide eyes. When she doesn't answer him, the Moon King smooshes the faces of the corpses against the glass barrier, which freaks the poor lady out even more. She slumps to the floor and hides her face in her hands, sobbing pitifully.

The Moon King sighs and steps back, still clinging to the corpses like a toddler with a doll in each hand.

Mama's attorney walks through the front entrance but doesn't notice the Moon King at first because she's heads down in her phone. She has dark-brown skin and a buzz cut, more curves than a go-kart track, and a passion for justice. Ursula's phone vibrates in her hand, and Namina's head snaps up to meet our dazed expressions.

"Oh, there you are!" she exclaims—then looks up at the Moon King, whose head is bent and shoulders brush against the ceiling. He looks down at her, and she screams.

Namina drops her phone and tears across the space to huddle beside me and Ursula.

Detective Sommers steps back through the secured door with a uniformed officer in tow. They both stop and stagger backward, wide-eyed incredulity on their faces the moment they see the Moon King.

"Ah, Jeida Sommers," he says, enunciating the syllables of her name as if analyzing the taste of them in his mouth, "just the sellout I've been looking for."

Sommers bristles, a deadly frown on her face. She and her partner draw their guns at point them at the Moon King.

He doesn't flinch. "Funny position you're in." He glances around the room with zero acknowledgment of me, as if I were invisible. "A person like *you* in a place like *this*, doing what you're doing." He moves closer and leans in, sniffing the air between them. Sommers glowers and quivers from nerves but stands her ground. Her partner looks ready to bolt any second. "Mmm . . ." The Moon King closes his eyes for a moment, relishing the scent. "I can still smell magic on you." He straightens and takes another step closer. "Faint. But it's there. What a waste. Silly girl."

"I'm not your girl," Sommers grumbles.

"Oh, but you *are* all my children," says the Moon King. "However, that's not why I'm here. You and I will have our time soon." He dumps the dead bodies at Sommers's and her partner's feet. They leap back, and her partner kneels to inspect the bodies while Sommers keeps her gun trained on the god standing in front of her.

"These two have committed a number of crimes," explains the Moon King, "but I think you're presently interested in this one"—he nudges Jack's lifeless head—"for the murder of your mayor. And while we're on the subject of murder, the demise of those insufferable scourges on my people, Edgewater and Thomas, was my doing, though I'm admittedly irritated you were incapable of appreciating my artistry. Those messages were not for you—they were left for my community. The god of justice is back, and things are going to start changing around this city."

My head swims, and bile rises in my throat, but I swallow it back down. I can't lose my head now. I slip underneath Ursula's arm and twist out of her reach when she tries to pull me back.

As I stalk up to the Moon King where he stands near Sommers, I hear her partner whisper-shout to her, "What do we do? We can't arrest a monster!"

"That's no monster," I say, drawing their attention. The Moon King looks at me for the first time, though his inhuman face is expressionless. "He's a god. And he's very dangerous." I stand rigid in front of him and stare up at his face. "Where is my brother?" He ignores me, and I bellow, "Hey! I'm talking to you!" I grab for his sinewy arm, but he vanishes.

He's gone. And so's Clem.

I clench my fists so hard, they tremble with fury. *You won't have him, Oberun.*

Mama's attorney wanders over with Ursula, but Sommers raises her hands, cutting them off before either of them can lay into her.

"I don't have the mental bandwidth to even argue with y'all after what the fuck I just witnessed here at"—she looks at her watch—"two thirty-three in the morning." She turns to her partner and says, "Start processing Marie Trudeau's release. Then we gotta talk about how the hell we're gonna deal with *this* situation." She turns back to us. "I'm still gonna need to take an official statement from you, so don't move."

"Okay," I say.

Namina pulls Ursula aside to chat, and Sommers breaks off with her partner too. I don't even get to process that Mama's officially coming home before my phone rings, which is odd given the hour.

It's Aurora. Even odder.

I answer, and the frantic breaths I hear on the other line startle me. "Cris," Aurora cries. "Thank the gods you answered. I need you to come to my house now. Just you. No one else. It's urgent."

"Are you okay?" I ask.

"Uh, that's a complicated question right now. I'll explain everything when you get here."

"Okay, I'm on my way now."

When I hang up, Ursula's staring at me, and Namina's stepped aside to make a phone call.

"Where are you on your way to at three in the morning?" asks Ursula. "And Sommers asked you to stick around to give your statement."

"Unrelated emergency," I tell her, already heading for the door. "But I have to go see about this. I'll be back. I swear."

"Okay, just go," Ursula says. "This process might take a while anyway. I'll wait here for your mama. Someone's gonna need to tell her about Clem."

I nod, guilty that I'm relieved Aunt Ursula gets the burden of breaking that news to Mama. Dealing with Ursula's reaction while managing my own grief was already difficult. I hope Mama takes it better, though I'll deal with that later. One problem at a time.

I'm rushing through the front door when Sommers calls after me. "Hey!" she shouts. "I told you not to leave! I still need to talk to you!"

"I'll be back!" I shout back over my shoulder, not slowing.

Thank goodness Aurora doesn't live far from the police station, but the drive is still too long for comfort. I'm too antsy the entire drive to sit still. I call her a couple of times along the way, but she doesn't answer.

*Damn it, Aurora. What is this about?*

A wild thought crosses my mind, and before I can talk myself out of it, I call Clem. I feel silly when it goes straight to his voicemail. I hang up on the canned standard mailbox greeting. Of course he never recorded a personalized message. Quintessential Clem.

I burst into tears.

I wipe my face and gather myself enough to keep driving, but I can't stop crying until after I pull into Aurora's driveway. I have to hold my breath to stop the flow of tears.

*Now's not the time to fall apart.*

I dry my eyes and glower at Xavier's SUV in front of Aurora's car in the circular driveway of their family's two-story brick colonial. The leafy green vines lording over the front of their home and the overgrown hedges bordering the driveway look extra uninviting in the dark. Aurora could've at least turned on the porch light for me.

I haven't been back here since she and I snuck into the garden shed in the backyard to collect the evidence she'd stashed there, which linked Lenora Savant to the murder of Alexis Lancaster thirty years ago. It feels strange casually walking up to the front door now.

I reach for the doorbell, but the porch light blazes on, drowning me in a flood of brightness. The door lurches open, and I rear back, breathless. I blink several times and look again before I can believe what I'm seeing. This can't be happening.

Not tonight.

"Aurora . . ." I say, far calmer than I feel. "Why are you covered in blood?"

She must still be in shock. Her lips and limbs quiver, and my friend's mottled-brown eyes are wide and glistening. The blood smeared across her face and neck and shirt is still wet.

"I need your help," she says, wringing her bloody hands in the doorway.

My heart drops to my knees, but I ask anyway. "With what exactly?"

"Xavier's dead," she says. "I killed my brother."

# FORTY-FOUR
## CRISTINA

Death stalks me like a scorned lover. I can't escape them. They're always there, haunting the darkened corners of my life when not bold enough to be front and center, a perpetual reminder that they'll come for me too one day.

But not tonight.

However, Death has tagged another person, one who, in my most honest of opinions, had it coming. I have enough bloody messes on my hands without tacking on this new one. But I won't let my friend down when she needs me. And as it turns out, I might need her too.

Aurora pulls me inside and closes the door, pressing her back against it. Shock still lingers, rendering her far more cautious and timid than I've ever seen her. She reminds me of a fawn whose brain scrambles for purchase when staring at a car's blinding headlights. Relatable.

"Where is he?" I ask.

"In here." She gestures for me to follow her to the kitchen.

Xavier Vincent's sprawled on the floor beside the island counter. He lies face up in a mess of his own blood, open-mouthed and glassy-eyed, staring blankly at the ceiling. A butcher's knife lies at his feet, covered in blood and bits of torn flesh stuck to the edge of the blade like crumbs of raw meat. I'm sure it was the weapon responsible for the gaping stab wounds in his stomach and neck. I reach a shaky hand to my own.

"Shit, Aurora," I say. "What the hell happened here?"

She can barely get the words out. Her eyes are stuck on her brother's corpse on the floor of their kitchen. Her mouth opens, and she stammers incoherently until I pull out a stool from the other side of the island counter, out of sight of Xavier's body.

"Here, sit," I tell her, and she does.

All this is a bit alarming for even me to see at first, but the initial exhilaration wears off faster this time. I guess I'm becoming desensitized to death and dead bodies now. Wonderful.

Aurora leans her elbows on the counter and hides her face in her hands. After she takes a long, deep breath, she sits back, and though slumped and visibly weary, a wilted husk of the girl I know (also relatable, unfortunately), she says, "He asked me to come by and talk." She frowns at the swirls of darkness in the light-colored stone. "I thought he meant to talk about how we could reconcile and end this ridiculous lawsuit." She shakes her head. "I should've known better."

"What'd he want?" I stand next to her, my nerves too revved up for me to sit right now.

"To confront me," she says. "He saw me talking to Detective Sommers at the Bean earlier this evening. I had no idea he was even there."

My brow wrinkles under my grimace. "Why were you meeting with her?"

"I wasn't," Aurora insists. "I was getting tea, and she cornered me while I was waiting for my drink to harass me about her stupid deal. I still haven't given her an answer, and I told her to stop bugging me about it. Xavier claims he was on his way in when he saw us from outside the window and got so mad that he left without coming in."

"Shit," I mumble.

"Right. He called me over here a couple hours ago and accused me of ratting him out to the cops to get rid of him so I can steal Dad's estate. He blamed Sommers's whole investigation on me." She sighs hard and rolls her eyes. "I was so over fighting about this shit that I was considering just letting him have it all and starting over somewhere else."

"You want to leave New Orleans?" I get it, gods know I do, but I can't stomach losing another person I care about. I wonder if this is how Clem's felt for so long, which makes me feel even more hollowed, if that's even possible at this point.

Aurora shakes her head. "Of course not. But it felt like he was leaving me no choice. Xavier doesn't know this, but Dad has an apartment in Barcelona he set up as a safe house. He told me about it before he died. And he said if ever a time came when there was no other safe place in the world, that that would always be my home."

A place to escape to sounds enticing, but what about when the trauma and would-be murderers follow? Our family was removed from the drama of the Gen Council for thirty years, and it still found us again. Maybe this is our destiny, and instead of running away from it, we should charge straight into it.

I pull Aurora into a hug. I don't care that she's sweaty and covered in blood. "It might be selfish of me, but I'm happy you didn't leave."

She sits back and runs a hand through her hair. We both could use a day at the hair salon and some TLC for our natural crowns, but that seems silly when people are literally trying to murder us every damn day.

"Yeah, but I might be going to prison now," she says, dispirited.

"We haven't gotten there yet," I tell her. "Back to your story. I'm guessing Xavier didn't believe you when you told him you weren't working with Detective Sommers."

Aurora shakes her head. "The more I insisted, the more he accused me of lying until he completely lost it and attacked me." She drags her hands to her lap and lowers her head. "He fought me like he didn't know me. Like we didn't grow up together. My own brother. And the whole time, all I could think about was how I couldn't let him do what he did to me before, how being crossed out of my mind and trapped in Chateau des Saints was worse than being damned to the never-realm, and that I could not and *would not* go back there. And knowing Xavier, he probably would do something worse the next time. I panicked and grabbed a knife"—she nods toward the wooden knife block on the counter across from Xavier's corpse—"and then I just . . . blacked out. Next thing I remember, he was on top of me, dead, his hands still around my throat." She rubs the purpling bruises on the fair skin of her neck, and it relights the fury inside me.

I know my friend is suffering right now, but Xavier got what he deserved. Fuckers like him and Oz, who take power from those they deem weaker, need to be taught a lesson. I would never tell Aurora this, but I'm glad that asshole is dead. The world's better off without him.

"Well," I say, "at least you did it the old-fashioned way, so we won't have Sommers on our asses screaming about magical serial killer nonsense."

"Yeah," Aurora says, "I didn't have time in the moment to be fancy and innovative like you."

Heat rushes my face. "Huh?"

"I've been busy, not comatose," she says. "I knew what you were up to. I'm just mad I couldn't be there with you. Tabitha and Dr. Thomas got what was coming to them."

I open my mouth to say something but stop.

"And before you say it, yes, I'm biased. Xavier was evil too, but he was still my brother. Despite what I said to him last summer when we took back the Council, there was a part of me that thought he could be redeemed—no pun intended."

I shake my head and groan.

"I don't care what that makes me," she continues. "But I'm not proud of killing my brother, and I don't know what to do now. I guess I should start thinking about life in prison, huh?" She looks out the window, despondent and taciturn, as if the paddy wagon just pulled up outside to load her up.

"No," I tell her. "We won't let that happen. You're one of the best parts of this world, of humanity. If anyone deserves to live and live freely, it's you."

She doesn't respond. She only stares out the window, frozen except for a subtle shiver.

"Damn, girl, I know I suck at consoling sometimes, but I at least thought—"

"We're *so* fucked," she whispers.

"What?" I turn to where she's staring, and what I see snatches my chest hollow.

Someone watches us from outside the kitchen window. Their head and shoulders are veiled in shadow, which makes them appear otherworldly at first. But then they shift in the darkness, and I see their eyes flit to Xavier's bloody corpse and then back to us.

"*Shiiit*," I mutter.

Detective Sommers followed me here from the police station.

# FORTY-FIVE
## CRISTINA

Before I can come up with a plan of action, Aurora zaps back to life and slips off the stool. She charges past me and throws open the glass doors to the patio and goes outside to confront Detective Sommers. I follow, calling Aurora back, but she ignores me.

Outside to my left, the pool lights throw wavering blue reflections through the water onto the back of the house. The Moon sits low in the sky, tucked behind trees, but Aurora doesn't need to have a clear line of sight to tap its power. As she strides toward Sommers, she reaches up in the general direction of the Moon. I gasp as several rivulets of moonlight crest the tops of the trees, spiraling through the air toward us.

"Aurora!" I cry. "What are you doing?"

She doesn't respond.

In front of us, Detective Sommers stands with one hand on her weapon, which is thankfully still holstered. She must not have noticed the magic sailing overhead yet.

"It's too late, girls," Sommers says. "I already saw the body. You got two seconds to tell me what's going on here before I call for backup. Don't make me regret giving you the benefit of the doubt."

Aurora, silent and singularly focused, lifts her hands on either side of her just as two streams of moonbeams finally arrive at her palms. She sends the first rocketing at Sommers's head. The detective leaps aside, but Aurora whips more magic at her. Sommers ducks underneath the attack, but Aurora launches another at Sommers's feet. The moonlight slips around her ankle, flipping her onto her back. I reach for the magic to try and take it from her, to stop her from doing something she'll regret, but it doesn't respond to me anymore. My connection's still cold.

It's really gone.

Aurora commands the rope of moonlight to lift Sommers into the air by her ankle, dangling the screaming woman upside down. Sommers unholsters her weapon, but Aurora jerks the moonlight, and Sommers drops the gun.

Aurora tosses more moonbeams at Sommers. These tighten around her throat and transform into a radiant azure cuff. It starts choking the life out of her at once.

"Aurora!" I shout. "Stop! Please!"

She clenches a fist in front of her, tightening the magic choker locked onto Sommers, who coughs and wheezes, clawing at the viscous moonbeams, which only shift and glimmer from her touch, as if she were merely trailing her fingers through moonlight reflected on the surface of water.

I stand in front of Aurora, and she shoves me with her free hand, but I grab her wrist and hold it tight. Since I don't have magic right now, I'll have to end this the old-fashioned way.

I squeeze her arm hard and stare into her eyes. "Listen to me." I jerk her close so she has no choice but to look me in the eyes. "Sometimes violence is the answer—but not always. Sometimes it just makes shit a hell of a lot worse." I glance over my shoulder at Sommers. Her eyes are bloodshot, and veins bulge on her face. I turn back to Aurora. "If you kill her now, then you *will* go to prison. Don't waste your life, Aurora."

She releases an angry breath and drops her hand. I let her go too. Sommers tumbles to the ground. She gasps, sucking in a shrieking breath and rolls over onto her hands and knees.

I run over and kneel beside her. "Are you okay?"

"Yes," she says, still breathless. "Thank you for that."

"I've seen enough death," I whisper to her. "Can we talk? Please. We will explain everything to you. Please just give us a chance."

She considers my request for a long, nervous moment before staggering to her feet and letting Aurora lead us back inside the house. Aurora takes us through the kitchen, Xavier's dead body unavoidable along the way, which catches Sommers's attention. While they sit in the living room on opposite ends of a long sectional sofa, I fetch them both a glass of water, which I make quick work of as my skin crawls every moment that I'm alone in the kitchen with dead Xavier.

When I return, Aurora's in the middle of recounting the story of what happened this evening.

"He attacked you first?" Sommers asks immediately once Aurora's done.

She nods. "I—I blacked out and don't remember anything until I came to, and he was dead on top of me with his hands around my throat and my knife in his." She trembles with anxiety, and I sit next to her and put the glass of water in her hands and rub her back. "He locked me in an asylum for nearly a year and got away with it, and I was terrified he'd do worse this time." She frowns at Sommers. "He lost it on me and tried to kill me tonight because of *you*."

Sommers sighs, and her surveilling stare switches between Aurora and me, but I have nothing but a grimace for her. This woman has created a grand mess in our lives in a record amount of time.

"I believe you," Sommers tells Aurora. "And I might've been willing to give you a break on the grounds of self-defense had you come clean instead of assaulting me."

Aurora's cheeks flush. She doesn't speak. I wonder if she feels ashamed of what she did to Sommers. I can certainly relate. Maybe that's why I speak for her. Maybe all we've been through over the past couple of weeks has led to this moment. Maybe in some situations, instead of violence, we can find a way to move forward with an enemy.

"The three of us are a lot alike," I say, nodding to them both. "Aurora and I want justice, just like you," I tell Sommers. "There's no reason we can't all work together, but not while you're legally hunting gen. You cannot be our community's oppressor and our savior."

"Oh, don't feed me that ACAB bullshit," Sommers retorts. "How do you expect to fix oppressive systems of the world if we don't have people trying to enact change from inside them?"

I shake my head. "The systems aren't broken, Detective. Everything's working exactly by design, including you leading the assault against communities of people who look like you. Aurora, me, my mama, and gen like us aren't the enemy. We're only trying to make our communities better and safer. It's people like Xavier Vincent,

Lenora Savant, Tabitha Edgewater, and Dr. Gregory Thomas who are the real criminals."

Sommers heaves a long, deep sigh.

"One day, the system's gonna come for you too," I tell her. "And when that happens, even though you haven't earned my trust, you can still come back to us."

"Back?" Sommers asks, cocking her head curiously.

Aurora raises a brow, intrigued as well.

"I heard what the Moon King told you," I say. "He smelled magic on you. Which of you were gen? Was it your mom or dad or grandparents?"

"All of the above," Sommers admits, the old grudge roughening her voice. "Gen magic ripped apart my family and shadow magic killed my little brother."

"No"—I shake my head—"people did that. Magic is only a conduit for our true nature." I pause, but Sommers offers no further words, only one of her signature scrutinizing stares that unnerves me despite myself. "Can we at least call a truce for the night?"

"Fine." Sommers huffs and stands up. "I need to call this in."

The onslaught of flashing emergency lights, official vehicles, and uniformed people parading through Aurora's home kicks off a mere fifteen minutes after Sommers calls for backup. While pictures are snapped and evidence is bagged, Sommers and another cop ask me and Aurora both a million questions, though I'm relieved to finally give Sommers all the statements she needs at once for my entire hellish night so she can leave me alone. And now that the Moon King's taken responsibility for Jack and Zac Kingston's deaths, it's much easier to switch my entire story to match his version, which Sommers appears more than ready to close the lid on—thank the gods.

*Not you, Oberun.*

A couple of hours later, not long after the Sun rises, the last cop leaves, and Sommers lets Aurora know she's writing this up as a self-defense on Aurora's behalf and leaving out the part about assaulting an officer, and we both thank her for the grace. I don't even mention how she owed us that little bit considering how she'd flipped both our worlds upside down, but I knew when to leave well enough alone.

I offer to drive Aurora back to our home, and she accepts. On the drive over, I tell her the true story of what happened at the cabin, including my attack on Sofia and the loss of my magic.

"I understand why you flipped," Aurora says at the end of my short but dramatic tale. "You just get so mad after being frustrated and hopeless for so long. And you feel backed into a corner, left with only the option to fight or die—and I pride myself on being particularly difficult to kill."

I can't help but chuckle. I wish the circumstances were different, but being seen this way feels like standing in the sunlight after spending too long in the cold of dark.

"That's weird about your magic," Aurora says. "I've never heard of anything like that happening before. Maybe you just burned out your magical batteries and they need time to recharge."

"Maybe," I mutter, though I don't believe that for a second. I fear the Moon King may have been right. The sudden loss of my magic feels like something more . . . deliberate.

"I'm sorry about Clem," Aurora offers. "I won't rest either until we come up with a plan to bring him back home. You all are the only family I have left now, so, yes, I will help fight for it."

"I appreciate that," I tell her. "Real family are the people who show up for you when you need them most."

Soon as we get home, Aurora dashes straight upstairs for the shower. I'm in the kitchen pouring a glass of juice and have barely had enough time to catch my breath before the front door opens. I step out into the foyer to see who it is just as Mama and Aunt Ursula walk inside.

The sight of Mama stops me for a moment. Her eyes are red, the skin around them puffy from crying, and her hair's in a messy ponytail. She's wearing the same dress she wore when she was arrested, but it doesn't fit the same, as she lost a few pounds in jail, enough for me to notice.

Some of the darkness dispels from her face at once when she sees me. She throws out her arms and cries, "Oh, Cristina!"

I throw myself into her, almost toppling us both. She ensnares me, squeezing so tight that I grunt from the pressure, but I don't dare complain. Mama's home.

I lied earlier—about only wanting a hug from Clem and no one else. I'll take one of Mama's. At times, they're more powerful than magic.

"Ursula told me what happened," Mama whispers. "I'm so glad you're okay."

Her embrace is the first place it's felt okay to shed every piece of my extensive armor, to let my posture slip and allow my raw, ugly emotions and vulnerability to lie exposed.

It's relieving and terrifying.

"The Moon King took him, Mama," I bawl, my cheeks sopping. "He took him from us."

"Do you have any idea where he might've taken your brother?" Mama asks, leaning away from our embrace to wipe my tears with her hands.

I shake my head. "I don't know."

Odessa comes downstairs, dressed to begin her workday. She stops at the bottom of the stairs and clutches her chest at the sight of Mama, then runs over and hugs her too.

"I can never thank you enough for taking care of our family—again," Mama tells Odessa when they part, still holding on to both her hands.

Odessa beams, then looks at me and Aunt Ursula. "Where's Clem?"

I give her the abridged download of Clem's fate this evening, despite the pain I see in Mama's face as I recount how the god tricked her child into eternal servitude.

"But why only Clem?" asks Odessa. "Not that I'm unhappy you're safe."

I hesitate for what becomes an uncomfortable, bloated pause, my answer to that question like a dead body floating in the ocean after a few weeks. I open my mouth to say something, though I don't know how to explain to my family that the Moon King saw no use in me because I've lost my magic.

The doorbell rings, startling everyone in the foyer and temporarily saving me from Odessa's inquisition.

"You expecting someone?" Mama asks, looking at Ursula, Odessa, then me—and we all say no.

I can't make out the distorted silhouette of the person who stands on the other side, but I can tell it's an adult with a distinctly feminine body shape. But who's visiting us at this time in the morning? It's barely after 6:00 A.M.

The three of us stand back while Mama answers the door. She opens it a crack and peeps outside at the person on the porch.

"How can I—" Mama staggers backward, her hands clasped over her chest, and shakes her head. "No . . . It can't be . . ."

She faints.

Odessa cries out in surprise and lunges forward, catching Mama as she crumples to the floor. I suck in a sharp breath, but my brain is sluggish from exhaustion, so it takes me a moment to catch up to what's going on. By then the door swings open, revealing Grandma Cristine.

But she's different from last time.

Her form doesn't waver around the edges, but instead, she's solid—and real. With the same kind round face and warm-tawny skin as mine and Mama's, though this time I can more clearly see the fine lines that mark her age, which make her appear even more gorgeous to me. They're a sign of longevity and wisdom. My grandma carries herself with the air of a grand matriarch, someone to be revered.

Grandma steps into our home—well, technically, *her* home—and closes the door behind her. She crouches in front of Mama, who's just now coming to, cradled in Odessa's lap. Grandma cups Mama's cheek in one hand.

"Ma?" mumbles Mama, blinking as if dazed and hallucinating. "But you died. How can this be?"

Odessa stares at Grandma too, shaking her head in muted disbelief, her lips trembling, tears streaming down both cheeks.

Grandma stands up and turns straight into an embrace from Ursula. They spend a few moments in one of Aunt Ursula's signature hearty rocking hugs that invoke equal feelings of love and irritation.

When they part, Grandma beelines for me. Her grin puffs up her cheeks. Up close, her skin is as smooth as glass and looks unreal. I feel light-headed and weightless.

A few weeks ago, my life went off the rails and is presently showing no signs of getting back on anytime soon. Maybe it's time I kick back and enjoy the ride. I could ask a dozen questions about how the hell my (dead?) grandmother is standing in front of me, very much alive, *or* I could do something I've never done and never thought I'd ever get to do.

I hug my grandmother.

And she wraps her arms around me. She smells of jojoba and clean linen. I shut my eyes in her arms and see nothing but the Sun, and its warmth, as if standing outside on a perfect spring day. I don't know how this is possible, but by the gods, I hope it's real because finding out this moment is a trick would be too cruel to handle right now.

Then my heart sinks anew because I remember Clem's gone. He needs a hug from Grandma Cristine most of all, but the Moon King took him from us.

"I've been watching you, Cristina," says Grandma in her light earthy voice that sounds like the wind blowing through a dense wood.

My body goes rigid, but she only clings tighter to me, not in a threatening way; somehow her grip makes me feel more secure than anything.

"It hurt me to see you so angry and not be able to comfort you," she tells me in a low voice, so only I can hear. "I hate that you had to process all that alone. Because, had I been there for you, you would've never gone that far." I drop my head, and she leans back and lifts my chin so we look into each other's eyes. Hers are a rich multifaceted brown like a mottled collage of different types of wood that's effortlessly hypnotizing this close.

"Was it you who took my magic?" I whisper, ignoring the prying stares of everyone in the room who tries subtly (and some not so subtly) to crane their neck to better eavesdrop on my conversation with Grandma.

She nods.

I let go of a heavy breath. I should be relieved to finally know how and why my connection to the spiritual realm dried up. But instead, I'm humiliated that I disappointed my grandmother, someone I looked up to more than my own mama, on such a massive scale that she stripped me of my magic on the spot. And now I don't know what I could possibly say that could vindicate me in her eyes. I find myself wishing Grandma could see me the way Aurora does.

She focuses her gaze and narrows her eyes on me. "Don't feel bad for being angry," she tells me. "It's a natural emotion that you're always entitled to feel—so long as you don't allow it to consume and mislead you. I saw you straying dangerously close to a line you didn't need to cross, so I saved you from yourself." She purses her lips, and her expression softens. "I understand how disorienting that might've been, not knowing what was going on, and I'm sorry about that. I'm not as meddlesome as the gods when it comes to these things, but I couldn't watch you make that mistake. You have too much life ahead of you, baby girl."

"What mistake?" asks Mama, butting in on our private conversation now that she's back on her feet.

"Never you mind," Grandma says, parting from me. She caresses my earlobe between her index and middle fingers and tells me, "You and I will talk more later."

"Yes ma'am," I say.

And then Grandma Cristine addresses everyone. "We have a great deal to discuss. I'm sure you all have a hundred questions, but I also know you're all exhausted. Don't even try to deny it. For now, you will sleep, and we'll talk once you're rested."

Despite feeling like an extra in a B zombie movie, I shake my head. "We can't rest yet. We were all about to come together to talk about how we're getting Clem back from the Moon King."

Grandma takes a deep breath in and blows it out through her mouth. "I know you're upset, but we are dealing with gods now, Cristina. I did try to warn you last summer. This is far more serious than a feud between ex–best friends. A spiritual war is coming, and the whole of two realms are at stake. And an exhausted mind is no good to any of us—Clement, especially. You kids don't need to worry anymore. I'm back now, and I'll bring my grandbaby home—even if I have to sacrifice myself a second time." When no one argues with her, she clasps her hands in front of her and says, "I'm cooking dinner tonight. I can't wait to get into that upgraded kitchen."

It feels like I'm dreaming. But a sinking feeling in the pit of me, a drain sucking out every positive emotion, drags me into a nightmare again because I can't help but think about how the Moon King robbed Clem of this moment. And I lost Clem to the Moon King because of Zac's pointless act of violence, which killed Yves—who, I guess is alive now? Oh, gods. I didn't even think to check if the Moon King upheld his end of the bargain. But the only way to confirm that is to physically drive to Jean-Louise's house, and I'm way too tired to get back behind the wheel of a car right now.

Grandma was right. It's past time I recharged for a bit. I've been running on E for a while, and our fight is apparently long from over.

I don't know what the gods are playing at, but they've officially fucked up by dragging my brother into their drama. My family is all I have, so even the gods need to understand that when you mess with them, I no longer have anything to lose—and that could get *very* dangerous.

Despite the sadness that lingers like a chill draft in an abandoned home, I feel stronger and more capable with the incredible women at my back, who will stop at nothing to protect this family. Grandma. Mama. Aunt Ursula. Odessa. Aurora.

It's frightening to imagine what the six of us stand to accomplish working together. The monumental task ahead of us suddenly feels slightly less intimidating and insurmountable.

*Hold on, Clem. I'm coming for you. I swear.*

The Moon King better take care of my brother while Clem's in his charge because blood justice can most definitely come for him too. Not even gods are exempt.

"Oh! One more thing!" Grandma's singsong voice snaps me firmly out of my reverie. She turns to Ursula with a disarming stare and raises a scolding brow. "Ursula, my little bumblebee, your loyalty is appreciated, but I never taught you to be so crass."

Ursula's eyes widen, and her mouth drops open, though in a rare occurrence, she's speechless. Mama and I exchange a bewildered expression, and Odessa looks away suspiciously.

Grandma Cristine cocks her head, still eyeing my aunt. "Please bring me Lenora Savant's head from off the mantle in your bedroom, darling."

# FORTY-SIX

## OSWALD STRAYER

Oz left the moment his parents went to bed. He rode in silence the entire way, choosing to listen to the frustration and anger crackling inside him like a bonfire.

He wasn't letting this shit go.

He was *not* going to just let Cris take away the *one* fucking thing in his life that mattered.

Halfway there, the storm started. When the wind kicked up, he almost turned back; but instead, he took it as a sign to keep pushing through adversity. This was his test.

Nothing and *no one* was going to stop him.

The storm still raged when he parked his car and got out. He didn't have an umbrella, but he didn't care.

He trudged to the front door, trembling from nerves and the cold rain battering him. He rang the doorbell and waited. His teeth chattered, and he clamped his mouth shut. His hands quivered, so he shoved them into his pockets.

The porch light blazed on, and Oz flinched, folding further into himself.

He hated feeling so small. Insignificant. Invisible. Fucking useless. Emasculated. And he hated Cris for making him like this. For making him do this.

But he was already here. This was the only way now.

He was nobody without magic. And he wasn't going to settle for being nobody anymore.

The locks clicked as they disengaged, and the door opened.

Oz's aunt squinted down at him, a confused look on her face. He must've been a frightful and pitiful sight to her, soggy mess as he was, standing on her porch in the middle of the night.

"Ozzy!" Madeline DeLacorte cried, clutching her robe tighter before peering around her nephew to see if he'd come alone. "What are you *doing* here? Do your parents know where you are?" He shook his head, and she looked him up and down and asked, "What's wrong? Did something happen?"

He gathered his courage and stared into her glistening eyes. "Aunt Maddie," he said, "will you teach me light magic? *Please?*"

# EPILOGUE
## YVES BORDEAUX

The words were hard to explain when he wasn't wholly himself, but Yves Bordeaux had come to learn that life had a taste. He believed everyone's existence bore a distinct flavor palette, one they craved to taste the way their bodies thirsted for oxygen. He'd discovered, in fact, that his own unique flavor was one with forward and lingering notes of a varied sort, that began as savory and buttery and ended quite sweet and decadent with hints of lemon and cream.

But the cruelest aspect of the entire setup was that people spent the majority of their lives unable to truly luxuriate in the elaborate flavors of their gift of mortality, that is, not until those final fleeting moments, when they're finally granted a petite sampling, the slightest of tidbits, merely enough to drive them mad with the singular thought that they will never taste it again.

From the moment the muzzle of that gun flashed that night in the back-alley parking lot and darkness began encroaching on Yves's world, he'd gotten a taste of his life; and it had been there, in that moment with Clem, that his senses heightened to overstimulating levels. Yves had read somewhere once about a restaurant where the lights were intentionally dimmed in the dining room because food tasted better in the dark. It was kinda like that.

And every moment since, a biting, gnawing hunger roiled inside him that he knew and feared would never be satiated. One that only grew louder and more famished with every passing day, threatening to drive him into madness and depression, the depths of which, in his partial state, were unfathomable.

So, when the moment came that he'd begun thinking would never happen, when the precious, familiar taste of his own life hit his tongue once more, he devoured every decadent morsel. And he ate his fill—until he was whole again.

And Yves Bordeaux leapt from the chair in which he'd been sitting in the spare bedroom of Jean-Louise's home, inadvertently knocking the newspaper he'd been reading onto the floor, the first headline of which read:

**DEMOCRATIC HOPEFUL, DESIREE DUPART, CONVINCES LOUISIANA SUPREME COURT TO VOTE FOR RE-ELECTION OF MAYOR OF NEW ORLEANS**

Yves breathed for what felt like the first time, and even the air tasted fresher, rejuvenating, as if he could feel it circulating through his body like an ocean breeze.

"I'm back," he murmured, then clapped his hands over his mouth to keep from crying out in shock at hearing his own voice again. "Oh, God," he whispered.

Clem did it. But *how?*

The signature leaden-footed thudding of Jean-Louise on the stairs resounded from the hallway. A moment later, he passed by Yves's door, his head downcast, and didn't bother to look inside.

Yves called his name.

Jean-Louise doubled back, tripping and nearly falling but catching himself on the doorjamb. He stood poised in the doorway, looking as if he'd just seen a ghost.

Yves walked up to him and stared into Jean-Louise's dark eyes, which scrutinized Yves with disbelief that dissipated the closer he drew. Yves shook his head at him, but Jean-Louise only stared in surprise at Yves's sudden and unexpected revival.

Yves punched Jean-Louise in the chest. Not hard, because he wasn't very strong, but the sad shadow that slunk across Jean-Louise's face signaled to Yves that it had hurt Jean-Louise more emotionally than physically, which was just as good. So he hit him again. And again. And Jean-Louise stood there and let him. He didn't flinch or fight back or yell or cry or try to stop him. He absorbed every blow like a sullen sandbag.

When Yves's tears blurred his vision, making it hard to see where he swung, Jean-Louise grappled him into a hug.

"You abandoned him," Yves whimpered into Jean-Louise's broad chest, his ear pressed against the rapid thumping of Jean-Louise's heart. "He *trusted* you, and you *abandoned* him!" Yves shoved himself out of Jean-Louise's arms and glowered at him. "How could you?"

He inched forward, his hands out, his sleepy eyes pleading. "I—I was scared. You didn't see what I saw—"

"Jean-Louise?"

Jean-Louise went stiff as a day-old cadaver. He turned slowly in the direction of the voice that came from the hallway behind him. Once he saw who stood there, Jean-Louise let out an inhuman cry that eviscerated Yves's heart on the spot.

Auguste Dupre had been restored too.

Jean-Louise leapt with what seemed a single bound from inside the room into Auguste's arms. Both men held on tight to each other, sobbing uncontrollably and unabashedly.

Yves watched, hugging himself and longing to hold Clem again.

Clem did it. Yves didn't know how, but Clem had kept his word.

*But what did that cost you, Clem?*

Jean-Louise and Auguste finally parted, but Auguste didn't look as cheerful as Jean-Louise, which drew a skeptical look from Yves.

Something felt off—because why the hell did Auguste look pissed?

"There's something I need to tell you," Auguste said in a low voice, smooth as aged whiskey. "Something I've been stewing in for four years now. Something I can't let go, not if I'm to have any semblance of life."

"What is it?" asked Jean-Louise, concern deepening his stress lines.

Yves wandered closer, though the idea of the answer frightened him. He had an unavoidable sinking feeling that Auguste's return to life would be anything but drama-free.

"Justin Montaigne murdered me," Auguste sneered. "And I demand *blood justice*."

# ACKNOWLEDGMENTS

The Blood Debts series, and especially *Blood Justice,* means so much to me as an artist, a reader, and a Black gay man, and I am so proud of this story, myself, and every single person who played a part in bringing it to life.

To Ali Fisher, rock star editor extraordinaire, I can never thank you enough for the guidance, trust, and grace you give me every single day. I feel so incredibly fortunate that I get to make magic with you. Cheers to many more stories!

To my impeccable agent, Patrice Caldwell, you already know how much I love you, but I'ma tell you again: I LOVE YOU! I can never thank you enough for all the career support and guidance and fearless protection. I appreciate you to the Moon and back.

To Trinica Sampson-Vera, every day that I get to work with you is such an honor, and I'm so grateful that even when I am an absolute gay mess, you never judge me and always have my back—you are the real MVP. Thank you for being you.

To Saraciea Fennell, thank you sooo much for everything you've done and continue to do for me and the Blood Debts series. You're truly a light and inspiration, not just for me or at Tor Teen, but in publishing in general. I appreciate you.

To Dianna Vega, Khadija Lokhandwala, Ashley Spruill, Isa Caban, Anthony Parisi, Eileen Lawrence, Lucille Rettino, and the entire Tor Teen team—thank you so much for your continued love and support for me, the Blood Debts series, and my career. I'm very proud to be a Tor Teen author and to have the privilege and honor to work with some of the best and brightest people in the publishing industry.

To Lesley and Tomasz, I can never thank you enough for the beautiful and enthralling way you've captured the essence of my fictional babies in both the *Blood Justice* cover and the *Blood Debts* paperback cover. I feel very fortunate and honored for the opportunity to work with you both.

Biggest of thanks and honor to Elishia Merricks, Maria Snelling, Amber Cortes, and the rest of the Macmillan Audio team. The audiobook production for this series is top-notch, and I'm so fortunate to have the opportunity to work with you all. Special thanks and appreciation to the incredible audiobook narrators: Joniece Abbott-Pratt, Zeno Robinson, Bahni Turpin, and Torian Brackett, who brought these characters to life in ways I could've never imagined.

To my husband, Kevin, you were the very first person to believe in me and continued to do so even when I began to doubt myself. This book and the past year were both really tough, but your love and support throughout truly made the difference.

To Adam Sass, my bunny . . . whew. I would've never made it through this book without you. I appreciate you keeping me motivated and sitting through so many long and in-depth conversations about plot and these characters (especially Clem) as I figured out what the heck I was doing, haha. Also, thank you for inspiring me through your own work and pushing me to always be the best version of myself.

To my favorite goober, Naseem Jamnia, like this story and this series, you mean very much to me. Thank you for being a perpetual light in my world. It was your warmth that got me through many a dark night, particularly when I was working on this one.

To my real-life Zac—who is in no way related to Zac Kingston, haha—thank you for holding me down always. Love you, fam.

To Sam and Raaven, this year was very tough for me, but the love and light you both shared with me throughout helped get me through some very dark times. I hope you love this one too. To David Nino and Beatrice Iker, thank you for the support behind the scenes on all the minor but super important details. To Jeida, thanks for letting me borrow your name, friend. :)

Highest of thanks and royal regards to every single teacher, librarian, and bookseller who's been promoting *Blood Debts* and *Blood Justice* and working tirelessly to put my work into the hands of the kids for whom I created this world and this epic story. I couldn't do this without you.

To everyone who read, blurbed, reviewed, posted, or shared *Blood Debts* or *Blood Justice*, thank you for sticking with me this long.

Until next time. Be easy.

## *BLOOD JUSTICE* TEAM

* President of TPG and Tor Teen Publisher: Devi Pillai
* Chairman/Founder of TPG: Tom Doherty
* VPs, Editorial Directors: Will Hinton and Claire Eddy
* Marketing lead: Anthony Parisi
* VP, Director of Marketing: Eileen Lawrence
* Publicists: Saraciea Fennell, Ashley Spruill, and Khadija Lokhandwala
* VP, Exec. Director of Publicity: Sarah Reidy
* SVP, Associate Publisher: Lucille Rettino
* Senior Production Editor: Jessica Katz
* Production Manager: Steven Bucsok
* Interior designer: Heather Saunders
* Jacket designer: Lesley Worrell
* Artist: Tomasz Majewski
* Publishing operations: Michelle Foytek
* Copy editor: Manu Velasco
* Cold reader: Melissa Frain
* Sensitivity readers: Bree Barton and Adriana M. Martínez Figueroa